USA TODAY bestselling author **Heidi Rice** lives in London, England. She is married with two teenage sons—which gives her rather too much of an insight into the male psyche—and also works as a film journalist. She adores her job, which involves getting swept up in a world of high emotion, sensual excitement, funny and feisty women, sexy and tortured men and glamorous locations where laundry doesn't exist. Once she turns off her computer she often does chores, usually involving laundry!

Marcella Bell is an avid reader, a burgeoning beader, and a corvid and honeybee enthusiast with more interests than hours in the day. As a late bloomer and a yogi, Marcella is drawn to stories that showcase love's incredible power to inspire transformation—whether they take place in the vast landscapes of the west or imagined palaces and exotic locales. When not writing or wrangling her multigenerational household and three dogs, she loves to hear from readers! To reach out, keep up, or check in, visit marcellabell.com.

Also by Heidi Rice

A Forbidden Night with the Housekeeper
Innocent's Desert Wedding Contract

Hot Summer Nights with a Billionaire collection

One Wild Night with Her Enemy

The Christmas Princess Swap collection

The Royal Pregnancy Test

Also by Marcella Bell

The Queen's Guard miniseries

Stolen to Wear His Crown
His Stolen Innocent's Vow

Discover more at millsandboon.co.uk.

THE BILLIONAIRE'S PROPOSITION IN PARIS

HEIDI RICE

PREGNANT AFTER ONE FORBIDDEN NIGHT

MARCELLA BELL

MILLS & BOON

First Published in Great Britain 2021
by Mills & Boon, an imprint of HarperCollins*Publishers* Ltd,
1 London Bridge Street, London, SE1 9GF

www.harpercollins.co.uk

HarperCollins*Publishers*
1st Floor, Watermarque Building,

Printed and bound in Spain using 100% Renewable Electricity
at CPI Blackprint (Barcelona)

THE
BILLIONAIRE'S
PROPOSITION
IN PARIS

HEIDI RICE

MILLS & BOON

To my wonderful Irish father, Peter Ronan Rice,
who died far too soon.

He would have blushed like a nun
if he'd ever had the chance to read this book!

But he would have told me
how much he enjoyed it anyway.

Miss you always, Dad. xx

CHAPTER ONE

'I WILL NEED you to be on call twenty-four-seven. If I contact you, I expect you to make yourself available to me immediately...'

'Really?'

But I'm an event planner, not your mistress.

The whispered word—and the inappropriate thought—popped out before Katherine Hamilton could stop either, interrupting the stream of instructions she had been receiving ever since she had been ushered into Conall O'Riordan's glass-walled office on the thirtieth floor of Rio Corp's headquarters in London's golden mile five minutes ago.

She regretted the impulsive question immediately, when O'Riordan's dark head rose from the pile of papers on his desk—which he had been signing with efficient flicks of his silver pen as he reeled off his list of requirements—and his scorching blue gaze met hers for the first time.

Her breath backed up in her lungs—the jolt of awareness both shocking and electrifying at the same time.

Oh... My!

She'd done her research as soon as she'd been told her fledging event-planning firm was in the running to receive a coveted contract from O'Riordan's company.

She already knew Conall O'Riordan, the agricultural-tech billionaire, was strikingly handsome, renowned for his magnetism, drive, ambition and charisma. She knew he'd come from humble origins to become one of Ireland's most eligible men at the age of only thirty-one. But nothing could have prepared her for the impact of having that intense cobalt gaze focussed solely on her. Or the heat that slammed into her chest and spread through her body like wildfire.

Uncomfortable sensations she hadn't felt since Tom's death. Or, frankly, since before Tom's death. The wave of sadness which followed the thought of her dead husband helped her to catch her breath and examine her unprovoked reaction to O'Riordan.

Her relationship with Tom had not been a wild passion—not even close. It had been a childhood friendship that had blossomed into love. A love they'd never consummated. Physical intimacy had been the least of the things they'd lost when Tom had become ill. Did that explain her shocking reaction to O'Riordan—her chronic lack of sexual experience?

O'Riordan's brows rose as his lips flattened into a line but the intensity in his gaze didn't dim one iota... Could he feel it too—the shot of adrenaline turning her insides to mush?

I hope not.

'Did you say something, Ms Hamilton?' O'Riordan asked, or rather demanded, his husky tone, low with command, only increasing the devastating prickle of awareness.

Breathe, you ninny! And stop staring at his lips.

Katie struggled to collect herself and her shattered equilibrium.

This commission could be a game-changer for her

company and life-changing for her. It was an opportunity she'd spent the last forty-eight hours prepping for with her team. She had a folder full of ideas propped next to her chair that they'd killed themselves to produce in record time, ever since receiving word of this interview from one of O'Riordan's management staff.

But, if she were to take this commission, they needed to establish some kind of working relationship—her shockingly inappropriate reaction notwithstanding.

She wasn't sure she liked the way O'Riordan had rattled off a string of outrageous demands. He hadn't even mentioned the event itself yet—which she had been briefed was a team-building week followed by a company reception in O'Riordan Enterprises' Dublin headquarters.

This didn't feel like an interview, it felt like an interrogation.

'I… I wondered why you would need me to be available to you twenty-four-seven?' she managed.

'This is a problem?' he asked, his gaze raking over her with a raptor-like focus that only made her more aware of the wildfire still rushing over her skin.

Katie drew in a steadying breath.

He's just an extremely attractive and powerful man. It's instinctive. The female of the species is hard-wired to respond to the alpha male. It just means you're still human. Still alive. Still a woman. No biggie.

'No, not exactly, it's just…' she began, attempting to fill the awkward silence. 'Usually when I accept a commission I work up an event plan, then you and I and my team discuss it, and then—once you're entirely happy with everything—my team and I take over…' She paused, aware his focussed gaze was making her babble.

Was he trying to unnerve her? Because it was definitely working.

'It's my job to handle all the details,' she continued. 'So, basically, I wouldn't be doing my job properly if you felt you had to contact me in the middle of the night,' she finished, finally managing to get to something resembling a point.

He placed his pen on top of the papers he'd been signing. But then his lips quirked. It wasn't a smile, exactly, closer to a sneer. Unfortunately, it only made that striking combination of intensity and dark masculine beauty more breath-taking.

'I run an international company, Ms Hamilton. We're currently involved in projects in eight different time zones and I travel extensively. What is the middle of the night for you might be the middle of the day for me. I also never sleep more than three or four hours a night,' he added, then frowned, perhaps because he'd given away a piece of personal information. She shifted in her chair, the rush of sympathy at the admission he had insomnia as inappropriate as all the other sensations that had assailed her since she'd walked into his inner sanctum.

'If I have a question about the event,' he continued, having recovered from the slip a lot quicker than she had, 'I will want it answered. *Immediately*. By you. Not one of your staff,' he clarified, the tone both condescending and laser-sharp. 'If that kind of availability is a problem for you, we can end this interview now.'

'It's not a problem,' she said instantly. 'I can be available if you need me to be. I'm just saying that shouldn't be necessary,' she added, aware she wanted this commission now more than ever, and not for entirely professional reasons.

Conall O'Riordan presented a challenge. Not just for her company but also for her. A challenge she had managed to avoid ever since Tom's death five years ago. Because in many ways she'd been dead too. She still wasn't ready to consider dating again. But navigating an inappropriate sexual attraction to a client—especially a client of Conall O'Riordan's calibre—was all part of the process of returning to the land of the living. Surely?

'Good, as long as we understand each other,' he said.

The tight feeling in Katie's chest released—a little. Her physical attraction to this man was nothing to be afraid of. Especially as there was no way on earth she'd ever act upon it. And no chance whatsoever that O'Riordan would ever see her in that way. From the copious research she'd done on him in the last forty-eight hours, she knew his dating history consisted mostly of supermodels and actresses and assorted other women who looked as sensational as he did.

She reached for the folder by her chair, desperate to direct their conversation back to where it needed to be. 'Would you like to see the concepts we were asked to put together for the event?' she asked, standing to place the folder on his desk. 'I understand it's for a week-long team-building event at your headquarters in—'

'It's not.'

'Excuse me?' She folded her arms over the portfolio and stood dumbly, staring at him, panic joining the unwelcome sensations still shimmering through her body.

Had Caroline Meyer, her assistant, got the details of the brief wrong? Surely not? Caro was brilliant, she didn't make mistakes. And, anyway, they'd spent forty-eight hours with very little sleep putting together this portfolio. If they'd got the brief wrong, there was no way he was going to give her this commission and all their work would have been wasted.

But, before she had a chance to spiral into a full-blown anxiety attack, he gestured for her to sit back down.

'I had you deliberately misinformed about the brief.'

'But…why?' she asked, not sure whether to be annoyed or astonished.

'Because I value my family's privacy, and I don't want information about the actual event or its location being leaked to the press. I'll expect you to sign an NDA before I hire you.'

'I… I understand,' she said, although she really didn't. Maintaining a client's privacy was part of any reputable event planner's DNA. Leaking that kind of information could destroy a company's reputation, especially a company like hers, which was hoping to plan exclusive, boutique events for a high-end clientele.

'Of course. I'll be more than happy to sign an NDA if that's what you require.' After all, it was just another of his unnecessary demands.

She knew how taciturn and demanding men like Conall O'Riordan could be, because her half-brother, Ross De Courtney, owned and ran the biggest logistic firm in Europe. Maybe Ross wasn't self-made like O'Riordan, having inherited De Courtney's from their late father. But Ross had the same drive and ambition, having grown the company's status and reach exponentially in the ten years he'd been its CEO, and he had the same demanding, inflexible personality.

But she'd never had to organise an event for Ross. She hadn't even been a part of his life for five years, ever since their epic falling out over her marriage.

What you feel for Tom isn't love, it's pity, Katie. You're nineteen. I refuse to give you my permission to do something so ludicrous. And I'm certainly not paying for a wedding.

I don't need your money for a wedding, or anything else, and I certainly don't need your permission.

She swallowed the lump of anxiety that always surfaced when she thought of the angry words they'd exchanged, and how easy it had been for Ross to cut her out of his life. Just like their father...

Katie sliced off *that* unhelpful memory before it could take root, knowing it would only make her feel shakier.

So not the time, Katie.

Clearly spending two sleepless nights working on her now redundant portfolio had not been the best preparation for this meeting.

O'Riordan wasn't her estranged, dictatorial billionaire half-brother—or the father who had refused to acknowledge she even existed. He was a billionaire client. They had no personal connection.

Thank goodness. Working with O'Riordan would give her a unique insight into this kind of commission, all part of the steep learning curve she needed to be on to snare clients of his calibre.

'But I'm afraid I'd need to know what the event actually is,' she said. 'Before I can work up a proper proposal,' she finished, just in case he thought she was some kind of magician and could pull proposals out of her hat without doing the necessary groundwork with her team.

She sat down and placed the unopened and now entirely pointless portfolio beside her chair.

'No need to bid for it. You've got the commission,' he said.

Astonishment came first, swiftly followed by the buzz of achievement. Her heart bounced into her throat. 'Truly?' she said. And then wanted to kick herself.

Way to sound totally unprofessional, Katie.

His lips quirked again in that almost-smile, which did mad things to her bouncing heart rate. But as he spoke the nerves and the sizzle of sensation returned.

'Yes,' he clarified. 'I want this event to be tailored specifically to my needs, to make a statement befitting the O'Riordans' standing in our community and in Irish life. I spoke to Karim Khan about the baby shower you organised for his wife, Orla, last month,' he added, mentioning the biggest job Hamilton Events had done so far. 'Before the birth of their son. He recommended you.'

'I loved doing that event.' Katie smiled, remembering the last-minute commission she'd got through a friend of a friend in the Irish racing community. It had been Hamilton Events' first foray into the echelons of top society events and had given her the courage to start pitching for other similar work. 'They're a wonderful couple,' she added.

The nerves continued to jiggle and jump in her stomach, however.

The Khans' baby shower had been a small, intimate family affair—albeit for an extremely exclusive client. Karim Khan was a billionaire businessman, and also Arab royalty, having assumed the throne of Zafar several years ago now. His marriage to Orla Calhoun—the oldest daughter in the Calhoun racing clan—had been a match made in celebrity heaven two years ago.

From what O'Riordan had just said about his event, though, it didn't sound as if he wanted small or intimate.

'We can discuss the fee once everything has been finalised,' he continued, still not mentioning what the event was. 'But I'm prepared to pay double your usual rate as long as all my demands are met, which I understand to be ten percent of the budget.'

'That's correct. If you're not willing to talk about the actual event, it would be great to get an idea of the budget and how many guests you're expecting,' she said. At least if she had an idea of costs she could get a handle on the logistics.

'Whatever it takes,' he said, in that matter-of-fact tone which told her money really was no object. 'But I had a ballpark figure of five million euro. And a guest list of approximately a hundred and fifty people.'

'I see,' she said, trying to remember to breathe again.

A budget that size would give Hamilton Events a commission big enough to expand and get new offices in Central London. She loved the quirky converted railway buildings they currently inhabited in Shoreditch, in trendy East London, but it sent out the wrong vibe to the clients she was looking to attract. Much more than the money, though, this event could be a stepping stone to get Hamilton Events into the big league.

Standing up, he extended his hand. 'Deal?'

It wasn't really a question, but she nodded anyway and popped out of her seat.

His fingers curled around hers in a strikingly firm, unyielding grip, and the wildfire flared again. Her thigh muscles tightened and her palm burned before he let her go.

'Would you like to tell me what the event is, or wait until I've signed the NDA?' she asked, discreetly rubbing her burning palm on her thigh.

It's a job, Katie. A really, really good job. Stop freaking out.

His head tilted to one side but, just when she was convinced he might be able to tell how unsettled she was, he shrugged.

'It's a wedding.'

The word reverberated in her skull. She had always avoided doing weddings because they reminded her of the first and only wedding she'd ever planned. Her own.

To Tom. Ten days before he'd died of the rare cancer which had snuck into his body a year before their wedding day—and had slowly robbed them of the lives they might have had.

'You're getting married?' she asked to stop herself from blurting out the truth.

Did he know she'd never planned a wedding professionally? Would he withdraw the offer if she told him? How was she going to cope with arranging all those details, that she'd once done for love, for a man like him? Who appeared to be as coldly unemotional as he was compelling?

The thought felt strangely intimate, when it absolutely wasn't... Which was only making her freak out more.

He laughed, the deep chuckle as bitter as it was amused.

'Absolutely not,' he said. 'It's a wedding for one of my sisters. I have two of them,' he said, the muscle in his jaw relaxing for the first time.

Her heart slowed, despite her best intentions. However cold and cynical this man appeared to be, he wasn't as cold and cynical as her brother, because he clearly cared deeply about his sisters.

She steeled herself against the wayward emotions at the warmth in his eyes. Just because Conall O'Riordan loved his sisters, enough to pay for an extremely lavish wedding, didn't make him—or planning this event—any less of a threat to her peace of mind. Or any less of a logistical nightmare. Even she knew securing a suitably stunning venue for a society wedding for a hundred and fifty guests two months before the event would be next to impossible.

'Her name's Imelda,' he said, interrupting Katie's thoughts. 'She's twenty-one and has made the insane decision to marry her childhood sweetheart. Who happens to be a local farmer near my home in Connemara. I don't approve,' he added somewhat unnecessarily given the disapproval dripping from every word. 'But she's headstrong, as well as a hopeless romantic, so I'm stuck with the situation and I've decided to let her use Kildaragh,' he finished.

Katie's mind whirred to a stop. She'd seen photos of Kildaragh Castle while researching O'Riordan in the last few days. The mostly Victorian building built on the ruins of a medieval monastery on Ireland's untamed west coast was stunning.

At least she wouldn't have to find a venue, then. Sourcing all the necessary services might still be quite challenging, but she would just have to call in every favour she'd ever had.

Then something he had said reverberated in her head. 'Is it your sister's marriage you don't approve of, or the relationship?' she blurted out.

He frowned, and she knew she'd overstepped the mark. But to her surprise he answered her.

'Both, Ms Hamilton. Imelda is young enough to believe the usual nonsense about love. Which is why she's too young to make this decision. But, even if she weren't, she'd still be making a mistake. I have nothing against farmers, and Donal's a nice enough lad but he lacks ambition. He's not good enough for her.'

'So you don't believe she's in love?'

'No, I don't—not least because romantic love doesn't really exist. It is simply a construct used to trap the unwary,' he supplied. 'And separate people from their hard-earned cash.'

It was a view so cynical she almost felt sorry for him. How could anyone go through life genuinely believing something so hopeless? She'd had the love of her life and lost him. And it had nearly destroyed her. She didn't expect to find another. Nor did she really want to. It would feel like cheating on Tom. But it saddened her to think that men like O'Riordan and her brother just didn't get that...for all their wealth and success.

'And to glorify the most basic of urges,' he added.

His mouth crinkled again in that coldly compelling almost-smile. And suddenly the atmosphere became charged. Charged with the shocking sensations that had derailed her as soon as she had arrived. His gaze roamed over her, penetrating, provocative and disturbingly intimate. Her body quickened in response, mortifying her.

'But you're still willing to pay a fortune to celebrate a marriage you don't approve of?' she blurted out, desperate to break the tension.

'Whether I approve or not, it won't stop Imelda making this mistake,' he said. 'And, anyway, why would you question that impulse, seeing as you're going to make a killing out of it?'

'Because I do believe in it,' she said, trying not to be offended by the remark.

'Believe in what, exactly?' he asked. 'Spending a fortune on a wedding?'

'No, in marriage,' she said. 'And love.'

He blinked, and she could see the flash of surprise in his eyes before he masked it.

'How quaint,' he said. 'And convenient—coming from a wedding planner.'

She wasn't a wedding planner—not yet, anyway. And she wasn't in the business of convincing her clients to believe in love. She might have been as hopelessly romantic as his sister once but she was a realist now. She'd had to become one. But, even so, she couldn't quite let the caustic comment pass.

'Perhaps, but at least it means you'll get your money's worth,' she said. 'Because I'll do my absolute utmost to make sure Imelda's special day is one she'll remember for the rest of her life.'

'Or until she gets divorced,' he supplied, but then added, 'But it's grand you intend to ensure I get my money's worth, because I always insist on getting what I'm paying for.'

His gaze remained focussed on her, and she had the strangest feeling they weren't talking about his sister's wedding any more. The atmosphere was crackling now with an electrical energy that was forcing her dormant body to wake up... In a way it had never been woken up before.

He sat and picked up his pen, his gaze returning to the papers on his desk.

'My assistant will be in touch with more details once you've signed the NDA,' he murmured as he began scanning the documents again and signing them.

Her body sunk, like a puppet released from its strings, the loss of his attention almost as jarring as having been the centre of it moments before.

'I'm taking the company chopper to Kildaragh next Friday—you can accompany me for the week to check out the venue and organise the details. I'd like to have everything finalised by the end of that week.'

'You want a wedding for a hundred and fifty people organised by the end of next week?' she asked, so shocked she wasn't sure how to respond. Did he realise he was asking the impossible? Planning any event took time and consideration. Even with a venue secured there were so many details to consider and so many choices to make.

His gaze connected with hers, pulling the puppet strings taut again. And she had the strangest feeling he knew he was asking the impossible and that he was enjoying it. 'I do,' he said. 'It's a short time frame, but I expect you to make it work… If not I can withdraw the…'

'I can make it work,' she said. She would just have to hit the ground running when she got to Connemara.

'Good, work up some concepts in the meantime so I can look at them en route to Kildaragh.'

'Absolutely. Would it be okay if I brought some of my team with me…?' she ventured. At least if she had Caro there to chase down the details, and Trev, one of their regular freelance coordinators, to help check out local suppliers…

'No, you may not. I'd prefer you come alone. I don't want hordes of people in my home,' he said.

Caro and Trev would hardly be a horde, and really, his home had to have about a hundred bedrooms, from the photos she'd seen online, but again, she suspected this was a test. And she refused to fail it, so she immediately acquiesced again. She did not want to lose this commission on a technicality.

'I can work solo if you need me to.' And there was always email and online conference calling to keep her team in the loop.

He gave a barely perceptible nod, as if he had expected no less. 'By the way, no Christmas themes, even if the event is scheduled for the first week of December.'

She nodded. 'We can do something with a winter theme, rather than Christmas, if that's what you and Imelda prefer.'

'I do,' he said, and she noted the emphasis on the 'I'.

So, he had a problem with Christmas as well as romance. *Quelle surprise*. And he seemed to think he could do this without the bride's input. The softening she'd felt towards him earlier seemed increasingly misplaced.

His gaze dropped back to his papers. 'See yourself out,' he said, and she realised she'd been dismissed.

She left the office, ignoring the spurt of indignation at the cursory command, stupidly grateful to be away from that all-seeing gaze.

As she arrived in the lift lobby the view of St Paul's Cathedral dome thirty storeys below, the grey expanse of the River Thames and the Shard standing on the opposite bank like an enormous phallic symbol was almost as vertigo-inducing as the thought of her trip to Connemara in five days' time. And all the challenges presented by this commission... And more specifically her taciturn and tactless—and far too unsettling—new billionaire client.

Pressing the lift call button, she noticed her finger trembling. She curled her hand into a fist to stop the shaking. She needed to get her reaction to Conall O'Riordan under control ASAP, or how the heck was she going to survive being in close proximity to him for a week and behave with any degree of professionalism whatsoever?

Her heartbeat jammed into her throat. She swallowed convulsively.

Don't be ridiculous, Katie. You're a professional. O'Riordan's a client. Your best client ever, in fact. You've worked hard for this opportunity and you are not going to muck it up thanks to a few inappropriate sizzles.

And anyway, what were the chances Conall O'Riordan would be that hands-on? Surely he wouldn't actually want to be that involved in the wedding planning? He'd already made it clear weddings were not his area of interest or expertise. And he was an extremely busy man.

Imelda, being the bride, was the one Katie would ultimately be working for, no matter who was paying the bills.

Or how overbearing and controlling and ludicrously hot he happened to be!

CHAPTER TWO

'YOU'RE LATE!' CONALL shouted above the noise of the helicopter powering up as Katherine Hamilton appeared at the entrance to the rooftop heliport on top of O'Riordan Tower and rushed towards him. She carried a small bag and a much bigger folder, like the one she'd had with her five days before—probably full of ideas he intended to reject. But, as satisfaction settled over him at the thought of how much he intended to enjoy putting Ross De Courtney's sister in her place, her coat flattened against her body in the wind created by the helicopter's blades and an unwanted shot of desire fired through his body on cue.

He frowned, finally forced to acknowledge his decision to hire her—five days ago, for a wedding he still wasn't sure he wanted to follow through on, when the original plan had simply been to quiz her for information about her brother—had been impulsive in the extreme. And he was not an impulsive man.

As she approached, it occurred to him she was considerably shorter than the women he usually found attractive, her figure soft and curvy in places where theirs were toned and taut, which only made the buzz of reaction in his groin more annoying.

Dusk had fallen a few minutes ago, and the reddish glow from the sunset over the City of London gave an added lustre to her chestnut hair. As if it needed it. The unruly curls cut in a practical bob bounced, drawing his gaze to the light flush of exertion on her cheeks.

I wonder if she'd have the same glow on her skin after making love?

He tensed, irritated even more by the unbidden thought—and the realisation that his knee-jerk decision to invite her to Connemara had as much to do with her unruly effect on his libido as it did with her connection to a man he needed to find out a lot more about—as discreetly as possible.

Inviting the man's only known blood relation to an interview had seemed like the perfect solution. Until he'd lifted his head, seen the shock of awareness in her eyes and his libido had gone off like a firecracker, too.

He steeled himself as the unwanted buzz of attraction turned into a definite hum. What was it about Ross De Courtney's half-sister that made her so damn tempting, when he knew he shouldn't be tempted? And he certainly didn't want to be.

And what was it about her obvious awareness of him five days ago that had made her seem vulnerable when he knew she was not?

She was an astute and ambitious businesswoman—her boutique company already making an impression in the circles he frequented—but much more than that she was a De Courtney. Which meant, unlike his own sisters, she had been privileged, pampered and entitled her whole life, even if she kept her connection to De Courtney on the down low, and no matter how hard she might be willing to work.

Although that remained to be seen. Perhaps his fact-finding mission had faltered at the first hurdle during their initial interview... But by bringing her to Kildaragh, he had bought himself more time. So what if his motivations hadn't been entirely practical? The plan was still a good one.

He would put her through her paces on this assignment and discover how much of her success had been bought for her by her brother. Meanwhile, he would find out everything he could about the man who had exploited his sister—a man he was already convinced was better off out of his nephew's life. But he needed to be sure.

If Katherine Hamilton did a good enough job, he might even consider following through on the wedding plans—after all, he hadn't lied to her about being unable to stop Imelda making this mistake. But he very much doubted she'd be able to impress him that much.

Katherine's green eyes connected with his when she reached him and she sent him an eager and hopeful smile—apparently undaunted by his irritation.

'I'm so sorry, there was a problem on the Tube. It won't happen again, Mr O'Riordan.'

He stared at her flushed face. What the heck was she doing riding the Tube? Was this a bid to persuade him she was a regular Londoner, when they both knew she wasn't? That she'd had to struggle to get what she needed, as he had?

Yeah, right.

'No. It won't happen again,' he said, signalling to his assistant to take her carry-on bag and the unwieldy folder.

He cupped her elbow to lead her towards the chopper. And felt the satisfying ripple of reaction at his touch, the way he had five days ago, when they'd shaken hands. This time, though, he didn't drop his hand until he had directed her into the aircraft.

Perhaps it was counter-productive to get satisfaction from her reaction. After all, he wasn't a man like her brother, eager to prey on young women, but then he didn't feel she deserved any pity. She knew how the game was played. He'd sensed her arousal too, during their last merry meeting. Why not use this inconvenient attraction to his advantage to get poetic justice for what her brother had done to Carmel? And little Cormac.

'I'm a busy man, Ms Hamilton,' he said as he fastened his seatbelt. 'I don't like to be kept waiting.'

'Absolutely, I understand,' she said as she took off her coat to reveal a fitted pencil skirt and an emerald silk blouse which matched her eyes. The ensemble should have looked slick and professional, but somehow didn't. He noticed the way the silk clung to her full breasts and how a tendril of hair stuck to her lips. She brushed the errant curl back behind her ear and seated herself opposite him.

'If you're going to be late, contact my assistant Liam and let him know,' he said, annoyed by the fact the hum in his groin had only got worse. 'Or, better yet, be on time. I don't like doing business with people who can't be punctual.' He was being unnecessarily surly; after all she was less than five minutes late. But the truth was, he did hate to be kept waiting, especially by a woman like her. And he wanted to test her response.

How would she react to being put firmly in her place? *Again.*

Although, truth be told, her reaction during their interview to his overbearing behaviour hadn't been as productive as he'd hoped. In fact, he'd ended up revealing far more than he had intended about his attitude to love and marriage, and even about his relationship with Imelda, of all things.

But he'd decided after she'd left, that all the starry-eyed romantic nonsense she'd spouted and those probing personal questions had just been part of her act. Of course a high-end wedding planner would pretend to be a romantic. She certainly couldn't know about his sister's connection to Katherine's brother. Not even Carmel was aware he had found out the truth a week ago about the identity of Cormac's father... *Yet.*

Even so, he shouldn't have let Katherine Hamilton's little act get a reaction out of him. And certainly not enough to engage in a personal discussion.

It wouldn't happen again.

She blinked, her gaze as guileless and earnest as it had been in his office. Damn, but she was good at her act. No wonder he'd momentarily fallen for it.

But then her gaze flashed with impatience.

Finally, he'd got to her.

Not so placid now, are we, Ms Hamilton? Let's see how long it takes you to show your true colours. And lose this commission.

But to his surprise she didn't rise to the bait. Instead the flicker of resistance disappeared and she said simply, 'As I said, I understand. I won't be late again. This commission means a great deal to me and my company. I want to get everything right. And I promise you, I will.'

He heard the sincerity again in her voice. And the eagerness and enthusiasm, which made him feel like a bastard—even though he knew she deserved his disdain... She was just another daughter of the elite playing at being a businesswoman. Seriously, could she have come up with anything more unoriginal than working as a party planner?

But how had he been so easily outplayed—and made to feel in the wrong, when he wasn't?

'I intend to hold you to that promise,' he said, but the threat lacked any heat. Somehow she'd defused the situation, which only annoyed him more.

She leant down to clasp the folder Liam had left by her

seat after he'd taken her coat. 'Would you like to have a look at the themes my team and I have been putting together?' she asked, launching into a professional spiel, belied somewhat by the chemistry thickening the air between them. She opened the folder and he got glimpses of colours and fabrics, sketches and notes, and some photos of Kildaragh she must have downloaded from the internet. 'Obviously, until I've had a chance to properly assess the venue,' she said. 'And spoken to Imel—'

'We'll have time for that tomorrow.' He cut her off, still annoyed. He certainly didn't intend to let her speak to Imelda, not until he had made a final decision whether to use her services or not. He reached into his jacket pocket to pull out his phone. 'I need to make some calls. We'll be at Kildaragh in about three hours. Until then I'd prefer it if you didn't disturb me.'

Her cheeks heated and her eyes flared, finally supplying the temper he'd been hoping for earlier. But this time it didn't amuse him the way it might have done before, because it made those emerald eyes spark with a green fire that only made her colouring more striking. And the hum in his abdomen start to throb. *Damn.*

'Of course, Mr O'Riordan,' she said, and closed the folder with more of a snap than was strictly necessary.

Breaking eye contact, she turned to stare out of the window just as the helicopter rose into the evening sky. The bird banked as it climbed, giving them a panoramic view of the city at dusk. The Houses of Parliament and the Millennium Wheel, floodlit on the opposite bank, appeared like sentries to the city's achievements past and present as the aircraft followed the bend in the Thames to head west for the journey to Ireland.

He heard her breath catch, the way it had done once before in his office when he'd first made eye contact with her. The sound of staggered surprise had a similarly visceral effect on him now. And the throb of unwanted sensation arrowed down.

Her fingers gripped her arm rest and he shook his head to remove the sudden vision of those same perfectly manicured nails digging into his shoulders as she rode his...

Sweet Jesus. He thrust his fingers through his hair but was unable to take his eyes off her.

She crossed her legs, revealing a glimpse of thigh above the hem of her skirt. The heat flooding his groin became painful as he imagined placing his lips on the inside of her knee, nibbling his way up and finding out if he could make her gasp again, this time with pleasure.

He looked away, furious now.

Did she know what she was doing to him? Was this all part of the act?

He flipped open his laptop and began the series of calls he had scheduled for the flight, determined to ignore her for the rest of the journey.

Katherine Hamilton's attractiveness, and his reaction to it, was a complication. No question.

A complication he would have to address sooner rather than later, he decided when he caught a whiff of her scent. With notes of orange, cinnamon and rosemary, the addictive aroma was subtle and earthy, and not at all the sweet, cloying, expensive scent he would have expected.

But then everything about Katherine Hamilton had been unexpected so far. And he was fairly sure he didn't like it—one little bit.

Katie's eyelids fluttered open at the judder of turbulence and her gaze connected with Conall O'Riordan's. She pushed her hair back behind her ear and straightened in her seat, embarrassed to realise she'd nodded off after the light supper she'd been served. And he'd noticed. How long had he been watching her? And why did that just make the uncomfortable sizzles even worse?

'I'm sorry,' she murmured instinctively, because he was studying her again with that assessing gaze that made her feel as if she had something to apologise for, although she had no idea what.

She was still mortified she'd managed to be late for their rendezvous at his heliport. And that he'd been so annoyed with her. She was never usually late for anything, certainly nothing as important as this assignment, but there was something about Conall O'Riordan that unnerved her quite apart from those sizzles... It was almost as if he were deliberately trying to provoke her with those unsettling looks and the curt commands.

She took in a careful breath. Let it out again.

For goodness' sake, Katie, get a grip. This isn't about O'Riordan—this is about you. You're just tired. And a little overwrought because you have a lot riding on this job.

Everything about this commission felt far too personal already—perhaps because of her daft and extreme reaction to O'Riordan, and the pressure to get this right. But that had nothing to do with him. She was projecting. And she needed to stop it.

After five fourteen-hour days working on themes and concepts for the wedding and sounding out suppliers, she wasn't her usual pragmatic, professional self, that was all.

He gave a slight nod, accepting her apology as if it were his due. Resentment flickered at his overbearing attitude. Yes, she'd been late, something she would make sure she never did again, and she was still struggling to make sense of her reactions to him, but he'd definitely overreacted.

As hard as it had been to hold her tongue, and not let

his surly attitude get to her, she'd managed it. So she could take some solace from that. Clearly handling bad-boy billionaires was going to be much more challenging than she had assumed. But she could do this. She had to do this.

'We'll be arriving in ten minutes,' he said, the first words he'd spoken to her since dismissing her after take-off—and then ignoring her for the last two and a half hours. The husky Irish accent rippled down her spine, as it did every time he deigned to speak to her, even when he was chastising her, which seemed to be rather often.

She inclined her head and forced herself to smile. 'I'm looking forward to seeing your home,' she said, in another attempt to strike up something resembling a rapport with him.

She was usually so good at forming strong working relationships with clients. She'd always been a people person—which was why event planning had been such an obvious choice of profession. Surely, if she really put her mind to it, she could soften him up enough not to constantly be getting on his bad side?

'The pictures on the internet made the castle look quite magnificent,' she continued. 'Certainly a wonderful venue for a wedding. Your sister is very lucky.' Buttering him up was a strategy she hadn't used yet. But surely it had to be a good way to start knocking down the brick wall of his disapproval? 'I understand you bought it several years ago and spent a fortune renovating it, using local craftspeople to bring it back to its former glory.'

Sycophancy didn't seem to be working either, though. His deep-blue gaze remained unmoved and was as unsettling as it had been earlier—when he'd been telling her off for her tardiness, as if she were an unruly child instead of a capable businesswoman.

But then his lips quirked in that devastating almost-smile, which didn't warm his gaze so much as make it even more intense. Liquid sensation sank into her lap, and she crossed her legs, desperate to stem the flow.

'I see you've done your homework,' he remarked.

'I wanted to find out as much as I could about the venue before I arrived,' she admitted, because his comment hadn't exactly screamed approval for all her hard work. 'I read the interview you gave to *Investor's Weekly* two years ago after beginning work on the renovations. It sounded like a daunting and yet exciting project,' she added, determined to draw him out if it killed her.

'Expensive and time-consuming would be closer to the mark,' he said, directing his gaze back to his laptop and dismissing her again.

Whoever said the Irish had the gift of the gab had obviously never tried to talk to Conall O'Riordan in a snit. Her heartbeat continued to rise, though, as she took the opportunity to watch him unobserved—and tried to decipher what exactly it was about his appearance that unsettled her so.

Perhaps it was that rakish curl in the thick dark hair that fell across his brow and touched the collar of his shirt. Maybe it was the sculpted lips, the designer stubble—which looked entirely natural, rather than deliberate—and gave him a wild, untamed air.

Perhaps it was the harsh planes and angles of his face, both unyielding and commanding and perfectly symmetrical but for a small scar on his top lip. Or maybe it was the length of his eyelashes? she wondered, noticing them for the first time as he concentrated on typing something out on his phone with lightning-fast thumbs. Seriously, most women would kill for those eyelashes, so how was it that they only added to the striking masculinity of his face?

Stop ogling him, Katie. It's not helping.

She dragged her gaze away from O'Riordan and stared out of the window, while trying to drag her mind back on topic and ignore the pounding heartbeat which had settled disconcertingly between her thighs.

Seriously, what are you? A glutton for punishment? The man's an absolute pill, despite his staggering looks. Since when have you found arrogance attractive?

'If you look out the other window, you can see Kildaragh coming up now.'

Her head jerked round, startled by the quietly spoken instruction—and the unmistakeable note of pride in his voice. It was an olive branch, of sorts, but she grasped it with both hands, scooting round in her seat to peer out as the helicopter banked to their left. She didn't have to fake her enthusiasm, though, when Conall O'Riordan's home came into view.

'Oh… Wow!' she gasped.

The staggering beauty of Kildaragh Castle was not unlike its owner, so perfectly proportioned it was hard to believe it was real… The palatial vision was like something from a children's story book or a Hollywood movie. Towers and turrets pierced the night sky, joined by the elegance of fortified ramparts in an amalgam of different styles and periods which, she already knew from her research, were a legacy of the castle's illustrious past.

It had first been the seat of an Irish king, then a monastery and then a boarding school, before falling into disrepair in the nineteen-eighties. The immaculate and extensive work Conall O'Riordan had had done to the building to bring it back to life was clear in every detail, highlighted by the silvery glow of the full October moon and the light from the arched windows as the helicopter approached.

'The pictures I found didn't do it justice,' she whispered, more to herself than him now, utterly captivated by the structure's artistry. 'It's absolutely gorgeous.'

She sighed. She sucked in another breath as she noticed a huge stained-glass window on what looked like a small chapel on the west side of the structure as the helicopter circled. Walled gardens covered the back of the estate and she could just about make out the cliff edge, where the promontory on which the castle was built dropped into the sea. 'Is that window original?' she asked, her artist's eye already in heaven as she swung back round to face him.

For the first time, she caught him with an actual smile on his lips—one that took the cynical chill out of his eyes and added a mesmerising dimple to his cheek.

A dimple? Seriously?

'No, the house and grounds were wrecked when I bought the place. There was stained glass there in the original structure, according to the records. The window was made by a young craftswoman on Innismaan called Elaine Doherty. She used original materials and did some research into the castle's history to come up with the images, which were inspired by the folklore surrounding the last High King of Ireland who, legend has it, built the first structure on this site.'

Pride thickened his voice and took away the cynical edge she had become accustomed to, which only made him more handsome.

'It's exquisite,' she said, trying to convince herself she was totally talking about the stained-glass window. 'She's very talented.'

She swivelled round in her seat to concentrate on the

amazing architectural achievements of his home, rather than that mesmerising dimple, as the aircraft settled on the heliport constructed near the cliff edge.

As the blades powered down, the crash of surf on rocks became audible, full of drama and energy, not unlike the clatter of her heartbeat—excited not just at the prospect of the magnificent wedding she could plan here but also at the small sign of his approval.

Calm down, Katie. This is a job, not an adventure! However dramatic the setting and captivating the client.

'I can't wait to see it in daylight,' she added. 'And start planning how best to use the location. Does your sister have a preference for where the marriage service should be conducted?' she asked, subtly trying to introduce the subject of the bride, and already imagining how incredible it would be if Imelda wanted to get married in the chapel.

'I expect so,' he said. 'We can discuss all that tomorrow,' he added as the door opened from the cockpit and the assistant who had served her dinner appeared.

'Conall,' the young man said, surprising Katie by addressing his boss by his given name. 'Geraldine Ahern at Amari Corp wanted to know if you could take a conference call tonight with Karim about the Zafar project.'

'Sure.' He unclipped his seat belt and lifted his jacket off the seat beside him. After slipping on his coat, he indicated Katie. 'See Ms Hamilton into the house and introduce her to Mrs Doolan.'

At last he turned back to her, but the smile was gone and he was all business again, making her feel oddly deflated. 'I'll see you tomorrow at five to discuss the details further. If you need anything, speak to my housekeeper.'

The door to the helicopter was opened by the ground crew and the wild scent of sea and earth rushed in with a splatter of rain, the rumble of surf turning into a roar. Before she had a chance to thank him, or even get her breath back, he had disappeared down the aircraft steps and was already making his way into the house, surrounded by a coterie of people who had obviously been waiting for their arrival.

'I'll get your coat, Ms Hamilton,' the young assistant said.

'Thank you,' she murmured, unable to take her eyes off the retreating figure of her new client. Silhouetted against the castle's floodlit splendour, he looked almost mythical. His tall frame took the steps up to the heavy oak entrance door two at a time before he disappeared inside.

Like the lord of all he surveys. Literally.

She shook the thought loose and struggled to even her breathing. Then tried to figure out why she felt so giddy… And disorientated.

Maybe this was a job and not an adventure, but weirdly it felt like the latter. Surreal and challenging, but also unbelievably exciting…

And she had a bad feeling that had nothing to do with the commission—and the virtually impossible task of organising a major society wedding in two months for a couple she had yet to meet—and everything to do with the taciturn man who had just walked away from her. And was even more fascinating and overwhelming than his home.

CHAPTER THREE

KATIE WOKE EARLY the next morning in the palatial suite of rooms in the castle's west tower that had been assigned to her, feeling more than a little groggy after a not entirely peaceful night's sleep. Who knew her inappropriate reaction to her new client would chase her in dreams? Her sleep had been disturbed by sensual images of Conall O'Riordan looking tall and indomitable while commanding her to do a lot more than just organise a wedding for him.

Taking a fortifying gulp of sea air from her window—and enjoying the magnificent view of the deserted cove below the castle—she huffed out a determined breath.

Work—that was what she needed. To take her mind off Conall O'Riordan's impressive presence. And it wasn't as if she didn't have a ton of things to be getting on with. Before her scheduled meeting with Conall that afternoon, she wanted to be up to speed on as many details as possible. For starters she needed to assess the castle's facilities and the grounds, work up some informed suggestions about where to schedule the different elements of the event, liaise with her team to discuss the logistics—now she finally had a confirmed date via email from one of O'Riordan's army of personal assistants—and hopefully meet the bride.

Even though Conall still hadn't mentioned a meeting

with Imelda, Katie felt that was the obvious next step. Imelda was the bride and surely she would want input on what kind of wedding this was going to be?

After jumping into the suite's power shower to wash off the last of her sleep haze, she dressed in jeans, boots and a smart sweater—all the better to check out the castle's extensive walled gardens and parkland while still appearing professional, just in case she bumped into her host.

It didn't take her long to track down the housekeeper, Mrs Doolan, who she had been introduced to the night before. Unlike her boss, Mrs Doolan, who insisted on being called Maureen, was a bubbly, chatty and welcoming soul who—after insisting Katie have a full Irish breakfast—was more than happy to give her a guided tour of Kildaragh.

Maureen introduced her to the ground staff and the castle's chef, Clodagh Murphy, who, strangely, had not yet been informed of the upcoming nuptials. Katie made a note to ask Conall if he wanted to hire an outside caterer or use Clodagh and her team with some supplementary kitchen and waiting staff.

While touring the castle, Katie was told that the east wing held Conall's offices, but according to Maureen and the other staff he was rarely in residence and neither of his sisters lived on the grounds either.

She took copious pictures and notes of the castle's two dining salons, four stunning antechambers and all the different reception areas in the two main wings, jotting down ideas and suggestions that she intended to incorporate into the themes and activities she had already worked out.

She also checked out the chapel, which could be an option for conducting the wedding itself. Not only was it beautifully appointed, right next to the castle—so even if it snowed there would be no problem getting people from the church to the reception afterwards—but it was tranquil and elegant. The stained-glass window she had admired the night before was illustrated with a king and his fairy court, only one of the building's many stunning features.

When Maureen showed her the castle's banqueting hall, Katie knew she had an equally perfect venue for whatever festivities Conall and his sister preferred for after the vows had been said—whether it be a formal sit-down meal or a more relaxed affair.

Four storeys high, the hall was as perfectly restored as the rest of the castle, from its vaulted timber ceilings, to the intricate stone carvings on the imposing walls, to the marble flooring and the bespoke mahogany furniture. She glanced around the magnificent chamber, imagining how amazing it would look once her floral and lighting designers had got to work, decorating the austere room with fresh winter blooms, candles and torchlight, and enough wow factor to bring out the venue's fairy tale appeal.

Conall O'Riordan might not be a romantic, but she knew his sister was, and his home would provide the perfect place to give her marriage a start fit for a fairy queen.

'Would you like me to serve you lunch, Miss Hamilton? It's past two o'clock and you must be starving.'

Katie glanced up from her smart phone, where she had been jotting down notes to share with her team, to find Maureen standing at the entrance to the hall.

'Oh… Goodness,' she said, saving herself from swearing just in time. 'Is it already two o'clock?' She had less than three hours before she was due to meet with Conall and she had yet to make contact with his sister. 'I would love a sandwich or something, if it's not too much trouble. But what I really need to do is maybe talk to Imelda. The bride. I'd love to arrange to meet her—and hopefully her fiancé—at some point.'

Conall really should have introduced them already, but she could imagine he would probably prefer for her to take the initiative at this point. After all, he'd made it clear he didn't want to be too bothered with the details… Midnight phone calls notwithstanding.

'Imelda and Donal live on Donal's farm not ten minutes' drive away. If they can see you once you've had your lunch, I could get the groundskeeper to arrange a car for you to use?' said the ever-helpful Maureen.

'That would be wonderful,' Katie said, already excited about meeting Conall's sister. And perhaps not entirely for professional reasons.

During the tour of the grounds earlier, the chatty Maureen had turned out to be a font of knowledge on the O'Riordan family's affairs, nattering away about the details of Conall's and his sisters' upbringing which had brought back the soft glow Katie had felt yesterday for her new client.

Apparently Conall and his two younger sisters—Carmel and Imelda—were extremely close. Their father had died when Conall was only sixteen and the girls much younger, and then their mother had passed away two years later. But, instead of allowing his sisters to be taken in by distant relatives or fostered out, he'd instead insisted on becoming their legal guardian while having to run the family farm single-handed.

She had a much harder time imagining the man she had met being a surrogate father to two little girls than she did imagining him managing to found and grow a billion-dollar agricultural empire.

It was a feat she couldn't help being extremely impressed by when she considered her own family's hopelessly dysfunctional past. If you could even call her and Ross a family anymore. She had to take her hat off to Conall, too, for not abandoning his sister when she had chosen to marry her childhood sweetheart against his wishes.

Meeting Imelda O'Riordan would give her an insight into Conall's softer side, a softer side he kept well hidden in business and which—as much as she knew she shouldn't—Katie had to admit she was intrigued to discover more about. A lot more.

'I'm sorry, who are you now?' Imelda O'Riordan's striking blue eyes, so like her brother's, narrowed as her gaze fixed on Katie's face.

Conall's sister slapped the haunch of a horse whose hooves she had been checking over when Katie had entered the barn and strode out of the stall, staring at Katie as if she had two heads. Lean and tall, with flowing black hair ruthlessly tied back in a serviceable ponytail, and wearing worn jeans and an old T-shirt splattered with mud, Imelda O'Riordan had the same stunning colouring—and intimidating stare—as her brother.

The frown on her brow was remarkably familiar too.

'My name's Katherine Hamilton,' Katie began. 'Maureen said she spoke to you about me popping over to discuss your plans for the wedding?' she finished, feeling almost as tongue-tied as she had with Conall yesterday. What was it about the O'Riordan siblings? Did intimidating frowns run in the family?

Imelda's brow puckered even more as she gave Katie a searching once over. 'Uh-huh, but no way are you from

Flaherty's. Paddy's far too tight to employ someone as fancy as you.'

'Flaherty's?' It was Katie's turn to frown, Imelda's tone had made the 'fancy' comment sound like code for 'stuck up'. 'I'm sorry, I don't...' she began.

'Flaherty's Pub in Westport,' the other woman said, removing the gloves she wore and tucking them into the back pocket of her jeans. 'The place Donal and I hired for our wedding.'

What the...? Katie swallowed, feeling sick as she gripped the folder of concepts she had under her arm.

Had Conall intended the lavish wedding at Kildaragh as a surprise for his sister and her intended? She'd never heard of anyone throwing a surprise wedding before, but perhaps it was an Irish thing. And now she'd put her foot in it and ruined his surprise. But, really, why hadn't he told her?

'I'm so sorry. I think there may have been a mistake.' She turned, stifling the urge to wring her new client's neck as she shot out of the barn. All she could do now was damage limitation until she found out exactly what was going on.

'Hey, wait up.' Imelda, with her much longer legs, caught up with her in a few strides and grasped her elbow to halt her speedy exit. 'You still haven't told me who you are.'

She jerked Katie to a stop so fast, the folder flew out of her hands.

Katie swore as her sketches, suppliers' brochures, photos and samples scattered across the muddy floor like so much confetti. She had everything backed up on her laptop, but even so, she was supposed to be showing this to Conall in an hour's time. And now it was covered in... Was that even mud? Because it didn't smell like mud...

'Really, I'm nobody,' she said, dropping to her knees. 'I shouldn't have come over like this…' She scrambled to gather up the papers, racking her brains to think of how to explain her presence to Imelda—and how she was going to explain the horse manure all over her work to Conall.

But then Imelda knelt beside her and picked up one of the sketches Katie had done of a possible mediaeval Irish theme, complete with fabric swatches and colour schemes to go with the castle's early history.

'This looks glorious,' Imelda murmured, the awe in her voice bringing Katie's frantic movements to an abrupt stop. 'And this,' she said, picking up another sketch which Katie had developed, centred around the local myths and folklore.

Katie managed to take a breath. 'Thank you,' she said as she lifted the two designs from Imelda's fingers.

'You're a wedding planner!' Imelda declared. 'A really grand one!'

Katie nodded, because what else could she do? She was totally busted. 'I'm an event planner. I…'

'Conall hired you, didn't he? To work on a wedding for me at Kildaragh?'

Katie sunk back on her haunches, dumping the last of the muddy paperwork back in the folder as the young woman's astute gaze fixed on her face. *Oh, damn.* She'd really messed up. 'Yes, although I suspect he'll *definitely* want to fire me now that I've totally ruined his surprise.'

'That sneaky, high-handed bastard,' Imelda declared, but her lips had lifted into a cheeky grin that made her look even more beautiful. Clearly devastating dimples ran in the O'Riordan family, too. 'Surprise my bum,' she added, her true-blue eyes sparking with mischief.

'I'm sorry, I don't understand…' Katie began, struggling to get a grip on the conversation now. She knew she'd screwed up and her big commission was about to sink into the horse manure with her sketches. No way was O'Riordan going to put up with an error of this magnitude after giving her so much grief for being two and a half minutes late. But why his sister found the whole situation so amusing, she had no clue.

'Don't be sorry,' Imelda said. 'This is absolutely not your fault. This is my brother messing with me. Or you. Or possibly the both of us,' she said. 'I have no idea what his game is here—because he's made no bones about trying everything in his power to stop this wedding—but he's up to something. I'm sure of it...'

'Perhaps he's changed his mind?' Katie offered, finally getting a grip on the conversation, but still not sure what was going on.

'Have you met my brother?' Imelda asked, giving Katie a pitying look.

'Yes,' Katie said, mortified when her mind chose that precise moment to replay an image of Conall O'Riordan demanding things of her in last night's dreams that had nothing whatsoever to do with event planning... Her cheeks ignited.

'Then you know what a cynical, controlling, sneaky bastard he is,' Imelda supplied, apparently not having noticed Katie's flaming complexion.

Thank goodness for the barn's low lighting or this would be even more excruciating.

'Well, he...' Katie hesitated. She didn't want to agree with Imelda, because that would be totally unprofessional. Conall O'Riordan was a client—or possibly an ex-client—but she couldn't quite bring herself to disagree with his sister's caustic assessment of her brother's character because... Well, he had been quite a pill last night and during their interview a week ago.

'He can be quite a demanding employer,' she managed. 'That's true.'

'Demanding is one way of putting it,' Imelda announced with a full-bodied laugh—part-scoff, part-snort. 'Put it this way,' Imelda continued, 'With Conall, there's always an ulterior motive. A hidden agenda. Some underhanded scheme to bend people to his will. And his will, last time I looked, was to oppose my marriage to Donal with every fibre of his being, because apparently only another gazillionaire will ever be good enough for his baby sister.'

Imelda scoff-snorted again, obviously as unimpressed with Conall's opinion of her choice of husband as Katie had once been with her brother Ross's opinion of Tom. 'So, if he's got you designing a wedding for me...' She lifted the grubby sketches back up. 'A really spectacular wedding, by the way, then he's doing it for a reason that has nothing whatsoever to do with actually giving me a wedding day to remember.'

'But are you sure he isn't doing it because he loves you?' Katie said, not quite able to let go of the conviction that behind Conall's taciturn, dictatorial, overbearing façade was a big softie just waiting to get out.

Oh, pur-lease... Is that for real, what you think, or is it just your hormones playing 'justify the inappropriate attraction'?

'Ah, sure, he loves me.' Imelda interrupted Katie's thoughts, her tone suggesting her brother's love was more of a burden than a benefit. 'But he also thinks he's the boss of everyone, especially me, and Carmel and even Mac. And your little man is only three!'

Your little man? Who is Mac? Does Conall O'Riordan have a child? A child he hasn't thought to mention?

Disgust had Katie's heartbeat galloping into her throat—and her sympathy drying up fast.

Her father had always refused to acknowledge her. She'd been the daughter of one of his mistresses, a 'by-blow', a 'bastard', a 'mistake'—all names she'd been called by the snooty kids in the boarding school Ross had insisted on sending her to after her mother's death.

At least Ross had acknowledged her as soon as he'd found out about her existence when her mother's solicitor had contacted him. How pathetically grateful she'd been for that when she'd been fourteen and alone. Until he'd decided to 'un-acknowledge' her five years later.

But it had never been Ross's job to recognise her. It had been Aldous De Courtney's, and he never had.

Was Conall a man much worse than her brother? A man like her father? Not just arrogant and cynical, but selfish and cold?

'Take it from me, Conall never does anything out of the goodness of his heart,' Imelda said, riding roughshod over Katie's latest internal monologue. 'Mostly because he doesn't have much of a heart. He's like the Grinch... It shrank after Daddy's death, and then again after Mammy's, and then again and again the richer and more powerful he became. Until finally it became almost invisible when Carmel got pregnant with Little Mac and wouldn't tell him who the father was.'

Little Mac is Conall's nephew—and someone else he feels responsible for.

'I see,' Katie said, the wave of relief that she hadn't completely misjudged her client followed by a wave of sadness, for Conall O'Riordan and his shrunken heart—even though she was well aware he would hate her pity as much as her lack of punctuality.

But is his heart really shrunken, or is it just guarded?

*The way any heart would become after too much trag-
edy? And so much responsibility?*

'Ha, I think I've got it!' Imelda announced, dragging
Katie back to reality and the problem at hand. Instead of
the one in her overactive imagination.

Why on earth was she concerning herself with the
workings of Conall O'Riordan's heart? When it would
be much more productive to concern herself with how
she was going to keep this commission?

'Got what, exactly?' Katie asked as politely as possible, as she noticed how Imelda's eyes had narrowed
on her face.

'Con's ulterior motive for employing you to plan me
a fancy wedding,' Imelda supplied patiently, as if Katie
were ever so slightly stupid. 'Which he probably has no
intention of following through on because he doesn't want
me and Donal to get hitched.'

'Which is?' Katie asked, intrigued now by the mischievous spark in Imelda's blue eyes. After the compre-
hensive briefing she'd had from Maureen earlier, on the
complete history of the O'Riordan siblings, she knew
Imelda was twenty-one, three years younger than her,
but she could suddenly imagine Conall's sister as a child
who had probably run her brother ragged.

'You!' Imelda announced as if she had just solved the
crime of the century.

'I beg your pardon?' Katie said, wary now, as well as
confused. Had Imelda figured out that Katie had never
quite been able to keep a professional perspective where
her new client was concerned? Her already vibrant cheeks
warmed even more at the compromising prospect. She'd
always been accused of being too transparent, but this
was becoming seriously awkward.

'You.' Imelda pointed at Katie and laughed. 'You're

the reason he's organising a wedding for me. You're really pretty and super cute and—from those sketches—obviously brilliant.'

'Well, thank you... I think,' Katie replied, not sure whether she was being complimented or insulted now, because...um... *Cute?* Who wanted to be called cute? Especially by a woman as stunning as Conall's sister? And where on earth was Imelda's pseudo-compliment leading? Because Katie was already getting a bad feeling about the knowing look in the other woman's eyes.

'You're welcome,' Imelda said without breaking stride. 'And, the biggest clue of all, Conall dumped his last mistress—Christy Cavanagh—a few months ago, when Christy started making noises about marriage.'

'You've lost me,' Katie said, humiliated by the ridiculous spike of jealousy when she recalled the striking supermodel she had seen in several of the photos she'd found of Conall O'Riordan on the internet while prepping for their first interview.

'Isn't it obvious he wants to date you?'

'He...? *Wh-a-a-at?*' The last of Katie's cool deserted her. Was Conall's sister actually serious? And where on earth had that spurt of excitement come from at the thought that Conall O'Riordan—the scarily hot and superdominant and overwhelming man she'd shared a difficult interview, one tense helicopter ride and a few wildly inappropriate wet dreams with—would be interested in *her*, in anything other than a professional capacity?

Forget wildly inappropriate. She'd just shot straight to insane without passing Go.

'Conall. He's planning to hit on you. That must be why he's hired you,' Imelda said, repeating her insane theory and making Katie's pulse rate hit the stratosphere.

'But that's...' *Pretty creepy, actually.* The truth was,

if Imelda were right, she totally ought to be insulted and not at all impressed or giddy.

No matter how drop-dead gorgeous Conall O'Riordan was, men who hired women because they wanted to sleep with them were basically creeps, whatever way you looked at it. She ought to know, after all—wasn't that how her father had met her mother? By hiring her to renovate a fresco at a *palazzo* he owned in Rome while she was backpacking through Europe after finishing art school. Then he'd seduced her, keeping her as his mistress for months while insisting he loved her, before dumping her as soon as she'd become pregnant with Katie.

'Does he usually date women who work for him?' she asked, trying to get her heartbeat under control and figure out exactly how freaked out she should be about Conall's motives—not to mention her insane reaction to them.

'No, never.' Imelda's brow creased, as if she were reconsidering her theory. 'Fair point. He's kind of a stickler for stuff like that. But there's always a first time… And Con never goes more than a few weeks without a woman, and it's been over two months since he dumped Christy, so there's that,' Imelda added, warming to her theme again. 'Plus, since he became a billionaire, women tend to chase him instead of the other way around, and he hates that. Did I mention he's a control freak?'

'Yes, you did,' Katie said, starting to realise she was getting way too much information about her client's dating habits from his little sister. And it wasn't helping to calm down her giddy pulse one bit.

'Really, Imelda, I think you're totally wrong about this. Your brother is definitely not interested in me in anything other than a professional capacity,' she said, deciding an intervention was called for, before this conversation got any more out of hand. And/or she had a heart attack. 'And I'm also not remotely interested in him,' she said firmly.

Surely she couldn't be held responsible for a few inappropriate sensations and one night of wayward dreams? She was under pressure and she'd never... Well, she'd never met a man quite like Conall O'Riordan before. As much as she had adored Tom, they had always been far too comfortable to create the kind of sparks that Conall O'Riordan clearly inspired in every woman he encountered. The man oozed testosterone. And she was obviously way more susceptible to that hormonal call to arms than she had ever realised.

She refused to feel guilty about it though. Or freaked out... *Much*.

It was a sign, that was all, that her body was finally ready to come out of hibernation. Numbness had been her friend for the year of Tom's illness... And the years after his death. It had helped her to deal with her grief and her anger, and eventually helped her channel what had once been her love for Tom into her love for her work. It had allowed her to concentrate on the important things in life. But she couldn't be numb for ever. Just because Conall O'Riordan—or rather her reaction to him—had made her realise that, didn't mean this physical yearning had any other significance. And it certainly did not mean she needed to act on it, or to get too hung up on Imelda O'Riordan's insane theories about her brother's dating intentions.

'But don't you see that makes you the perfect candidate?' Imelda said, still flogging her dead theory.

Katie glanced at her watch pointedly, and rose to her feet, still shaky but a little less freaked out. 'I should go. I have an appointment with your brother at five back at the castle.'

An appointment she was looking forward to even less now. Not only did she have to explain to her client she'd told his sister about his plans—and deal with the possible fall out from that, because he had obviously intended to keep it a secret for some reason. But now she would have Imelda's mad theory in the back of her mind, which she suspected was not going to help her deal with the hormonal overload Conall O'Riordan inspired just by looking at her. And that was before she even factored in showing him the portfolio that she'd been waiting to wow him with for over a week, which was now covered in horse dung.

She brushed her hair back from her face, then tried to brush the mud off her jeans. *Terrific.* She didn't have time to change into the more professional outfit she had planned to wear for their meeting, because one thing she absolutely refused to be was late... Again.

'I'm really sorry to have bothered you and created a problem between you and your brother,' she said carefully to Imelda.

'What problem?' Imelda asked, looking nonplussed.

But Katie chose not to elaborate—and point out all the things Imelda had said were wrong with her older brother. She'd crossed about a hundred lines by coming here already. That would teach her not to act on her instincts and indulge her curiosity.

She reached out a hand. 'I really hope we get to work together on your wedding. I think Hamilton Events could do an amazing job for you and Donal and Mr O'Riordan.'

'Oh, I'm sure you could. Your designs are glorious. I love them,' Imelda said, taking Katie's hand and giving it a firm shake. 'And with Con footing the bill, it'll be so much grander than what we had planned at Flaherty's.'

The unguarded and effusive praise lifted Katie's spirits a little. Perhaps she could still salvage this job, if she worked her socks off and Conall never discovered exactly how personal her conversation with his sister had become. Because she had a sneaking suspicion that if he ever found *that* out he would have even more cause to fire her on the spot. And frankly she wouldn't blame him.

'I *am* the bride,' Imelda said. 'And, even though my opinion won't matter to my arrogant, control-freak brother, when you speak to him tell him I think the fairy theme is the best,' Imelda added, finally letting go of Katie's hand. 'And that he should definitely dress as a leprechaun to give me away.'

Katie opened her mouth to say she hadn't intended to include leprechauns in the theme. She was going for classy and mythical, not clichéd and crass—but then she spotted the mischievous twinkle in Imelda's eyes.

A laugh bubbled to her lips. 'That's not remotely funny. He'd definitely fire me if I suggested that!'

Imelda laughed too, and Katie realised that somehow or other, during their very short acquaintance, she'd made a friend. And that she really liked Conall's sister. Having never had a sister, but always having wanted one, it was a good feeling—even if this friendship turned out to be very short lived.

'Ah, go on now, I was only messing with you,' Imelda said, slapping Katie on the back in what she was beginning to realise was a typically easy-going gesture.

As Katie made her way back to the car she had borrowed from the Castle and climbed in with her muddy folder, she wondered how it was that Conall's sister was such an impetuous and enthusiastic sort when her brother was so guarded and cynical.

But then she remembered the details of their past. Imelda and her sister Carmel had been orphaned when they were only six and eight respectively, according to Maureen. And then Conall had become their guardian. So the way Imelda had turned out would be largely down to Conall's influence. Whatever friction there was now between the two siblings, Conall must have been a wonderful surrogate parent, no matter how over-protective and controlling, for his sister to be so confident and well-adjusted after losing both her parents when she was so young.

Imelda now stood at the threshold of the farmhouse beside her fiancé Donal, who had his arm slung around her waist. A strapping young farmer, whom Katie had met earlier before being directed out to the barn, Donal Delaney obviously adored his bride-to-be.

Imelda waved goodbye as Katie backed the vehicle out of the yard. 'Good luck with Con, Ms Hamilton,' Imelda shouted after her. 'Even though I'm guessing you won't need it, because he's totally planning to hit on you—take my word for it.'

No, he's absolutely not. And I so don't want him to.

Katie frowned, attempting to concentrate on negotiating the rocky road in the late afternoon sunlight, rather than the wayward thoughts conjured up by Imelda's cheeky parting comment.

But as the castle came into view—gilded in reds and golds as the sun started to sink into the Atlantic behind it—her heartbeat kicked back up to warp speed and a hot weight swelled between her thighs.

Gee, thanks, Imelda.

CHAPTER FOUR

Good luck with the new romance, big bro! FINALLY you've found someone to hit on who isn't a sour-faced stick insect. I approve—&, btw, thx for seeing the light & offering to bankroll a fancy wedding for me and Donal at Kildaragh. I love your girl's ideas—at least as much as I love you. We accept! Immy x

CONALL STARED AT the text from his sister that had just popped up on his phone and tried to make head or tail of it.

New romance? Your girl? *What* girl? And how had she got wind of the wedding planning?

Imelda had taken great joy in messing with him ever since she'd been six years old and had realised how far out of his depth her big brother was trying to be both father and mother to two little girls. He'd had to learn everything from scratch, and fast—from how to plait an eight-year-old's hair at seven in the morning, when you'd already been up for three hours milking cows, to how to deal with night terrors and bed-wetting when you were cross-eyed with exhaustion and grief-stricken too. Imelda, with her eagle-eyed attention to detail, had spotted all his failings, pointed them out at great length and then told him how to fix them.

But she hadn't messed with him in a while. In fact, they'd hardly been speaking—ever since their latest falling out over her decision to marry Donal Delaney. Donal was a nice enough lad, but nowhere near good enough for her. And did she really want to be some man's wife for the rest of her life when Conall had been grooming her to take over O'Riordan's Irish division ever since she'd graduated from Trinity this summer with a first in Agricultural Science?

Of course, even when she wasn't speaking to him, Imelda usually had a lot to say about his choice of girlfriend. Both his sisters did. But where had she got the idea he needed her approval to date anyone? And who the heck was she talking about? He didn't do romance and he hadn't yet had time—or frankly the inclination—to find a replacement for Christy after their bust-up. He hadn't meant to hurt her, but when had he ever given her the impression he was interested in more than superficial sex and entertaining company?

'Conall, Miss Hamilton has just arrived for her five o'clock appointment.'

He looked up from his phone to see his assistant step aside and the woman who had crowded into far too many of his thoughts appear in the doorway.

He tensed against the now familiar ripple of awareness. He was annoyed when he noticed the way the casual outfit of jeans and a soft sweater hugged her voluptuous curves—and the ripple turned into a definite jolt.

He stood and tucked the phone into his back pocket. Whatever Imelda's game was, he would have to deal with it later, because he had a more pressing problem. Somehow his sister had found out he'd hired a wedding planner, and now she was expecting him to follow through on hosting an event at Kildaragh he didn't even agree with, when he hadn't yet made a definite decision about it.

But the way she had finished the message had got to him.

Immy.

It was the nickname he'd given her when she'd been a baby, a nickname he hadn't used since their mammy's funeral, when she'd looked up at him with a solemn tear-streaked face and announced she was 'too grown up' for silly nicknames.

The wave of emotion at seeing that nickname again was something he liked even less than the arousal still charging through his body, because it was going to force him to rethink his strategy and host this damn wedding after all. And that meant working with this woman for a lot longer than a week. A woman whom he didn't want to notice, let alone be attracted to, but somehow was.

'Hello, Mr O'Riordan, I hope I'm not late?' Katherine Hamilton said as she walked into the room and sent him a tentative smile that still somehow managed to light up her heart-shaped face.

The comment seemed guileless, but he had to wonder if she too was messing with him now.

If she was, it was a mistake, because he did not take kindly to having the mickey taken out of him. And, frankly, he was already on edge enough after Imelda's cryptic text not to appreciate the dig at his surly behaviour yesterday before their flight.

He glanced at his watch. 'No, you're not late this time,' he said bluntly, being sure that he did not react to the smile—which even more annoyingly made her cheeks glow with a becoming flush.

Her make-up had been immaculate the day before and during their interview a week ago—but this afternoon she did not appear to be wearing any. For the first time, he noticed the sprinkle of freckles scattered across her nose. The tiny blemishes on her clear dewy skin, coupled with the dishevelled casual clothing—was that mud on her jeans?—and the eager smile made her seem even younger and hotter than she'd been during last night's helicopter trip.

The blood pounded beneath his belt on cue and he straightened.

Don't be a sap. She's not sweet, or innocent. How can she be if she's a De Courtney? This is desire plain and simple—and the emotional sideswipe of having Imelda use her old nickname.

'Sit down,' he said, indicating the seat in front of his desk, before he sat behind it, determined not to lose sight of his motivations for bringing Katherine Hamilton to Kildaragh.

He wanted to find out more about her brother. And maybe part of him also wanted to punish her for being a De Courtney, for having all the privileges and opportunities his own sister Carmel had been denied when she'd had a child at nineteen. Just because he might have to go through with Imelda's wedding at Kildaragh now, didn't mean he couldn't still put Katherine Hamilton through her paces while he was employing her.

He certainly didn't intend to make this commission easy for her. She didn't deserve easy. She'd had enough easy in her life already, while her brother had ensured that Carmel's life was far too hard.

He gave her far-too-hot jeans-and-sweater combo a scathing once-over, making sure she knew he was not impressed with the informality of her appearance—even if his groin was giving it a round of applause.

'I'm sorry for the casual attire.' She gave a nervous

huff. 'I didn't have time to change into something more suitable,' she added, her cheeks igniting. 'I've been so busy today, checking out the castle. I wanted to get a head start on all the logistics, working out a schedule for the events, planning possible venues for the different activities...'

He interrupted her babble. 'Next time find the time to dress appropriately.' Had he flustered her? *Good*.

'Okay,' she said, the obedience in her tone somewhat contradicted by the flash of something provocative in her eyes. Indignation, irritation, rebellion? Whatever it was, that flash had made his groin pulse harder.

Then she hooked the wild hair behind her ear and he caught a tantalising whiff of her delicious scent—orange and rosemary—which had intoxicated him on the chopper ride. And he had to bite his tongue to stop himself from drawing in a greedy lungful.

Good God, what was wrong with him? This woman was the privileged, pampered sister of a man he despised. A man who had wronged *his* sister and abandoned his own child.

How could he feel anything for her but disgust?

'Did you bring the portfolio with you?' he asked, suddenly keen to get this meeting over with and her out of his personal space, until he'd got this unfortunate reaction under control. And figured out what exactly he was going to do about her, his sister's wedding and Imelda's typically confusing text.

That was all this was—Imelda had unsettled him with that text, and it was impacting his ability to control his unwanted attraction to Katherine Hamilton.

'Um...no,' she said, taking the laptop she had under her arm and flipping it open.

But, as she placed the laptop on his desk and clicked

the power button, heat rose up her neck—giving her dewy skin a pink glow.

What was that about? What had she done to feel guilty about? Because he would recognise a guilty flush like that from thirty paces. After all, he'd been the legal guardian of two teenage girls for nine never-ending years.

'I thought I'd show you my ideas on the laptop...' she began, her gaze fixed firmly on the computer screen as she opened a series of files and documents.

'What happened to the portfolio?' he asked. Why was she avoiding eye contact?

The guilty flush exploded in her cheeks as her gaze darted to his. Not just guilt. What he saw also looked like a compelling combination of shame and maybe even panic. Katherine Hamilton was nothing if not completely transparent.

'It got a little muddy,' she said.

'How? And where?' he asked as the pieces suddenly began to slot into place.

The new romance? Your girl's ideas? There was only one new person on the estate at the moment. Only one person he had brought with him from London. And only one person who was likely to have shown Imelda the ideas for the wedding and told her about his plans to use Kildaragh Castle.

Katherine Hamilton had spoken to his sister, had pitched her ideas to her, without asking him first.

How dared she take such a liberty?

Fury flooded through his system, exacerbated by the sharp stab of desire that arrowed down when she licked her lips—the guilt and panic in her gaze like that of a doe who had just spotted the hunter. Why that should make the pulsing in his groin start to pound only made him more furious.

'Did you speak to Imelda,' he asked, because she hadn't replied, 'without my permission?'

You have really blown it this time, Katie.

Conall O'Riordan looked really mad. And utterly magnificent.

For goodness' sake, Katie. Mad and magnificent do not go together, at all.

'Yes, I'm afraid I did. I went to the Delaney farm this afternoon,' she rushed to continue as his steely frown became catastrophic and the twitching muscle in his jaw hardened. 'I just wanted to meet her. To pass a few of my ideas for the themes by her, before consulting with you. It seemed appropriate, as she's the bride. I had no idea the wedding was supposed to be a surprise.'

'It's not supposed to be a surprise.'

Then why are you so mad?

'I see, well, it's definitely not one now,' Katie replied, desperately trying to sound upbeat and not apologetic or flustered, even though her pulse rate had hit the stratosphere. 'But the good news is Imelda loved some of the ideas. She's particularly keen on the myths and folklore theme.'

'Oh, is she, now?' he snarled. He literally snarled, still glaring at her with those deep-blue eyes as if she'd just shot his dog or something.

She didn't get it. Why was he so furious? And how could that frigid gaze feel as if it were incinerating every inch of exposed skin when it was so chillingly disapproving?

The unsettling reaction forced her to breathe and regroup...as she frantically tried to figure out what on earth was going on. Conall O'Riordan had been obstructive and unforthcoming about every detail of this commission so far. He'd put her off, treated her with disdain and got worked up about what were ultimately fairly minor issues.

Normally she would avoid conflict. She was not the sort of person who thrived on confrontation—she worked in events, for goodness' sake. But she'd dealt with arrogant, overbearing men before, Ross being a case in point, and she happened to know that giving ground when they had effectively backed you into a corner was not a good strategy.

If she'd allowed herself to be bullied by Ross, she never would have had those few precious days as Tom's wife. She would never regret those moments, even though it had cost her dearly in terms of her relationship with her brother. And, while she desperately wanted this commission, she could not do it with any degree of success if she couldn't communicate with Conall O'Riordan honestly and openly.

Taking a deep breath, she gathered every ounce of courage she had, determined to stand up to him. 'If the wedding's not a surprise for Imelda, why is it a problem that I consulted her?' she asked, pleased when her voice sounded clear and direct—despite the ball of nerves tying her stomach in a knot.

If Imelda was right, and Conall O'Riordan had some ulterior motive for hiring her, she needed to know what it was. Because even thinking it might be the one Imelda had suggested was making her panic and her anxiety increase, along with those unwanted jolts of sensation that had plagued her whenever she was within two feet of this man. And she could see the fire in his eyes or smell the enticing scent of clean pine soap and spicy juniperberry cologne.

She held her breath, trying to resist breathing in the

intoxicating aroma, and braced herself, ready to be fired on the spot.

His brows lowered even further, his gaze so sharp now she was surprised it didn't slice through the last of her composure, the only sound in the room her breathing and his.

The stand-off seemed to last for several eternities, the silence stretching tight as the spark of something real and vivid sizzled over her skin.

She had no idea what that something was, but her body felt as if it were about to burst into flames as his gaze raked over her. Her staggered breathing slowed, her heart pounding painfully in her chest. The tight feeling in her ribs becoming as addictive as it was terrifying.

Then he broke eye contact.

Her breath released in a rush. And her stomach flipped over, the roar of triumph in her soul as unmistakeable as if she had faced down a dragon—an extremely hot dragon—and won.

Two heartbeats later, his gaze met hers again but, while his expression was still intense, still disturbing, he no longer looked as if he was about to explode.

'My sister and I don't always see eye to eye. She's passionate and tough, but also impulsive and reckless, and she likes to make my life hell on a regular basis, so I prefer to manage her involvement,' he said, so carefully she knew she wasn't getting the whole story. But this at least was a start, a basis for communication rather than conflict.

And, to be fair, he had a point about his sister. As much as she had enjoyed meeting Imelda, the woman was almost as much of a force of nature as her brother.

'I'm really not here to create difficulties between you and your sister,' she said, trying to be as conciliatory as possible now. He hadn't fired her. She could still do this wedding. But she needed to be one hundred per cent professional now.

Somehow she'd already crossed a line with Conall O'Riordan. A line that kept shifting and changing in ways she didn't really understand because, even though she was officially a widow, she had never had to deal with this level of physical attraction before. An attraction that was not just electrifying but volatile. The only way forward now was to establish boundaries, for her own protection.

'I'm just here to plan a wedding, but Imelda *is* the bride, so I think it's vitally important I consult with her as well as you.'

He continued to stare, his gaze seeming to peer into her soul, as if he could see things she had never known were there. But then he nodded, the movement stiff and forced, but enough of a concession to make Katie's heartbeat hit double time.

'Point taken,' he murmured. 'You can consult with her on all the details.' He indicated the laptop. 'In fact, you might as well put that away. You can show those files to her and Donal for approval.'

'Okay, good,' she murmured, closing her laptop and tucking it back under her arm, a little deflated at the realisation she would not be consulting with Conall O'Riordan in future—which made no sense at all, because consulting with him so far hadn't exactly been a picnic.

'Work with her this week, and once you've agreed everything give me a rundown of the costs involved,' he said.

'Absolutely. I'll make sure we stick closely to the budget you outlined,' she said.

His brow creased. 'The budget isn't an issue. I want

her to be happy, even if she is determined to waste a perfectly good education,' he said, the brittle edge still there but blunted with resignation. 'If the costs go above the budget, just let me know.'

Katie nodded. She needed to leave now. His disagreements with Imelda over her marriage were none of her business. But, as she turned to go, she heard the sigh behind her—frustrated and weary—and she couldn't stop herself from turning back.

'For what it's worth, I think you're doing a wonderful thing, Mr O'Riordan,' she said. 'And that you're a really incredible brother.'

One sceptical eyebrow arched and that hot gaze sharpened again. 'Why?' The cynical tone was back with a vengeance. 'Because I'm willing to spend a fortune on a wedding that could quite probably ruin my sister's life?'

'No,' she said, absorbing the caustic comment and the implied criticism of what she did for a living, convinced his frustration wasn't directed at her. 'Because you're willing to support her choices, even though you don't agree with them. That's huge, and much rarer than you might think.'

He blinked, and she realised she had surprised him with her compliment. She wondered why.

'Maureen told me about how you became your sisters' guardian when you were little more than a boy yourself,' she continued, suddenly wanting to explain, even if it meant dancing over that line again. Maybe she wouldn't be working that closely with him, but if she couldn't get him on board with the wedding plans at least she might be able to make him less hostile to them…and her.

'Maureen told me how you brought them both up while working your family's farm and eventually building your business. It's obvious that you love them, and that Imelda loves you back, even if she does enjoy making your life hell.'

She wound to a stop, because he was now staring at her blankly, as if she'd completely lost her marbles. Maybe she had. The swell of emotion in her chest was choking off her air supply.

'Mrs Doolan talks too much,' he said, but the muscle in his jaw had stopped twitching. What she saw in his eyes wasn't cynicism and impatience any more, it was rich and intense—and not entirely disapproving, giving her the courage to finish what she'd started.

'What I'm trying to say is that Imelda's confidence and determination and independence are all a testament to the sacrifices you made. She's her own woman, and that's down to you.'

'Exactly—I've created a monster,' he murmured, but his lips quirked in that almost-smile that told her, while he probably still wasn't happy about the wedding, he wasn't entirely opposed to it.

My work here is done.

But what should have given her relief gave her anything but when he continued to stare at her with that raptor-like focus, as if he were trying to look past the professional to something a great deal more personal.

'We can meet at the end of the week to go over the budget,' he said, his tone curt and business-like, but his eyes continue to study her…making her far too aware of the sensations still rippling over her skin. 'Work out the event details with Imelda and Donal. I have a few people I should include on the guest list, but otherwise that can be Immy's domain.'

'Who's Immy?' she asked before she realised it must be Imelda. To her astonishment, he tensed at the innocuous question, and colour slashed across his tanned cheeks.

He cleared his throat. 'Imelda,' he said, his voice gruff. 'It's a nickname.'

His gaze slid away from hers at last. But Katie's heart skipped several beats as she watched his reaction to the unintentional slip.

No one could ever describe Conall O'Riordan as sweet. He was forceful, demanding, taciturn, supremely cynical and he did not suffer fools gladly. She'd certainly experienced how overbearing and uncompromising he could be after working for him for little more than a week. But in that moment, as she realised how uncomfortable he was at having her witness the unguarded use of his sister's pet name, she couldn't help being deeply touched. He might want to be a hard ass, might want to believe he could control every emotion and bend it to his will, but even he couldn't do that all the time.

He's human, even if he doesn't want to be.

The tender thoughts were quickly dispelled, though, when his harsh blue gaze locked back on her face.

The whisper of arousal arrowed down through her abdomen and became a roar.

'You can see yourself out, Ms Hamilton,' he said, the abrupt dismissal bristling with frustration.

She nodded and left, rushing out of the room, all of a sudden stupidly glad she wouldn't have to spend too much time in his company going forward, as the heat pulsed in her sex and rose up her torso to hit her cheeks.

What just happened?

She shot up to her suite of rooms—knowing she was more than likely going to have another disturbed night's sleep. Because it felt as if she hadn't just stepped over the line this time, she'd crashed over it, and now she was in no man's land. Stuck in a territory which she had no idea whatsoever how to get out of again. The endorphins charging through her were completely out of control—all as a result of one harsh, uncompromising, assessing look that probably hadn't meant anything to Conall O'Riordan but meant far too much to her.

But, more than that, she felt an emotional connection to this man now that made no sense whatsoever.

Because somehow, during just one day in Kildaragh, thanks to Conall's talkative housekeeper, his indiscreet sister and his own unbidden reaction to a perfectly innocuous comment, she'd discovered things—intimate and inappropriate things—about this overwhelming man that didn't just captivate and excite her far too inexperienced body...but also her far too open and easily bruised heart.

CHAPTER FIVE

FOR WHAT IT'S WORTH, I think you're doing a wonderful thing, Mr O'Riordan. And that you're a really incredible brother.

Conall strode out of the churning surf onto the sandy beach of the private cove below the castle, the words Katherine Hamilton had spoken to him a week ago still bugging him.

Why couldn't he get her, and the expression on her face that day—earnest, compassionate, sincere—out of his head? Why should he care what she thought of him, or his family?

The rocky cliffs which hugged the headland and the winter wetsuit he wore provided some shelter from the rain and wind that had picked up since he'd entered the water twenty minutes ago, but not nearly enough to stop him shivering violently as he stripped off the clinging neoprene and grabbed his towel.

After drying off as quickly as possible, he donned the sweats he'd left sheltered under the rocks—the now damp sweats.

Perhaps he should go for a run to work off some more of the energy still charging through his body—a by-product of thinking about the wedding planner? Which he seemed to be doing all the damn time.

But as a gust of wind laden with the cold, fine spray of the October drizzle brushed over his skin he decided against it. This was madness. Hypothermia was not the way to keep thoughts of her out of his head, and his pants. And, anyway, he had controlled it this long. Just about.

He'd all but been forced to abandon plans to quiz her about her brother after their incendiary showdown in his office, deciding that creating distance between them was more important. He'd been swimming in the cove every day of the last week to leash the hunger that had blindsided him during their last meeting. And invaded his dreams every night since. And most of his waking hours as well.

He'd kept himself busy and made a point of staying away from the parts of his home he knew she was using to prep for the wedding and hold meetings and brain-storming sessions with a host of local suppliers, artists, catering staff and craftspeople, making her vision for the event a reality.

But despite his best efforts he'd caught glimpses of her, and they had tortured him, keeping her front and cen-tre in his thoughts when he didn't want her to be there.

Such as when he'd spotted her from the window of his suite on Tuesday morning as she'd chatted expansively to his head groundskeeper in the walled gardens below, and her short curls had whipped around her face in the autumn breeze.

Or as she'd scribbled in her ever-present sketch book when he wandered past the entrance to the banqueting hall yesterday afternoon. She hadn't spotted him, but he'd paused to watch her for one breathless moment until the sight of her small, white teeth chewing on her bottom lip had sent a shaft of desire through his system so sharp it had taken him most of the afternoon to get over it.

Of course, his efforts to forget her had not been helped one iota by the fact his housekeeper, his personal assistants and pretty much every other person that worked in Kildaragh kept informing him how much they enjoyed working with her—despite the scowl on his face every time her name was mentioned, which must have told them he had no desire to discuss her.

Even his sister had rung him several times to sing the woman's praises, so excited now about the prospect of the wedding they were planning together that she seemed to have completely forgotten she wasn't speaking to him. Either that or Imelda had somehow guessed the best way to rile him was to talk non-stop about the woman he'd made it perfectly clear he had no interest in whatsoever.

Except that isn't true. You do have an interest in her. A volatile, incessant interest in her which has only got worse over the last seven days, despite freezing your backside off each afternoon and becoming a prisoner in your own castle.

He slung the wet towel over his shoulders and scooped up the sandy wetsuit, then trudged up the beach towards the steps carved into the rock.

Avoidance wasn't working.

Even those fleeting glimpses only stoked the flames that had been torturing him ever since the afternoon in his office when he'd been furious with her—until the fury had turned into something wild, visceral and untamed. And so uncontrolled he'd let his guard drop, enough to blurt out that daft nickname, and have the things Katherine said about what he'd done for his sisters mean something.

He didn't need her approval, or her sympathy. He certainly didn't need to be captivated by the sincerity in those wide, slightly tilted emerald eyes—devoid of make-up and guile—or the sadness.

But somehow he had been. And now it wasn't just this incessant hunger driving him nuts. It was the thought she wasn't who he had decided she was. That he'd made a mistake, and couldn't punish her for her brother's sins. No matter how much he might want to.

Because for that split second, when she'd spoken so compassionately about his sisters and him, he'd looked into her face and seen honesty and regret…and not the entitled carelessness he'd wanted to see.

And now he wanted to know why.

Why had she looked so sad in that moment?

Why had what he'd done for his sisters moved her so deeply?

And why the heck should it matter to him?

He'd resisted the urge to pull out the investigation report for six days. The one he'd commissioned four years ago when Carmel had run away from art college in London, pregnant, alone and devastated, refusing to name the father of her baby. The investigation that had finally led him to the man he was now convinced was Mac's father.

But, when he'd pulled out the report again last night, it had given him no more details than he already knew about Katherine Hamilton. Just her name, her business address and the fact that she was Ross De Courtney's only known blood relation. A half-sister who Conall had assumed the man must love very much, as he'd paid for her to go to an extremely exclusive boarding school—even though she was his father's illegitimate child.

But now he wasn't even sure about that.

You're willing to support her choices, even though you don't agree with them. That's huge, and much rarer than you might think.

Somehow those quietly spoken words—and the other things she'd said that afternoon—had pierced through the wall he kept around his heart.

A wall that he'd constructed brick by tortuous brick, ever since he'd walked into his mother's bedroom one Christmas morning thirteen years ago and found...

He cut off the cruel memory and smothered the wave of self-loathing which came with it.

Yeah, so not going there. Not when my mind is messed up enough already by this woman.

He made his way up the castle's back stairs to his suite of rooms in the east wing. After dumping the towel and wetsuit in the basket for the housekeeping staff, he stripped off the damp sweats then walked into the *en suite* bathroom and turned on the power shower.

He stepped under the needle-sharp spray and washed the salt and sand out of his hair and off his skin. Then he switched the dial down to frigid, to control the pulsing ache in his groin which was back, despite the freezing swim.

Grand, just what I need before I see her again.

He got dressed then checked the clock on his smart phone. He was late for their appointment. An appointment he'd considered cancelling a ton of times. He didn't really need to okay the wedding budget. He could easily pass that responsibility off to his financial director. But each time he'd contemplated cancelling he'd known he didn't want to... Because now, as well as the hunger, there was the curiosity, that nagging feeling that there was much more to Katherine Hamilton than he'd realised.

She was scheduled to leave Kildaragh tomorrow morning once they went over the budget—and he would have no need to see her again until the wedding itself in several weeks.

Which should have been a good thing. The perfect excuse to get her out of his mind, as well as his sight. But, try as he might, he couldn't deny the deep pulse of yearning. And the even more disturbing desire to know much more about her. He wanted to discover the secrets that lurked behind those guileless emerald eyes…

Surely this yearning was really just about him finishing what he had started by hiring her in the first place? he told himself. Nothing more, nothing less.

Had her brother let her down too? And, if he had, could Katherine Hamilton give him information he could use against Ross De Courtney if he needed to?

And if the hunger turned out to be mutual…? Would it really be so wrong to use it to get closer to her, for Carmel's sake? For Mac's?

He made his way back down the castle stairs towards his office in the east wing. So what if he wanted her? It could be useful, especially if she wanted him in return. She couldn't possibly be as innocent as that flush of awareness had suggested when he'd first met her. And she wouldn't get past his wall again, because he was ready for her now.

He thrust open the door to his office and she jumped up from her seat, her fingers wrapped around her laptop and her face a picture of surprise and… Was that pleasure?

Something surged up his torso…and he knew. This meeting didn't have to be an end, it could be a beginning.

An idea formed in his head as he recalled the ball at the Hotel de Lumière in Paris, which he was attending on Sunday night. He hadn't wanted to go to the event, as he usually hated those kind of dressy, pointlessly fancy affairs, but he'd been strong-armed into it by his PR team. Apparently it would help if he was a lot more visible in the French media before they floated O'Riordan's European division on the Paris Stock Exchange in two weeks' time.

'Good afternoon, Ms Hamilton,' he said, spreading his arm out to indicate she sit down again. 'Take a seat.'

He marched round his desk but, as he watched her brush her pencil skirt over her bottom before taking her seat, and saw her blouse stretch over her breasts, the thought of seeing her in something glittering and a lot more revealing had the idea becoming fully formed.

Maybe it was impetuous, even a little reckless—which was not at all like him—but why not?

Katherine Hamilton was a romantic. She'd said it herself. And, while he'd doubted it at first, he had become convinced of it in the last week, after the way she had bonded so quickly with his love-struck sister. From the few glimpses he'd been given of the fanciful fairy-tale design they'd settled on together for the wedding, from that heartfelt look when she'd spoken of family and commitment and love, and from the flush warming her cheeks now.

He hadn't imagined the awareness in her eyes when she'd turned round a moment ago, either.

Why not give her a little of the romance she craved? And get them both what they wanted? Seducing more information about her brother out of her wouldn't be that hard. And they could both enjoy the results immensely, if the desire pumping through his veins was anything to go by.

She placed the laptop on the desk, powered it up and started talking about the budget she'd worked out for his sister's wedding in that business-like tone—somewhat belied by the vivid flush on her face and the rapid rise and fall of her breathing beneath her blouse. He asked what he hoped were pertinent questions, while considering how to invite her to Paris and get her to the ball without scaring her off.

Because he had the definite impression Katherine Hamilton found him intimidating as well as exciting.

He smiled, as on cue she bit into her bottom lip, while bringing up a spreadsheet of estimates from the local suppliers and contractors.

Intimidating is good, Con... All the better to sweep her off her feet with.

Keep talking, don't look at him and stop blushing, for Pete's sake.

'As you can see, we've managed to find a lot of really terrific and also cost-effective suppliers in Galway and Mayo. Imelda was particularly keen on sourcing locally and I agree with her.'

Katie took a much-needed breath, the figures on her spreadsheet starting to blur—probably from lack of oxygen. Why did she find it so hard to breathe when she was near him? And to remain professional? Perhaps it was the smile he'd treated her to when he'd walked into his office—as if he'd been genuinely pleased to see her—that had sucked all the air out of the room.

Or maybe it was the memory of him walking out of the surf half an hour ago, from her vantage point in her room as she prepared for this meeting, the contours of his muscular frame perfectly displayed in a leave-nothing-to-the-imagination wetsuit.

It was a guilty pleasure she'd got into the habit of indulging every day now, ever since she'd spotted him taking his swim on Sunday afternoon, and had discovered the next afternoon—when she'd just happened to be watching from her window again at precisely the same time—that it was something he scheduled every day at around four p.m.

A guilty pleasure she was now paying the price for, big time.

How was a woman supposed to concentrate on euros and cents and the intricacies of finding the perfect florist when all she could see was Conall O'Riordan's magnificent physique displayed in clinging wet neoprene as he battled the elements, and when all she could smell was the clean, spicy scent of soap and man?

She sucked in a breath and forced herself to conclude her presentation. 'So, as you can see, I've got some really competitive quotes and Imelda is very happy with the progress so far.'

'Grand, email the spreadsheet to my financial director.' The deep voice concluded, ending the presentation she'd been practising for over an hour—before she'd got distracted by the sight of him in a wetsuit, his dark hair plastered to his forehead, his muscular chest gilded with moisture as he'd stripped down to his...

Focus. On the work, not the six-pack reveal.

'Um...yes, of course,' she managed, forcing her gaze to his face and that far-too-knowing blue gaze.

Unfortunately, his features—and the cobalt blue of his irises—were no less breath-taking than the sight of his naked chest half an hour ago, now tattooed on her frontal lobe.

'I've given him the budget and you can liaise with him now about the details,' he added, his lips quirking in rueful amusement that had all her freak-out vibes freaking out more.

Did he know that she'd been spying on him every day at four? Could he see the compromising image inside her head—seared there for all eternity—of rippling abs, bulging biceps, the sprinkle of chest hair that arrowed down past his hip flexors to...

Stop! And say something... Preferably something relevant and coherent, if possible.

'Um...absolutely. *You* don't need me to email you my spreadsheet, then?' she asked.

One dark eyebrow arched, and his lips curled on one side—turning the rueful quirk into a definite smile. 'Your spreadsheet?' he said, the teasing tone doing diabolical things to the heat in her face, which chose that precise moment to start wending its way down her torso. 'No.' He paused, his amusement unmistakeable. 'Although your spreadsheet looks very...accomplished,' he finished, almost as if the word 'spreadsheet' were a euphemism for something else entirely.

'Thank you,' she said, not entirely sure what they were talking about any more, because it definitely didn't feel like spreadsheets. 'Well, I suppose...' She switched off her laptop, trying not to regret the fact their meeting was effectively over. 'I should go then, unless you had any other questions about the budget? Or the wedding plans?' she asked, trying not to wince when she heard the eagerness in her voice. Exactly how desperate was she to spend a few more precious minutes in his company?

'I don't have any other questions about the commission, no,' he said.

She nodded, not able to speak round the stupid regret now as she shoved her laptop back into her briefcase, keen to get out of his office before she did something really mortifying. Like beg... Or hyper-ventilate.

Seriously, Katie, haven't you already been unprofessional enough with your recently discovered Peeping Tom tendencies?

'But I do have another question that has nothing to do with the wedding.'

She looked up to see those intense blue eyes locked on her face. Her still burning face.

'Actually, it's more of a request than a question,' he said, his eyes darkening. 'I need a date for the Lumière Ball tomorrow night in Paris.'

'I'm sorry…what?' she asked sharply, so shocked she was fairly sure she must just have had an audio hallucination of some sort. Either that or she'd got totally the wrong end of the stick.

Had he just asked her on a date—to the Lumière Ball, the most prestigious and exclusive event in Europe's winter season? Only billionaires, movie stars, royalty and other assorted very, *very* important people attended the Lumière Ball.

But it wasn't really the thought of the ball—any event planner's dream to attend—that was giving her breathing difficulties. It was the thought of going with *him*. She blinked, struggling to shake the fanciful thought loose. No, it wasn't possible. She was his event planner. An event planner whom she wasn't even sure he really liked very much. She must have misunderstood him.

'I don't know anyone you could ask,' she said, wondering if perhaps he thought she ran an escort service on the side.

Asking her to find him a date was odd—especially as he was probably one of the world's most eligible bachelors, so must have a string of glamazons at his fingertips to call on at a moment's notice. But it was probably not the oddest request she'd ever had, if you included the septuagenarian couple who had asked her if they could celebrate their golden wedding anniversary by abseiling down Tower Bridge.

'Katherine...' he said, the lip quirk turning into another slow smile. 'Do you mind if I call you Katherine?' he asked, getting up to walk round his desk and perch on the corner of it—right in front of her.

'Katie,' she murmured. He was so close she could see the dimple in his cheek peeking from the five o'clock shadow. And the sparkle of amusement in his eyes— which reminded her of the sparkle in Imelda's eyes. Except not. Because Imelda's sparkle didn't give her goose bumps.

'Sorry?' he said.

'Katie.' She cleared her throat to stop her voice from rising even more. 'People call me Katie. No one calls me Katherine.'

'That's a shame. Katherine suits you better,' he said. 'Katie sounds like a girl's name, instead of a woman's.'

'You can call me Katherine if you'd rather,' she replied, her voice so breathless now she was surprised she hadn't passed out.

'Good. So, just to be crystal-clear—it's you I'm asking on a date, Katherine. No one else.'

'Oh.' So she hadn't misunderstood him. 'I see,' she said, even though she really didn't see. How could he want her to go with him when he was just so...? Well, so...*much*. Of everything. And she so wasn't.

'You'd be doing me a huge favour,' he added, clasping his hands together and resting his bare forearms on his thighs, drawing her attention to the way the strong muscles stretched the fabric of his suit trousers and how the fly settled over the bulge of his...

Look away from his crotch! Are you insane?

'I have to go to this damn thing,' he said. 'And I prefer not to go alone.'

She stared at his face, hoping her heart wasn't going

to punch right through her ribcage. He was actually serious. He wanted to take her to the Lumière Ball.

A part of her knew she should say no for the good of her health. How on earth was she supposed to survive an event like that on this man's arm when she found discussing a spreadsheet in front of him a major challenge to her lung function?

Good Lord, had Imelda been right all along? Had he hired her to hit on her?

But, just as the coronary-inducing thought occurred to her, she recalled something else Imelda had said during their first meeting about her brother's dating habits.

Since he became a billionaire, women tend to chase him instead of the other way around, and he hates that.

Her lungs began to function again as Conall's motives became clear. He wasn't *really* hitting on *her*. He just didn't want to go to the Lumière Ball alone, because then he'd be fair game. And he hated that. This wasn't a real date, it was just a stunt date—to keep other women at bay. After all, he had said she'd be doing him a favour. That was all this was.

You've got this! No need to go to pieces. You can do him a favour and do yourself a massive favour too.

Because going to an event like the Lumière Ball would be the ultimate busman's holiday—event-planning-wise.

'The ball is tomorrow night...'

He was still talking in that deep, husky Irish accent that seemed to brush over her skin like a caress. She tried to listen.

'If your work schedule is a problem, I can ensure you're back in London by—'

'I'd love to go with you,' she interrupted him. 'If you're sure,' she added, suddenly scared he might change his mind.

His eyebrows rose up his forehead, but then he smiled.

It was the first truly spontaneous smile she'd ever seen on his face. It set alight the mischievous sparkle in his eyes, adding silver streaks to the true blue and turning that damn dimple into a lethal weapon.

She couldn't breathe again, of course. But now she didn't care. The excitement flowed through her like an electrical current. Maybe this was a stunt date for him. But she intended to make the most of it. Why not? It had been so long since she'd been the focus of any man's attention.

Somehow Tom's attention had been different. Not electrifying but cosy, comfortable and kind.

She felt the inevitable wave of melancholy. But she could almost hear him talking to her again, the way he had on their wedding night, as they'd lain together on his hospital bed and listened to the monitor beeping.

'No guilt or sadness after this is over, Katie. And no sack cloth and ashes either, you promise? You deserve to find someone else who can give you all the things I can't. Adventure, travel, a grand passion, lots and lots of kids... And really spectacular sex.'

She hadn't kept that promise, of course. Not for five years. Because she'd been gutted after losing Tom—and far too busy once she'd started her business—even to *want* to look for any of that stuff.

Plus, she was not daft enough to look for grand passion or great sex with a man like Conall O'Riordan. Because he was so far out of her league, it was ridiculous. And way too overwhelming. Making love for the first time with a man like him—who probably knew all the moves and could give a woman a multiple orgasm from thirty paces—would be dangerous. Because she was just vulnerable and chronically inexperienced enough to read far too much into it.

But adventure. And travel. And maybe even a little stunt passion. For one glorious heart-stopping weekend in Paris? That she could totally do.

'Grand,' Conall said. Then touched a thumb to her cheek. He slid it down to her chin to capture her face and lift it to his. For one glorious moment, anticipation squeezed her rib cage. Her heart stopped beating then started again at warp speed and her lips parted of their own accord. His gaze narrowed, the pupils dilating as her tongue darted out to wet suddenly arid lips. But, after staring at her mouth for what felt like a millennium or two, he cleared his throat, blinked and then dropped his hand.

And her heart dropped into her stomach, the intense yearning followed by devastation.

Yup, she definitely could not risk real passion with this man, or she would be risking so much more.

'How long will it take you to pack?' he asked.

It took her several moments to process the question— after her ludicrous overreaction to that almost-kiss.

'Not long,' she said. 'I don't have too much with me.'

'Grand,' he said again, then stood up and strode back around his desk to press the button on the intercom. 'Liam, get the chopper ready to take us to Knock, and then make sure Joe is available to fly us to Paris. Then call Etienne at the Hotel de la Lumière and extend my booking for the suites on the top floor to include tonight.'

'Yes, Con. What time do you want to leave?' came the prompt reply from his assistant through the speaker phone.

Con glanced at his watch. 'In about forty-five minutes.'

Katie stood slowly, feeling dazed now as well as giddy. They were leaving *tonight*? In less than an hour?

Conall's gaze connected with hers as he signed off, and he let out a rough chuckle that sounded a little strained. 'You should probably get out of here and start packing, Cinderella.'

'Right, absolutely. On it.' She nodded and flew out of the office.

But it wasn't until she was in her suite, busy throwing things into her suitcase like a crazy person, while simultaneously tapping out a text to Caroline, her PA at Hamilton Events, to rearrange her schedule for Monday and trying not to hyperventilate, that it occurred to her Cinderella had a problem.

Not only did she not have anything remotely appropriate to wear to something as exclusive as the Lumière Ball in her luggage… She didn't have any spare *haute couture* lying around at home either.

And no fairy godmother to speak of.

Terrific. Cinderella has a ball-gown emergency.

CHAPTER SIX

'IT'S ALL SO much more magnificent than I ever imagined. And I imagined a lot.'

Katherine Hamilton's whisper was hoarse with awe, her head swivelling backwards and forwards to get the best possible angle to view the Arc de Triomphe as Conall drove across the intersection at L'Etoile.

'As you imagined?' Conall asked, far too aware of his passenger's scent, which had been torturing him for the last few hours and was now filling up the car's interior. 'Haven't you ever been to Paris?'

Surely that couldn't be true? Was that why she'd been so quiet on the flight over?

He'd wanted to quiz her about so many things. But he'd decided against it, until he could figure out how best to approach this situation. The decision to bring her to Paris had been done on the spur of the moment. A knee-jerk reaction to the desire that had been flooding his system for days now, and which he had finally acknowledged.

Why not admit it? The urge to bring Katherine to Paris had a lot less to do with getting the information he wanted about her brother than it did with the spike of need and determination that had assailed him the minute she'd said yes.

She'd looked so excited, so eager… And so nervous

when she'd joined him in the chopper for their flight to Knock and then onward to Paris in the company jet. And somehow so young.

She had also seemed oddly overwhelmed by the luxury, which made no sense at all. Surely the lifestyle he had now wasn't that far removed from the one in which she'd been brought up? Surely it was a lifestyle she would be very familiar with, given the kind of clients she worked for? Event planners needed to look confident in this environment, and she had up till now. But, as they'd flown over the Irish Sea and English Channel and finally arrived at Orly an hour ago, she had seemed utterly captivated by the whole experience.

Was this another act—the awestruck ingénue? He was trying to convince himself it was. But something about the glow of enchantment in her gaze and the flush of excitement on her cheeks seemed entirely genuine. And it was starting to bother him.

Seducing her in his office at Kildaragh had seemed like a good idea three hours ago. Sex, after all, was nothing more than a biological urge. One they both appeared to have for each other. But now he was beginning to second-guess the impulse. Exactly how innocent was she? He knew from the detective's report she was twenty-four—very young to have founded her own event-planning business and made such a success of it. He had simply assumed she was worldly, given her work, her background and her business.

But now, seeing the wonder on her face, he was concerned he might have miscalculated. What if she wasn't as worldly as he had assumed? He'd already begun to suspect that, while she was incredibly good at what she did, she wasn't as hard-nosed as she should be.

But innocence would be far worse. Unlike her brother,

he wasn't interested in seducing women with no experience. Women like his sister had been, who were vulnerable and naïve.

What was it about her that made him feel protective of her? Made him want to enhance this experience for her? He wasn't supposed to be that invested. It wasn't something he'd felt before for any woman—except maybe his sisters—and what he felt for Katherine certainly was not fraternal.

'Oh, no,' she said, that easy, even slightly shy smile spreading across her features and captivating him even more as she finally settled in her seat. 'Tom and I always talked about travelling, and we had Paris at the top of our list...' The glow on her cheeks dimmed. 'But we never got the chance.'

Who the hell is Tom?

Something that felt far too much like jealousy made Conall's hand jerk on the car's gear stick, the wistful tone telling him that, whoever this Tom guy was, he meant a great deal to Katherine.

The engine grunted in protest as he shifted back into gear to accelerate round a large delivery truck as they drove down the Champs-élysées.

'Who's Tom?' he found himself asking. Then wished he could take the question back. Tom, whoever he was, was clearly out of the picture now. Surely that was all that mattered?

She sighed, her eyes glittering as they headed down Paris's famous boulevard of lights—at a snail's pace, because it was choked with traffic. As always the bustle of movement and energy on the wide tree-lined avenue was intense. People filled the pavements, milling in and out of the street's grand terraces that housed cafés, theatres, cinemas and designer shops all buzzing with activity as night fell. Scooters zipped in and out of the traffic, irate drivers honked their horns and gesticulated and intrepid pedestrians stepped into the fray with typical Parisian *savoir faire*.

In the car, the mood had stilled, though becoming thick with an intimacy Conall had never intended but was somehow powerless to stop. He couldn't take the question back because he wanted to know the answer.

She glanced at him, the soft smile on her face both sad but so unguarded and full of compassion, it made him tense…and the jolt of envy increase. What was that about? Why should he care that no woman had ever looked at him like that, when he certainly did not want them to?

'Tom's my husband,' she said, so quietly he almost didn't hear her.

What the…? She was married. His fingers fisted on the steering wheel, but before he could even process his reaction to the shocking revelation she added, 'Or rather he was my husband. He died, five years ago. Not long after we were married. He was…'

She cleared her throat and he could hear the strain in her voice when she continued. 'He'd been sick for a long time.' She let out a rough laugh that sounded impossibly brave. 'But it's weird. I still can't think of him in the past tense.'

'You got married and widowed at nineteen?' he asked, unable to keep the incredulity out of his voice, and still not able to get his head round the furious envy caused by this insight into her past.

Why should he care about the man she'd married? Especially as the guy had died years ago. He already knew the woman was a romantic—she'd said so herself. Surely this just confirmed it?

But why did what she had done seem moving instead of desperately misguided? After all, if one of his own sisters had decided to marry some guy at that age, he would have advised against it. He didn't believe in love, and he believed even less in throwing your life away on a romantic idyll that could only bring you pain.

'You sound like you disapprove,' she said, her voice so devoid of judgement, he found himself defending his position, even though he knew her ill-advised marriage was none of his business.

'I do disapprove.'

'Why?' she asked. 'If I loved Tom, and he loved me, why wouldn't I marry him?'

He glanced at her. 'Do you really want me to answer that question?' he asked, knowing he probably shouldn't give her his opinion. After all, this wasn't meant to be more than a casual affair. Did he have the right to question her choices, however foolish?

But something about the way she'd phrased the question, as if she really couldn't figure out why marrying this guy had been a bad idea, got to him.

Seriously, there was romanticism and then there was self-destructiveness. And making a decision to hitch yourself to someone at that age, especially someone with no future, seemed naive in the extreme. It was pretty clear she was still hung up on this guy. Probably still thought she was in love with him. And that was mad, for all sorts of reasons.

'Yes, I really do,' she said.

'Then I'll tell you why.' He bit out the words, suddenly furious, the hole in his own chest that had been there for so many years making his tone sharper than he had intended. 'Because if your man Tom had ever really loved you, he would never have asked you to marry him in the first place.'

'Why not?' she asked, as if she really didn't get it.

'Because he knew he was going to leave you. That's a pretty crummy thing to do to someone you love. Don't you think?'

'You can't blame someone for dying, Mr O'Riordan,' she said with such dignity he felt a strange yank in his chest. He denied it, though. What the hell foolishness was this?

'Call me Conall, Katherine,' he said. 'And, yes, you can,' he added, suddenly angry with the man she'd married for putting the sheen of sadness in her soft green eyes. Which reminded him far too much of his sisters' faces as they stood over their mother's grave.

'Tom didn't have a choice,' she whispered.

'He had a choice about whether to take advantage of you, though, didn't he?' He could just imagine her—a young woman barely more than a girl, compassionate and easily led, just like his sister Carmel when she'd had the misfortune to encounter Ross De Courtney's charms.

'He didn't take advantage of me! We were best friends and I was the one who suggested marriage.'

'Why, though? So you could watch him die?'

'No, so I could watch him live what little life he had left.'

Good Lord, was she really that soft-hearted and that soft-headed? The man had exploited her. Used her. He said he'd loved her, but he'd hurt her. Wasn't that always the way when someone said they loved you?

She shifted round in her seat as the car cruised past the Jardin des Tuileries, the panoramic park crowded now with evening joggers, parents herding hyperactive children home and couples strolling arm-in-arm in the twilight.

'It's so beautiful,' she all but purred. 'And so romantic,' she added, their conversation about her marriage clearly over.

He sealed up the anger in his heart and the painful memories. She was right. Giving her his opinion of her marriage wasn't what he had planned this evening.

She continued to remark on the sights—carried out of her sadness by the splendour of the City of Lights—and determined not to talk about her marriage any longer.

He'd always enjoyed Paris himself—perhaps because its cosmopolitan energy and sophistication were the antithesis of where he'd grown up in rural Ireland. But hearing the enthusiasm in her voice, seeing the excitement light up her face, had him seeing it in a new light.

'The French are so wonderfully sophisticated, aren't they?' she remarked. 'So steeped in culture, and yet so at ease with it. I love that about them.'

She turned back to him, her face flushed but her expression clearly keen to paper over the cracks their conversation had caused. 'I went on a skiing holiday once to the French Alps as a teenager. But I couldn't ski like the other pupils, so the teachers let me hang out at the resort while they took to the slopes. I adored it—going to the little *boulangerie* in the town square, trying out my faltering French on the shop keepers, checking out the local market.'

Something about her reaction—so genuine and fascinated—made the pulse of yearning in his chest intensify.

Don't be daft, Con.

Perhaps she'd never been to Paris before, but she had lived a privileged life. His sisters had certainly never been on a skiing holiday as teenagers. And neither had he.

'Why didn't you learn to ski as a child?' he asked, finally getting it together to press her for more information. 'If all your peers did?'

She laughed, the sound light, musical and self-deprecating. 'Mum didn't have money for skiing holidays. We basically lived from commission to commission—she was a talented artist, but she didn't believe in commercialising her work. And, anyway, I'm not exactly the sporty type.'

But your father was a millionaire...

He had to bite back the question before he gave away the fact he knew more about her background than he should. But even so the question tormented him. He knew Aldous De Courtney hadn't publicly acknowledged her when he'd been alive, but he'd assumed the bastard would have paid some kind of maintenance. Was abandoning their children a trait of the De Courtney men, then? Because it was beginning to appear so.

'If your mother didn't have money for skiing holidays, how did you end up on that one?' he asked, risking a glance at her face as the traffic ground to a halt again.

The smile became wistful, the delight in her expression faltering. 'She died when I was fourteen and my brother became my guardian. My half-brother,' she clarified. 'Luckily for me, he was loaded.'

The tone suggested she was joking, but her voice caught. And he could hear the grief that still lingered for the woman who had died when Katherine had still been a girl.

'That's tough,' he said.

'What is?'

'To lose your mother so young,' he murmured. 'The same thing happened to my sisters and it was very hard on them.'

He'd known about the basic facts of her life from the detective report—all except her marriage—but somehow he hadn't really made the connection, until now, that she had suffered the same loss as his sisters. Why hadn't he? And why did it make him feel even more protective towards her?

It was stupid, just an unfortunate coincidence.

'And you,' she said, so softly he almost didn't hear her over the din from the traffic outside the car. 'It must have been very hard on you too.'

'I was eighteen when my mother died,' he said, trying to quell the emotion in his chest. He didn't require her sympathy...or her compassion. He didn't even deserve it. And he certainly hadn't brought Katherine Hamilton to Paris to have a heart-to-heart with her about his childhood. Or to open up old wounds he had sealed up a long time ago.

He'd paid his dues to his sisters as best he could. Had worked hard and sacrificed to give them everything he was capable of. Maybe money and security would never compensate them for the loss of their mother, but there was nothing more he could do, so there was no point beating himself up about it. Especially in front of her.

'I was a grown man. It didn't affect me as badly.'

'Were you really a grown man at eighteen?' she asked.

He turned to find her watching him, her eyes so full of understanding, he flinched.

What the...?

'I earned my first million by the time I was twenty-one,' he said flatly, determined to take that soft glow from her face. 'I am driven, ambitious and ruthless when I need to be. But, most of all, I stopped being a boy long before my mother died.'

He dragged his gaze away, aware that he was saying

too much, that he was overreacting, but somehow unable to stop himself.

He crossed the Place de la Concorde and drove onto the forecourt of the Hotel de la Lumière. He braked the powerful BMW in front of the magnificent four-storey building that took up a whole city block—originally a neo-classical palace built for Louis XV, the landmark hotel's arches and columns had been designated an historic monument by the French government over a century ago.

O'Riordan Enterprises had booked out the whole top floor of the landmark hotel for the Lumière Ball.

This was the man he was now—able to afford the trappings of royalty. A luxury he had worked so hard to earn, always aware of how far he'd come from that ambitious farm boy who had wanted so much more for himself than four a.m. wake-up calls, mucking out stalls or herding cows into the milking shed before he'd even had breakfast. The boy who had fallen asleep over his school books each evening, which he usually had to read by the fire because the farm's ageing generator had cut out again...

He'd done what he'd needed to do to get away from the path his birthright had set him on. A path every O'Riordan had followed until now.

He wasn't ashamed of that. And he refused to apologise for his ambition or his success. But Katherine Hamilton needed to know that, while he might be prepared to wine and dine her this weekend, to seduce her with a little of the romance she obviously craved—to get everything out of her he desired—he was no hero. And no grief-stricken child either. Nor had he ever been.

She had stopped gazing about, all her attention on him now. It made him uneasy, unsettled, and yet also strangely energised. No woman had ever been foolish enough to romanticise him before—not even Christy, who had wanted to marry him—but then Katherine didn't know him. Perhaps he should give her a taste of what she was getting herself into.

'I don't believe you,' she said.

The comment was audacious. And personal. Both delusional and yet also forthright.

He laughed, but the sound had no humour. The arousal darkening her irises made the yearning in his gut twist and tighten.

'You can believe what you want,' he said. He touched her cheek with his thumb, slid it down to glide across her lips.

She gasped, her irises dilating to black. The need in her gaze was as vicious as the tangle of desire in his gut.

Gripping her chin, he pulled her closer.

To hell with it. He'd been waiting to taste her for hours now, ever since she'd agreed to go with him and he'd seen the yearning in her eyes. Hell, even before that. Ever since he'd raised his head that first day to find her watching him in his office, when he should have been focussed on finding out more about her brother, and instead all he'd wanted was to find out more about her.

He dipped his head, giving her time to object, but all he could hear was the staggered pant of her breathing, encouraging him. He settled his lips over hers.

She opened for him instinctively, the sob of excitement firing his senses as he ran his tongue across the cupid's bow that had tormented him all evening and tasted her.

He delved deep, controlling the kiss, satisfaction turning to desperation as her palms flattened against his abdomen and her fingers gripped his shirt, drawing him closer.

He cradled her neck and angled her face, desperate to take everything she had to give him.

The kiss became more, so much more than he could ever have imagined. The fire in his gut turned from a slow burn to a raging inferno. He explored the recesses of her mouth, sipped at her lips, tangled his tongue with hers. She shuddered, moaned, the sound both desperate and excited and...*shocked.*

He drew back sharply.

Her eyes were glassy, dazed, stunned—more awestruck than when she'd seen the Arc de Triomphe for the first time—but then she blinked and jerked away.

'You... You kissed me?' she said.

He frowned, forced himself to drop his hand and deny the urge to grip her waist and drag her across the console into his lap, to press the hard weight of his erection into the hot cradle of her sex.

He could smell her arousal, which was even more addictive than the intoxicating scent of orange, rosemary and the taste of her lips.

But the shock was there, too.

He'd turned into an animal. The sophistication he'd worked so hard to attain over the last thirteen years— ever since the boy had made a vow to become a man— had deserted him as soon as his lips touched hers.

'Of course I did,' he said, realising he'd said it more sharply than he'd intended when he saw her blink. 'I've been wanting to for hours.'

She touched her finger to her lips, sill dazed, drawing his gaze to where he'd reddened the skin on her chin and cheek. He'd mauled her like a needy boy, instead of the man he knew himself to be.

What the heck was wrong with him?

'But I thought... I thought this was a stunt date?' she said.

'A what?' he asked, confused now as well as frustrated,

with himself as much as her. When had he become a slave to his own appetites, unable to control his desires?

As much of a bastard as her brother.

'A stunt date…' she repeated, still making no sense whatsoever. 'I thought you asked me to the ball so you wouldn't have to fend off advances from other women. Your sister said you don't like to be chased. She said—'

'Imelda was wrong,' he cut in. Trust Imelda to have something to do with the shocked look in Katherine's eyes. 'This isn't a "stunt date", Katherine,' he added, drawing on the last reserves of his patience, still not sure how everything had got out of control so quickly and so comprehensively. 'I want you, and I believe you want me,' he continued, determined to be open with her. Or as open as he could be in the circumstances. 'And I'd say that kiss confirms it.'

He waited for her to deny it.

'I… Yes, I suppose it does.'

He noticed the parking valet standing patiently beside the car, waiting for them to get out. The boy seemed flushed.

He'd probably seen that kiss.

Conall might have been annoyed—he didn't usually maul women with an audience—but the craven hunger still pounding in his groin was making it hard for him to think about anything but finishing what they'd started.

'I'm not in the business of pressuring women,' he said. 'If you want to go back to London, now you know this is not a stunt date, it can be arranged.'

He'd never considered himself to be a particularly gallant man, but something about the way she had kissed him…her response so fresh, so eager, so unguarded…had shocked him a little…and only made him more hungry.

But still he waited patiently for her answer, or as patiently as he could with the need throbbing like a sore tooth.

At last, she shook her head. 'I don't want to go home.'

'Good.' He signalled the young man and concentrated on getting out of the car before he took what he wanted too soon. She needed time to adjust to the inevitable, and clearly so did he. When they made love, he intended to be in control.

'Bonsoir, mademoiselle,' the boy said to Katherine as he opened the car's passenger door.

Conall stepped out the other side, only too aware that he was still sporting a fairly impressive erection. A blast of the cold night air helped it to subside as two doormen took their luggage and the parking valet got into the car to drive it away.

He directed Katherine into the marble and gilt-edged lobby, the antique furniture in keeping with the hotel's historic grandeur. But, as he placed his palm on the small of her back, he became far too aware of her shudder. And had to steel himself against the desire to move his hand lower and cup the lush weight of her backside in the form-fitting coat.

They were whisked to the front of the queue to check in and then directed to the top floor. He walked her to her suite, keeping his hands to himself.

Gone were her gasps of astonishment, the babbling commentary on everything she saw. Instead she was quiet, subdued, contemplative. But he could still sense the ripple of reaction as they stopped at the door to her rooms.

He turned her towards him, touched his thumb to her lip and then brushed it tenderly over the skin of her chin.

'I should have shaved. Your skin is very sensitive,' he said, rather inanely. It was about as close as he could get to an apology for taking her mouth in the car like a madman.

She nodded, watching him with those wide, transparent eyes again.

'Liam suggested you might need a stylist,' he managed, remembering the enquiry he'd had from his assistant, suddenly not wanting to let her go. Knowing it was going to be a very long while before he could get to sleep after that kiss. 'To get you something to wear for the ball,' he prompted. 'He figured you might not have anything appropriate.'

He could have asked one of his assistants to deal with this tomorrow. He'd always intended to when Liam had mentioned the problem. But, when the blush lit the sprinkle of freckles on her nose, he was glad he hadn't.

'Actually, that would be great. I need to buy something to wear. But I have no idea where to go in Paris.'

No way are you buying your own ball gown, he thought, but didn't say. Women's fashions were hardly his forte, but he suspected a suitable gown would be well outside her budget, and he'd be damned if he'd feel guilty about that too.

'Liam can handle it,' he said, still not quite able to draw his finger away from her flushed flesh.

What else was there to say? The kiss had been phenomenal. Much more than he had expected. But he needed to get this yearning under control before he saw her again. 'I'm going to be busy tomorrow, in meetings, so I'll be here at eight to take you down to the ball.'

'Okay,' she said.

Leaning forward, feeling her heartbeat pummelling against his thumb, he pressed a chaste kiss to her forehead then let her go. 'Enjoy yourself tomorrow.'

So saying, he turned and strode away.

Somehow, between now and eight tomorrow night, he needed to get a grip on this hunger. Or they were never going to make it to the damn ball.

Katie closed the door, caught the breath she had been holding and sunk down onto her bum, her back dragging against the door as her knees turned to water.

The city lights glittered through the huge arched windows that looked out onto a stone terrace. Moonlight lit up the palatial living area, glowing over bespoke antique furniture, luxury fabrics and expertly displayed art.

She drew in a staggered breath, catching the whiff of lemon polish, to inflate lungs constricted with shock and awe... The view of Paris from the penthouse suite was almost as breath-taking as Conall's kiss.

Almost.

She touched one trembling finger to her chin, smarting from the sting of beard scruff. Then ran it across her mouth, her lips burning from the ferocity of his kiss.

Almost? Who was she kidding?

The view of Paris—a city she'd wanted to visit for years—was nowhere near as spectacular as Conall O'Riordan's kiss.

He'd devoured her, as if he couldn't get enough of her, his lips hungry, seeking, branding her and demanding her surrender. And it had lit a fire inside her body which she hadn't even realised was there. And had made it burn.

She crossed her legs and sat dumbly, trying to get her breathing to even out, aware of everywhere her body buzzed, pulsed and throbbed.

She should get up, switch on the light, explore the suite—which was probably as magnificent as everything else about this trip—and check out the no doubt heart-stopping view from the terrace.

But she couldn't move. Her body was like warm butter—melted, insubstantial, a puddle of sensation.

What had happened? One minute he'd been chastising her about Tom and her marriage—reminding her far too forcefully of her brother—and the next... She sighed, the guilty flush working its way up her neck.

'Oh, Tom, I'm sorry,' she whispered into the darkness. But Tom's face seemed so hazy now.

Tom had never made her feel the way Conall O'Riordan just had. He'd always been a boy, never able to grow to manhood. He'd been her best friend. But had he ever really been her husband? she wondered. In any meaningful sense...?

The trickle of guilt became a flood. Not because she'd responded so readily to Conall's kiss—his scent, his texture, his taste, all so addictive—but because she couldn't even really remember any more what it had been like to kiss Tom.

She'd loved him so much. But she was beginning to wonder if she had ever really *loved* him. Like an adult. Their life together felt like a dream now—a short, tragic, far away dream—with no conflict, no disagreements but also in some ways no substance, no excitement.

Why had she really married him? Had it been because he needed her, or because she'd needed him?

She cut off the thought. Her life with Tom was over, but one thing was for certain—that part of her life had not prepared her to deal with kissing a man like Conall O'Riordan.

And not stunt kissing either. *Real* kissing.

She took a few moments more to get her bearings back—which took a while, as her mind kept reliving that kiss—but after about five minutes she finally managed to drag her aching body off the floor.

She still felt shaky as she made her way through the huge room to the terrace. Sliding open the glass doors, she found herself on a large stone balcony furnished with elegant loungers and huge flower arrangements made up of winter blooms and pine branches. But it was the view that took her breath away…

The Eiffel Tower stood like a beacon in the distance, the nearby glass and wrought-iron dome of the Grand Palais also lit up in the night.

Paris was a staggeringly beautiful city. And she was here for the first time. With a man who quite literally took her breath away. And he wanted her. *Really* wanted her, with the same urgency she wanted him.

She should be cautious and careful. She still wasn't sure the ethics of what she was doing were exactly right. Was he her boss? Would she jeopardise the commission if she took what he was offering this weekend?

She had to hope not. She knew she was doing a good job with the wedding planning, and he'd seemed a lot less interested in any of it once Imelda had taken over.

She had to believe whatever happened in Paris would stay in Paris. He'd said as much. She certainly knew he wasn't a man who did long term.

Her heart slowed as she recalled the frustrated expression on his face when they'd talked about her marriage. It had been so weird. Perhaps she should have taken offence…his objections to it were not unlike her brother's… but somehow she'd had the strangest feeling they weren't really talking about her choices, her past, but his…

He'd been determined to convince her he was ruthless, unfeeling, unemotional. That his interest in her past had been pure curiosity or arrogance. But it had felt like more than that, especially when he'd spoken about being a man at eighteen.

Maybe he believed that. But she wasn't convinced.
She shut off the direction of her thoughts.

Stop over-thinking this weekend when you're already in danger of being swept off your feet.

She wanted to enjoy herself. To go to her first ever ball. To finally find out what all the fuss about sex was, something Conall O'Riordan could surely show her.

But she had to remember this was a fleeting moment, a glorious adventure, nothing else.

It didn't mean anything more than some spectacular chemistry and a hunger which she would finally have a chance to feed.

She took a deep breath and let it out slowly, her gaze taking in the spectacular view, her body remembering another view even more spectacular: Conall's deep-blue gaze fixed on her face before he'd branded her with his kiss.

You deserve this chance...these two days out of real life.

A smile snuck onto her lips, making her even more aware of the burn from Conall's ferocious kiss.

Cinderella, eat your heart out! Katie Hamilton is going to the ball.

CHAPTER SEVEN

'THIS COLOUR LOOKS incredible on you! The jewelled bodice is perfect to bring out the emerald in your eyes, *mademoiselle.*'

The stylist, Celestine Dupre, purred next to Katie's shoulder as Katie gazed at herself in the gilt-edged full-length mirror in Madame Laurent's luxury boutique in the Marais. Her fingertips touched the beading on the gown's bodice, then traced the neck line that dipped to reveal the swell of her cleavage.

A blush mottled the skin. Thank goodness for the bustier Celestine had insisted she put on, or she'd be spilling out of the gown all together.

She swished her hips from side to side and watched the gown's hem glide over the jewelled slippers which Celestine had insisted she wear with the outfit.

Katie let out a shuddery breath. She wanted this gown. It gave her confidence and made her feel...*special.* 'How much is it?'

She forced herself to downgrade her excitement. The designer creation was exquisite, the beaded emerald satin fitted to make her curves look like a work of art. She'd never felt more like a princess in her entire life. But the stylist Conall had hired, and Madame Laurent, the boutique's French couturier, and her staff had been super-cagey about the cost of every gown she'd tried on so far.

She ran a successful company. She wasn't a pauper, but paying thousands for a gown she would probably only get to wear once was not a good use of her resources.

Celestine sent her a benevolent smile. 'Monsieur O'Riordan's assistant said you are not to worry about the price, that Monsieur O'Riordan is paying for...'

'She'll take it.'

Katie gasped and swung round at the assertive statement, delivered in a far too familiar Irish accent, as goose bumps rioted over her skin.

Conall strode towards her. He looked tall and indomitable in black jeans, a dark polo-neck sweater and a leather jacket—a stark and defiantly masculine presence in the boudoir's elegant cream and satin interior.

'Conall?' she murmured, the goose bumps going haywire as his penetrating gaze raked over her, and she suddenly became far too aware of all the places where the gown clung. And every inch of skin it exposed, which was rather a lot.

'It looks perfect for tonight, and it suits you,' he said, taking her fingers and lifting her arm away from her body so he could get a better look.

'Why...? Why are you here?' she asked, feeling stupidly shy and yet also ridiculously happy to see him. Whatever the gown cost, she would find a way to pay for it. She wanted him to look at her like this all night.

'The meetings finished early,' he said, his assessing gaze finally rising back to her face. 'I thought I could give you a tour of Paris. As you've never been to the city before.'

'Really? That would be amazing,' she said, her heart lifting into her throat and battering her collar bone.

Today already felt like a fairy tale. She'd been introduced to Celestine by Conall's assistant Liam, and the stylist had whisked her off to a luxury spa straight after breakfast where she had been buffed, primped and polished to within an inch of her life by a team of beauticians and hair stylists. Then Celestine had taken her to the Marais in a limousine and introduced her to one of France's most famous *modistes*. They'd been working out an outfit for the ball ever since, beginning with shoes and underwear and finally moving on to the perfect gown.

She'd always been a bit of a tomboy when it came to clothes. But she knew amazing craftsmanship when she saw it.

She turned to the couturier, whom she knew didn't speak English. *'D'accord, madame. Je voudrais l'acheter,'* she said in her faltering French, hoping the woman understood. Then she spoke to Celestine. 'Could you ask her to send the bill to the Hotel de la Lumière?'

Celestine nodded but, instead of translating the information, her gaze moved to Conall. 'Monsieur O'Riordan?'

Conall rattled something off in fluent French to Celestine and then the couturier. The older woman beamed, nodding and smiling, and then clicked her fingers to have her assistants help Katie out of the gown.

But before Katie was led away she turned back to Conall. 'What did you just say to her?'

'I have an account here, Katherine,' he said. 'The gown is on me.'

'But I can't let you pay for it…' she began, shocked at the thrill that worked its way up her spine at the thought that he would even offer.

What was wrong with her? She was an independent woman. Conall wasn't her boyfriend, not really, and she certainly did not need him to buy her clothes.

'Consider it a business expense,' he said, riding rough-shod over her objection as he spoke again in French to the couturier and her assistants.

'But it's not...' she said. She didn't even know how much it cost yet, but it had to be in the thousands, and how was he going to justify that as a business expense?

Then something else he had said occurred to her. 'Why do you have an account at a ladies' couturier...?'

His lips twisted in a mocking grin that made him look even more devastating than usual and he dropped his voice, leant close and murmured in her ear. 'Why do you think, Katherine? FYI, I don't wear a lot of designer gowns myself.'

She choked out a laugh. But the blush already glowing on her collar bone blazed its way up her neck, making her feel like the most gauche woman on the planet.

Of course he had an account at one of Paris's most exclusive boutiques. Because she wasn't the first woman he'd invited here and she wouldn't be the last.

'I'd... I'd still prefer to pay for my own ball gown,' she managed.

The smile became rueful. But then he spoke again to the couturier and got a reply. Turning back, he said, 'It costs a hundred and fifty thousand euros.'

'It... *What?*' Her jaw almost dislocated, it dropped so fast. Her stunned gaze dipped to stare at the exquisite gown. At the intricate stitching, the jewels glowing in the sparkle of afternoon sunlight.

Good grief, are they real emeralds?

'I... I should find something less expensive,' she managed. Her company made a decent profit but a hundred and fifty thousand euros for one dress? She couldn't possibly justify that kind of expenditure.

'No need,' he said, still grinning and making her feel

even more ridiculous. She worked on luxury event-planning, so she knew a little bit about how these people lived. Why on earth hadn't she figured out the price would be much more than she could afford?

'We really don't have time for you to look for another one if we want to see any of the sights this afternoon. And why should we, when this one is grand?' he said, stepping back and treating her to another oxygen-depriving assessment. 'I've got this.'

Before she had a chance to argue further, he placed warm, callused palms on her bare shoulders, turned her round so that she was facing the changing area and then gave her a soft pat on her bottom. 'Now, go get changed, so we can get the hell out of here. There's so much I want to show you and we only have four hours before the ball.'

The giddy thrill that blossomed under her breastbone at his playful tone propelled her towards the changing room before she had a chance to argue.

Perhaps she could work out a payment plan, she thought frantically as the assistants helped her out of the gown, and she watched them box up the exquisite dress while she tugged on her jeans, boots and jacket.

She really couldn't accept a one-hundred-and-fifty-thousand-euro gift, but she could always arrange to return the gown once she'd worn it, or auction it online and recoup some of the cost to pay Conall back that way.

The giddy thrill worked its way into her stomach. She'd figure it out somehow. One thing she refused to do was let a little thing like an astronomically expensive ball gown get in the way of their afternoon adventure.

She couldn't wait to see Paris with Conall O'Riordan and take the opportunity to get to know him better. She already planned to sleep with him tonight but, given that he was going to be her first lover, why shouldn't she want to know more about him?

Maybe this wasn't a proper relationship, but it was a proper date—leading in one very intimate direction later tonight. Surely she was entitled to satisfy some of her curiosity?

'But where's the car?' Katherine chewed on her bottom lip, sending the usual spike of adrenaline straight into Conall's gut. Not good when he had to negotiate Parisian traffic while she clung on to him for dear life.

Conall mounted the gleaming vintage Harley-Davidson he'd had delivered to the hotel an hour ago—as soon as he'd called off the rest of the day's meetings, knowing he had been struggling to focus all morning and was not going to be able to stay away from Katherine for another twenty-five minutes, let alone four hours.

Perhaps it was indulgent and reckless, but he'd been rewarded when he'd walked into the exclusive boutique, where his last two girlfriends had enjoyed shopping, and had seen the woman he was taking to the ball tonight in all her glory.

She'd looked stunning in the figure-hugging gown… He'd pay a million euros to escort her in that dress tonight, let alone one hundred and fifty thousand. And a million more to ease her out of it later.

He cut off the rampant direction of his thoughts with an effort.

Not the time.

First, he had to give her the tour of Paris he'd offered her. Why hadn't he just suggested going back to the hotel? But something had stopped him. Even though he knew, from last night's kiss and the flushed determination on her face after it, she was more than willing…

Something he wasn't quite sure of. Maybe it was the surprising way she'd reacted to his perfectly reasonable decision to pay for the gown. Or the way she was now chewing her delectable bottom lip, as she stared at the bike as if he were asking her to ride a fire-breathing dragon.

'But I've never ridden on a motorbike before,' she murmured, raising her panicked gaze to his.

He had to choke back a laugh at her look of concern. 'It's perfectly safe. And the best way to see Paris when we're this close to rush hour.'

After straddling it, he adjusted the clutch, flicked up the stand and stamped down on the ignition peddle. The bike roared to life, making Katherine jump.

He grinned. He couldn't help it, this was going to be fun. And when was the last time he'd had fun with a woman, or anybody, for that matter? His life had been so damn serious and focussed for so long, but there was something about Katherine Hamilton—her eagerness, her earnestness, but also her determination and guts— that made him want to show her Paris his way. Because he knew she'd appreciate it.

He grabbed a helmet from the bike's saddle bag and lobbed it to her. She caught it instinctively. 'Put that on and climb aboard.'

'But…' She glanced down at the helmet. 'The stylist spent an hour this morning doing my hair for the ball,' she managed.

He studied her hair. The curls had been scrunched in some concoction and arranged to halo around her head in artful disarray. The do was great, drawing attention to her peach-soft skin, high cheekbones and those eyes— now wide with panic and astonishment, but also curiosity and excitement.

She wanted to do this. She just needed a bit of a nudge. Katherine had curtailed her adventurous spirit for years, the way he'd curtailed his own. He could feel it in his bones. Married at nineteen to a man who had died a few weeks later, struck down by grief and then focussed on making a success of her business. She hadn't had the time to indulge herself any more than he'd had after becoming guardian to his sisters at eighteen and working flat out to make his mark.

This afternoon was a chance for them both to throw off the chains of responsibility and cut loose for a few hours. And he wasn't going to let her chicken out.

'The hair can be fixed,' he said, knowing full well the hair wasn't really the issue. She hadn't struck him as a woman who was vain about her appearance. If she was, she would never have turned up for their meeting in Kildaragh in muddy jeans, and she would have known the cost of the gown—and been more than happy to have him foot the bill.

Her gaze met his, purpose igniting the gold streaks in her emerald eyes and banishing the last of her indecision.

Damn, but he loved how transparent she was. How easy she was to read. There seemed to be no subterfuge with this woman, no desire or inclination to hide her feelings or hold back. Why he should find that so captivating, he had no idea. But he chose not to question it too deeply. She was just refreshingly different from the women he usually dated, that was all. The novelty would wear off soon enough once they'd fed this insistent hunger. But why not enjoy the ride? He'd once loved the chase, after all, he just hadn't had the chance to indulge in it for a very long time.

She placed the helmet on her head, the determined

expression almost as beautiful as the flush highlighting her cheeks. 'Okay, fine, let's do this thing.'

He laughed, the chuckle a little rusty but still making his ribs tighten. 'Grand. Climb aboard, Cinderella,' he said, getting into the spirit of the thing. 'Your steed awaits.'

CHAPTER EIGHT

'COME ON, NOW. Just a few more steps...'

'I'm so unfit!' Katie smiled, her heart bursting with something that felt strangely like hope as Conall gripped her hand and dragged her the rest of the way to the top of the never-ending stairs.

She craned her neck to take in the glorious dome of the Sacré-Coeur Basilica in front of them. Up close, it looked even more staggering than it had at the bottom of the five thousand steps they'd just climbed.

'Wow, it's huge.'

'Spoken like a true tourist,' Conall said, but the wry smile on his face was full of approval. 'But you're missing the best bit now,' he said then, taking her shoulders in strong hands, he swung her round.

She gasped. Paris lay before her like a carpet of wonders. Montmartre's labyrinth of eighteenth-century terraces—made famous by the artists of the Belle Epoch—gave way in the distance to the architectural triumphs old and new of the Eiffel Tower and the Montparnasse skyscraper. The late-afternoon light was so bright, the day so clear and crisp, and the angle so steep, she could even make out the greenery of the Bois de Vincennes on the outskirts of the city. All places she's read about in books, and seen in films and on TV, but had never imagined would look so stunning in real life.

She let out a heavy sigh and heard him give a rueful laugh.

'I've finally silenced you,' he said.

She glanced at him over her shoulder. Her heart did a giddy two-step in her chest. She'd always known he was an incredibly handsome man. But something about seeing him so relaxed, the teasing glint in his eye without any edge to it, made her own smile broaden.

The whole afternoon had been magical—like a vivid, waking dream full of sound, colour and heart-stopping excitement. But it wasn't really the series of stunning Parisian sights he'd shown her or even the thought of tonight's ball that was making her heart swell.

They'd had so much fun together, Conall's knowledge of the city almost as captivating as discovering that he had a light, playful, sometimes wicked sense of humour.

She knew she mustn't romanticise these moments. Or make too much of the sense of connection that had grown during the afternoon. But for once he looked completely open and unguarded.

'How do you know Paris so well?' she asked. 'Do you come here a lot?' she added, then felt her cheeks warm.

Fabulous, Katie, why not just ask him if he comes here often?

He simply stared at her for a moment, making her sure he was going to deflect the probing question, as he had the few times she'd already asked him about himself today. They'd shared a strong coffee on a barge on the Seine in the shadow of Notre Dame and toured the haunting statuary in the Père Lachaise Cemetery, where he pointed out the burial places of everyone from Jim Morrison to Abelard and Héloïse.

But anticipation rose like a bubble in her chest as he turned away from her to look out across the stunning vista. The smile had been replaced by a pensive look—was he finally going to answer a personal question?

When he spoke, his voice rough with memory, she found herself letting go of the breath she hadn't realised she was holding... Why did this feel so important?

'I lived here for a year, after I sold the farm in Galway. I'd set up Rio Corp two years before, and it was doing well. We had patents for a lot of really innovative agricultural equipment, but I wanted to learn French so we could base our European hub in Paris.' He let out a slow breath. 'My sisters weren't too happy about it. At that point they were fourteen and sixteen and they'd never left Ireland—learning French was not high on their list of priorities,' he finished, the wistful chuckle filled with affection.

'You brought your sisters with you?' she asked, stupidly touched. She'd always longed for a close-knit family who chose to stay together, no matter what. But still it surprised her to think he hadn't simply had his sisters carted off to boarding school while he'd taken his business to the next level. He had been a young man, still only twenty-three, already burdened with so much.

Conall's head swung towards her, his brows lifting. 'Of course. Why wouldn't I?' he asked, the simple question making the inadequacy she thought she'd conquered a lifetime ago squeeze her chest.

Why not, indeed?

While she'd yearned for her brother's attention in the early years after her mother's death, and had been unbearably lonely at the exclusive school he'd sent her to, she had always believed she'd understood why he'd had to send her away. But now she wasn't so sure. She could still remember those pitiful phone calls when she'd begged him to let her stay with him over the holidays, not to leave her at the school when all the other kids had gone home to their families, but his answer had always been the same.

'I'm not your father, Katie. And I'm not cut out to be a parent. Believe me, you're much better off where you are.'

Why had she never realised until this moment that the problem hadn't been with her, it had been with him? If Conall O'Riordan could be a parent to his sisters, why hadn't her brother been able to step up to the plate too, even if only for a few weeks over the holidays? She'd asked him for so little in the way of emotional support. But he'd given her even less.

'Well, I guess…' She stumbled as Conall's eyes narrowed on her face, almost as if he could see into her thoughts, her feelings. Instinctively she tried to mask the stab of inadequacy and hurt, that painful instinct that told her she was 'less than', that she was somehow unlovable.

Ross had been right about one thing: he had never been capable of being a brother to her in the truest sense of the word. How stupid of her not to realise that until this moment.

'It just seems you would have had a lot on your plate already,' she managed. 'Relocating to Paris with two teenage girls must have been tough. Especially if they weren't keen on the move.'

'You have no idea.' He let out a gruff laugh, but it was so full of affection, her heart squeezed again. What must it be like to have someone love you no matter what?

Even her mother had always set conditions on her affection—showing it only as long as Katie didn't get in the way when she was busy with a piece, didn't ask too much or make a fuss when they moved again on an artistic whim. She'd been uprooted so many times as a child, she had been forced to learn resilience and adaptability. She'd gained the ability to settle into new places with optimism and hope, always determined to see the best in any new spot.

But it had also left her yearning for stability. Maybe just not the stability of an exclusive boarding school where everyone judged you for your 'common' accent, your complete failure to conjugate a Latin verb correctly and the fact that your older brother, who paid the fees, didn't seem to be interested in spending any time with you.

'Imelda came around a lot quicker than Carmel,' Conall murmured, the warmth in his voice unguarded now. 'Immy could be a troublemaker, but it isn't in her nature to sulk. She's too much of a livewire. Mel, on the other hand, is a born rebel—super-smart, super-headstrong and super-independent. Boy, did she know how to crucify me for all the wrongs I was doing her by taking her away from her mates. She's nobody's pushover,' he continued. 'Or at least she didn't used to be,' he said, so softly she almost didn't catch the words.

'Mel is the one who has a son?' she asked, keen to keep him talking about his sisters, if for no other reason than it softened those gruff edges and gave her another precious insight into his family life.

His gaze locked on hers, the suspicious look startling her as the expression on his face hardened. Had she said something wrong?

'Yeah,' he said at last, the sharp tone unmistakeable. 'Some rich, entitled bastard seduced her when she was nineteen, a virgin, got her pregnant, then insisted Mac wasn't his son. It changed her. But she's so damn tough, she refused to take any help from me. She wouldn't even tell me who the guy was.'

She could hear the brittle fury in his tone. Whoever his nephew's father was, the man was probably very lucky Carmel had never told her brother his name, or she doubted he'd be able to father any more children.

'I'm so sorry. He sounds like a jerk,' she said.

'He is, but Carmel and Mac are better off without him, so there's that. And she's a terrific mammy,' he said, his admiration for his sister clear. 'Mac doesn't need that bastard in his life.'

'Especially as he has you,' she said, remembering what Imelda had said about how close Conall was to his nephew.

She stifled the silly sting of envy, for everything the O'Riordans had. How foolish, she thought, to be jealous of a little boy, especially one who had been rejected by his father. She knew what that felt like.

'Yeah, he has me,' Conall said. 'I'd never let anyone hurt him, certainly not that son of a...' He cut off the curse word, but his gaze remained locked on her face, and for one awful moment it seemed as if his anger was directed at her...

But then he broke eye contact and murmured, 'Sorry, it's a sore point.' The apology was grudging at best, but she took it at face value. Because if she had learned one thing about Conall O'Riordan in the last twenty-four hours it was that beneath the veneer of control was a man of fierce passions, especially where his family was concerned.

'I understand,' she said, because she really did. She placed her fingers on his arm, the jolt of awareness arrowing down when his forearm flexed. 'My father never acknowledged me,' she said gently.

Perhaps it was too much information. It was also something she never spoke about to anyone, but she became convinced it was the right thing to do when he looked at her again and the raw fury had dimmed.

'It hurt to know that he didn't ever want me. That he didn't ever value me. That I was a mistake. My mother always insisted it didn't matter, that it didn't make me "less than", but it felt like somehow it did. And when she died I was terrified I'd have to go into care. That I was totally alone. So when my brother Ross got in touch...'

She sighed. She could still remember that day—how she'd run up to this tall, handsome stranger and hugged him too tightly. And how he had stiffened but hadn't drawn back. Instead he had patted her shoulders awkwardly. He had tried to make things right, even though he'd had no idea how to deal with a grieving child.

Ross could have abandoned her—she had no doubt he had wanted to, but he hadn't —and for that she would always be grateful. He'd fed her, clothed her, paid for the most expensive schools and then college and, most importantly of all, he hadn't hesitated to acknowledge her as his half-sister. Ross had tried to be there for her in the only way he'd known how, even though it had clearly gone against every one of his instincts. Instincts she was sure had been drummed into him by a man who she was probably very lucky had never wanted to be her father after all.

'Well, it made a difference,' she said. 'We haven't spoken in a long time... Ross was as opposed to my marriage to Tom as you were.' She huffed out a breath, determined to forgive her brother his failings. She was a grown woman now and she had survived. It was foolish to still need his approval.

'But he was there when I needed him the most.' She sent Conall what she hoped was an easy, well-adjusted smile—strangely gratified to see him watching her intently. 'A strong male role model is what children need. Ross wasn't up to the job of surrogate father, not really, but the fact he tried is what mattered. The thing is, Mac knows that you love him. So you're right—he doesn't need this man, if he has you.'

So that bastard abandoned her too.

Conall's heart pulsed hard as he tried to contain his violent reaction to her quiet revelation.

Her loyalty to a man who clearly didn't deserve it disturbed him in a way he wasn't sure how to handle. Because it only made him feel more protective towards her. And that couldn't be good.

Katherine is far too sweet and forgiving for her own good.

He touched her cheek, letting his thumb glide down the flushed skin—finally forced to let go the last of the resentment he'd wanted to feel towards her.

'Good to know,' he murmured, a little choked up by her faith in him, however misplaced.

He cleared his throat, let his hand drop. 'So, where do you want to go next?'

She smiled, the spontaneous grin as trusting as the rest of her. 'Where do you want to take me?'

Back to the hotel.

He stifled the thought and the shudder of need that went with it. What was it about her openness, and her honesty, that made her even more desirable to him?

That way lay danger, he realised. The feeling of connection, and the riot of emotions she caused, was not something he should take too lightly until he knew how to handle them.

'How about we get some food? I'm starving,' he said, even though he knew food wasn't going to vanquish the driving hunger in his gut. 'I know a grand little brasserie—looks like something out of a film—where they do the best *moules-frites* in town.'

'That sounds fabulous,' she said, her eyes sparking with delight again, her pure *joie de vivre* infectious. 'I certainly worked up an appetite with all those steps,' she added. But he could hear the heat in her voice, too, matching his own. And knew the meal was going to be pure torture.

'The Eiffel Tower was so much bigger than I expected,' Katie said breathlessly, unable to contain the burst of joy as Conall gripped her freezing fingers, his hand warm against hers, and steered her through the hotel lobby. Heads turned, probably because she was with the handsomest man in the whole of Europe… And perhaps also because they were trailing a puddle of water behind them on the marble tiles.

'I wish we had been able to go up it. I bet the view's phenomenal,' she added as he stabbed the call button for the penthouse lift.

'It is… But are you mad?' he added, but he was smiling, that rare smile she had become addicted to. 'We would have drowned.'

She laughed. She didn't know why she amused him so much—probably her total inability to be remotely sophisticated or blasé about all the amazing things he'd shown her today—but she was glad she did. Because she suspected that, despite all his wealth and success, and the strong, loving family he had spent his life nurturing, Conall O'Riordan didn't smile nearly often enough.

They'd wound their way across Paris on his powerful bike after leaving Sacre Coeur, to a brasserie tucked away on a side street near the Place de la Bastille. It was all chrome fittings and leather booths separated by glass etched with drawings of elegant ladies straight out of a Toulouse-Lautrec painting. The smoke-stained walls and delicious plates of mussels and French fries had made her feel as though she'd stepped back to an elegant time of dancing girls and top-hatted gentlemen.

Back on the bike they'd wound their way through the cobble-stoned streets of the Marais, and the bustling markets of Les Halles. The Eiffel Tower had been their final stop but, just as Conall had been bribing the attendant—because apparently billionaires didn't queue—the heavens had opened. She'd been soaked through within minutes, clinging to Conall as they'd raced back to the hotel, all her senses focussed on the feel of his body—strong, solid, smelling of clean pine soap and motor oil and wet leather—and the pulsing ache between her thighs that had been building all afternoon.

Could any day have been more wonderful?

She hadn't managed to prise any more information out of him about his life, his past, himself. While he was fairly comfortable talking about his sisters, she had soon realised Conall was almost preternaturally close-lipped when it came to the subject of himself. But then he hadn't asked her for any more confidences either... So, after a few more faltering attempts that had been easily rebuffed, she'd resolved not to pry. If this fling was going to work, she needed to stow her curiosity about him and live in the present, live in the now. Enjoy what this weekend was—and not get hung up on what it wasn't.

Conall O'Riordan had given her Paris. But, so much more than that, he'd made her feel seen, feel special, feel like a woman—who was desired—for the first time in her life. She let the excitement swell in her chest and pound between her thighs as he dragged her into the lift.

He tugged her back until they were standing against the back wall of the ornate steel enclosure, then tipped up her chin and wiped the moisture from her cheeks with his thumbs.

She shuddered, the ripple of reaction shooting up her spine, as it had so many times during the afternoon, every time she'd felt his back shift against her breasts or his arm fall across her shoulders to tug her to his side when he was pointing out some interesting sight or other.

'You're freezing,' he murmured. 'And soaked.' He glanced at his watch. 'The ball begins in twenty minutes,' he said. 'How long do you need before I can come and get you? I have no problem being fashionably late.'

It took her a moment to register what he was saying, as her chest deflated like a popped party balloon.

But I don't want to go to the ball. I want to spend the rest of the night just with you.

The fanciful thought flashed into her head, the yearning so intense it took her a moment to process it. She blinked, struggling to get a grip on the desperate longing.

Don't be ridiculous.

They had come to Paris to attend the Lumière Ball together. It was one of the most prestigious events in Europe's social calendar. *Of course* she wanted to go to it, if for no other reason than it would be an incredible networking opportunity.

'Not long,' she managed at last, all her attempts to talk herself out of the reckless need doing nothing to silence the thrum of anticipation in her sex, or the hollow ache in her chest.

They had all night. There was no need to rush any of this. In fact, it might be better not to. Her emotions were already too close to the surface, her desire for this man well beyond the physical already.

He guided her down the corridor, stopping at the door to her suite. 'Good,' he said. 'I can't wait to see you in that dress…' His voice lowered to a husky purr as his gaze roamed over her, igniting all the spots that wanted to beg him to stay. 'And get you out of it again.'

The desire in her belly ignited at his parting comment.

Goodness, how am I going to survive the biggest social event of my life while imagining Conall O'Riordan seeing me naked?

CHAPTER NINE

THE LUMIÈRE BALL was everything it had been cracked up to be, and so much more.

Beautiful people graced the hotel's elegant parlours and ball rooms, dressed in the finest designer gowns and expertly tailored tuxedos. The huge glass atrium at the centre of the historic building had been turned into a lavish banqueting salon worthy of the stone palace's original owner, Louis XV.

The guests spilled out after a five-course *cordon bleu* supper into the main ball room, its vaulted ceiling lit by an array of antique chandeliers. Two wide, sweeping staircases—their stone balustrades entwined with glittering lights and winter blooms—led down from a first-floor balcony crowded with waiting staff in nineteenth-century livery, who served yet more glasses of vintage champagne in crystal flutes, delicate canapés for anyone still hungry and exotic cocktails in dazzling primary colours.

The whole experience was an event planner's dream—each stunning design aspect and creative detail brilliantly combining the venue's grandiose history with the needs of guests used to gold-standard customer service.

But as Katie tried to capture every detail, and file them away for future reference, her heart continued to clatter in her chest and her whole body throbbed, not from the event itself, but from the overwhelming experience of being Conall O'Riordan's date.

She had expected him to use the event for networking. After all, the people in attendance were surely his crowd, not hers? But he seemed almost bored with the proceedings, his attention focussed solely on her—and the comment he'd made earlier in the evening before leaving her at the door to her suite kept repeating in her head.

The emerald-gown constricted around her ribs every time his hand landed on the small of her back to lead her through the crowd. The bustier she wore—which had been so comfortable in the boutique that morning— all but cut off her air supply as they'd sat down to dinner. And his gaze had kept dropping to her lips while she'd nibbled at the array of rich, beautifully flavoured dishes, none of which she'd wanted to eat. Her nipples had squeezed into hard, swollen peaks as soon as he had arrived at her door to escort her down over four hours ago.

She felt both exhausted and energized, speechless and at the same time unable to stop talking, her nerves increasing the deep yearning sensation tightening her skin and making it impossible for her to focus on anything but him.

They danced together to the music of a full orchestra in the main ball room, the low lighting going some way to hiding her vivid blush as his hand trailed across the sensitive skin of her back where the gown dipped— sending the familiar riot of sensations deep into her sex.

At last, he drew her close to whisper against her earlobe, 'How about we call it a night?'

She nodded, not able to reply, her voice suddenly trapped somewhere around her solar plexus. It was a loaded question. They both knew where they would end up if they left the ball. The hunger in her abdomen tangled with the sudden spurt of panic and apprehension.

Should she have told him she'd never done this before? Did he have a right to know she might be terrible at it?

'Are you sure now?' he said, the husky Irish brogue thickening. He studied her face, waiting patiently for her answer, the amusement fading to be replaced by that focussed intensity that had unsettled her so much when they'd first met—but which only made the heat swell and pound in her veins more fiercely now. 'I believe they have fireworks to come in the courtyard…' he added, his dark-blue gaze now so hot with purpose she imagined it sizzling over her skin. 'We can stay if you wish to see them.'

The ball wasn't due to end for another hour…at least.

'I don't want to wait…' she managed to whisper, her own voice so raw she didn't recognise it. 'And I really don't need any more fireworks,' she added.

He laughed, the sound gruff, but then stopped dead in the middle of the dance floor. The other couples glided past them, but her focus remained solely on him, now mesmerised by the heated purpose in his gaze. Almost as if in slow motion, he lifted her hand to his mouth, opened her trembling fingers and murmured something in a language she didn't recognise… Then bit softly into the swell of flesh beneath her thumb.

She jolted, the heat ricocheting through her over-sensitised body like an Exocet missile and exploding at her core.

'Let's get the hell out of here, then. I think we've waited long enough,' he murmured, his gaze never leaving her face.

She nodded.

The next ten minutes seemed to last several eternities, her mind spinning through all the things that could go wrong tonight as he clasped her hand and led her off the dance floor. As he had done all evening, he dodged the greetings of famous people from politics, film and sport she recognised as they left the ballroom and made their way through the crowd back towards the hotel's private suites.

He took her up a dark staircase. She felt like Cinderella again, but this time she was running away with her prince.

Stop romanticising, Katie.

She tried to tell herself this wasn't a dream, it was reality, but still she struggled to focus on anything other than the pounding beat of her heart and the realisation the moment she had waited for so long was rushing towards her now at breakneck speed.

Was Conall O'Riordan really the right man? She still knew so little about him. And yet she trusted him. But did she trust him too much?

She was breathless and more than a little shaky when he shouldered open the door at the top of the staircase and she found herself in the corridor leading to their rooms.

His fingers squeezed hers, his hold both determined and reassuring as they arrived at the door to her suite. She stood dumbly for a moment, everything inside her clutching and releasing, the heavy weight in her sex almost as disturbing as her racing pulse.

'You'll have to open the door, Katherine,' he said, the lilt of amusement roughened by arousal.

She scrambled to find the key card in her clutch bag but her fingers were trembling too much to slide it through the slot. He took it from her, swished it through then handed it back.

'Thank you,' she said, tucking it back into the clutch.

'You're welcome,' he said, the rumble of humour only making her feel more gauche, more exposed.

Opening the door, he let her step inside. She stood on the carpet as he closed it behind them. The view of the City of Lights from the suite's stone terrace looked like a carpet of stars rolled out to the horizon.

But all she could concentrate on was him as he stripped off his tux jacket and approached her.

'Let me,' he said as he took her purse and dropped it onto a nearby chair, then ran his thumbs under the gown's jewelled straps.

She nodded, even though it wasn't really a question. Her breathing accelerated again as he brushed the straps off her shoulders and then found the zip under her arm. The bodice released, drooping down to reveal the lacy bustier. She drew in a jagged breath.

'Beautiful,' he said, tracing the soft swell of her cleavage above the lacy prison. Her ribs contracted, her nipples already begging for his touch.

Threading his fingers into her hair, he tugged her head back, his gaze—hot, demanding, hungry—roaming over her face.

He swore under his breath. 'The last four hours have been pure torture.'

The desperation in his tone spurred her senses. She flattened her palms against the rigid muscles of his abdomen and felt them tense against her seeking fingers beneath the starched shirt. He clasped her face in rough palms and covered her lips at last.

The kiss was forceful, demanding, as furious as the night before but so much more overwhelming. The fire at her core sparkled and glowed, spreading up to her breasts, down to her toes, making her shaky and desperate.

She tugged his shirt out of his trousers, needing to feel

him. Her fingers touched his abs, exploring the velvet-soft skin rippling with strength.

He tore his mouth away, his breathing as hard and thready as hers. Then he stepped back to tug off his tie and rip open the shirt. Buttons popped, the violent action making her breathing ragged as he threw the shirt away.

The moonlight gilded the ridged muscles of his six-pack, the bulge of his pecs and biceps. Katie looked her fill as he unbuckled his belt.

He dipped his head to undo the zip and open his trousers to reveal tight black boxers moulded to the thick outline of his erection.

How is that going to work?

She blinked several times, the question only making her more giddy as she stared at the hard evidence of his desire.

'Hey.' He lifted her chin. 'Is everything okay?'

She nodded again. 'Yes, wonderful.'

'You've got too many clothes on.' He smiled that devastatingly intense smile that turned all her misgivings to mush.

Everything inside her tightened and pulsed.

The erection will fit and it will be wonderful.

She wanted him inside her. She wanted to know what it felt like to be possessed by a man. Especially this man. She'd waited long enough. Far too long, really.

He toed off his shoes and stripped off his trousers. Standing before her in only his boxers, he looked magnificent in the pre-dawn light.

Stepping back towards her, he clasped her neck and murmured against her lips, 'Your turn.'

She felt his smile as her own lips curved. He continued to kiss her, light, fleeting, hungry kisses across her nose, her chin and her neck, the rasp of his stubble livening up her skin as she struggled to get out of the dress with clumsy fingers.

'Do you need some help, Katherine?' he asked, the strained humour in his voice going some way to dispelling the embarrassment scorching her skin.

She nodded dumbly. Emotion welled in her throat when he dragged the gown off, then dropped to his knees. 'Let's handle the shoes first, *mo mhuirnín*,' he murmured.

She grasped his shoulder to steady herself as he slipped off one jewelled slipper. 'What does that mean?' she asked.

'Huh?' he said as he discarded the other shoe.

'*Mu-voor-neen...*' she replied, trying to pronounce the strange words.

He frowned, colour shadowing his tanned cheeks. 'Did I say that?'

'Yes', she said, wondering where the guarded look had come from.

'It's nothing, just some nonsense in Irish,' he murmured as he stood and turned her round to unhook the bustier.

She folded her arms over her breasts as the garment loosened, aware of her nipples tightening, the hard peaks clearly visible through the lacy fabric. She ducked her head, trying to hide her embarrassment. She'd never undressed in front of anyone before.

But as she faced him again, he touched her chin, nudging up her face. 'I've been wanting to see the rest of you ever since you were all but spilling out of this gown this morning.'

The small joke had a chuckle bursting out of her mouth. She let her arms drop, the bustier falling away. But the intensity, the sparkle of sensation, returned as he stripped off the last of her undergarments.

He swung her round again so she could see their

reflection in the terrace doors. The hard ridge of his arousal pressed against her back as he traced her ripe nipples, plucking and playing with the taut peaks. Her head dropped against his shoulder when he covered her aching breasts at last, caressing, weighing the swollen flesh, his lips finding the pummelling pulse in her neck.

She gasped and bowed back, all her senses focussed now and yearning as one large hand slid down her torso and located the aching, tender, melting spot between her legs.

She sobbed, the spiral of need, of desperation, tightening, throbbing, so perfect it hurt as he found the slick, swollen nub with sure, certain fingers and circled it... So close and yet not close enough.

Teasing, torturing, tormenting.

He lifted her arm and draped it over his neck, leaving her open, her back arched, her breasts begging for his attention as he covered one turgid nipple, while one thick finger entered her and drove her wild.

'Please... I... Please...' She begged for the release which beckoned just out of reach.

'Shh, *mo mhuirnín*,' he said again, the endearment as raw and desperate as she felt.

Then he touched the very heart of her. His thumb flicked the spot where the heat gathered and pulsed. The orgasm cascaded through her, making her buck and moan, dragging out the pleasure in titanic waves of a release so strong, her knees gave way. She groaned as the last wave finally washed over her, retreating, leaving her limp.

He scooped her up and placed her on the couch. She watched, dazed, transfixed, as he kicked off his boxers, his hands as shaky as she felt.

The huge erection sprang up, long and thick, the swollen head glistening with moisture. Cursing, he scooped up his trousers again, found a small foil packet, ripped it open with his teeth and sheathed himself.

The emotion clutched in her chest again at the realisation that he had thought to protect her, when she'd been too lost in sensation, too dazed by need, to think of protecting herself.

She wasn't afraid any more, nor unsure. The yearning built again, swiftly and surely, her body clutching on emptiness, desperate to be filled.

Sitting down on the couch beside her, he dragged her up and over his lap until she knelt above him, her hands on his shoulders. He kissed her, his tongue possessive, demanding and, clasping her hips with firm hands, guided her onto the huge erection.

She sank down, the recent orgasm easing the way despite the stretched, full feeling. She ignored the pinch of pain, the fullness almost more than she could bear as she impaled herself to the hilt.

He swore softly and tugged her head back to stare into her eyes. 'Am I your first?' he demanded, his face a picture of need, hunger but also…something else, something she didn't understand. Was that shame? Shock?

She could have lied. A part of her wanted to—he did not look happy—but she knew she owed him the truth. Maybe she owed herself the truth. She wanted him to know he was the first man she'd ever trusted with this part of herself. And he'd already made it magnificent.

So, she nodded. 'Yes.'

No… Damn it.

Conall's mind screamed in denial. But it was already too late. He could feel the desire licking at his spine, impossible to deny a moment longer.

She was so hot, so tight around him. He had to move. Had to finish this now. It was too late to take it back.

He pressed his forehead to her chest, kissing the peak of one ripe nipple, then lifted her off him and placed her on the couch, his whole body clamouring now for release. She looked dazed, sweet, giddy and so brave. She had no idea what she'd just done. But it didn't matter now. It was too late to change.

He cupped her cheek. 'Tell me if it hurts.'

Surely it had to hurt? He was a large man, and she'd been so tight.

But she shook her head as he pressed inside. 'It doesn't, it feels good.'

He thrust into her, slowly, carefully, or as carefully as he could when his whole body was a mass of desperation.

Like their kiss the day before, and everything that had happened since, he could feel his control slipping but was powerless to stop it. Forced to move, inside the grip of her body, he thrust harder, faster, needing her to take every inch of him. The bad as well as the good.

He rocked out and back, the desire like a tsunami now, rolling through him, the approaching climax more powerful than any he'd ever felt before.

He found the slick nub of her clitoris, clumsy and desperate to make her go over first. Her muscles clenched as she sobbed out her release, bucking beneath him as the wave took her. He let go at last, everything he was, everything he believed himself to be, shattering as he soared.

But as he crashed to earth the last words his father had ever spoken to him echoed in his head—damning him.

'Women are the heart of us. Remember that and protect and respect them always. Do you promise me, lad? Never take what you can't give back.'

* * *

Katie lay sated, exhausted, her body limp and her mind a mess of fuzzy thoughts and emotions. Conall's head lay heavy on her shoulder, the erection still firm, still *there*, inside her. Their panting breaths filled the heady silence.

Her heartbeat battered her ribs as her breathing finally began to slow. She touched his cheek, stroking his damp hair back from his forehead with tender fingers. And tried not to lose herself in the swell of emotion making her chest hurt.

Only chemistry. And a marvellous adventure. Just because he's your first, it doesn't make this more than sex.

He shifted, then lifted himself up. His gaze—assessing, intense and not entirely happy—searched her face. The expression in his eyes made no sense... She would have expected surprise, possibly even annoyance, because she hadn't mentioned her virginity. She'd realised her mistake as soon as he'd questioned her in that raw, shocked tone while buried deep inside her.

But he didn't look like that now... If anything, he looked...resigned? Did he regret what they'd done already? A heavy weight dropped into her stomach, but before she could say anything he rolled off her. And sat up.

'Conall, I'm sorry...' she said, confused now, as well as wary. Did it really matter that he had been her first? Surely her virginity was her business? It wasn't as if she'd set out to deceive him... And why should he even care? This was maybe a bigger deal for her than she'd realised. She hadn't expected her first experience to be quite so— well, so overwhelming, the passion and pleasure so intense or so intimate. But she doubted it could have been that intimate or overwhelming for him. Surely he was used to these sensations, more than aware of how transformative sex could be? He'd had girlfriends before her.

He glanced over his shoulder. 'Sorry for what, now?'

'For not telling you about…' The words came out on an embarrassed whisper. 'Well, about you being my first. I didn't think it would matter that much to you.'

'Uh-huh,' he said, then reached down to scoop up his boxers. He stood up to put them on, then walked off into the bedroom without saying anything, without even looking at her.

The bubble of panic pressed against her breast bone as she heard the toilet flush and the water run in the *en suite* bathroom. She imagined him getting rid of the condom and washing his hands. Then she waited.

Was he angry? Why?

Finally, he reappeared, wearing one of the hotel's plush bathrobes with another in his hand. He gave it to her. 'You best put this on, so we can talk.'

She tugged the robe on, grateful for the coverage, far too aware of all the places her body still burned from his focussed, forceful caresses. And how much it still yearned for his touch, despite the tenderness between her thighs. But even that felt more like an ache than a pain, an ache that was already eager to be filled again.

Who knew sex with Conall O'Riordan would make me insatiable?

The silly thought helped her to relax a little as he sat on the couch and beckoned her over. 'Come here,' he said. Gripping her fingers, he pulled her down to sit beside him.

He didn't sound angry. Not exactly. But the look he sent her wasn't really putting her at ease either. Because she had the strangest feeling he could see right into her soul at that moment. And that she was powerless to protect herself from that probing, oddly dispassionate gaze.

'How come you're a virgin if you were married?' he asked.

The question came out of left field, making her think of Tom for the first time in all of this. The pulse of grief was there, but right behind it was the cruel stab of guilt.

Intellectually, she knew she had nothing to feel guilty about. She'd made her peace with Tom a long time ago. She had never considered taking this step until she was ready. She hadn't betrayed her husband, because they'd never had that kind of a marriage, but still it felt like it would be a betrayal of the friendship she and Tom had shared to tell Conall the whole truth. So she attempted to tell him the lie she'd told herself all these years.

'He was very sick when we got married. He c-couldn't…' She stammered to a stop as his eyes narrowed on her face and the flush of guilty knowledge heated her cheeks. 'It wasn't that type of…'

She cleared her throat and stared down at her hands, which were clasped so tightly in her lap the knuckles had whitened. She'd always been a terrible liar, unfortunately. 'He wasn't able to…' She stopped abruptly when his knuckle touched her chin and he raised her head, watching her again with that all-seeing gaze.

'*It* wasn't that type of marriage, or *he* wasn't able to? Which was it?' he asked, his tone calm but insistent, instantly picking up on the inconsistency in her statement.

She shrugged and looked away, the guilt now like a boulder in her throat. She'd lied to Tom, as well as herself. They'd lied to each other with their marriage. Perhaps it was time she admitted that. She drew in a steadying breath and twisted her fingers. 'Both, I suppose.'

He placed a hand over hers, rubbing his thumb over the skin. 'Explain it to me,' he said. 'Why did you marry the boy if you didn't want to sleep together?'

'Because he was dying, and he was my best friend,' she murmured. 'He didn't have anyone else. No family. And I didn't want him to be alone.' She sniffed and wiped her eyes with the sleeve of her robe.

And I didn't want to be alone either… The reality of what she'd done echoed in her head, clear for the first time.

'So you married him out of pity,' he said.

The stark truth sounded so harsh, so unforgiving, so childish and foolish when he said it like that. Shame thickened the guilt in her throat.

It was the same thing Ross had accused her of all those years ago. Back then, she'd been so angry with her brother. Annoyed that he would reduce what she felt for Tom to something so crass. She had convinced herself at the time that Ross was simply incapable of love himself, so he didn't understand it in others. She'd told him he was wrong, that what she felt for Tom was something he didn't understand. But she could see now, all too clearly, what she'd felt for Tom wasn't the kind of love which should have led to marriage, not even close.

And she wasn't even sure any more she'd done it for Tom's benefit. She'd been so determined. She'd wanted to make everything better, to give him something to live for, but she'd also been determined to prove her brother wrong. To do it in spite of his objections. And Tom had been stuck in the middle. All she'd really done was give him false hope and a fake marriage that had made *her* feel better about losing her best friend.

'I think I thought, if I married him, I could fix everything. That even if I couldn't make him better, I could make him happy.' She choked out a laugh that lacked any warmth or humour as she thought of Tom's words on their wedding night—how guilty she'd made him feel because he'd always known he couldn't be a real husband to her. 'God, I was so young. What the hell was I thinking?'

Conall squeezed her fist. 'Don't beat yourself up too much. There's no point in regretting things already done.'

She sighed. 'No, I suppose not.'

'And marriage is best without that nonsense about love anyway. At least you know that now, which'll make our situation a lot easier.'

She turned to him, shocked by the statement and the prosaic way he'd said it. And the indomitable look on his face. 'I don't understand—what has my marriage to Tom got to do with us?'

Especially as there wasn't really an *'us'*. Even if a tiny part of her heart pulsed at the thought there could be... there might be.

Terrific, now I'm delusional as well as insatiable.

'Not a lot,' he said. 'Except I think you should marry me now.'

CHAPTER TEN

'WHAT?' KATHERINE STARED at Conall as if he'd just suggested she jump off the balcony with him.

He had expected her to be surprised, had been ready for some push back. After all, they hardly knew each other. What he hadn't expected, though, was the blank look of absolute shock on her face.

But he'd given it some thought in the bathroom while calming himself down—after the tumultuous orgasm, the hideous reality of her virginity and the discovery of the risks he'd put her through—and it was the best solution. And the only way to honour the sacred vow he'd made to his father on his death bed not to exploit a woman's innocence.

At the time, his father had made him make the vow to protect his sisters and his mother. But how different was Katherine from them? She'd been abandoned by the same bastard—her half-brother—who had abandoned Carmel.

Plus, there were other more prosaic benefits to a union between them. He'd been thinking for a while now that a marriage would be a good business move as it would stabilise his personal life. Christy had put the thought into his head with her constant questions on the topic—but he'd discarded the idea because she wasn't the right candidate.

But, unlike Christy, Katherine was refreshingly low-maintenance. The only thing that had given him pause was the thought of her romanticism—the eager, artless, sweetness that had captivated him that afternoon could be a problem going forward.

But after talking to Katherine about the reality of her marriage he had become convinced she might be a good candidate after all. She'd already married one man for something other than love. She might be innocent when it came to sex, she might even love the trappings of romance, but she also understood marriage could be a prosaic, practical arrangement. They shared a rare chemistry which would no doubt fade in time, but until it did it could be a strong basis for their union. And she amused him. They'd had fun this afternoon, her quick wit and optimistic nature something he had enjoyed. That had to count for something, right?

The truth was, he had never looked for a grand passion in his relationship with women. Had never wanted it. He knew what that kind of devotion could lead to, and he wanted no part of it. But he'd also never really considered the possibility of friendship with the women he dated. He'd certainly never enjoyed a woman's company the way he had enjoyed Katherine's today—she had entertained him with her quick wit and artless sweetness and made him eager to explore so much more than just their incendiary chemistry.

Until this moment, he'd never considered marriage seriously, despite its obvious benefits to his business and personal life, because even the thought of it had bored him. He couldn't see himself getting bored with Katherine, though, unlike all the other women he'd dated.

'Are you joking?' she asked, still staring at him as if he'd lost his mind.

'Not at all. I took your innocence, Katherine,' he said with all the gravity he felt. 'That means something to me, something very profound.' He took her hand in his and covered her trembling fingers, even more sure that this was the right course of action. How was what he'd just done any different from what Ross De Courtney had done to Carmel? His sister had been seduced by Katherine's bastard of a half-brother—a man much more worldly than she was—and then discarded. The only real difference here was Conall hadn't *intended* to risk a pregnancy. But that didn't alter the fact there was still a reckoning to be paid.

'I made a vow to my father, on his deathbed, when I was a boy of sixteen, that I would protect the women in my life. I failed my sister Carmel.' *And my mother.*

He paused, quashing the errant thought and the turmoil of emotions it caused. She didn't need to know how comprehensively he'd failed *all* the women in his life.

'I refuse to fail you too.'

'How did you fail your sister?' she asked, her wide eyes so full of concern, he found himself squeezing her fingers. Damn, how did she get to be so innocent, so compassionate, after everything she'd already been through in her life?

'You know how, I told you. She was only nineteen when she got pregnant. I refuse to be a man like the guy who seduced her. Ever. Do you understand?'

'But Conall…' She tugged her fingers out of his grasp, and he felt the loss immediately. 'I'm not nineteen, I'm twenty-four. And you didn't seduce me. I wanted to have sex with you…' Her skin lit with a vivid flush. 'Very much. And I'm not going to get pregnant because you had the good sense to use a condom, remember?'

'It split,' he said, and watched her skin pale.

'Oh,' she said, her throat contracting as she swallowed.

'In my haste to get the damn thing on, I must have punctured it. You'll be glad to know I've never been dumb enough to open the packet with my teeth before,' he said, because she had to know he'd hardly been celibate up to now. 'But pregnancy is a possibility. Unless you're using contraception?'

'I...' She swallowed again, her eyes widening to saucer-size, and he could see every emotion flit across her features—worry, guilt, regret, embarrassment. 'I'm not, no, but it's probably only a small chance.' She cleared her throat, the flush on her cheeks endearing despite the circumstances. 'I'm at the very beginning of my cycle.'

The blush turned the sprinkle of freckles on her nose to beacons. And he had the strangest realisation he was actually pleased he was the first man she had ever had such an intimate conversation with.

Neanderthal much, boyo?

Not a reaction he would have expected, but he decided to go with it. After all, everything about his interaction with this woman had been unexpected so far, and weirdly—given that he was a man who didn't usually enjoy unscheduled surprises—it was another thing about her he found fascinating.

'I could take emergency contraception,' she offered.

'If you wish, yes,' he agreed. 'But do you want to?'

He guessed on one level it made sense. And, truth be told, if he had ripped a condom with any of his other girlfriends his reaction would have been very different. But when he'd taken if off in the bathroom and realised the problem, the panic simply hadn't come. He hadn't felt trapped. Instead, the prospect of a pregnancy had seemed oddly inevitable, even fortuitous.

He'd already felt the weight of the vow he'd made to

his father, the fact of her virginity determining what he had to do next to make amends. But, more than that, he'd been able to picture the child they might have, with his focus and her optimism, his drive and her compassion.

He adored Mel's son, Cormac. Family was a hugely important part of his life. It was the bedrock on which he'd built his empire. After his mother's death, he'd never shirked that responsibility, had never wanted to.

It was one of the reasons he had worked so hard to amass the fortune he had—more than any man could ever spend in a lifetime. Up until this point, he'd avoided the inevitable question of when or even if he planned to have children of his own. But as he'd examined the torn rubber and realised what had happened a strange calm had settled over him—at the thought the choice might already have been taken away from him.

Fate was a powerful thing, something he had always believed in—well, he was an Irishman born and bred, after all. And if fate had determined they should have a child, then so be it.

'I… Are you saying you don't want me to take emergency contraception?' she managed, the shock replaced by confusion.

He cupped her cheek and brushed his thumb across her lips, suddenly needing to touch her, to make this moment more tangible, more real.

'It is your choice, Katherine… But, honestly, I suppose I realised when I saw the condom had split I would not be averse to the prospect of a pregnancy.'

'But… *Really?*' Her voice came out on a squeak of shock. 'You're not upset? We've only just met, and we're not even dating properly…'

'We are now,' he said, just in case she was in any doubt. 'And, no, I'm not upset,' he said, a little surprised himself by how sure he was of that. 'Family means everything to me. And being a father is something I think I would be good at,' he added. 'After all, I've had quite a bit of practice already.'

Maybe he had made mistakes and dropped the ball with Carmel and his mother, mistakes he would always regret. But here would be a chance to make amends in so many ways.

'I don't know what to say,' she said with an honesty he had come to admire.

'I've given you a lot to think on, for sure,' he said, smiling at her perplexed expression. 'You don't have to make a decision tonight. You have time.' He glanced at the clock on the wall behind her head. 'I need to leave early in the morning—for a business trip to Australia. Let Liam know when you're ready to return to London—and he'll make all the arrangements.'

He stood, dragging her up with him. He brushed a curl behind her ear, trying to ignore the soft rise and fall of her breathing, the glimpse of cleavage and the desire to strip her out of the robe and take her to bed. There would be time enough for that when he returned.

'I won't see you in the morning, then?' she asked, sounding disappointed. The surge of possessiveness was swift and unequivocal.

'No.' He leaned forward and forced himself to brush his lips across her forehead rather than tasting her mouth. The shudder of response, the flash of arousal in her eyes, sent the inevitable shot of heat straight to his crotch. He forced himself to ignore it as he scooped his clothing off the floor. 'You've a week before I come back,' he said, knowing he would be unable to leave her alone longer than that, already stupidly eager to have her again. 'Which will give you time to heal. And consider my proposition.' He was rushing her, and he knew it, but he saw no reason to wait.

He strode out of the suite, leaving her silent behind him, already able to hear her mind galloping to keep up with him.

Good luck with that, Katherine.

He was a determined man—ruthless, successful and goal-orientated. Once he had set his sights on something, he never failed to achieve it. And he had just set his sights on Katherine Hamilton.

All he had to do now was get Katherine to agree to their union. Perhaps he couldn't offer her the romance she craved but he could offer her so many more tangible benefits—companionship, friendship, financial security and, of course, a chance to explore their spectacular chemistry.

He wasn't even bothered that she was Ross De Courtney's sister any more. He'd have to tell her eventually of her brother's connection with Carmel and Mac. But the bastard had abandoned her too, so she owed the man no loyalty whatsoever.

CHAPTER ELEVEN

'KATIE. OH. MY. God. You looked stunning yesterday. The pictures of you and the "Irish Bad Boy Billionaire" are all over the internet this morning. Why didn't you tell me you were going to the Lumière Ball? And that you're dating O'Riordan? What's he like? Is he as brooding and delicious as he—?'

'Hi, Caro.' Katie's face heated as she interrupted her best friend and top executive assistant Caroline Meyer's stream of consciousness long enough to hook her coat over the rack crammed into their tiny office in East London. 'How's everything been?'

The question was punctuated by the ring of the phone. Caro grabbed the handset on her desk because, as well as being her top executive assistant, Caro also doubled as their receptionist.

'Hi, Hamilton Events, Caro speaking, could you please hold?' she said, then covered the receiver. 'Are you kidding?' She grinned. 'The phones have been ringing off the hook ever since I got in two hours ago!'

Her face beamed with a combination of curiosity and excitement. 'O'Riordan's company account put it out on social media this morning that Hamilton Events is organising some top-secret family deal for him. And that's how you guys met. Ergo, we are now the go-to company for high-end event planning. Everyone who's anyone wants to hire us.'

She gave a deep sigh, hugging the phone to her chest. 'Honestly, it's actually like a fairy tale. You both looked so into each other. It's so romantic.' Another big sigh. 'And after only a week? Love at first sight really does exist.'

Except he doesn't love me.

'Oh, hi,' Caro added as she spotted the man who had walked in behind Katie.

'Caro, this is Jack Mulder, my new...um...' Katie hesitated, still not quite able to believe how her life had changed so much in the space of one tumultuous weekend.

'Bodyguard and driver, Ms Hamilton,' Mulder supplied with a friendly smile.

'Right. Yes.'

'You have a personal bodyguard and driver now?' Caro sounded as stunned as Katie had felt when she'd been introduced to her new professional shadow and his team after Conall's private jet had touched down at Heathrow.

She'd come straight from the airport after dropping off her luggage at her flat, keen to get back to some kind of normality. But Jack Mulder's presence wasn't the only thing making that impossible—her thoughts and feelings had been in turmoil ever since Conall had proposed marriage and insisted he was perfectly okay with an unplanned pregnancy.

It was probably a good thing she hadn't seen Conall this morning—after a sleepless night at the Lumière, the text she'd received from him on the plane had been disconcerting enough.

In transit/meetings for the next few days. Will call you at home Friday evening. Eight p.m. UK time. Liam is making necessary arrangements for your safety and will put you through to me if you need to get in touch. Con

At least she now knew what the second sentence had been about. Liam had informed her it wasn't safe for her to travel by public transport any more—and that Conall insisted on certain security measures being in place for all his close acquaintances.

While part of her had wanted to object when she'd been introduced to Mulder—because her safety wasn't *really* Conall's responsibility—another part of her had been deeply touched he'd gone to the trouble of arranging security for her.

Ultimately, she'd spent the long drive back to her flat from Heathrow with Mulder at the wheel, arguing with herself about her reaction. She needed to be careful not to be a total push-over. Conall's attention was overwhelming enough without her letting her own insecurities get in the way.

She'd always been a sucker for any kind of male attention, perhaps because she'd been denied it throughout her childhood. She'd already married one man for the wrong reasons. She mustn't fall into the trap of thinking Conall loved her simply because he clearly had a bit of a 'white knight' complex.

As a result, what should have been exciting news— that Conall's and her romance had inadvertently given her business the boost she'd been hoping and planning for for months—felt anything but. In truth, all it did was pile on more pressure and make her feel even more overwhelmed. Because this wasn't a real romance any more than her first marriage had been.

The sex had been spectacular, maybe a bit too spectacular, because she should have rejected Conall's proposal straight away. Instead of which she'd given him the impression she could be won over, that she could be as pragmatic and cynical as he was. And she knew she couldn't... Not least because, she was very much afraid, she already had more feelings for him than she knew what to do with.

Feelings which had to do with much more than the two spectacular orgasms he'd given her while she made love for the first time, or the cherished way he had made her feel by insisting he employ a driver-cum-bodyguard to keep her safe... And everything to do with the fierce passion in his voice when he'd spoken of his sisters, his family, the possibility of children and marriage.

She'd always wanted to have children too...always dreamed of having a family she could love unconditionally and who would love her unconditionally in return... Enough to know she wasn't going to take emergency contraception, even though it had to be the smartest option.

But the truth was, her decision to risk an unplanned pregnancy—however slight the possibility—with a man she hardly knew wasn't even the scariest thing about this situation. By far the most terrifying thing was the fact that when Conall had offered her marriage—had offered her a life with him—in that firm, practical, no-nonsense and defiantly anti-romantic tone, her foolish, unguarded heart had shouted 'yes'.

Not because he was a billionaire who could turn her boutique business into the go-to company for high-end events. Not because he was the hottest—well, the only—lover she'd ever had. Not because he was sinfully handsome, wonderfully compelling and wildly charismatic, or even because she knew he most likely would make a far better father than her own father had ever been to her.

But because she had done something really, really stupid over their one tumultuous weekend together.

She'd fallen in love with a man she wasn't sure was even capable of loving her in return. And, if that wasn't delusional enough, she was very much afraid she was already in danger of persuading herself she could make this work… That maybe Conall could learn to love her back if she just gave him a chance. She knew she wanted desperately to give him that chance, to give *them* that chance. Despite the fact that her cock-eyed optimism— that love could always find a way, despite all evidence to the contrary—and her belief in happy-ever-afters had left her devastated once before.

And she had no guarantees whatsoever it wasn't going to kick her in the teeth all over again.

CHAPTER TWELVE

'CONALL! YOU CALLED!' Katie's heartbeat leapt into her throat as her lover's face popped up in the video-chat app on her phone at exactly eight p.m. on Friday evening—then wanted to kick herself.

Why had she thought he might not call? And what was he going to want to talk about? Because, even after five days apart, she did not have a coherent answer for him yet. About anything.

She'd arrived home an hour ago, having worked her butt off all week handling the never-ending stream of new clients—which had thankfully helped deflect the constant playback of every detail of their twenty-four hours together in Paris. What had comprehensively failed to redirect her thoughts in the last week, though, was the constant calls and emails she'd had to field from all her friends and acquaintances enquiring about the new man in her life.

Once she'd arrived home, she'd veered between exhausted, excited and panicked as the time scheduled for their call had drawn closer. She'd also spent far too much time debating what to wear while she showered, and put on make-up, then took it off again, only to settle on brushed cotton PJs and bunny slippers.

Seductive, much?

'Of course I called,' he said, the deadly dimple appearing in his cheek as he flashed her a weary smile. He looked rumpled and even more gorgeous than usual, bright sunlight shining off his dark hair. 'I said I would.'

'Yes, yes you did.' And she'd discovered even on their short acquaintance that Conall was a man of his word. 'Where are you?' she asked.

'Take a look,' he said, then flipped his phone around. 'It's a place I own on the Gold Coast—kind of soulless, but better than staying in a hotel when you're battling epic jet-lag.'

She took in a luxury open-plan living area complete with a spotless state-of-the-art granite-and-steel kitchen. The view of an infinity pool and a wide, empty golden-sand beach fringed by palm trees—the summer sun sparkling off crystal clear water—visible through the glass wall at the end of the space was almost as breath-taking as Conall's face when it filled the screen again.

'It looks amazing,' she said.

'Come with me next time,' he offered. 'I'll teach you how to surf.'

'How do you know I can't surf already?' she asked, surprising herself with the teasing comment, pleased when she heard his rough chuckle. 'What time is it there?' she asked, trying to dismiss the spark of joy in her chest which always came when she made him smile.

'Too early.' He yawned and her galloping heartbeat slowed at the comforting domesticity of the moment. 'Liam tells me you've been busy?'

'Yes, very,' she said, then began to babble about all the new clients they'd taken on. Her words tumbled over themselves, the need to keep talking about inconsequential stuff suddenly paramount. But eventually she wound down, noticing that his gaze had dipped.

'What?' she asked, able to feel the heat in his perusal even from the other side of the globe, the familiar pulse and throb in her core no less intense than it had been five days ago, or every night since—when she'd woken up hot and sweaty, her sex slick and swollen, the memory of their one night together still so vivid.

'What are you wearing?' he asked, his voice having dropped several octaves.

She chewed on her lip, wishing now she'd opted for the thong and see-through negligee she'd momentarily considered buying for tonight's call. 'My PJs,' she managed, unable to hide the apology in her voice.

'Cute... Show me,' he said, the tone becoming even huskier. Apparently he was undeterred by her complete inability to dress appropriately for a late-night video call with her lover.

'They're not remotely sexy,' she said, almost as embarrassed now as she was turned on.

'I'll be the judge of that.'

She lifted the phone up to give him an arm's length view of her totally unsexy PJs. 'See what I mean?'

'Hmm... The flying pink pigs are kind of hot, actually.' His deep voice—playful and yet intense—rumbled through her over-sensitised body and gathered like a warm weight in her sex.

'Really?' she asked, and he laughed again, the sound as strained as it was sexy.

'Katherine, how do you feel about losing your phone sex virginity with me too?'

'Yes,' she whispered, the weight in her sex pulsing now, the command in his voice as unbearably hot as the wicked intent in his eyes.

'Are you sure? Because you're going to have to do exactly as I tell you. No hesitations?'

'I… Yes,' she managed around the lump of lust forming in her throat to match the boulder now jammed between her legs. 'I can do that.'

'Good girl,' he all but purred. He ran his thumb across his lips, as if considering his options. 'Find somewhere to prop the phone, so I can see all of you. You're going to need both hands for what I have in mind.'

After two frantic minutes, she managed to position the phone to his satisfaction and found herself lying down on the sofa, still wearing the fluffy PJs, the brushed cotton like sandpaper now against her skin.

How did he do that? How did he turn her into a mass of throbbing desperation with a single look, a simple command?

'As much as I love the pigs,' he said. 'We're going to have to lose them. Take off the pants first,' he murmured.

She did as he instructed, the purred words of encouragement only adding to the torment as she stripped off the pyjama bottoms, finally lying in front of him in her panties and the pyjama top.

She could smell the musty scent of the moisture flooding between her thighs. Could he see it? Did he know what he did to her? But what might have embarrassed her once only made the hot weight heavier when he spoke again.

'Now the top—unbutton it for me, *mo mhuirnín*,' he murmured, using the Irish word he'd used before in passion. 'Slowly,' he added, when her trembling fingers popped open two buttons in quick succession.

She tried to slow down, but the feel of his gaze was pure torture, her breath becoming ragged as she finished unbuttoning the top.

'Show me your breasts,' he said, the demand back in his voice. She brushed the sides of the top away to reveal her swollen nipples. The peaks pebbled into bullets of need under his commanding gaze, the slight draft from her windows like an arctic storm on her over-sensitised flesh. He swore softly, the curse word full of approval and passion.

'Do they hurt?' he asked.

'You have no idea,' she all but groaned, earning another rough chuckle, this one even more strained than the last.

'Play with them for me,' he demanded.

She rolled the stiff peaks between her fingers, caressing, pinching, aware of his dark gaze spurring her on. The hot centre of her sex swelled and throbbed, the slick bundle of nerves somehow attached to the hard peaks, so achy now she began to move on the couch, thrusting her breasts up, offering them to him, so desperate for his touch she entered another realm. His words of encouragement and demand were the only thing tethering her to reality, until she could almost feel his lips, firm and strong, unyielding and relentless, working their magic on her turgid breasts.

'Lose your panties. Do it now.'

She struggled out of her underwear, fully displayed now, and yearning, her whole body one throbbing bundle of need.

'Now stroke yourself where you need me the most.' His voice cut through the fog of sensation, the swell of desperation.

She dragged her fingers through the slick folds and found the swollen nub begging for release.

'Rub it harder, make it burn. But don't go over, not until I tell you.'

She arched her back, struggling to hold on, to hold back, her movements his to command like a puppet and its master. Her staggered breathing was the only sound.

She circled the sweet spot, delved, flicked right at the heart of her pleasure, drenched in desperation. The orgasm flickered so close, but just out of reach, as the torture increased.

She heard his grunts, knew he had to be pleasuring himself too as he watched her, commanded her. Somehow the thought that she could devastate him the way he devastated her gave her a strange jolt of power, just as he groaned.

'Now, go over now!'

The command had the orgasm crashing through her, wave upon wave of harsh, painful pleasure. Too much and yet not enough.

At last she lay, limp, exhausted, shuddering, on her couch. Her galloping heart finally slowed, but her body remained raw, tender, uninhibited.

She heard the stunned curse and lifted her heavy eyelids, still too shattered to summon the energy to cover herself as his gaze coasted over her flushed skin.

He swore, sounding almost as dazed as she felt. 'That's the best phone sex I've ever had. You're a natural.'

She choked out a weary laugh, stupidly pleased. Perhaps in this much at least, they could be equals.

'Get some sleep,' he said, the tone still commanding, but maybe less sure of itself than it had been at the start of the call. Why she should take even more pleasure from that flicker of uncertainty than the virtual sex, she had no idea, but she did.

'You're gonna need it,' he added. 'Because I've decided to leave early. And, when I get to your place, I intend to keep you very busy, doing that for real.'

CHAPTER THIRTEEN

'WHERE ARE WE going, Jack? I thought we were meeting
Conall at the Opera House,' Katie said to her driver, all
too aware of the buzz of anticipation.

Tonight was the four-week anniversary of the night
she and Conall had first made love in Paris. And she still
hadn't had her period. Not that that really meant anything, she told herself staunchly. Her cycle was often ir-
regular. It wasn't uncommon for her to have a six-week
gap between periods. Of course, she could totally put
them both out of their misery at this point and just take
a pregnancy test. But Conall hadn't asked her to. In fact,
he hadn't even mentioned the prospect of a baby again,
since he'd returned from Australia three weeks ago, so
she'd decided to wait and see.

Every time they'd made love since—and they'd made
love a lot—Conall had worn protection. It had made her
feel both cherished and yet unsure of where he really
stood on the prospect of a pregnancy. He wasn't pushing
it, she'd decided, and neither should she, because she really wasn't sure where she stood either. They were still
in the honeymoon stage of their relationship, and what a
honeymoon stage it was.

After so many years of being unaware of her sexual
needs, she'd discovered a side to her personality she hadn't

even realised existed. A sensual, exciting, erotic, insatiable side which she had been satisfying to her heart's content at every available opportunity. But, more than that, for the first time ever she felt truly a part of a couple.

Her experience as Tom's wife had been so brief, and also so fraught with tragedy, there had been no time to simply be with him, to have normal conversations the way she did with Conall.

They talked about everything, from where they would spend their weekend—at Conall's eight-bedroom Grade-Two-listed Regency town house in Kensington, or her one-bedroom flat in Shoreditch—to whether they should cook in or eat out at one of the many sumptuous restaurants where Conall was a regular.

Her social life had also become turbo-charged, with Jack Mulder arriving at her office several evenings a week to whisk her off to some red-carpet event in London or Dublin, or even one spectacular evening in Milan, which Conall had asked her to attend with him. After some initial nerves—because she was used to organising events, not participating in them—she'd become almost as blasé as Conall about travelling in his private jet or helicopter, having her own driver or hobnobbing with stage and screen stars, political grandees, pop divas, sports heroes and assorted other famous faces. She was also getting accustomed to the intrusive attention of the paparazzi and the press.

But the best moments by far were the private moments she got to spend alone with Conall, just the two of them. They both had busy careers, so it always felt as if those few evenings they got to share together—usually in his house, not hers—were a rare and special gift.

She still hadn't got too much more information out of him about himself, but in some ways she didn't care.

They were getting to know each other and all those big questions could wait. Just being with him and discovering the little things—such as that he could cook a mean Irish stew, liked to nod off after sex while wrapped around her and had an encyclopaedic knowledge of the film *Mean Girls* because his sisters had watched it on a loop in their teens—was more than enough for now.

'Mr O'Riordan asked that I bring you to the town house first,' Jack replied as the car headed past Kensington Gardens. Her chauffeur-cum-bodyguard, who had become a trusted friend, sent her a gruff smile. 'The opera doesn't start for over an hour.'

'Okay.' Katie smiled back, thrilled at the prospect of seeing Conall alone—for a whole hour. Her cheeks heated at the thought of what they could do in that time, especially as she hadn't seen him in two days, after he'd had to make an impromptu trip to Ireland without her.

The car pulled into the driveway of Conall's elaborate stucco-fronted house. She bid goodbye to Jack and jumped out of the car as soon as it stopped. As she rushed up the stone steps, the front door opened and Conall appeared in the doorway looking beyond gorgeous in the tuxedo he'd donned for the opera.

Her heart danced into her throat.

'Hey, about time. What took you so long?' Conall murmured, before she barrelled into him.

He huffed out a laugh as she wrapped her arms around him, absorbing the delicious smell of juniper and pine that clung to him—the well of emotion blind-siding her, along with the familiar spurt of heat. He drew her into the house's warmth and slammed the door behind her with his foot, before lifting her face to his. 'Good to see you too,' he said, before his mouth covered hers.

The kiss was deep and demanding, full of promise and

need. Her hands explored the ridged muscles of his abdomen beneath the starched linen of his dress shirt as he cupped her bottom through her dress, the desire as sharp and desperate as always. But as her fingers found the buttons of his shirt, clumsily flicking them open, her hands desperate to touch his naked skin, he tore his mouth away and drew back, holding her trembling hands at arm's length.

'Hold on. We're going to have to take a rain-check until after the opera,' he said, his pure crystal-blue eyes fixed on her face—the flare of passion contradicting the strained smile.

'Why?' she said, unable to hide her devastation.

He let out a gruff laugh. 'No pouting, Little Miss Ravenous.' His thumb skimmed over her bottom lip. 'I've got something for you.'

Threading his fingers through hers, he led her into the library off the main hallway. The musty smell of old leather and lavender polish filled the room.

'Sit down,' he said, and let go of her hand. After crossing the room, he clicked the dial on the safe built in to the shelving then produced a small velvet box.

Katie's heartbeat bounced back into her throat, her gaze fixed on the box as he walked towards her then knelt in front of her.

'Conall?' she whispered, so stunned she could hardly breathe, let alone talk or think coherently.

He hadn't mentioned marriage again, not since their first night in Paris. She'd simply assumed he'd changed his mind. But when he flipped open the box, to reveal a vintage ring studded with diamonds, her breathing stopped altogether, trapped somewhere around her diaphragm.

He touched her chin, lifted her startled gaze to his face then ran his thumb down her cheek.

'Breathe, Katherine,' he murmured in that husky voice

that had the power to make her ache, and she suspected always would. He took the ring out and discarded the box, then lifted her trembling fingers with his other hand.

'It's my mother's ring,' he said. 'I went to Ireland to collect it, and to check with Immy and Mel they were okay for me to have it.'

'You did?' she said, still so stunned, she had to force herself to breathe before she passed out.

She hadn't yet met his sister Mel, or indeed his young nephew Cormac. And while she'd developed a great relationship with Imelda—the younger woman apparently overjoyed her brother was finally dating a 'real woman'—her words, not Katie's—the idea that he had discussed their marriage with his sisters felt huge. Too huge in a lot of ways.

'Uh-huh. I'd like you to wear it, as I want to marry you, Katherine.'

'But…' Her hand instinctively roamed to her stomach, her mind racing to catch up with her staggered breathing.

When he'd first proposed marriage it had seemed like a kneejerk suggestion. Something she hadn't really considered seriously since. Partly because it would have been far too easy to allow her romantic heart to say yes when it felt like the wrong thing to do. He had told her he didn't love her and had made a point of saying he didn't even think love was necessary in a relationship. But since then, her feelings for him had become so much deeper. She knew now this relationship was about more than just sex. But was it still too soon? Especially as she still couldn't be sure he wasn't doing this out of a sense of duty, a sense of responsibility. She knew he cared about her, he'd shown it in so many ways in the last month, but…

'I might not be pregnant, Conall,' she managed, trying to gauge his reaction. Was that the real reason he was asking? Because he thought he had to, after what had happened to his sister? 'I should have taken a pregnancy test.' Why the heck hadn't she? 'I can take one tomorrow. Then we'll know for sure if...'

'Shh...' He touched his finger to her lips to silence the panicked stream of words. 'This isn't to do with the possibility that you might be pregnant,' he said, covering the hand she had on her belly with his. The gesture had her heartbeat slowing to a crawl. 'As I said, I've no fear of fatherhood, would welcome it, in fact. I'm not getting any younger,' he added with a rough laugh that belied the serious expression. 'But this is about you and me. I want you to be my wife.'

She released a shuddery breath. The panic retreated to be replaced with something even more disturbing... *Hope.*

'But... *Why*, Conall?' she forced herself to ask.

He frowned, as if the question made no sense to him, then stood up, the ring in his fist as he paced away from her, then back again.

'Because we suit, Katherine. Surely it's obvious?' He ran impatient fingers through his hair. 'I can't keep my hands off you and, even when we're not tearing each other's clothes off, I like you. You're good company, funny, sweet, compassionate. And most of all smart and independent. This past month has proved to me we'll make an excellent team.'

It was hardly the declaration of love she might once have dreamed of, but then she knew that Conall was a practical, pragmatic man. And it wasn't really his words that mattered, she realised, but the emotion behind them. His agitation, impatience and the frustrated frown were somehow more compelling than the beautiful ring still clutched in his fist.

'And…' He knelt in front of her again and took her hands in his, his gaze so hot and determined she could feel her heart punching her chest and her resistance crumbling. 'And if we should be blessed with children. Now,' he added, glancing at her belly, 'or in the future, I know you'll make a good mother. You're strong, which is important, because sometimes motherhood can be so tough. My own mother struggled—' He stopped abruptly and looked away, the colour highlighting his cheeks making the emotion swell in her throat.

'Conall? What were you going to say?' she asked softly as he swore under his breath and got back to his feet.

He'd never spoken about his mother. All she knew was that Maeve O'Riordan had died a scant two years after her husband. Over the last few weeks, on the rare occasions when they'd spoken about anything personal, he had talked freely about his father. Enough for Katie to know Ronan O'Riordan had been a hugely important figure in Conall's life. She knew how much Conall had looked up to his father, how much he had respected and admired him—and how traumatic Ronan O'Riordan's sudden death in a farm accident had been for his only son, even though Conall seemed unwilling or unable to acknowledge that trauma himself.

But Conall's relationship with his mother had remained a mystery until this moment. Katie hadn't pressed him to talk about her. She knew how harsh unresolved grief could be, especially if your relationship with the person who had died was problematic. After all, she'd had to come to terms with her own issues with her mother after her death. Forced to acknowledge that in many ways Cathy Hamilton had always been more dedicated to her art than she ever had been to providing a secure and stable home.

'Nothing,' he murmured. But she could see it wasn't

nothing. The colour highlighting his cheeks was so unlike him, she knew there was much more to his proposal than he had let on. This wasn't just about practicalities or great sex, or even the companionship they'd shared over the last few weeks.

Was it possible Conall might actually need her, in a way she already knew she needed him? The pounding in her ears became deafening.

She placed her hand on his arm. 'Conall, you do know you can trust me, don't you?' she said softly.

'I don't want to talk about it,' he said, sounding frustrated, but also unsure of himself—which wasn't like him at all.

'I understand,' she said, determined not to push or be hurt by his denial. But when she dropped her hand from his jacket sleeve, he grasped her wrist to pull her closer.

'No, you don't,' he murmured.

He searched her face and ran his thumb down her cheek, the turmoil in his expression totally transparent for the first time since she'd met him. She knew he always held himself back, in a way she never had, but her lungs constricted, shocked by what she saw. Not just grief, and sadness, but also guilt and shame.

'She killed herself,' he said, the turmoil in his eyes as vivid as the confusion in his voice. 'Left my sisters and me, because she couldn't stand to live without him. She was always so fragile...' He let her go and stood up, his voice so full of pain now she could feel it tearing at her own composure.

'She miscarried two babies between having me and my sisters. I think it destroyed a part of her. And he always made allowances for that. Some days she couldn't even get out of bed, so he would do it all. I asked him once why he put up with her moods and he slapped me across the face for saying such a thing about my mother. It was the only time he ever hit me.'

He sat down heavily on the couch and sunk his head into his hands, running his fingers through his hair. 'He loved her so much, he forgave her everything. And I never understood it.'

Katie knelt in front of him. She placed her hands on his knees, her ribs squeezing at the shame and confusion on his face when his gaze met hers.

'I miss him, every day. But I don't miss her, even though I know the depression wasn't her fault,' he said so simply, her heart hurt. 'If that's what love does to you, I want no part of it in my marriage. If that's what you need from me, I can't give it to you.'

He opened his fist to reveal the beautiful ring nestled in the centre of his palm, the diamonds having reddened the skin where he had gripped it too tightly. 'This ring is probably cursed—why didn't I realise that?' he murmured, sounding so lost her heart broke—for the young man, not much more than a boy really, who had lost so much, so quickly and had never had the time and space he'd needed to come to terms with his loss.

Love wasn't about weakness, she thought. It was about strength. It couldn't heal depression or mental illness, but it could heal a heart. And it wasn't something you received but something you gave. His father had understood that, and so did he, even if he didn't realise it—or why would he have worked so hard to keep his family together after his parents' deaths?

But she couldn't tell him any of that, she realised. All she could do was show him.

And suddenly she knew she loved him. For better *or* for worse, and even if he didn't love her back... *Yet...*

Some day he would surely take that leap too? Because he was more than capable of it.

He was terrified right now of feeling that deeply again, for anyone other than his father, his sisters and even his mother, but she could wait for those feelings to grow.

She cupped his jaw, the zing of awareness never far from the surface as his stubble abraded her palm and his gaze lifted.

'I'd love to wear her ring,' she said simply.

His frown deepened, but then the heat, hunger and something that looked very much like triumph turned his gaze to fire. 'You'll marry me?'

'Yes,' she whispered.

He gripped her neck, dragged her to him and devoured her mouth with a hunger and purpose that made her heart slam into her breast bone.

Standing up, he lifted her with him and growled. 'Put your legs around my waist. We're going to be a late for the opera.'

In the end they were close to an hour late for the opera. Conall had made himself drag Katherine out of bed— even though he'd never been that keen on opera, he knew she loved it, and he was scared if they had stayed in bed he might never want to leave it.

The hunger that had controlled him for over a month hadn't abated one bit. He'd had to force himself to leave London without her this week, after ignoring his businesses around the globe for three whole weeks—ever since he'd raced back from Australia two days ahead of schedule just to be with her.

He had hoped, once he got his ring on her finger, the driving hunger would begin to fade… No such luck, he realised as he showed her to her seat in their private box and watched her eyes glitter with emotion as the soprano on stage hit a stream of fanciful notes.

His fiancée wore a blue satin dress that skimmed her thighs, her curly hair still sexily rumpled from their love-making. How could she be even more beautiful every time he looked at her?

As he seated himself, his gaze snagged on the ring he'd placed on her finger. Why had he blurted out all that stuff about his mother?

And why had she accepted it all so readily?

He sat through the remainder of the opera's second act, the urge to skim his hand under her dress and touch her, taste her again, fizzing in his veins.

Why was the longing to be with her still so intense? To be near her? To brand her as his the only way he knew how at every possible opportunity?

It was madness. And he had a bad feeling it went way beyond their extraordinary chemistry. Or the practical benefits of a marriage between them. And had everything to do with the wide-eyed look on her face—so open, so unguarded, so full of hope—when he'd told her what he could never offer her and she had agreed to marry him regardless.

He'd known in that moment, Katherine had persuaded herself he could be the man she needed, the man she wanted, when he knew he could not. He should have told her the truth, made her understand that deep down he wasn't worthy of love, would never be worthy of love. Because he couldn't give it back.

He'd failed his mother, blaming her for something that had never been her fault, never realising how bad the grief had hit her until it was too late... And he would fail Katherine too—because he would never be able to open himself to that kind of pain. But he hadn't been able to say anything, because he'd wanted her bright, lively, compassionate presence in his life so much.

She glanced at him and smiled, applauding the performers as they left the stage and the theatre began to empty for the intermission.

'Well, at least we didn't miss the *whole* of the first half.' She grinned.

'Come on.' He stood and offered her his hand. He needed to get out of their box before he got ideas about kissing her again, because that way lay more madness—and possible arrest. 'Let's get a drink.'

After leading her through the crowds, they entered the exclusive private members' bar reserved for the people who owned the boxes.

'How about champagne?' he asked, keen to celebrate their engagement.

He was being an idiot. She'd agreed to marry him. Why was he complicating this? They would make a good team. There might even now be a child growing in her womb... He needed to tell her about her brother's connection to his family, but that could wait until after the wedding—which he planned to expedite as quickly as possible. He wanted her in his home, wanted his ring on her finger and his name on her passport.

She nodded, the blush lighting the sprinkle of freckles he had come to adore over the past four weeks, but as he lifted his hand to signal the barman her face paled as she spotted someone over his shoulder.

'Ross?'

He swung round to see a tall man standing behind him with a woman on his arm. She looked vaguely familiar, but it was the man's face that drew his attention, the shock of recognition going through him like a bullet.

'I didn't know you like the opera.' Katherine's distressed whisper came from a million miles away, muffled by the fury thundering in his ears.

'I don't,' the man said, the rigid muscle in his jaw softening as he stared at Katherine. But then he blinked, recovering himself. 'Katie, you look… Well…' The man's blue-green eyes, so like his nephew's, landed on Conall, his lips twisting in a caustic smile. 'Hello—O'Riordan, isn't it?' he said curtly, the conversational tone belying the focussed gleam in his eyes, as if he were assessing Conall's suitability to date his sister.

Conall's fury started to choke him. Who the hell did this bastard think he was?

'I saw in the press that you two were dating.' The man held out his hand towards Conall. 'I'm Katie's brother,' he added. 'Ross De Courtney.'

'I know exactly who you are.' Conall ground out the words. He glanced down at the offered hand, then shoved his own hand into his pocket. His fingers curled into a fist as he grasped hold of the last thin threads of his control to stop himself from ploughing his fist into the bastard's face.

'You do?' The man's brow wrinkled, the muscle in his jaw working overtime now. 'Have we met?'

'Thankfully, no,' he said. 'But I know what a bastard you are.'

'Conall?' Katie gasped beside him, clearly shocked by his rudeness, but Conall didn't care. How dared this man call himself her brother? He had no right.

And how dared he look at Conall as if he weren't good enough to date his sister, when *he* was the one who had failed her so spectacularly?

'What's wrong?' Katie asked, confused now, the concern in her voice making the anger in his gut twist into something a great deal more volatile.

He should have told her, he realised. Long before now. Told her that Ross De Courtney was the bastard who had seduced and abandoned Carmel. But it was too late for explanations now. All he cared about was keeping this man the hell away from her. Because he'd seen the surprise in Katherine's face a moment ago, swiftly followed by the soft glow of pleasure. She was ready to forgive the bastard, a man who hadn't spoken to her in years, who had never been any kind of a brother to her, by the sounds of it. Because she was too soft-hearted, too sweet, compassionate and kind.

Which is the same damn reason she's willing to marry you. When you can't love her.

He dismissed the sickening thought. And forced his righteous fury with De Courtney to the fore to cover the wave of shame that followed hot on its heels. Maybe he couldn't love Katherine, but he would protect her from her bastard of a brother.

'Stay away from her,' he snarled, unable to recognise his own voice. 'You've no right to talk to her.'

'What the…?' De Courtney swore viciously, shock wiping the cynical smile off his face. 'Who the hell are you to tell me that?'

'I'm the man who's going to marry her.' Conall spat the words, his fist flexing.

The thundering in his head began to clear, though, as he became aware of Katherine's fingers digging into his other arm. And he looked down to catch the sparkle of diamonds on her finger.

'Conall?' He turned to see horrified shock tempered by the sheen of moisture in her eyes. 'What's going on? How do you know Ross?'

She blinked, the moisture sparkling in her eyes crucifying him.

He took her hand in his, suddenly desperate to get away, to get out, the shame rising up again to choke him. 'We should leave,' he managed around the brutal knot forming in his stomach. 'We need to talk.'

'Katie, don't be an idiot, the man's obviously insane,' came the brittle comment from her brother.

Conall stared at her, the urge to punch De Courtney all but consuming him now, but he held on to the fury as the shame in his stomach curdled to sick dread.

De Courtney didn't matter. What mattered now was getting Katherine out of here, so he could explain. Even though he wasn't even sure himself any more what he was supposed to say… Because this all suddenly felt like so much more than he'd ever meant it to be. So much more than he knew how to deal with. Because he hadn't been thinking about Carmel, or little Mac a moment ago. All he'd been able to think about was protecting Katherine. And that made no sense.

She glanced at her brother, but when her gaze returned to his, his heart galloped into his throat, the absolute trust he saw in her eyes crucifying him all over again. 'Okay,' she said. 'Let's go.'

He led her out of the bar, ignoring Ross De Courtney behind them calling them both lunatics. But, as he gripped her hand, his galloping heart began to choke him… And the pain in his chest became so real and visceral, it terrified him.

CHAPTER FOURTEEN

KATIE SHIVERED, WRAPPING her arms around her stomach, trying to hold the shattered pieces of herself together as Conall's car drew up to the kerb outside the Opera House.

She'd left her coat in their box, she thought inanely, but it wasn't the winter wind, bitter against her skin, that had the cold wrapping around her heart.

'Here, you're freezing.' Conall's coat covered her shoulders, his strong arm banding around her waist to direct her into the car as Jack Mulder opened the passenger door.

The familiar scent of juniper and pine invaded her senses, but the inevitable rush of sensation from the warmth of his body heat that clung to the fabric refused to close the chasm opening up in her chest.

She sat stiffly in the seat, her movements somehow no longer her own, as if she were acting on autopilot.

A part of her knew she was in shock. The look of pure, unadulterated rage contorting her fiancé's face into someone she didn't recognise, as he'd confronted her brother and said what he'd said, replayed over and over in her head.

'I know exactly who you are.'

How did Conall know her brother? Why hadn't he said anything?

The truth was, she'd been considering contacting Ross ever since her conversation with Conall in Paris. She knew he lived in New York now, and she had even gone so far as to get his contact details. Their estrangement was stupid, she'd decided, a product of their foolish pride. She could see now he'd objected to her marriage to Tom to protect her. She was the one who had pushed him away, not the other way around, refusing to speak to him until he recanted—which of course he'd refused to do, because he'd never been very good at admitting he was wrong.

All those thoughts and feelings had been rushing through her head at breakneck speed but, before she'd had a chance to voice any of them, Conall had intervened.

And now the only word that kept racing through her mind was...*why?*

Where had that rage come from? He'd made it sound as if it had something to do with her relationship with Ross. But how could it, when they'd hardly spoken about their pasts? And he'd certainly never asked her any questions about her relationship with her brother.

The car sped through the evening traffic in Covent Garden as Conall placed his hand over hers, gathered her fingers and squeezed.

'I'm sorry,' he said, but the words sounded brittle, unconvincing, forced, said out of necessity rather than apology.

She glanced down at their joined hands, noticing the ring she had accepted so readily, so eagerly, only hours before on her finger.

She tugged her hand out of his, placed it in her lap and stared out of the window. Christmas decorations adorned the shop fronts along Piccadilly—expensive gold and silver satin bows, sprigs of lush red holly, lavish green pine boughs all lit by swathes of colourful fairy lights—as the car drove past Fortnum and Mason, the Wolseley, the Ritz. But what had enchanted her on the way to the theatre did nothing to lift the leaden weight in her chest now.

'How do you know my brother?' she asked dully.

The silence in the car stretched tight, the pain in her stomach becoming agonising as she waited for his answer. She forced herself to look at him and saw the flicker of indecision.

'Please don't lie. And tell me that was about me,' she managed round the weight that had somehow risen up to jam itself into her throat.

The intensity of his gaze seared her skin, but she refused to look away, refused to break eye contact. Finally, resignation and regret shadowed his eyes.

'Your brother is the bastard who got my sister Carmel pregnant four years ago...' he said in a voice low with fury.

Katie sucked in a torturous breath, surprised she could still be shocked, but she was. Not just by his words, but the chilling anger in his eyes.

And in that moment a slew of memories came tumbling back. His words, his actions over the last month right from the first moment she'd met him, which she had interpreted one way—excused them in her ignorance and naivety, and forgiven them so easily in her determination to see the best in him, in *them*. But those words and actions looked so different now, the actual motivation behind them revealed in the cold, harsh light of reality.

'That's why you hired me?' she murmured, barely able to breathe now around the catastrophic weight pressing down on her chest. 'Why you made everything so hard for me. Why you invited me to Paris...'

'Maybe at first. I persuaded myself it was about him, but then...'

He stopped and stared down at his hands. But when he reached out to run his thumb down her cheek, as he had done so many times before, she reared back.

'Katherine, don't...' he murmured, his tone as broken as she felt. 'He's not why I...'

'Yes, he is,' she said. That brutal feeling of inadequacy that had dogged her throughout her childhood and adolescence—every time her mother hadn't seen her, every time her father had refused to acknowledge her, every time Ross had pushed her away, even when Tom had died when she had wanted so much for him to live—all came tumbling back.

'*He's* why you seduced me, why you wanted to marry me. It was all about him, wasn't it? You wanted revenge for your sister and your nephew, and I was it.' She was struggling to breathe now, the tears scoring her cheeks as she gulped in each painful breath.

Because she was that small, insignificant child again. The one no one had ever really wanted. She'd worked so hard to lose that girl, to be her own woman. She'd built a business, had stayed strong even after losing her best friend and had been prepared to give everything she was to Conall, but it had never really been her he wanted.

'That's nonsense, Katherine,' he said, and tried to reach for her again.

Her back slammed against the car door as she shifted away from his touch. She hit the button to open the driver's partition. 'Jack, stop the car. I need to get out.'

'Miss, is something wrong?' Jack glanced back, his voice concerned and wary.

'Stop the car, Jack,' Conall said.

As soon as the vehicle stopped moving, she jumped out. Hearing the door slam behind her, she raced forward, then turned to see Conall approaching her, his palms up.

He looked concerned, probably because she was behaving like a crazy lady. She swallowed down the wellspring of emotion, knowing she had to deal with these feelings, had to find a way back—but she couldn't do it with him there, and that hurt, more than anything else about this whole mess. Because she loved him so much, and he had never loved her.

'Katherine, calm down please. Let's talk about this. I want you to be my wife.' His gaze dipped to her belly. 'Even now you could be pregnant with our child.'

The comment was like a body blow. Oh God, was the child he had said he wanted all part of this too? She shook her head. No, she couldn't think about that now.

'Did you ever love me, even a little bit?' she asked, her voice breaking on the pitiful plea.

He tensed, as if she'd hit him. And the catastrophic weight seemed to implode, bleeding its misery into the deep well of sorrow in the centre of her chest.

How could she have been so foolish? So misguided? God, he'd even told her he could never love her, and she hadn't listened.

She grasped the ring on her finger, twisted it off and held it out. 'You can take it back. I don't want it any more.'

Instead of taking it, he planted his fists in his pockets and stared at her. 'I won't take it. Not until you get back in the damn car and listen to reason.'

A part of her wanted to throw the ring at him, to match his anger and impatience with her own. But the twisting pain inside her was too draining even for anger now. So she placed the ring in the pocket of his jacket, took the garment off and dropped it onto the pavement.

'You're not listening to me, Conall,' she said with all the strength she could muster. 'I can't be your wife any more. Because I love you. And it's very clear now, you can never love me.'

She hesitated, giving him a moment to contradict her, but he said nothing, and her heart finally shattered into a thousand tiny pieces.

'If there's a child, we can discuss visitation rights through lawyers,' she managed. 'But I never want to see you again.'

She forced herself to turn and walk away from him. To hail a cab and climb in, drawing on the last reserves of her strength to tell the cabbie her address.

But as the taxi sped off, and she watched Conall staring after her, his discarded jacket in his hand, she knew she was lying to herself as well as him.

And when she sent him a text two days later, to tell him she'd started her period and there would be no child, her heart was still in bits and the agony was only more overwhelming.

Because she still wanted him, and the life she had believed they could make together, even though none of it had ever been real.

CHAPTER FIFTEEN

Two weeks later

KATIE DROVE THE small hire car along the driveway and gulped down the inevitable lump in her throat as Kildaragh Castle appeared—the glorious peaks and turrets highlighted by the cold December sun. As she braked in front of the main entrance, and spotted the path down to the secluded cove where she had once watched Conall battle the surf every afternoon, her breathing accelerated. The twin tides of panic and bone-deep sadness—a sadness she wasn't sure she'd ever be able to shake—was all but destroying her.

He won't be here. Imelda promised.

She sat in the car, taking several moments to regain her composure and some semblance of her usual professionalism.

The wedding was in two days' time, and Imelda had begged her to come and oversee the last of the preparations. After her split with Conall, Katie had arranged to have the rest of Imelda's wedding arrangements handled by a well-respected wedding planner in Galway who had jumped at the chance to take on the prestigious commission.

Stepping out of the car, she picked up the folder that

contained the final checklist she'd done to reassure Imelda everything was going to go brilliantly the day after tomorrow. The guests were due to start arriving this afternoon, so she'd left London on a five a.m. flight, determined to put Imelda's mind at ease and leave as quickly as possible.

It wasn't the pre-dawn wake-up call, the mostly hassle-free journey to Knock or the drive down the coast to Kildaragh, though, that was causing the fatigue dragging her steps as she headed towards the chapel where she and Imelda had agreed to meet. She'd barely slept in the last two weeks, her dreams as well as most of her waking moments filled with memories of him—some hot, others painful, all devastating.

Stop thinking about him. It won't help.

She berated herself for about the five thousandth time in the last fourteen days. Running through every second of their relationship wouldn't change the inevitable outcome or make her feel less of a gullible fool. He'd hurt her, yes, but she'd let him, and she had to take responsibility for that.

She pushed open the heavy oak door to the chapel and walked down the aisle, already expertly decorated with green satin ribbons and the beautifully arranged sprays of winter blooms she'd helped design with a local florist. *Before.*

'Hi, Imelda, it's Katie!' she shouted, glancing at her watch to check she wasn't early. 'Are you here?'

The musty interior was cool and dark, overlaid with the scent of roses and jasmine, shards of coloured light from the magnificent stained-glass window she had once admired lighting the dust mites.

'She's not, no.' The low reply ripped through her consciousness—stiffening her spine and making her heart slam into her breastbone.

She spun round to see Conall's broad silhouette standing in the vestibule behind her, before he stepped into the light.

Her heart stuttered, then stampeded.

He looked the same, and yet not. His usually expertly styled dark hair was in disarray, and the thick stubble on his jaw had become a beard, but when those pure blue eyes locked on her face the familiar jolt returned.

She dropped her folder, her whole body starting to shake.

'What are you doing here? Imelda p-promised...' she stammered. 'She said you would be in Rome,' she rambled, not sure she was making any sense, her heart beating so fast now it was gagging her.

She couldn't do this again. She didn't want to.

'She lied,' he said, walking towards her, his steps cautious but unrelenting, as if she were a wild animal he was determined to tame. 'I asked her to lie, to get you here. So I could talk to you.'

'No, I can't...' She shook her head, feeling the tears she'd already shed so many of stinging her eyes again.

It would break her.

But as she went to dash past him he grasped her upper arms in gentle hands to prevent her escape. 'Don't run from me again, Katherine, please.'

She braced her forearms against his chest and balled her hands into fists, struggling against his hold. The lungful of his scent—juniper, pine and clean citrus soap— making her frantic. He'd held her hopes and dreams in his hands and he'd crushed them. She wasn't strong enough to survive that again.

'Please, let me explain, let me apologise... There's so

much you don't know, so much I should have told you.'
The agony in his voice pierced through the fog of panic,
and her struggles turned to shudders of anguish and grief.

'Katherine,' he murmured, letting go of her arms to
cup her cheeks and lift her face into the light. 'You look
shattered. Did I do that too?'

She could hear the devastation in his voice, see the
harrowing regret in his eyes. She tugged her head out
of his hands and wrapped her arms around her body, to
hold onto all she had left... Her pride.

'It's okay,' she said. 'I'll be fine,' she managed, trying to salvage the last remnants of her dignity and stop
the shaking.

'It's not okay, none of this is okay,' he said, thrusting
his fingers through his hair. His shoulders slumped as
he stepped back to give her space, and it occurred to her
for the first time how shattered he looked too—as she
noticed the bruised smudges under his eyes, the lines
around his mouth, and the unkempt appearance, which
was so unlike him.

She stifled the foolish kernel of hope that he had been
as devastated by their parting as she had. Because how
could that be true? And did it really make any difference?
He'd lied to her, about everything.

'I ruined it because I didn't trust my own feelings,' he
said, his voice, barely a whisper now, echoing in the old
church. 'I want to explain,' he offered. 'But I don't want
to hurt you any more,' he added. 'I guess I shouldn't have
tricked you into coming here, but I was desperate. And I
knew the stuff I wanted to tell you couldn't be said over
the phone or via email.' He stepped aside and shrugged,
the sincerity in his eyes making her heartbeat stutter and
her stomach hurt.

He wasn't the charismatic, compelling man she had

persuaded herself she had fallen in love with, but someone who was as confused and unsure as she was right now. He lifted a weary arm, presenting the door to her. 'If you need to leave, if you don't want to hear what I have to say, I won't stop you.'

Her body stilled as she searched his face. The glimmer of irrepressible hope, though, was somehow as painful as the devastation that had gone before. But then something twisted inside her, and suddenly she knew he wasn't the only one to blame for the mess they'd got themselves into.

She'd put him on a pedestal, allowed her romantic imagination to take over. Had she ever really looked at him for who he really was, instead of who she wanted him to be? Ever really admitted to herself the mistakes she'd made too? She'd rushed into this thing—had become addicted to the glamour, the excitement, the spectacular sex and the sheer adrenaline rush of being with him, being wanted by him—and had never stopped to ask herself what she needed, what she deserved.

She sighed, the staggered huff breaking the tense silence.

'You're not the only one at fault here, Conall.' She looked at her feet, scared to admit the pathetic truth but knowing she had to. 'I was willing to accept so little from you,' she said, her voice soft but firm. She needed to admit her part in all this. 'Maybe you didn't tell me the truth about Ross. But you told me you couldn't love me, that you didn't even believe in love.'

She raised her head, knowing she had to look him in the eye, for her own salvation as much as his. 'And yet I was willing to marry you—even to have a child with you—without once demanding more. I've always accepted less than I needed—from my mother, my father, my brother, even Tom—and I did the same with you. And that's on me.'

He'd probably brought her here to try and persuade her that his offer of marriage, the suggestion they have children together, hadn't just been about her connection to Ross. She'd given it some thought over the last two weeks—well, a heck of a lot of thought, to be honest— and she had come to realise he hadn't been lying about that. Her reaction after she had discovered the truth had been about her own insecurities as much as his lack of openness about Ross's connection to his sister. After all, he'd outlined in forensic detail exactly why he had wanted to marry her, to have children with her, all those weeks ago when they'd first slept together. She was the one who had taken that practical explanation and tried to make it mean more.

She brushed away the errant tear that leaked from her eye, knowing despite the pain she was a stronger woman than she had ever been before.

'But I can't… I won't…' She paused, took a breath. 'If you've brought me here to tell me your offer of marriage…' she swallowed heavily '…of a family wasn't just about getting your revenge on Ross, I've already figured that out for myself. But I'm afraid it's not enough to make me change my mind about us. Because I won't settle for less any more.'

Conall shoved his hands in his pockets, the sick feeling of dread in his stomach, tempered by the painful burst of longing, making his ribs hurt as his heart thundered in his chest.

Had she ever looked more magnificent than she did in this moment? The exhaustion in her eyes did nothing to dim the aura of strength and beauty that emanated from her like a bright, shining light.

He'd always known she was smart, funny, captivating and hot enough to make him ache constantly... But had he ever really realised what an amazing woman she was? Not just intelligent, compassionate and kind, but also so strong?

She was telling him where he could shove his proposal of marriage at the exact same moment he had figured out how much he needed her bright, shining light in his life. It would be ironic...if it weren't so terrifying.

He fisted his fingers, resisting the urge to touch her dewy skin, to kiss the sprinkle of freckles across her nose that had always fascinated him, to take her to those places she'd only ever gone with him, to use their electric chemistry to stop her from looking too closely...at him. At them.

But he knew he didn't have the right to touch her again until he made amends for all the wrongs he'd done her, which he knew now were legion... Because he'd had two never-ending weeks to tally up every single one in a mental ledger entitled, *How Conall O'Riordan Screwed Up the Best Thing that Ever Happened to Him*.

He'd planned to start off by telling her his offer of marriage hadn't been about Ross, or Carmel, or Mac. That he'd all but forgotten about his anger with her brother when the guy had appeared out of the blue in the bar at the Opera House. But she'd already nixed that easy out. And anyway, he knew it was a whole lot more complicated than the lies and omissions, the things he hadn't told her and the things he should have.

'Understood,' he said, because he could see she was waiting for an answer.

'Okay, then,' she said. But when her shoulders drooped and she went to walk past him again, he said the only thing he could think of that would stop her—the God's honest truth.

'Truly, Katherine, I think I fell in love with you the very first day I met you.'

'You…what?' She stopped, her eyes widening as she stared at him. The doubt on her face hurt as it occurred to him that, while she was all the things he couldn't live without, she had no idea of her own worth. And that was on him too. And every other person in her life who hadn't given her what she deserved.

That ends now.

And, just like that, the one thing he'd dreaded having to say, the feelings he'd avoided even acknowledging to himself, let alone her, came pouring out without any filter at all.

'I didn't realise it at the time, because…' He hitched his shoulders, the complete shock on her face making it somehow easier to admit how badly he'd screwed up.

'I was a man who had always convinced myself love wasn't needed. That it was a trap, a burden best avoided. My father tried to make me understand, but I wouldn't listen. He told me over and over again women were the best of us, that they had to be honoured and respected and cherished and protected, and I took that literally. But he wasn't talking about women as such, what he was really talking about was love.'

'He sounds like an incredible man,' she said gently and touched his arm, the soft brush of her fingertips like a balm. 'I know how hard it was on you to lose him.'

He could see the unguarded compassion which was so much a part of her personality. It would be so easy right now to tell her about his mother, about how he'd been the one to find her that awful Christmas morning. To unburden himself of all the guilt, fear and trauma that still haunted him from that terrible discovery—how badly he'd let his mother down, because he'd blamed her for something she'd never had any control over. And maybe he would tell Katherine one day, because he knew she'd listen, and know exactly the right things to say to finally help that young lad put the pain, sadness and guilt to rest.

But he bit down on his lip and kept that darkness inside for now, because he knew if he told her about that terrible day now a part of him would still be using her compassion against her, manipulating her emotions to avoid having to bare his soul completely, and he couldn't do that any more. Not when he loved her so much.

So he satisfied himself with tugging one hand out of his pocket and gathering her fingertips in his. He lifted her hand to press his lips to her knuckles. He felt the inevitable shudder of response and found the strength to smile.

But for once, instead of exploiting their devastating chemistry, he dropped her hand from his mouth and told her what he should have told her weeks ago.

'He *was* an incredible man, and an incredible da,' he said. 'Because he was brave and honest and unafraid of love. Just like you are.'

'What are you trying to say?' she asked, but he could see the hope shining in her eyes again, and he knew he'd already been forgiven.

As the joy surged through him, he promised himself he would never, ever take this feeling for granted again. He would never belittle it, or ignore it, or side-line it, or try to argue himself out of it. Or be afraid of it. Never. Because protecting himself wasn't as important as protecting her.

'Ah, *mo mhuirnin*,' he murmured, lifting his other hand out of his pocket to cradle her cheek, letting all the love he felt show in his eyes. 'Isn't it obvious? I'm try-ing to tell you I absolutely adore you. And I know I al-ways will.'

She still looked taken aback, but he could see she be-lieved him now because, as well as being smart, beau-tiful and strong, his one true love was also remarkably intuitive.

What a woman!

'Really?' she said, the way she had the first day he'd met her, but the doubt had disappeared.

'Yes, really,' he said without pause or equivocation. '*Now* will you please marry me?'

The smile that spread across her face was like a beam of sunshine on a rainy day, bringing with it rainbows and pots of gold—*but no leprechauns, thank god.* 'I suppose so,' she said as if she were playing hard to get, but the joy sparking in her eyes told him everything he needed to know.

'Thank goodness.' He banded his arms around her waist and lifted her off the floor.

His whoop of joy joined her gasp of delight as he swung her around then deposited her back on her feet.

Their mouths met, sure and eager. The kiss turned from sweet to carnal in a heartbeat but he made himself make one final vow— before his mind turned to more urgent stuff.

I vow to show her how much I value her, cherish her and love her, every single day for the rest of our lives. Do you hear me, Da?

* * * * *

PREGNANT AFTER ONE FORBIDDEN NIGHT

MARCELLA BELL

MILLS & BOON

To all the stories I've loved before

CHAPTER ONE

FOR THE FIRST time in his life, Sebastian Redcliff gave another human being a second look.

And then he stared.

She wore the dark blue uniform of the royal guard.

Thick layers of colorful Kevlar, utility pockets, and polyester obscured the shape of her body and she wore her near-black hair in a severe and simple low braid that swung down her back. There was nothing remarkable about any of it.

Her sloe-eyed gaze was wide, like a forest doe's, and her nose straight at the bridge and rounded at the tip.

Her lips were wide, and her mouth a natural dusky rose.

In fact, if it hadn't been for her incredibly thick eyebrows, the kind that could catapult a model to international fame, there would be absolutely nothing unique or particularly remarkable about her looks.

But it wasn't her physical appearance that had led to Sebastian's uncharacteristic pause.

He was the head of intelligence for the island nation of Cyrano.

Appearances were particularly superficial to Sebastian.

But, blessed—or cursed—as he was with above average gifts in the art of seeing beneath the surface of things, he found himself ensnared upon laying eyes on her.

A blinding prism of light lay beneath *her* surface.

He had never encountered a person—man, woman or child—who exuded goodness with the intensity that she did.

Confronted with all of that earnest intention—so much delicious passion for hoping and trying, not for gain, but simply because it was the right thing to do—wrapped up in one person filled Sebastian with an imperative and irresistible urge to dive into her light.

The sky was up, gravity held the universe together and he had to quell the first thing that had ever distracted him from carrying out his duties.

His presence at the event tonight was a matter of business, an opportunity to debrief with the king while *hiding in plain sight*, as they said.

There would be no hiding, however, with a light like hers around.

Fortunately, if Sebastian had learned anything in his life to date, it was that things tended to only look bright from far away.

Looking deeper, learning more, was all it typically took to dim the glow.

It was only the most incurable fools who remained transfixed on the item of their obsession after scratching the surface, and he was many things, but not a fool.

In all his life, he'd found nothing so effective at dimming his interest in a person as having sex with them.

Intimate knowledge, he'd found, quickly tarnished illusions.

And whatever else he knew and thought about her—which was a surprising amount given that vetting royal security records was one of his many duties—it was very certain that, paragon of dedication though she may be, she was still just a wretched human like the rest of them.

It was his job to keep that in mind, just as it was his

job to remain impenetrable, inscrutable and always one step ahead.

That she'd penetrated him with her glamour, wreaking havoc on any semblance of inscrutability, was therefore an intolerance that required redress.

Right now, inscrutable was the furthest thing from what he was.

Watching her, he was filled with the feeling that if she decided to aim the high beams of all that goodness at him, he might disintegrate like a vampire in sunlight.

Or even worse, he might be flayed open and revealed with no place left to hide.

Her name was Jenna Noelle Moustafa—she was of good Cyranese stock and a dedicated member of the Priory, a small religious group, and had a record to prove it.

Sebastian had reviewed that record personally but he had never met her in person.

Officially, he still hadn't.

But he would. Within the hour, he decided then.

Jenna, as he now called her in his mind, stood watch over the Queen of Cyrano, on solo duty as her guard partner and captain, Helene d'Tierrza, was the hostess of the gala they were currently attending.

While Helene was off duty, the full complement of the king's security team supported Jenna in her role of safeguarding the queen, but even from across the balcony, it was evident that Jenna had the duty well in hand.

Her entire attention was focused on the monarch, eyeing the queen with a mixture of adoration and responsibility that went beyond what was typical of her position, almost as if she were guarding a sister.

This was apparent in not only her gaze but the way her body remained poised, ever ready to leap to defense, offense or sacrifice—whatever the situation demanded.

She did not guard her liege. She guarded her friend.

Sebastian could almost taste the dedication and commitment from across the crowded balcony.

It wasn't nearly enough.

He wanted the whole thing.

He wanted every ounce of the attention she gave the queen and more focused entirely on him.

The queen accepted dainty hors d'oeuvres from a server, and Jenna said something low to her. The queen responded with a shake of her very curly head and let out the loud, open, commoner's laugh for which she was becoming famous.

King Zayn could not have picked a better queen himself—and he had not picked her. To the king's surprise, at thirty-six years old, Zayn had learned that his father, the late King Alden, had betrothed him to a common woman, the daughter of the man who'd saved Zayn and his mother's life before he had even been born.

Queen Mina was perfect for the role—beautiful and incredibly intelligent—but more importantly for Sebastian's current purposes, she was a lovely and reliable distraction to the king.

Turning now to the king, he commented, "Queen Mina looks lovely this afternoon."

And it was true.

The queen stood out, a breath of fresh air and lively intelligence among a sea of jaded wealth. The king's violet gaze traveled in her direction before snagging on her with the hunger of a starving man.

It was clear he wanted to breathe her deep.

Sebastian almost smiled. It was all too easy.

People often made the mistake of thinking that his was the work of shadows and lies when, in fact, spy craft was and ever would be the arena of truth—who held it, who wanted it kept secret and what they might be willing to do to ensure that it remained that way.

Lies blew over, fell apart at the slightest pressure.

Truth made grown men weep and cry out for their mothers.

Truth was what snagged the monarch's attention now, made his violet eyes go dark and intense, his entire focus, at least temporarily, fixed on his much-adored wife.

"Indeed, she does, and like she needs a break. She's been in high demand this afternoon," the king added.

Sebastian smiled. To all the world, it would appear he'd shared a private joke with the monarch. But, as was often the case, all the world would have been wrong.

Sebastian kept smiling as the king made his way to his queen with his own guards alert and at a discreet distance—precisely as Sebastian had wanted. Things were going according to plan.

He loved it when things went according to plan.

He loved it almost as much as he would love the sensation of things returning to normal after he'd seduced Jenna. Once would be enough. Once was always enough.

Tasting her would disarm the intrigue and render her ordinary. Then he could forget about her.

She would cherish the memory forever because he had standards.

Afterward, he would no longer feel like he'd been scraped raw and exposed to the world, all of his shields ripped clean off by the simple fact of her existence.

He would return to being Cyrano's most notorious playboy—wrecker of marriages and despoiler of hearts.

Every spy needed a cover and with the family history he had, his mother's infidelities and wildness well known, it was only natural that his cover would be that of the heartless Casanova cad. He had become known more for being free with compliments and enjoying hedonistic delights than for his intelligence or dedication.

Covers worked best when they fulfilled people's expectations and the Redcliffs had earned a reputation thanks to the previous generation.

To the eyes of society, he was everything Jenna was not—her polar opposite.

She was a royal guard, her full heart in her duty, on proud, uniformed display. As a Priory woman, she was dedicated and faithful to her unusual upbringing and religion, as evidenced by the fact she'd made a stipulation in her employment records that she be allowed the Priory's weekly day of rest and important holidays off. The Priory were a family-focused and conservative religious minority in Cyrano, famous for still encouraging chastity before marriage in their youth and refraining from many of the modern pleasures that men like Sebastian lived and breathed.

No woman had ever cared to resist him. The sheltered, serious guard would be no exception.

And if she did turn down the pleasure he offered, well, he knew how to walk away. He was just confident she would not.

In fact, the ease with which he anticipated he'd achieve his ends only urged him to get it done sooner.

Her incessant brightness drew him like a moth to a flame, tempting him to come closer, luring him out of the shadows and threatening to both reveal and destroy the darkness he moved within.

It was his job to move in the shadows. He could not be drawn out.

The king reached the two women, and Jenna created space for him with a slightly awkward shuffle of her feet. Her frown, with those unbelievable brows coming together just so, her lips pursing, revealed that she wasn't pleased to be pushed away from her charge, even by the king himself.

Adorable.

And everything was progressing as Sebastian had designed.

After the incident with the Farden chancellor's son, it had become a joke that the queen needed no security when her husband was nearby. Like all jokes, it was funny because it was true.

Sebastian was counting on it.

Despite the libertine affectations he presented to the world, Sebastian was severe when it came to his work.

He had taken a vow to safeguard the nation and its monarchs, and no personal distractions could ever be allowed to supersede that, particularly not something as superficial and fleeting as attraction—even an unprecedented attraction.

Sebastian waited until the king leaned close to whisper in the queen's ear, watching for color to come to her cheeks as she gave a little nod, and then waited still longer for the king to lead the queen away from the party.

Then he crossed the balcony toward where Jenna stood, hoping the triumphant glint in his eyes didn't look too wolfish.

Sebastian intercepted Jenna's path into the interior of the manor as she followed the monarchs from a discrete distance. He positioned himself so that she bumped into his shoulder.

The move was obvious but had the desired effect.

"My apologies, Your Grace." Her words were automatic, delivered with a slight bow, stiff and formal, her eyes cast at the ground. She hadn't looked him in the eye, and though he'd anticipated that ingrained deference, he found himself irritated.

He wanted to see her eyes.

"Yes, well, if you'd been looking where you'd been going…" He infused his words with the aristocratic drawl that he'd been born to as much as the winning smile he'd been employing to get his way since he was a child.

Her eyes flashed up to his face.

Up to that point, things had been going according to Sebastian's plan.

Abruptly, they no longer were.

If her brightness had caused him to do a double take, her eyes froze him to the spot and tore him apart.

It would be tempting to assign their clarity, the unflinching truth in their sable depths, to her profession, but that would be a fantasy.

Jenna's goodness was her own.

Astonishingly open and clear, her gaze demanded nothing less than complete truth. So crystalline and deep were the dark brown orbs that they tempted him to imagine that she saw things others didn't, that she could see through his layered masks, straight through to the true core of him.

But he did not give in to the temptation to believe.

She was no more aware of his multilayered existence than anyone else in their circle.

If she had been, a rose blush wouldn't have dusted her olive cheekbones, and her moistened lips wouldn't have parted.

Her stunning eyebrows came together, confusion clouding her gaze, her pupils dilating as she sucked in a quiet breath of air.

Already, his seduction was working, and if there was a level of unexpected thrill in the success, he attributed it not to the woman but to the reward of getting what he wanted.

He always excelled where he chose to put effort.

"Again, you have my apologies. I wasn't looking where I was going," she said. Her voice was sweet, as musical and genuine and unguarded as her stare.

It tasted like wildflower honey.

Lifting an eyebrow, he said, "I'll forgive you for not noticing me once. Not again, though."

His words startled her again, enough so that this time, he knew he'd caught her attention, truly caught it. Instead of brushing him off to return to her duty, she looked at him and *saw* him. Her pupils dilated, and her eyes narrowed before she said, "I'm sorry. I don't understand."

"We're in that together then."

Outright confusion creased her brow. "Excuse me?"

"I wish I could. But that would be like excusing the sun for rising and bringing all of this chaos to life. Impossible."

"What?" She had no idea what he was talking about, as his words were absurd.

Oddly, he found he couldn't help it. She made him feel strangely foolish.

Being absurd did not make him any less effective, though. "I find myself drawn to you with an intensity I cannot comprehend, Jenna Moustafa," he said.

Her expression shuttered. "Very funny," she said flatly before turning from him.

For an instant, he felt utterly adrift at her abandonment.

With his access to the strange creature he found so alluring suddenly cut off, his mind went momentarily blank, ceasing to process its various inputs as if transported to an all-white room with no windows or doors.

And then he was back on the balcony staring at Jenna, surrounded by the very wealthiest of Cyrano's very wealthy, with a strange cocktail of sensations swirling in his gut and his hand wrapped around her slender wrist.

She had started to leave, had begun to walk away from him without a backward glance.

It was no less than he would have expected from a royal guard.

She was on duty.

It wasn't her job to engage in cryptic back-and-forth with cynical aristocrats.

But when she had turned from him, a foreign thing had happened to him.

He had panicked. And in that blank instant, he had reached out for her hand.

She stared at his grip in surprise.

It was a small thing, barely the touch of a hand, but he had not meant to do it. It was—unconscious, or not—a deviation from his plan.

She met his eyes again and, as before, whatever it was in her that needed to protect and serve shone out from them, bright and clear, with one critical difference: this time it was for him.

At that moment, she was his.

He knew it. She didn't.

"Are you okay?" she asked, searching his face.

The truth was a weapon. He knew that better than anyone else on the balcony. And though a strange, rusty, locked-away voice inside him pleaded with him to hold back, to refrain from what he was about to do, he ignored it.

"No," he said, and the word was a raw and rough syllable ripped from him. It was only the truth.

And like it always did, his weapon found its mark.

Confusion skittered across her gaze.

As suddenly as they had gone awry, his plans were back on track.

All he had to do now was tell the absolute truth, reveal how excruciatingly vulnerable he was to her, how fascinated and ensnared she had him—how helpless he was in the face of his need to be beside her. All he had to do was show her that she was in utter control of everything between them, and let himself be seen and touched.

And then he could be done with it, and no one would be the wiser.

"How can I help?"

Of course, she would ask like that, leading with goodness.

"Come with me to the library."

CHAPTER TWO

"COME WITH ME to the library."

Jenna's instincts screamed at her in warning in a voice oddly reminiscent of her mother's. The awareness of potential danger that she had honed through her training roared to life as if she stood on a catastrophic and furious battlefield rather than beside one of the most handsome men in the country on a balcony filled with pampered rich people.

Perhaps it was that those same instincts sensed a powerful undercurrent of strength in the man beside her—an undercurrent that warned her against dismissing this capital aristocrat as playing games despite the fact that his only occupation, as far as she had ever been able to discern, was seducing women.

His exploits were infamous, most so outrageous as to be unbelievable.

Encountering him in the flesh for the first time, however, coming face-to-face with his crystalline green eyes, dark heavy brow, fashionably cut and carelessly swept-back burnished-gold hair, and cheekbones that were so hollowed-out that they looked like they had been slashed into existence by a temperamental and sensual god, she was suddenly willing to believe that every single story was true.

Perhaps *that* was what the alarm was about—the natural reaction of a cautious woman in the face of a handsome playboy.

He was the kind of handsome that encouraged sinful thoughts and reckless behavior, but she knew that for three very practical reasons he posed no threat to her: she was poor, she was plain and she was Priory.

Nearly three years into serving the palace after completing her training at the Capital Military Academy before that, Jenna had become very aware that those three facts disqualified her from being considered as anything other than service personnel. Just as her desire for the wider world, a faster pace of life and something more than the ordinary disqualified her from life as a good Priory woman.

Being only the second woman ever to earn a position in the royal guard didn't help matters, either.

Unlike her partner, Helene d'Tierrza, who was so stunningly beautiful and wealthy that even being in uniform could not put off appreciative stares, Jenna's womanhood disappeared as soon as she strapped in.

The denizens of the capital lived for the latest trends, the hottest fashions and a fast-paced lifestyle. Here, the most attractive woman in the room was the one who had mastered all of it.

That was not Jenna.

So, overriding her internal alarm systems, she nodded crisply to the handsome aristocrat.

Calculating with a private blush that the queen would be *otherwise occupied* for the next little while, Jenna determined that it would be no problem to offer her service to the duke—temporarily. Her first duty, of course, was to the queen.

But things like assisting wayward nobility improved the reputation of the royal guard, and kept her mind from the fact that if it weren't for her duties guarding the queen, she would never have believed that royals would spend so much time *otherwise occupied*.

That kind of attraction was something she expected from ordinary people, like her parents, who had six children to show for it—not from aristocrats. The lives of the rich and famous seemed driven less by warmer, homier passions and more by a relentless drive to increase their power, status and wealth.

Of course, it was different for Queen Mina who, like Jenna, was a common woman.

Perhaps that was due the credit for the earthy enjoyment so apparent in the monarchs' relationship.

Raising the wrist that the duke still held, his hand a strangely electric shackle, Jenna offered him a smile. "Certainly, Your Grace. However, you'll need to lead the way as I am not familiar with the d'Tierrza estate."

The words struck Jenna's ears like stones, accurate though they were. The d'Tierrza estate was her best friend Helene's home, and yet today was her first time visiting, and she was here not out of friendship but duty.

It was just another small reminder that while she lived and worked in this glittering world, even among those closest to her she would never truly belong.

But that was the price a Priory girl paid for venturing so far from home.

In that world, friends knew each other's homes and families and gathered together as frequently as possible.

When one was best friends with a duchess and a queen, though, both of whom were also one's supervisors, things went differently. Jenna only wished she could be satisfied with the closeness they did have, without longing for something that felt more familiar to her.

She had all the reason in the world to be satisfied with her relationships.

Jenna spent her entire days with the queen and ate dinner

with Helene in the guard's common room every night, after which she retired to the quarters she shared with Helene. The three of them virtually lived in each other's pockets and continued to enjoy each other's company. That had to reflect a deeper relationship than visiting each other's houses.

Shaking herself free of this tangent, she brought her attention fully to the duke, finding it an easy thing to do with the heat of his skin a hot pulse around her wrist.

Rather than release her wrist, though, the duke briefly tightened the pressure of his fingers around her.

One corner of his mouth lifted, drawing her gaze to his sculpted lips and the carved hollows of his cheeks, where she noticed a faint hint of shadowed stubble grew.

The detail struck her. She would have expected him to be perfectly presented and clean-shaven. Like the undergirding of strength she sensed in him, the detail was at odds with his reputation.

In her experience, there were two kinds of men who allowed stubble: lazy ones and busy ones. She would have thought a man who made a profession of sexual pursuit would be neither.

Not that he didn't look good. That would be far from the truth.

And he didn't just look good. He smoldered. The longer Jenna stood in his presence, the more confident she grew that, handsome though he was, he owed his attractiveness to another thing entirely. His was the primal allure of the big bad wolf.

Thankfully, bad boys held no appeal for Jenna.

"Of course," he said, scanning the balcony as he spoke, assessing the crowd before leading them toward the interior of the manor.

And all of it without releasing her wrist.

People moved out of their way, noticing their joined hands but quickly dismissing it.

Her uniform was a form of invisibility. No eyebrows need lift at a royal guard being led away by a duke. The rigid roles and hidden layers of intrigue in the capital made the strict demands and expectations of growing up Priory seem light by comparison.

She liked to think the one had prepared her for the other. However, memorizing their route as she followed behind the duke, she reflected that nothing had prepared her for the mystery in front of her now.

What could the Duke of Redcliff possibly need from her?

She imagined she would find out soon enough as he pushed open a door that looked just like the other doors they'd passed thus far.

Like every room in the d'Tierrza mansion, this one was enormous, but the library put all of the others to shame.

Inside, curved walls rolled like waves all around them, lined floor to gorgeously painted classical ceiling with books. A massive domed skylight drew in the seaside sun, and every nook boasted a uniquely comfortable reading area—a plush leather love seat here, a wing-backed chair next to a small table there, a cushioned and pillowed bench tucked beneath a many-paned window across the room.

The air was heavy with the hush that only tidily shelved books and blankets of fresh, undisturbed snow seemed to convey, deep and tangible, yet comforting, like a weighted blanket or a fire on a windy evening.

The library was a reader's paradise, but the Duke of Redcliff dragged them through it with a single-minded purpose that suggested he had a more specific destination in mind than just the privacy the stunning library offered.

"If I'm not mistaken, we've made it to the library," Jenna said, faintly breathless in anticipating what he might say.

What could she possibly have to offer the Duke of Redcliff?

He didn't turn to answer her, merely replied, "What I need to tell you requires more privacy than this echoey dust trap."

Jenna bristled. She might not know the floor plan, but this was still her best friend's home.

"The library is beautiful," she protested.

He didn't spare it a glance. "A library's beauty comes from its use—from the experiences and memories enveloped in its folds, the myriad worlds it contains. This library, however, is a mausoleum, built in honor of ego and enjoyed even less. Neither the current duchess nor the dowager duchess utilizes nor loves this room. Therefore, it is not beautiful but an echoey dust trap."

Casting him a sharp glance, Jenna retorted, "You seem to know an awful lot about this library for someone who doesn't live here."

At her words, he slowed and turned, mouth pressed into a firm line, expression shadowed. "I studied architecture at university. The d'Tierrza estate is one of Cyrano's most famous structures—certified Heritage. The library was built and stocked by the fourth Duke of d'Tierrza nearly seventy-five years ago. Look around."

Jenna did, the hush of the room and the quiet seriousness in his voice weaving around her like a spell. The shelves were not, as he'd accused, dusty, but upon looking more closely, she saw that the books were indeed old, most with heavy cloth and leather bindings with gilded gold lettering.

There were thousands and thousands of volumes and, scanning them, not a single modern title among them.

The duke confirmed her assessment with his next words. "There hasn't been a book added to this collection since they finished the library—a great showpiece for a grand, pointless gala much like today's. Lovely to look at, but lifeless."

It was impossible to imagine him as a student or even as

a younger man. He gave the impression of having sprung into existence, fully formed as he was: leonine, feral and pitiless.

Whether or not he'd intended to reveal it, though, she now knew that buried so deeply that she couldn't even say she could see it, there was a young man who loved buildings and libraries.

"Are we nearly there? I would love to help you but will need to return to my duties soon." She tried to create distance with words while he led them around a final turn and into the most private reading nook she'd seen yet.

Hidden by bookshelves on all sides save the one they had approached from, this nook had a long, deep burgundy velvet settee centered beneath a breathtaking stained-glass window. The window's large, central motif, a dazzling kaleidoscope of vibrant reds, came together in the form of a rose exquisite enough to put Notre Dame to shame.

That this stunning window was hidden far away from the atrium, located in a place that one would have to know about to find, underscored the luxury and extravagance of the whole library.

Idly, her mind enchanted by the perfect little spot, she wondered what other treasures this "dead" library hid.

Leading her to the sofa, the duke guided her to sit.

He remained standing, directly in front of her, for a moment, just silently staring, his eyes drinking her in, his pupils dark and dilated like those of a hungry child standing outside a bakery window.

She fidgeted under the intensity of his regard, and then asked again, "What is it you want from me, Your Grace?"

His emerald eyes direct and unflinching, he said, "Everything."

He said it as if the statement was clear, explaining everything to everyone's satisfaction, and because it didn't, not in the least, she was irritated when she said, "What specifically?"

Infuriatingly, he said, "You," though this time, a hint of confusion had crept into his voice. "I need you."

Her eyebrows came together, each one so thick and slashing that she had given up trying to tame them years ago, resigning herself to merely plucking stray hairs here and there to prevent a unibrow.

Suddenly, she wished she had spent more time on them.

His eyes burned with an unfamiliar heat that brought a strange fluttering sensation to her stomach.

She forced herself to stay still, refusing the urge to squirm, but the intensity of his stare set off rivulets of sparkling sensation along her skin.

"What do you mean?" she said quietly, her voice losing the earthy, steady quality she was known for in the on-slaught of the man's regard.

He laughed, and the sound was as unexpected as it was entrancing.

It was creamy and musical, warm and baritone, like honey mixed with something naughty and decadent, in-toxicating and dangerous like a cocktail. Or at least what she associated with the idea of a cocktail, as she kept with Priory tradition and didn't drink alcohol.

The laugh transformed him, shaved years from his jaded angles.

Sounding surprised himself, he said, "I mean I want you, Jenna, naked. Now."

For a moment, she simply stared at him, dumbfounded. His words buzzed around inside her, trying to land, trying to wash her away in sparkling sensation and pooling heat, but she was held fast by the absurdity of a man like him speaking those words to a woman like her.

And so, she began to laugh, stopping only when she realized he was just waiting for her to finish laughing and answer, absolutely earnest.

Staring up at him, laughter chased away by his gravity, she said, "You're joking."

His eyes bored into hers, his expression hovering in the land between intense desire and deep frustration. "I am not. I have never needed a woman as much as I do you."

She hadn't known until that moment how much she'd been craving words like that, how they would enter and expand inside her, warm and enveloping, grabbing hold of the stirring place deep inside her and squeezing and pulsing with a hold and rhythm she never wanted to end.

"That's absurd," she whispered, her voice losing its strength in the face of this unbelievable situation. "You don't even know me."

He shook his head. "Believe me. I am as surprised as you are."

She frowned, not liking the sound of that. "You don't make it sound like a compliment."

"It's not."

He was strained, tense, even irritated about it all—like he meant what he said about not wanting it but being powerless to do anything to stop it.

Why that did things to her, activated places that had no business activating, she had no idea.

The Casanova type didn't appeal to her. When she eventually settled down, as much as her family despaired of that ever happening, she wanted what her parents had: an enduring flame kind of love, one built entirely on mutual understanding, respect and compassion. A place to belong.

And, captivating though he was, she knew she was not going to find that with an aristocrat she'd only just met—especially one who was famous for his shocking and temporary sexual exploits.

Shoving aside the ring of truth to his words and ignoring

the honesty of the attraction she saw burning in his eyes, it occurred to her with disappointment that this entire episode was likely some part of a cruel joke.

Too smart to fall for something like that, and too strong to waste any hurt feelings over it, Jenna was nevertheless frustrated with herself for not recognizing the signs earlier.

She'd witnessed plenty of playing with people's emotions, a kind of casual cruelty, amongst the glitz and glam of the upper crust.

There were some reasons she was glad she didn't truly belong in the life she lived.

Infusing stiff formality into her words, she remained seated—she didn't need to stand to be powerful—and said, "You're being completely inappropriate and, if you are lying, cruel. I am on duty and as such, you have no right to approach me with this. It is my job to protect the queen, and I am disappointed that you prioritized your pursuit of pleasure over that important task."

Her words were bold and direct and, even with all of the rule following and deference to rank and authority that she'd been imbued with at birth, still true to her nature. She might not like to rock the boat, but she wasn't weak. Whether it was her upbringing, her faith, or just because she'd lived twenty-nine years on this planet and seen the proof that lying got you nowhere repeated endlessly, Jenna believed in telling the truth. She put her whole heart into everything she did and followed her inner moral compass, no matter the pressure.

Her mother compared her to their old mule back home.

"Well said, Jenna, and I appreciate it even more as it confirms my evaluation of your character, but we both know that the queen is...*otherwise occupied*. You have the time, and you are not a coward."

That he had used the same words she'd thought privately confused her usually clear and direct perception.

He must have seen the king and queen leave the balcony, but the way he spoke hinted at more than mere observation. And what did he mean by *evaluation of her character*? Before today they had never spoken. While he lived in the capital, haunting the palace when not *otherwise occupied* himself, he had no connections to any Cyranese government branch that Jenna knew. He had no reason, nor right, to assess her.

Multiple times now, he had spoken as if he knew her, knew her mettle. How would he know if she were a coward or not?

And where did he get off dictating what she did and did not have time for?

Her temper, usually slow to rise, caught fire, as hot as the blush that scorched her skin.

He was right about one thing. She was no coward.

Coming to her feet, she said, "I don't know what kind of game you're playing right now, Redcliff, but I'm over it." Anger burned through the respect for tradition that she had, and in its void she'd imitated Helene's irreverence, dropping his title when she'd spoken to him.

Stepping closer to her, forcing her to tilt her head up to retain eye contact, he smiled before saying quietly, almost reflectively, "If you knew the kind of games I play, you'd know how ludicrous it is to suggest that I am anything but serious right now."

"I don't care if you're serious or not," she said drolly, "it's not happening." Her words were sharp and final, precisely as she'd intended, so she had no idea where the next ones came from, nor why they came out heavy, laden with an unspoken invitation. "I'm not that kind of woman."

He smiled then.

She shivered, the sensation running down her spine like the ripple of awareness through a herd when a predator neared.

He leaned forward, breaching the barrier of her personal space to bring his wicked lips close to her ear, close enough that the breath of his every word danced across her skin when he said, "I already know what kind of woman you are, Jenna Moustafa." He paused. "But what I don't know, what I long to find out, is how you taste. How you feel. How you sound when lost in pleasure."

What he said should have been outrageous.

Absurd.

But he was telling the truth.

The part of her that always knew, that was so entwined with truth itself that she could not help but know its taste and texture when she encountered it, was as certain as it was foolish to be.

She shook her head, the movement jostling the small gold hoops she wore, a gift from her mother, and marveled that such a slight sensation could rise to the surface amidst all the turbulent sensations warring inside her. "That's... crazy..." Her words were light, airy, the breathless, flimsy things that a different kind of person might utter.

He nodded, still so close that she could feel the heat of his skin on hers. "Utterly insane and true nonetheless. No woman has ever had this effect on me."

"You've slept with hundreds of women..." The words should have been enough to dampen the heat of the moment. Nobody liked to have their past thrown in their face, but he only smiled, the absolute lack of shame in his gaze an aphrodisiac in itself.

"All the better to please you with, my dear Jenna."

Breath escaped her, fled her parted lips like a caged bird who'd noticed the door had been left unlatched.

"I—" she started. His lips brushed against the point where her jaw met her neck, butterfly light, and her eyelids fluttered closed.

"You are singular, in the entire world, Jenna. This has already gone beyond a mere seduction."

Desperate to escape the spell he was spinning, she grasped at straws. "I can't. I've never—" And yet, she realized with astonished horror, her body coming alive in ways she'd never known possible, she *could*.

"I know," he said, the look on his face hungry and dark.

In the face of all that power and gravity centered on her, she realized she could all too easily.

He didn't just want her. *Want* was too weak a word for the fire that burned in his eyes.

The pull of it was overwhelming. She wished she could claim the magnetism between them stemmed completely from outside herself, that his need for her, how it poured off him, was responsible for the force of *her* attraction to *him*, but she could not. It would have been a shameful lie to blame what was building and blossoming entirely on him—though his words flowed over her like silk—when she knew that at least half of it erupted from within her, a seed of desire heretofore unknown bursting to life.

Who was this man, this creature of pleasure and luxury—a man she had only ever seen in passing and the exact kind of man to whom she had been invisible over these past three years—who seemed so driven to have her?

And why did the fact of it make her body smolder and heat?

Like glass in a kiln, the reasons, even the need for reasons, could not withstand the growing fire between them.

There was nothing gentle in her resistance melting away, just like there was nothing gentle about the way he was seducing her. Everything between them was up front and direct about its own dangerousness. Just like the man himself.

As if a dam had burst within her, twenty-nine years of chastity exploded at him, rushed at him in a wave so powerful that he was no longer the one driving the momentum of their seduction, but her.

Her fingers came to his hair at the exact moment his hand cupped the back of her skull and tilted her face upward.

She caught the flash of fierce green fire in his eyes before he descended, devouring her in a kiss that was more like a conflagration.

Her skin ignited everywhere on contact, exuding heat and glow so intensely that she knew that despite the circumstances, despite everything that was so very wrong with this, this moment and this man were exactly right— the union for which she had kept faith all these years.

And even still, there was no time for any of it. They had already wasted too much time talking. All too soon she would need to return to her duty.

Urgency drove her fingers, as confident and persistent in removing buckles and releasing the latches of her gear in front of him as they were in writing reports and disarming sparring opponents.

Her inner voice had spoken and she wasted no time with trepidation.

Like with the bawdy pre-wedding rituals that Priory folk guffawed through, her faith taught that there was nothing wrong in physical love, no practice taboo, so long as both parties entered into it with their hearts joined and open, willing and eager to find joy in each other's bodies.

Her faith also taught that physical intimacy was a sacred bond between paired souls, each made to soothe and comfort the other. She accepted that, took it as fact, but she had never anticipated that she would recognize her pairing at first meeting—let alone feel it with such certainty. Nor had she ever imagined that she would feel her partner's hunger for her as a tangible thing.

But she did. Awareness and, of all things, understanding of him thrummed through her body and bones and even teeth. Hot, electric, almost magical—in no way like the practical fantasies of a woman whose greatest romantic hope up to this point had been to end up with someone she found both attractive and kind.

Instead, her destiny stood before her—gorgeous, dangerous, and as far from kind and tame as it was possible to be.

He was nothing like she had imagined, yet he was hers, matched her in a way that she didn't understand and had never experienced before—neither in the world of the capital nor her Priory community.

And they had already delayed this moment for too long. Not merely over the afternoon, but throughout their lives up to this point.

CHAPTER THREE

SEBASTIAN HAD SEEN more naked women than he could count or remember.

Jenna erased any recollections that remained.

Her body was a work of art.

Her efficiency, her matter-of-fact lack of artistry in removing the layers of her uniform, should have been off-putting to a man who had been entertained by the world's most accomplished sex kittens.

It wasn't.

Instead, the deft and direct work of her fingers was the most erotic dance he'd ever witnessed.

Fully revealed, she was swarthy, her freckled skin olive, the soft hair on her arms, legs, neck dark, and at the V of her thighs thick and glossy.

Like her eyebrows, the liberal hair on her body simply accentuated rather than detracted from the perfect and straightforward beauty of her form. It drew the eye to the slender length of her forearm, the elegant arch at the nape of her neck, the shadowed and graceful contours of her shoulder blades, a natural accent and frame to her raw beauty.

As feminine as it was, her body was also extremely fit—toned and defined, as he would have expected of any person who had made a profession out of using their body as a weapon.

Her breasts, on the other hand, defied her chosen life, full and round, each one more than a handful and proud of it. Those breasts spoke of happy families and sunny hill-sides—images that generally repelled him but somehow now only enhanced the fantasy of the moment.

Unsurprisingly, her bra was simple and white.

However, whilst he would have expected plain cotton, the garment was made of lace and paired with a matching pair of lace panties. Unusually, thick and durable, the material he was so familiar with seeing on women looked new on her and he suspected it was handmade.

What a security guard was doing wearing a small for-tune's worth of handmade lace undergarments, he had no idea, but the effect was breathtaking.

In her ability to arrest him, to stir him past control merely by seeing her—she was truly as singular as he'd claimed.

Nothing he'd said to her thus far had been a lie.

He was, however, beginning to wonder if one taste would have the quelling effect he anticipated. Putting to rest the mystery of what lay beneath the stiff blue of her uniform certainly hadn't.

It had only stoked the fire.

When she moved to take off her bra, he stopped her with a fingertip to her plump lips. Her eyes fluttered to his, and he felt the earth shift, filling him with an urgent need to hold on as everything changed around him, though the only sound in their secluded library alcove was their weighted breathing.

Having undressed faster than her, he stood nude, en-tirely at ease in his form. A lover had once teased him that it was easy to be comfortable when one was built like he was, but his ease went deeper than that.

He was comfortable in the nude because it was possible to learn so much about people when one was naked. *What they liked…* Jenna's eyes lingered over his chest and shoulders, trailing across his skin like the brush of a feather. *What they were ashamed of…* Her cheeks flushed as her gaze traveled down his chest, slowly, painstakingly if he were being honest, before lighting on the appendage that stood out proudly at the apex of his thighs. *What they were afraid of…* Her breath stopped, her pupils dilated and froze, eyes remaining locked on his sex organ for an eternity before she finally gave a small gasp and her eyes darted back up to his face.

Again, her stare captured him, in a way only hers seemed to have the power to. This wouldn't stop, not until he had experienced the profound uniqueness of encountering her.

Why did her eyes freeze him in time and space?

They were an unflinching walnut color, each iris lined in kohl as if an Egyptian queen had designed their depths.

Shielding the enormous almond-shaped windows of her soul were eyelashes so densely packed it looked like she wore mascara when, in truth, she wore no makeup at all.

Everything about her was fresh and honest—her entire self, out on display for the world to see.

For him to see at the moment.

"Take out your braid." His voice was a rasping command, harsh and more desperately revealing than he would have liked.

She shook her head. "You do it." Her voice was thick but smooth; sweetness turned into nourishment like honey.

Though he noted the defiance, he chose to comply, turning the act of reaching slowly behind her to grasp the end of her long braid and draw it to him, over her shoulder, cool and soft between his fingers, into a seduction.

She was breathless before he began to release the braid.

When he loosened the last of its weave and brought his fingertips to her scalp to massage and shake her glorious mane free, she moaned.

The sound was a molten rod down the center of him, threatening to melt and combust at the same time, but his fingers kept their rhythm and she leaned in closer, her pebbled nipples grazing the fine blond hairs on his bare chest.

He couldn't have her all the ways he wanted to, not like this, not in the library on her ever-shortening break, and the thought infuriated him. Made him want to steal her away for as long as it took to exorcise this strange demon she'd freed.

Her hair was magnificent. Long, flowing down to her waist at its longest point, it was so dark brown it was nearly black and shined like an heirloom sable. There was a wave to it, and standing there before him, her hair flowing around her, breasts free, nude but for her white lace panties, framed on both sides by the enormous stained-glass rose, he knew how man had felt upon his first sight of woman.

And at that moment, he realized he would be willing to follow *this* woman out of paradise and into the very depths of hell if she wanted him to.

She had the power of a destroyer.

It was his duty to worship her.

Dropping to his knees in front of her, he pulled the panties down over her hips and began to pray.

She tasted like peaches and fresh cream, slick, sweet and addictive.

In answering the question of how she tasted, instead of satisfaction, he only found the knowledge that hers was a flavor he wanted more of. Perhaps an endless supply.

On either side of him, her knees buckled, and he steadied her, his long, strong fingers digging into her firm thighs to the chorus of her stifled gasps and moans, her fist clenched in her mouth to muffle the noise she couldn't quell.

In no time at all, she was cresting, tipping, falling into the abyss, her body desperate to melt, her legs full of electric jitters, her breathing ragged, even around her fist. But she remained upright, steadfast even in the face of the most pleasurable death.

His grin was wide. He would bring her to her knees.

But first, he would lift her up.

Coming to his feet, he tugged her left leg up his side, enjoying the silk caress of her thigh sliding along his body. He lifted her other leg quickly, carrying her weight easily, impatient now that he'd tasted her.

He wouldn't have her standing, though.

He carried her to the scarlet settee and laid her down, captivated by her utter refusal to look away.

Eye to eye, she let him see her every response. Such openness, such intense vulnerability, made his skin feel stretched and tight.

Without words, her eyes told him that she trusted him.

A raw, rejected thing in him snarled in the face of that trust, was tempted to warn her away, even as he laid her back with the utmost care. That was the kind of naivete that got one in trouble.

She believed in him. She accepted the unfamiliar and overwhelming energy that flared between them every time his skin made contact with hers, trusted it to keep her safe.

He, at least, now knew enough to recognize the energy for what it was—folly.

He had been wrong about seducing her.

He realized it as his hand fisted in her hair, releasing its aroma as if he'd crushed the petals of a bouquet instead of angled her chin upward to feast on her neck, covering her with his kiss.

They were where they were, and there was no going back, but he should never have tried to taste her. He realized that now.

He should have excused himself from the king's presence and left the gala immediately.

Like with every great tragedy, hubris had led him to

this downfall. Rather than sating his curiosity, his sample of her had him addicted.

But it was too late to turn back now.

Too late, as his hand trailed down her neck and chest, stopping only to cradle and adore the full globe of her breast before continuing on its silken exploration, destined for the sensitive bud at the top of her center.

She moaned when his fingers found their goal, his gentle circular caresses a blend of soothing and pressure that acted like a bellows on the still-glowing embers of her pleasure.

As he'd intended, her body tensed as the intensity built once again.

He brought her to the precipice once more with his hand, watching her face, her eyes having shut tight in pleasure, with the sharp focus of a raptor as he held her, teetering, on the edge. With his other hand, he maneuvered the condom he'd left discretely by the settee, hidden in the folds of his earlier discarded clothing. Other lovers had been impressed by the dexterity with which he could unpackage and apply the contraceptive one-handed, but the skill was more for his cover as a playboy than any desire to impress.

Rising over her while keeping her balanced on a delicious razor's edge, he repositioned their bodies before leaning down near her ear once more.

"Sweet Jenna," he murmured.

She moaned, the sound as sweet as the name he'd called her.

"Jenna, I'm going to have you now."

He felt the rush of heat, the flush of her skin, the catch in her breath at his words. She was trembling beneath him, and it was still not enough.

Her strong legs hooked around his waist, instinct urging her to close the space between them, but he still held back, retaining what was left of his fraying control.

With one hand, he played her like an instrument. With the other, he positioned himself at her entrance, rubbing along the molten crease at her center.

It was a torture, of sorts, but one he relished.

This was a singular moment between the two of them. He knew once would never be enough, but never again would he have her for the first time.

He was helpless in the face of her so he made them both suffer—edging until her lips wept for release, above and below.

Taking her in, her skin flushed and taut, her dark nipples erect peaks at the top of her full breasts, he growled, "I'm going to have you now, Jenna. You're all mine."

Once again, she cried out, her body tensing, her arms grasping and holding on to him for an instant before her hips found the rhythm.

Then they were dancing, her body's eager athleticism and soul's open brightness combining to make her a natural lover.

As natural as the fit of her—hot and slick and gripping him as he slid in and out.

Losing himself to the sensation, he only gradually became aware of the fact that his mind played a single word on a loop in rhythm with each thrust: *mine*.

He struggled to reject the idea. He was aware enough to know that something dangerous lurked in the shadows of this desire, even if his body was too busy staking a claim to heed his mind's warning.

He had made a mistake in tasting her once. It would be an easy thing to not do it again.

She was *not* his.

His mind disagreed.

His body disagreed.

The shriveled and dry thing in his chest disagreed.

With a final desperate thrust, he seized control, wrestling it back from the demon that hunted him. He was intent on denying these possessive feelings.

He was the spider in the nest. He was the shadow man pulling the strings.

He was not the one ensnared.

But when he opened, casting himself over the precipice, his mouth and soul in unison cried, "Mine."

And because she was his, she came, too.

CHAPTER FOUR

THE EMERGENCY ALARM system went off at the end of Jenna's long, contented sigh, robbing both of them of the liquid ease that seemed to have melted their bodies together on the sofa.

Separating and leaping to their feet in one motion created an awkward space between them that, for Jenna, the heat and contentment she had been filled with rapidly drained, was replaced with a sense of unease, like soapy water spilling over the edge of a mop bucket.

The alarm pattern did not signal the type of emergency she needed to rush away to deal with, but it certainly brought home a few sobering realities.

Royal emergency or not, it was her duty to be beside the queen when an alarm went off, which she was decidedly not.

And the reason for that was because she had just made love for the first time in her life in her best friend's library.

With a stranger.

No longer caught in the spell of his regard, aware only of the tingling wreckage of her own rapidly chilling passions—the emergency system sounding around them—the truth of that was becoming harder to ignore.

She didn't know this man at all and yet now she *knew* him. Biblically.

But that's not true at all, her suddenly wonky inner compass argued. *Your body recognized him as The One.*

I literally met him today, she argued with herself, unwilling to allow any excuses as she rapidly dressed. If anything, her body had merely recognized him as sexy.

She had been irresponsible at the very least, because as she continued to dress, she was most importantly not where she was supposed to be when an emergency alarm sounded. She should be at the queen's side.

She had no idea where the queen even was.

But you found him, a dreamy inner voice sighed.

The sweet, girlish part of her didn't seem to care that she'd neglected her duty and compromised her morals.

Because you haven't, it insisted. *He's The One.*

Her voice of reason gave a mental snort.

She didn't believe in that nonsense.

Not believing it was just one of the myriad reasons why she had eschewed Priory tradition—and the advice of both her parents and her older brothers—and gone to the military academy rather than straight into marriage.

She had tried to tell them that while she didn't see anything wrong with their choices, for herself she wanted a full life and career—opportunities to meet people with common interests and values—rather than chasing after notions of soul mates and rushing headfirst into motherhood.

They had called her foolish and insisted that the right life partner was the key to finding those things. They'd agreed to disagree and shaken their heads even as they sent her off with care packages.

But she hadn't minded. She'd been sure she would prove them wrong.

Back then, before she'd spent years living as an equally unrealized human being for the opposite reasons, she had been confident in her sense of the path—prideful even.

She had thought of herself as above the limiting conditioning of her childhood.

If the last few years and whatever had just happened between her and the duke were any indication, however, she shouldn't have been so sure.

Clearly some of that childhood conditioning had taken root, lying in wait to strike, ready to jump at the first opportunity to blossom and bloom in her psyche.

Was it any wonder she had given herself away to a virtual stranger then? Was it any different from all the other Priory girls she'd grown up with?

And did it even matter now that she'd gone wrong from both ends?

She'd eschewed and scoffed at finding The One, and then jumped into bed with the first man to notice her since she left her hometown.

And there hadn't even been a bed.

No matter how different life was in the capital, there was no equation in which she could make her behavior with the duke square with that of the woman she had always been.

He's not a stranger.

The persistently hopeful voice inside her was getting irritated.

He is an absolute and literal stranger.

The practical voice could get irritated, too.

But instead of offering a fiery retort, her voice of hope gave up, flipping her stomach over in the process. She suddenly felt sick, ashamed and overwhelmed.

Both voices spoke in unison now.

What were you thinking?

But she would sort the answer to that question out later, when she had some time and was alone.

Right now, she needed to get back to the queen.

She should have never come to the library with the duke. His devilish green eyes, his mesmerizing words, his thrilling touch, his magnetic desire—all of it was none of her business.

Her business was the queen.

"Jenna!" His exasperated tone brought her attention back to the real, flesh-and-blood man, as opposed to the mental image she could neither rectify nor justify.

"What?" Her tone was short, snapping, the one she used on family when they irritated her, not on the Cyranese nobility it was often her job to protect and serve.

"The alarm. It's not for the queen."

"What?" she repeated with the same crossness.

"The queen is not in danger."

"What? Yes, I know." She frowned, his words finally penetrating her growing fog of self-recrimination. "Why do *you* know, though?" she asked. He didn't, as far as she was aware of, have any kind of background in security or defense to interpret the alarm.

"It was not a royal defense code."

She paused her furious movements, reassembling the layers of royal blue to at least look like a guard even if she couldn't seem to behave like one.

He was right. But why did he know that?

The oddity of his insider's knowledge only emphasized the *off*-ness of everything she'd done with him.

Her awareness of the enormity of it was only growing.

Something was wrong with her mind. It had to be, for one person to have knocked her so far awry from her usual way of being.

Looking around their sensual alcove, she had no justification for how she'd come here.

In the streaming light and hush of the library, hindsight made it clear what the kryptonite had been.

A savior complex, a lifetime of baseless fairy tales, and the practiced seduction of a consummate professional.

She'd been an absolute fool.

He was *not* the one. He was the Duke of Redcliff.

Frowning, she worked her way through the buttons of her shirt.

His long hands—the wicked hands that had forever changed her—came to her shoulders, pulling them forward just slightly to angle her face up.

His expression was as shuttered now as it had been clear and readable to her earlier—handsome, yes, but inscrutable, like the moon.

She didn't know anything about this man she had shared herself with.

But it was too late to take it back now.

"I'll take you back to the balcony. With the alarm, the king's guard will have ensconced her. No one ever needs to know."

His words were barbs, even if they were practical. He spoke not of the turmoil in her heart and mind—or *his*— but of the matters at hand.

She opened her mouth to say as much, but no sound came out.

His expression cracked, pain and need once again raw on his face, and he too seemed on the verge of saying something, only to be cut off by the sound of rapid footsteps approaching.

Quickly, he thrust her behind him, blocking her, if only partially, from the person coming for them directly.

"I thought I'd find you here, Sebastian. It's Hel, she's gone—" King Zayn's voice, crisp and concerned, had preceded him, but when he came around the corner, his hands occupied with buttoning the final two buttons of his own shirt, he saw the two of them, Jenna's blue uniform unmistakable, and stopped.

Famous violet eyes darted between the two of them, taking in their state of undress.

Weariness and disappointment darkened his expression.

"So, this is where you were," he said, the words clearly directed at Jenna. He sounded tired, his voice so filled with disappointment that Jenna's heart cracked.

"Your Majesty—" she began, but the king stopped her with a palm.

"We looked for you before I left the queen with my guard. She wanted to know you were safe."

Jenna's heart turned to stone in her chest. "Your Majesty, I—" she repeated.

He shook his head, shoulders burdened by what she saw was coming.

The weight came, she knew, not because he respected Jenna as a professional, though he had already shown he did by appointing her to the queen's guard in the first place, but because he knew that what he was about to do would hurt his wife. Until this moment, it had been Jenna's privilege to come to know how deep their unspoken bond was.

The crack in Jenna's heart fissured.

The king was the king, light-years away from those tasked with guarding him.

She had known, respected and protected him for the bulk of her career but felt no closer to him than the sun.

But the queen…the queen was her friend.

Jenna's throat thickened with tears, but she straightened her spine, coming to full attention for what she knew would be her final address from the king.

"You know it pains me to do this, Moustafa…"

"Zayn," the duke spoke up, the king's given name as casual on his lips as it was on Helene's. Every time it was uttered, it was a small reminder that while she had a role in the room, she wasn't like the others.

With a word, he cautioned against the king's haste, but Jenna shook her head, the gesture firm and serious. What had happened between the two of them in the alcove was between them, just as what transpired now was between her and the monarch.

And though she dreaded what was coming, she knew the king was right. Regardless of the fact that it seemed that the duke had greater access to it than most, Jenna refused to give him all of her integrity by letting him try to save her from the consequences of her actions.

"It has been an honor to serve Queen Mina. Please tell her that." Jenna's voice caught on *please*, but she would not hold the request back. Mina had to know. "And Hel—"

Her friend's name brought the monarch's attention back to the business that had him seeking out the Duke of Redcliff in the first place. "That's right. Someone kidnapped Helene."

The words were a blow to the gut.

Someone had kidnapped Helene? She would not have thought that possible. Helene d'Tierrza was not a woman who was easily taken.

But then again, Jenna hadn't been, either.

"Zayn, you can't really fire her. You were busy. If I'm not mistaken, her contract stipulates that your guard staff is sufficient in such instances—"

Surprised, the king's natural abruptness escaped in his reply to the duke. "There are more pressing matters at hand. We're meeting in my office to strategize a plan. Be there as quickly as you can be."

If it was odd that the playboy duke knew about her contract stipulations and was being invited to a war council on what to do to rescue her partner and best friend, it was nothing compared to the devastation that the king was not inviting her.

With a final sad glance her way, the king did a rare thing and repeated himself. "We looked for you." And then he turned and left, and it was once again just Jenna and the duke in the not-so-private library alcove.

"Jenna, I—" the duke started. She forestalled him with her own raised palm.

Sebastian, she thought, recalling the name the king had used. The Duke of Redcliff's first name was Sebastian.

Shaking her head, she said, her voice thick with the knot in her throat from her whole world falling apart, "Helene."

The name was all she could get past that knot, and even that came out as a croak.

His emerald eyes locking on hers one final time, he nodded, his Adam's apple moving as he swallowed whatever it was he wanted to say.

She didn't want to hear it. Whatever it was, it wasn't as crucial as Helene.

He had asked her to come to the library. The least he could do was help save her friend, whatever strange role there was in that for a Casanova.

And she would go home. There was nowhere else to go. In the dusty old library, she had burned her life to ashes.

Nothing would ever be the same.

Stepping close one last time, he kissed her on the forehead between her eyebrows. The impression of his lips branded her as surely as any scarlet letter. There was no apology in the motion.

Watching him go, the bits of everything she'd built ashes in his wake, she pondered the reality that she—steadfast, trustworthy, dependable, never-make-a-fuss Jenna—had proven every cautious mother of the world right today.

She had torched her reputation, lost her calling and home, and lost both of her best friends—one literally—in one fell swoop.

Nothing in her life would ever be the same, and it wasn't even five o'clock.

CHAPTER FIVE

IT HAD BEEN forty days since he been with Jenna in the library.

In just forty days, his entire world had collapsed.

Sebastian stared at the report on his screen without seeing it.

Blood roared in his ears, but the only sign of his agitation was the single finger rapping on the gleaming hardwood of his desk.

Jenna was carrying his child.

He was going to be a father.

Pinching the place between his eyebrows with the other hand, he released a long sigh and pushed his chair away from the desk.

He was going to be a father.

The reality of it, here and now as opposed to an unmoored and vague concept happening *somewhere in the future*, was nothing like he had imagined it would be, and, as usual when things weren't going according to his plans, Jenna was at the root.

He would never marry—not after a childhood spent as the collateral damage of the sloppy and public disaster that his parents' marriage had been—but he had always anticipated fathering children.

Continuing the family line was the only thing he truly

owed his ancestors in exchange for his life of incredible wealth and privilege.

The next head of the Redcliff clan, however, had been going to be born of a surrogate, chosen with the utmost care by himself, a man with access to all the information in the country.

He would then raise his child himself, keeping said child at his side because that made the most sense, and was the safest option for the offspring of a man in his line of work and in his wealth and status bracket.

His decision had nothing to do with being thrust away from his own home at such a young age—never to be with his parents at home again—nor did his decision have anything to do with the circumstances under which he had been sent away.

He had simply spent enough time revisiting the mistakes of his parents and past to ensure that he avoided their pitfalls and failings entirely. Love and marriage had destroyed his parents, and in particular his father. The emotion and the institution had constricted both of them, squeezing every last drop of decency out until all they had left to give their child was resentment, guilt and spite.

Sebastian's child would fare better.

His choices were simply a matter of practicality.

But then there was Jenna.

Jenna was everything he would have chosen in a surrogate and more—beautiful, exceptionally healthy, fit and strong, highly intelligent, determined, diligent, steady, compassionate, honest…the list went on, and on, and on, and on.

In fact, it was the endless list of on and on that was the problem.

Jenna was *too* ideal, too much of everything he wanted crammed into one woman.

He'd spent enough time brooding about it since leaving her in the library to know for certain.

In fact, the only way he'd been able to focus up to this point had been to review her intelligence file daily, noting every small new detail as to where she was and what she was doing. As former royal security, it was procedure to monitor her whereabouts and activities for the first two years post-employment. That review just didn't typically fall to the director of intelligence.

Outrageous though his behavior had been, the instinct had been sound. How else would he have learned about his child? From Jenna?

Would she have come to him on her own?

Given what he knew of her, he trusted so.

But how long would it have taken her?

She hadn't taken or returned any of the calls she'd received from the palace, nor from her now returned former partner in the queen's guard, the newly minted Duchess Helene Andros, very recently d'Tierrza—that family name was now defunct.

If Jenna was not speaking with those closest to her, how long would it have taken her to tell him she was carrying his child?

Whatever the answer, it didn't matter now. He knew, and therefore he was compelled to act.

If it was his job to know things, it was also his job to pivot in the face of new information.

He was going to be a father.

Though most would never have believed it, he liked children. They were honest and, in some ways, more skillful at manipulating the people around them than his most talented operatives. Obviously, *his* child would be even more so.

The corners of his mouth quirked up at the idea, followed by a flashflood of images of what a child of his and Jenna's might look like.

They would have their mother's eyes, he decided.

Fathomless brown eyes, a brilliant mind, and if they happened to exude the same glow of goodness as their mother, he would simply protect it with all of the vast resources he had at his disposal.

He had planned on a surrogate because he would never subject himself or his child to the humiliations of love and marriage—that part of his plan would remain intact. So, while he hadn't anticipated Jenna's presence, nor the timing, she had not entirely upset his plans. In fact, she'd enhanced them. Now his child would have a mother as well, and in that, they could do no better than Jenna.

He did not even need to be around examples of good mothering to know, and he never really had been.

After his experiences with his own mother, he had avoided seducing or even associating with mothers. The idea of being the kind of man his mother brought home—the ones who weren't his father, as well as his father himself—filled him with disgust.

While he knew many wonderful mothers socially, their love and care for their children very evident in their behavior, they didn't move in the kind of circles he did. The ones in those circles were like his own.

The danger in Jenna being the mother of his child was not an issue of her character, however. It was in her appeal to him. In the way he hadn't ceased craving her, his desire only growing in her absence.

The danger with Jenna as the mother of his child was that he might disappear into her as his father had his mother.

His parents had fallen into each other like dolphins into a fishing net, a deadly entanglement that had ended in a wreck at the bottom of the sea and left no room for anything—or anyone—else.

And while the sea might be a metaphor, his mother *had* died in a wreck. A nasty one involving a motorcycle and winding cliff-side roads, strong intoxicants and a much younger man.

Not the cliffs of Redcliff, though. That was where her then thirteen-year-old son had been in residence, alone for his spring break.

She and her lover had died in Greece.

His father had called him from the capital to tell him, drunk and weeping.

In a way, it was true too, to say that his father had drowned. It had happened slowly and in alcohol, but it had been a drowning nonetheless.

Sebastian might not know exactly how to parent, but his parents had given him a stunningly good example of what not to do.

And, if he was lacking in the basic necessary traits that inspired a parent's love, he was at least *deeply* effective at existing. He collected and digested information like no other, was a virtuoso in effectively disseminating its nutrients to their highest and best use with a speed and efficiency unmatched.

Just not when it came to Jenna.

When it came to Jenna, his plans had the strange habit of backfiring wildly.

It wasn't an understatement to say that she had entirely upended his life—more so, in fact, than he had already been willing to acknowledge. And that was considerably, as he could admit to himself that he hadn't been right in the head since the moment he'd laid eyes on her at the gala.

He had intended to rid himself of an intoxicating mystery.

If she had been like any other woman, he would have lost interest in her and moved on.

It had been a logical, if mistaken, course of action.

He had wanted to return her to invisibility, so that she was just another body in blue he barely saw. He had not intended to make her disappear from her own life. He had certainly never intended for her to become a permanent fixture in his.

He'd used protection, for heaven's sake.

But, as he was slowly beginning to understand, where Jenna was concerned, his plans and intentions didn't matter.

Of course, their encounter would constitute a statistical anomaly.

It hadn't been enough that she'd already intruded on his mind constantly.

How could he be expected to function at all, now that he knew she was going to have his baby?

As a future duke or duchess, his child would be vulnerable. As the child of the head of Central Intelligence, even more so.

To his own mind, Sebastian was first and foremost an intelligence professional. However, it was an inescapable reality that he was also a Redcliff—*the* Redcliff. Regardless of the circumstances of their conception, any child of his would become a duke or duchess after him and would require all the appropriate protection. Managing that and keeping tabs on Jenna, both at a distance, while running his espionage empire would be impossible.

Therefore, he wouldn't do it.

CHAPTER SIX

SHE WAS PREGNANT.

After dragging her feet and then overcompensating by using more at-home tests than was recommended, Jenna had still refused to accept the positive results, but was now faced with the family doctor's prognosis, which now replayed in her mind on a continuous loop—relentless and undeniable.

Jenna was pregnant. She was going to have a baby, and not just any baby, but the Duke of Redcliff's baby.

She was intimately familiar with how it had happened, but it was still unbelievable.

And to think, she'd been under the impression that the worst had already happened, that losing everything she'd worked and built toward her whole life was the bottom of the pit.

Here was proof to the maxim then, that things could *always* get worse. She'd been caught in flagrante delicto with a man she'd just met by a man whom she had sworn to protect—a man who she respected and whose respect in return had mattered to her—and that was all in addition to losing the career she had worked for her entire life.

But if there was an oldest crime in the book, then there was also an oldest consequence, and what had befallen her thus far wasn't it.

Babies were.

Happy, chubby babies who thundered into the world and left nothing the same in their wake. Babies who deserved the entire world and the best start.

And all Jenna had to give hers was a disgraced single mother.

As to what their father would be willing to give, she realized, nauseous and dizzy at the same time, she had no idea… She didn't even know his phone number. Had no idea how she would get in touch with him to let him know.

How would he react? Numbly, it occurred to her that he might deny it. What if he forced her to prove it? Or worse, what if he asked her to end it?

Her hands came to her belly protectively. She might not have planned for it, but she would not lay down the responsibility now. She had transgressed her code of conduct, but she had not completely given up the values she had been taught. While the Priory taught that individuals had God's blessing in the governance of their bodies, they also taught that children were gifts from God.

She had apparently been chosen to receive such a responsibility-laden gift as a result of proving just how far into the depths of irresponsibility she had been willing to travel.

How easy it had been to go too far with Sebastian.

Making a disgusted noise, she tried to shake the thought of Sebastian out of her mind, scrub away the lingering want of him, to snuff out the terrible candle burning inside her, a flame at both ends—one, the ever-present desire to taste him again, the other shame.

Shame that her recklessness meant that the father of her child was a virtual stranger to her—regardless of how magnetically attracted to him she had been at the time. Shame that she had been so caught up in him that she'd not even considered the possible outcomes, but most of all, shame that in the face of the most transformational news she had ever received, the one feeling she could not seem to muster was joy.

CHAPTER SEVEN

THE TEMPTATION TO watch her sleep existed but Sebastian resisted the urge. He'd come to talk, not to gawk.

She *was* beautiful, though, in her lilac-colored nightgown.

That she wore a nightgown surprised him. Almost as much as his reaction to the bare foot and calf that peeked out from beneath her quilt. The intimacy of her bare foot struck him with more power than he'd have thought possible. He'd seen it before in the library, but had barely noticed. There had been no time to savor the full feast of her then. Now, as the only bare skin he could really see, he could appreciate that her foot was shaped like an artist's model's, defined with a high arch. The more he observed her up close and personal, the more he saw of her subtle hidden beauties—hidden not because they were hard to find but because they were so far from the first thing you noticed about her. It came as a surprise to realize that a woman who was so kind also had the kind of features that artists adored.

Because of his work, he knew her records and personal history like the back of his hand. Her bare foot, though, was new.

She was natural and earthy, this woman who had become an unexpected obsession and the future mother of his child.

The image she presented asleep fit the setting like a perfect peg—a Renaissance beauty in classic repose inside a sixteenth-century farmhouse with huge aged beams, a picturesque thatch roof and happy little farm critters. It was at least as ideal a setting for her as standing as the knight in blue armor in front of the queen. She oozed tradition and old-fashioned values. It shouldn't have captivated him. It was boring. And yet, here he was.

That she could inhabit each space so fluently was a quiet marvel to him. Jenna was natural wherever she was because she brought the characteristic of naturalness to everything she did.

What must it be like to walk into any arena and be so easily loved? He would have to add it to the short list of things he didn't know.

He had imagined she would be a T-shirt and panty type rather than a pretty nightgown type, but he appreciated the unexpected. There was more *feminine* and *wild* and *free* blended into the *good* and *honest* and *upright* in her than he had realized at first glance.

Jenna had a unique way of surprising him at every turn.

It was the special light she had, the lack of self-consciousness that was so unlike anything else he'd ever encountered throughout his jaded life.

It blinded him every time he came near.

And he'd gone and gotten caught up staring at her after all, he observed wryly.

She stirred, subconsciously sensing his presence, even while she remained asleep.

He had moved to wake her, silently repositioning himself at her bedside, when she sat up suddenly in bed.

"Sebastian?" she asked groggily. Her voice was sleepy and sweet and confused. Here, at least, was a surprise he could use to his advantage.

He sat down on the bed beside her. "Present," he said.

"What are you doing here? How did you get in?"

Only truth worked with Jenna.

"I'm here because you're pregnant."

He had not expected that she would leap back from him into a defensive posture, but supposed he really should have. She was a security professional.

"Who are you?" Her voice had become fully alert and dropped into her lower register, full of fearless menace.

Lifting his hands, palms up, he kept his voice even as he replied, "Relax, Jenna. We have a lot to talk about."

Her eyes narrowed, shadowed and cold. "Who are you?"

"You know who I am, Jenna," he soothed.

She bared her teeth.

He gave her what she wanted. "I'm Sebastian Redcliff. I am also the Director of Central Intelligence."

She wasn't buying it. "Cyrano doesn't have Central Intelligence," she countered, losing none of her defensiveness.

He gave her a half smile. "Not officially."

Her ferocity popped like a balloon at his words, leaving her collapsed against the bed with her hands over her face in its wake. The information was new, but he imagined it answered too many of her unanswered questions to deny.

"I'm such a fool," she said softly.

It wasn't the first time someone had said the words as a result of a conversation with him, but he hated the weary self-recrimination in her voice.

"For not knowing national secrets?" he asked softly.

"I work in national security."

"Exactly why you shouldn't know. It'd be a disaster if the front staff knew about what went on in the back of house. Otherwise, how would it sound genuine when you insisted to the public that Cyrano has no intelligence program?"

Their breathing and heartbeats were the only sounds for a moment.

Then she let out a dry, joyless laugh and said, "We had sex."

"We did. We're consenting adults, it's not against the law. Or did you mean you expected to know through some kind of sex osmosis?"

"You're a complete stranger." She sounded horrified at herself, as if she had lost herself in the woods.

Reaching toward her, he took her hand. In truth, she was taking his revelation well. "Get to know me, then. Come to Redcliff with me. Stay there throughout your pregnancy. I will take care of you and our baby and you can meet the father of your child."

She scoffed. "If that's even possible. Do you let anyone know you?"

He didn't, but strangely it stung to hear her say so when she was the one person he'd made the offer to. "No," he said.

She sat up again slowly.

A long silent beat passed during which she stared at him, a dusky rose blush blossoming across her cheeks. "You could have called. Or even come by during normal visiting hours."

Eyes locked on hers, he shook his head. "You would have ignored me or had your mother tell me you were sick."

She sucked in a breath at his words, her glorious chest lifting and pausing there, her body gone rigid at his accurate summation. "You tapped my phone."

He didn't bother to deny it. "Years ago, when you applied for a position on the royal guard."

"That's appalling."

He shook his head. "No. It's intelligence. Unless you're suggesting we let just anyone become a royal guard?"

She laughed again and though it remained a sarcastic sound, this time it carried some amusement.

"None of us knew," she said.

He nodded graciously. "Thank you. I take pride in my work."

"Helene?" she asked.

"Not even the famous duchess guard knows."

"But she has the highest-level security clearance."

He quirked a brow up. "Does she?"

Jenna laughed again, light and full for its low volume, and the sound soothed something unsettled within him.

"You broke into my room," she pointed out.

He nodded. "I did, and at great peril to myself, as you're one of the most dangerous women in the nation."

She smiled, as he'd intended, and he felt the same thrill of accomplishment he did after coordinating a successful intelligence mission.

But soon her smile faded, her eyebrows coming together before another long moment passed in silence. Then she said, shaking her head, "I can't believe I just took it all at face value."

She still felt like a fool, that was obvious, but she no longer hated herself for it.

It was an improvement at least.

Then she said, "This makes you my boss, you know. I could sue you."

He stared at her blankly for a moment before he chuckled. "That's a new reaction."

"To?"

"To learning my job title."

"I should hope this is a new situation," she said primly. "You could have called or sent an email. You didn't have to break into my house."

"Your parents' house."

"My home."

He looked around, noting the girlish decor, the discrete boxes of items that obviously did not belong to her, were merely being stored in a space that was rarely occupied.

"Your *childhood* home. You might have put your clothes back in the closet, but you don't live here."

"Your parents' house is always your home," she countered.

He looked at her pityingly. "Is it?"

Instead of fire, sympathy flashed across her eyes. "It's supposed to be."

Irritated by the unintended shift in subject, he waved her off. "I didn't come here to discuss our parents. I came here to discuss us as parents."

Her abruptly tired eyes narrowed as she tilted her head to one side, her arms coming to cross in front of her stomach in a protective position. "So talk."

"We have a lot to go over."

"So you broke into my house in the middle of the night?"

"It was the only way I could be sure of reaching you. You left the capital and have refused every call from there—barring the single instance of contact you had with Helene d'Tierrza upon her return—including three calls directly from the palace."

"As the head of intelligence, do you personally take such a close interest in all of the severance monitoring?"

He could appreciate that she was as intelligent as she was good, even while she challenged him. "Absolutely not, that would be ludicrous. 'Severance monitoring,' as you so eloquently put it, is normally rookie work. But I have never encountered anything with the power to distract me that you have, Jenna. You fascinate me. And that was before I learned you were carrying my child."

He spoke the truth.

Honesty was his only course with Jenna. And yet every time, he was left holding his breath and waiting for her response. It wasn't a particularly welcome sensation.

For another long stretch of heartbeats, she said nothing, only stared. Then she sighed, long and slow. Then she nodded.

"I'll go with you," she said.

The breath that had stuck in his chest eased free. "Thank you, Jenna."

"I've got to get my bags and leave a note," she groused.

"What will you tell them?"

"My mother knows about the baby. I'm just going to tell her the truth, that I've gone with the baby's father to sort things out."

Of course, she would tell the truth. Jenna valued it as much as he did, though she rarely weaponized it.

She stuffed a bag full of clothes and wrote a longer note than Sebastian had anticipated, but soon they were heading through the window.

As she went through before him, he asked, "Can you manage?"

Lifting an eyebrow, she said cockily, "With my eyes closed."

Smiling, he followed her through the window carrying her bag, feeling lighter than he had upon entry even with the extra weight. He hadn't been sure she would go with him.

He didn't know what he would have done had she refused. Seduction was no longer an option, not when he'd resolved to resist the dangerous attraction that remained between them, and he could not bodily force her.

It was fortunate, then, that he had not needed to devise an alternative. The fact that he felt the relief of that acutely, as if it were a matter of luck that things had gone smoothly, was a testament to how perilously footed he became when dealing with Jenna.

But if it emphasized the danger of getting closer to her, it also showed that he could navigate the thin middle way. He had underestimated her allure in thinking a single taste would render her harmless, but he had learned from his mistakes.

He would not touch her again, would not feed the hunger that he could now recognize as the same kind of obsession that had driven his father. Instead, they would work together to give their child the kind of childhood that produced a soul like Jenna's. Jenna had earned his trust long ago— enough to appoint her to the most important security detail in the nation. She would be an excellent mother. He would keep them safe and provide them with what they needed.

They moved in silence to where he had parked his Trevita a distance from her house. The sleek and stealthy car was a ghost gray that was a one-of-a-kind deviation from the extremely limited three-car run that the greater public knew about. The King of Sweden had gifted Sebastian the rare car as a thank-you for information services rendered and it was stealth incarnate.

"Nice car," Jenna said, a little breathless at its passenger side. Her tongue came to her lips, wetting them, as they took in the vehicle, and the eroticism of her perusal hit him like an invisible wall.

At a glance, the car looked like a standard luxury sports model, as common as any slate-gray Lamborghini. Upon closer examination, however, the infinite superiority of its craftsmanship was evident in every gorgeous fiber of its diamond-weave exterior. It wasn't paint that gave it its distinctive color and texture, but strands of woven carbon fiber. The handling was so responsive that he felt like he could drive it with his mind—a pleasure that was almost as unique as Jenna.

He was grateful for it for more practical reasons tonight, however. He was also appreciative of the moonless night above. The vehicle had been made to move invisibly through a night like this. But tonight, what had pleased him the most about the car was the way Jenna's eyes lit up when they'd landed on it.

Its top speed was outrageous for Cyrano, but tonight he would get close to it, if only to please the gearhead he suspected lurked beneath Jenna's exterior.

The journey passed quickly enough that they left the picturesque country lane in a blur.

A drive that should have taken him forty-five minutes took him twenty, and just as he'd planned, between the vehicle's color and the darkness, and the speed, no one saw him as he took the long dark road to the Redcliff estate. He didn't want to deal with the fanfare of arriving during regular hours.

The forbidding wrought iron gated entrance to the walled estate opened for him, the massive *R* in their center splitting to welcome the prodigal son home.

Named not for seaside cliffs, as most assumed, Redcliff was landlocked, located to the northeast of the seaside capital, so-called because of the high, clay-rich cliffs that slashed through the center of its boundaries, carved into the countryside over thousands of years by the Soleil River.

As they climbed the curving road that followed the river at an incredible height toward the main residence, the shocking cliffs were invisible in the darkness. Just as was each and every one of the other small details about Redcliff that generally never failed to bring a smile to his cynical mouth. The vibrant green of the grassy hills and clifftops, all the more luminous for the contrast of the red soil beneath. The trees packed together in dense patches and groves sporadically dotted across the landscape, clinging to the hills for dear life. The faded brown brick and terra-cotta tiled rooftops of the village homes. The structures lined the roadway, tight together, often so close they touched, built atop and into the sturdiest of the cliffs, connected by families, clotheslines, Wi-Fi passwords and busy lives.

He couldn't remember the last time he'd come to Redcliff. Possibly not since his last annual tour.

Too long.

At the top of the cobblestone drive was the ducal complex. Neither a manor nor a palace, the Redcliff compound was a sleek and contemporary structure that had been designed to blend seamlessly into the landscape. Boasting the very best of every modern convenience, with everything tastefully built into the structure itself, the luxurious space ensured that one could remain entirely connected to the world while feeling absolutely free from human society.

He knew this because he was responsible for its design.

Tearing down the old manor—a stately and stiff monstrosity that had been drafty, sat uncomfortably with its modern additions, and was haunted by memories of his mother and father's failures—had been his first act when he'd taken over the title upon his father's death.

He had been younger then, still passionate about architecture, before he'd realized that even a perfectly designed house did not make a home.

He had thought it would somehow change his memories of Redcliff if he replaced the house, that it would eradicate the persistent sense of isolation which dogged him every time he climbed the hill from the village and saw the ancestral grounds come into view.

He had been young and wrong, but the complex he had built was beautiful.

Elegant and comfortable, it had been designed for a family, a thing he could admit now that it was on its way to becoming a reality, but stepping inside with Jenna at his side, her bag slung over his shoulder, he realized immediately why it had always remained so cold.

Jenna had never been here.

And because she was with him, it felt profoundly different when he crossed the threshold this time.

He didn't know if it was because she carried his child or simply because she transformed every space she entered with her presence, but her magic was working already, her wide-eyed wonder at his creation finally proving his youthful idealism right.

His creation could become a home.

The glass entry doors slid open silently, admitting her like a temple goddess, the movement of air their motion caused strangely worshipful.

They strolled down hallways that appeared to be open air but were truly cleverly laid-out indoor spaces, perfectly climate-controlled in a way a stroll through the surrounding hillsides would never be, and she trailed her fingertips delicately along the gleaming wooden handrails while gazing at the outer world. He felt her touch as if she caressed his skin rather than his design.

Did she appreciate that he had made nature into a performance? Did she know that he had never invited anyone into his private project until her, that she was the sole audience he had intended to impress without ever knowing? He only realized it himself now.

He led her to the bedroom that was nearest to his office—near enough that he would hear her if she needed anything.

"I thought you would like this room."

It took her a moment of looking inside, mouth slightly ajar, before she turned back to him. "Thank you. We never talked about—"

He shook his head, anticipating her concern. "My room is in another part of the house. My office, however, is next door should you need anything. I'm in there most often."

"About the baby—"

"Tomorrow," he forestalled her. "When we're fresh. Make yourself comfortable. There's a private bathroom adjacent."

She looked at him, brown eyes serious, and opened her mouth as if she wanted to say something but then closed it with a shake of her head. "Thank you. Good night, Sebastian."

He tried to stick this image of her in his mind, as she was now, a lovely woman in a virginal nightgown, as opposed to the version of her performing erotic dances that had filled it as of late. Her proximity would be a challenge but perhaps in easing into a daily routine with her, one populated with encounters comprised of mundane pleasantries and virginal nightgowns, he could conquer the dangerous desire. "Good night, Jenna."

Leaving her there to settle in, he made his way to his office. Along the way, he passed the high wall of family portraits.

Comfort, aesthetics and a grudge against his parents might have motivated his youthful renovation of the homestead, but beyond that, he didn't bear any ill will toward his family history.

He was proud of it, in fact.

He certainly appreciated the fact that it made him rich.

Despite the renovation, he had saved the paintings and various heirlooms, even going so far as to preserve a stained-glass window from the oldest portion of the original structure.

The design of the window was simple and lovely, a white lily at its focal point, the petals of which were shapes cut from three types of glass—an opaque white, a mottled and sparkling translucent, and a softly transparent ivory. Brassy burned-orange glass for a stamen and pale sage for the leaves completed the image, which was surrounded and framed by an array of assorted translucent blues and greens.

It was the cliff lily of his family crest, and the first stained-glass window ever brought to the island of Cyrano, even before the island had become a unified nation. The

Redcliff family was a part of Cyrano's history, at least as much as the royal family and its relations. His family had been the spark and ember of what would later become a rich and artistic cultural tradition.

Sebastian had studied stained glass for months, practicing restoration techniques on the rose in the d'Tierrza library before he dared preserve and move the Redcliff lily. It was one of the reasons that he had become so familiar with the d'Tierrza library in the first place. Why it was his most treasured location for meetings in the capital.

At the thought of the library, his mind, of course, turned to Jenna.

It seemed all roads led to Jenna and the child she carried, no matter what direction he turned.

It was fortunate, then, that he had the power to redraw the map so that every one of them ended where he wanted.

CHAPTER EIGHT

THE BEDROOM SEBASTIAN had given her was incredibly beautiful.

Large rectangular paneled windows offered a stunning panoramic view from where she sat in the center of a massive bed. The bed itself, covered in stark white plush downy bedding, jutted out from a wood-slatted wall that supported it, appearing to float in the air.

In addition to the bed, a number of various-sized flat and cubed shelves were arranged tastefully along the slats. They boasted vibrant potted plants, decorative sculptures and books. There were no photos but, though she'd looked, she hadn't really expected to find any. She did not picture Sebastian as the family photo type.

Sliding her legs out of the bed, Jenna slowly stood.

Blessedly, her stomach remained where it was supposed to be.

Between her pregnancy and the effect Sebastian had on her system, she was grateful for any moment she felt steady. She felt like herself for this moment, and she would take it. Her baby and her onetime lover both seemed happy to engage in a constant battle for supremacy inside her consciousness, and the opportunity to anchor down and hold on to herself, even briefly, was a deep relief.

They had yet to discuss the details of their arrangement, but it was obvious to Jenna that reining in the out-of-control flares of attraction between them would be of paramount importance.

Giving in to those urges, that lunacy, really, had wreaked enough havoc in their lives. And more than that, she couldn't afford the risk of losing herself in him again.

Digging inside her old academy duffel bag, she grabbed the first dress that came to hand—a bright red loose-fitting linen maxi dress with three-quarter-length sleeves that her mother had made for her years ago.

It was voluminous and airy, intended to be worn at the end of summer when the family could spend entire days in the heat, preparing and storing their annual harvest.

With the right layering, she could wear it through a chill morning, the heat of the afternoon and into the coolness of the evening comfortably. It was practical, as well as lovely and durable, just like everything her mother made.

After dressing, she headed through the door Sebastian had indicated was the bathroom.

Like the bedroom, the bathroom boasted large land-scape-view windows that looked out over the incredible rust-colored cliff sides that surrounded the building, but when it came to focal pieces, the bathroom put even the bedroom to shame.

A gorgeous wooden tub—huge, square and deep, and a smooth, creamy honey color that a high-end hair salon would have been proud of—was raised in the center of the room. The inner lining of the tub was made from what looked like smooth gray stone, the same material from which the sinks appeared to have been made. Rather than a traditional faucet, the tub could be filled via a large wooden spigot, controlled by a pull chain with a matching wooden handle.

Jenna had seen many examples of astounding luxury over her life as a royal guard, but this bathroom was by far the best marriage of wealth and design that she had ever encountered.

Bringing herself to leave the bathroom to find Sebastian was hard, especially after discovering the shower alcove with its scandalous full-length cliff window—a complete outdoor shower experience without ever leaving the house. In exchange, all you had to do was bare your naked self to the entirety of the natural world.

She could not help but suck in a slow breath, in awe at the audacity and appeal of the space.

Without having to be told, it was clear to her that Sebastian had designed the house. It was just like him—breathtakingly audacious.

The man was an absolute hedonist.

As if the thought brought him to life, she caught a whisper of his scent in the air. Backtracking the way she had come, forcibly ignoring the artistry and details of the walls, she looked for him in the room he'd labeled his office the night before.

Upon entry, she gasped aloud.

Inside, the sprawling space overlooked the Soleil River. Cherry-stained built-in bookshelves spanned the length of the wall to her left at the doorway, but it was the desk that stole her breath.

It was centered in an entirely glass-walled space that was cantilevered out boldly over the river's deep ravine, seemingly with no support beneath its gleaming hardwood floor. The desk itself was large and heavy, parked with authority on the gorgeous rug that lay in the center of the hardwood. To preside as duke in situ here was to be king of the sky—to conquer the raging elements, to survey and command all that the light touched and more.

It was awe-inspiring and terrifying at the same time.

The rest of the office, the part that behaved like a normal room, was dominated by gleaming cherry woods and smooth leather. The contrast, everything right and proper that one might imagine in a traditional office on the one hand, and terrifyingly futuristic on the other, somehow screamed both conflict and triumph, and Jenna wondered what battle it was that Sebastian was fighting through the space.

With a start, she realized she'd been standing there at the entryway gazing in astonishment at an empty room.

She'd never been interested in decorating or design, but it was impossible not to be while inside Redcliff. It was the most incredible home she'd ever entered, a masterful work of art that revealed Sebastian's signature style, his passion and sensuousness, with every brushstroke.

Leaving the room, she went in the opposite direction, retracing last night's steps down the long skywalk that was even more enchanting in its integration with the outside world by daylight than it had been the night before. Between what felt like the miles of windows and the vibrant tropical potted plants, the walk felt more like a summer stroll than a passage to the front door.

She followed the way down the long hall until she stepped out into the large open living area that they had passed through the night before. Empty of Sebastian too, this room, while impeccably decorated and obviously to the highest taste, was almost disappointing in its normalcy. Even with its elegance, it was just a place to watch television, nothing like the bathroom and bedroom and office she'd seen.

She followed the flow of the architecture around a bend and partial wall to step into a home chef's wonderland.

Like the bedroom she had woken up in, the enormous chef's kitchen faced out toward the cliffs, with a wall of windows providing a panoramic view from pretty much every potential cooking and preparation area.

An enormous kitchen island dominated the center of the

room, situated in front of a massive range and oven that were equipped with a restaurant hood.

The sink was sunken into the island and everywhere else was clear, open counter space—miles of it, in fact. The glossy marble was thick and ivory colored with a subtle beige pattern. None of the standard countertop appliances one might expect marred the clean expanse. She suspected that they existed in abundance, however, but were merely hidden amongst the myriad of unique custom cabinets.

As incredible as it was, however, what struck her most about the grandiose kitchen was that it was made to be cooked in. It wasn't a showpiece, and it wasn't a sterile professional workspace tucked away from view where the staff worked like in many of the homes of the super-wealthy she had visited in service to the queen.

This kitchen was meant to be the place where the people who called the place home gathered and created memories.

It was the height of luxury, and yet it was also somehow normal—wholesome, even—and to find it right smack-dab in the middle of the home of one of Cyrano's wealthiest aristocrats and oldest families… Jenna would not have expected it.

Even more astounding, Sebastian leaned against the counter, fingers deftly typing something into his phone.

In the kitchen's morning light, which was extensive and bright since this room—like all the others she had been inside—had floor-to-ceiling panoramic landscape windows, he looked fresh and handsome. Certainly nothing like the kind of man who might sneak into your room and ask you to run away from home. Nor did he particularly look like the kind of man who might ask you to make love with him in a library.

Instead, he was tan and tall and green-eyed, his blond hair tidy, his jeans and button-up relaxed despite the fact that everything he wore was perfectly tailored to his long, lean

frame. He was stunning and wealthy in equal measure—
the kind of man who could look impeccably put together
with almost no effort—but here in his own kitchen he was
approachable, just a regular man somehow, as if this were
an ordinary morning and she were just now joining him
for breakfast after spending extra time luxuriating in bed.

The vision her eyes presented was all a lie, though. It
had to be. The aura of normalcy that clung to him, the way
that coming upon him in the morning felt more comfortable
than even returning to her own childhood home—none of
that coincided with the enigmatic denizen she knew from
the city.

But she didn't really know him at all, did she?

She was going to have to get that through her head before she did something even more foolish than she already
had with him. Coming with him had been about getting
to know the father of her child, not falling for a man she'd
had no business being with in the first place. And certainly
not on the first day.

Shaking her head, she chastised herself mentally.

He looked about as normal as Adonis masquerading as
a human man, and the sense of comfort and rightness was
just her hormones and desires switching on at the sight of
a man she was obviously infatuated with.

A mother didn't let those kinds of urges guide her,
though. Particularly not when the man in question wanted
everything his way and was good at making it happen.

Armed with the reminder, she dared look again.

His jeans were a dark wash and at their base, his high-
quality leather work boots looked supple from use and
care.

She had never seen him in jeans and boots.

Did wealthy city people wear jeans and boots? Only
eight weeks from living in the palace and it seemed she

couldn't remember any of the wealthy people she had ever seen.

There was only Sebastian.

His shirt was a buttery-soft green flannel, a shade darker than his jaded dragon eyes.

All but the top button of his shirt were closed. There was nothing seductive about the shirt, and yet her mouth watered. His unexpectedly muscled forearms felt indecent, revealed by his rolled-up sleeves.

She sucked in an audible breath, her resolutions forgotten in the face of the full power of him in the light of day.

He looked up from the device in his hand.

Their eyes locked and the jolt of electricity and understanding was as bad as it always was, worse even.

Attraction was not what lived between them. The word was too soft and flirty. Whatever it was that existed between them was thick and demanding and relentless. They hooked into one another and squeezed and tangled like ivy until she was sure they would both be lost in a vortex of green.

He stole her breath, her body instantly coming alive, making her wish she'd chosen something else besides the airy dress to wear—twelve layers of something else.

The same intensity of need burned in his stare, perhaps ever greater now than it had that day in the library, the dangerous green orbs dancing with the shapes of all the dirty things it was clear he still wanted to do to her.

Searching for the frayed strands of her intentions with no luck and irritated by everything delicious and fascinating about him, she snapped, "Good morning."

He laughed and she was momentarily mesmerized. "Good morning. Did you sleep well?"

She hadn't, but that wasn't for lack of comfort so she was polite when she said, "Yes, thank you. And you?"

His eyes lit with mischief. "Well, thank you. Can I interest you in something to drink, Jenna? I've got a number of options. Ginger lemonade?" He should never have been able to pull off mild mannered and charming, and yet here he was.

"That's sounds wonderful, actually. Thank you."

He got the glass for her himself, and when he turned to return the lemonade to the refrigerator, she was filled with a longing for this all to be about the energy that still sizzled between them rather than making arrangements for their unborn child.

But that wasn't for women like her. She was a sidekick, not a main character.

She took a sip and steadied herself. The lemonade was fresh and delicious, exactly the thing her stomach had been searching for as her occupied system woke up.

"Your home is astounding. I feel a little out of place," she admitted.

"You shouldn't, someday your child will own it."

He said it so casually, completely nonchalant, as if he was entirely comfortable with the sudden redirection of his life and permanence of their bond. Perhaps he was?

It was taking her longer to adjust.

Hollowly, she wondered where she would fit into the life of a child who would one day own Redcliff. It didn't compute that that child and her child would be one and the same. Would they be embarrassed that she was so obviously not from their world?

She would have to work and wait for the answer, like everything else in her life.

Regardless, there had been something warm and tender about Sebastian's words. He had a gift for making it difficult for her to see the lines that separated her from the world she now walked through.

"I've downloaded your checkup schedule and updated

your records with your new address and my emergency contact information."

Jenna gasped. "That's completely inappropriate, you know. The public would be horrified to know you could access that kind of information."

With complete seriousness he responded, "You're absolutely right, and because of that, I am going to have to ask you to keep the information to yourself. I know I can trust you, of course. You've taken an oath to protect and serve."

"Those are pretty words after you've already risked state secrets."

He squeezed her shoulder, the contact lighting the smoldering flame inside her. "I have absolute faith in you," he said.

He meant it, and he was right to trust her. They might be strangers, and yet in so many ways he knew her, understood her.

She couldn't say the same about him, though.

And chipping away at that imbalance was just one of the Herculean tasks she had to accomplish during her time with him.

"You know more about me than I know about you," she said aloud.

"I know more about most people than they know about me."

"Most people are not going to be the mother of your children."

A moment of silence greeted her statement before he said, "Agreed."

"So, I should know you."

"I am unknowable," he said.

Jenna snorted. "Only God is unknowable. Tell me about yourself."

He sighed, sounding bored. "What do you want to know?"

She shrugged, sipping at her lemonade. "What do you love? What's your favorite color? Only the truth." She pictured her questions landing on him like birds, beginning as a singleton then building into a flock.

Beside her he stilled. His eyes narrowed, scanning her, while the wheels of his mind turned. When he spoke, less than a heartbeat later, he answered her questions in rapid-fire succession, though she knew he'd thoroughly processed and controlled just what he would reveal.

"I love knowing things other people don't and the color of your eyes," he said, his words rough where before they had been cultured and smooth.

Once again, he'd floored her with the truth. Multiple truths, in fact.

Each one was meaty, too much to take in at a time, let alone in rapid succession. Especially since he had moved behind her and threaded his fingers through her hair to massage her scalp.

His fingers were gentle though she sensed annoyance coiled in his touch.

He didn't want to share with her, even as he endeavored to open.

His fingers were strong and deft and she couldn't help the quiet moan that escaped, even as she sensed she should keep the evidence of her weakening will private—for both of their sakes. But she didn't, and in response, he let out a sound of frustration before tilting her head up and taking her lips in a kiss that was soft and restrained for all of the denied passion clamoring behind it.

When he pulled back, slow and lingering, she held still for a moment, savoring the thing that shouldn't have happened—lips parted, eyes closed—before she opened her eyes with a frown.

"Sebastian, we can't—"

A strange expression came to his face—intense, needy

and deep—but flickered away before he pulled away from her to say, "You're right, of course."

"We should talk about—" she started.

"Not yet," he said, voice taut, expression mildly pained. His nostrils flared as he drew in a long, slow breath. "Space. A change of scenery. I have something I want to show you," he said.

"What?" she asked, her body still yearning toward his while her mind did its best to pull everything back in after their slip.

"The rest of the house," he said. "I designed it."

Grateful for the obvious diversion, Jenna jumped on it, exclaiming, "I suspected that!" And it wasn't even work to force a smile at the confirmation. Though there was a sin in pride, it felt good to be right after such a long spell.

Her bruised instincts were grateful for the vindication.

When he spoke again, it was a beat too late and only after he'd cleared his throat and taken her hand. "This way."

The rest of Redcliff was as astounding as the small portion she had seen.

As she'd expected, Sebastian had stamped himself everywhere.

Shadows played everywhere, lovely and peaceful, while the materials he'd chosen and natural light through the various slatted shoji walls and abundance of stunning cliff-view windows ensured that light was always available to create them.

She said as much as he led her through, her voice tinged with awe, as he led her around. "I understand the light, everyone wants natural light, but I would have never imagined how shadows could be used to enhance a room."

Another odd expression sparked across his face at her words, but he only said, "It's observant of you to notice. Not many do," before showing her the next wondrous delight.

Every room was astounding. He had an incredible, high-tech conference room, separate from his office. There was a workout room with fantastic equipment. At one end of the incredible home, two stories had been built around the tallest tree Jenna had ever seen on the island of Cyrano.

As a former royal guard, Jenna had entered some of the most extravagant and expensive houses in the world, but this was the first to make her wish she had the kind of money to create something like it for herself.

Through Sebastian's clever design, the mansion was situated and arranged so that nearly every room he showed her included an astonishing cliff view.

The stunning and rugged rust-colored terrain, the dramatic drop and roar of the river—all of it did far more to trumpet just whose home this was than any stodgy coat of arms ever could.

Like Sebastian, the Redcliff estate was too powerful to be subtle and was utterly unconcerned with pretending otherwise.

But if you like the view, her inner romantic purred, sliding itself out of the corner she thought she'd beaten it back to, *it's perfect.*

After he'd shown her far more rooms than she expected there to be in one house, he tugged her just a bit farther into the fully shadowed part of a hallway, where she was surprised to see another door.

"Another room?"

"One of my favorites," he said.

Reflecting on the glorious rooms he'd just shown her, she was skeptical that it would outdo them. "It's got a lot to live up to."

He replied mysteriously, "I think you'll find it as arresting as I do."

When he opened the door, she sucked in a breath, her cheeks flaming at the same time.

Inside was a library.

Smaller than the one that was now burned into her memory, Sebastian's library was a cozy, plush and private sanctuary. Each and every book boasted a cracked spine and a siren allure, enticing, calling to its reader. Scanning the titles proved that though new, the collection was as eclectic and broad as any discerning reader might desire.

Whereas the d'Tierrza library had emphasized many reading nooks, this cozy room was centered around a decadent central space, arranged as if intended for a group of readers to gather and quietly read together. A sofa, two large cushioned armchairs, and two large floor cushions encircled a luxurious Turkish rug, each seating area equipped with a small table beside it and a bevy of pillows and cushions. Whatever position a person might desire to take, they could achieve it with the plethora of options, each one designed to accommodate the pleasure of reading.

Or making love, she added to her mental observations, her body near combustion with sensual overload and determined to once again break down her common sense.

If the d'Tierrza library had been built for show, the Redcliff library had been built to be used and enjoyed, and not just by anyone, but Sebastian—and, she realized with a start, her eyes landing on the one bay of shelves filled with new books, their spines unbroken, her.

He'd been awfully confident she would come with him.

The assumption that the new books were for her trickled into certainty as the titles in the collection began to sink in. They covered subjects she had excelled in at the academy, as well as those she had not done as well in, but maintained an interest in. He'd included popular fiction titles she'd been meaning to check out by authors she'd bought before. She was impressed by his selection. He might have access to the best intel in the country, but it was another thing entirely to pick out a book for someone.

But of greater interest to her than even the excellent

books he'd selected for her were the ones he had chosen for himself through the years.

Those were fascinating for a whole different reason—for what they revealed about him.

He watched her silently as she walked along the shelves reading titles, running her fingers along shelves and up and down spines.

Language, foreign policy, world history, politics and—of course—architecture, dominated.

Was it any wonder he was interested in espionage?

Though it made sense that it would take quite a lot of study to know so much that he had no business knowing, she was impressed by the amount of time he spent continuing to learn.

It was an admirable thing to do, far more so than many of the other things she'd witnessed wealthy people do with their free time.

In front of the reading area, a massive fireplace, already set with logs for a fire, sat quietly.

He had outdone himself with the house, but it was this secret inner garden that slipped past the defenses she had erected around her heart.

He had created space out of time, and welcomed her into it—and this time, there was a lock on the door.

Whatever they got up to in this oasis, there was no chance they would be interrupted.

In the face of all the emotion, all she could say was, "Very bold of you."

He smiled with one side of his mouth. "I think we've established that."

She did her best to remember to be professional, to recall that she didn't need to want this man. She needed to get to know him, she needed to work together with him to plan a future for her child. This wasn't about them.

It wasn't about the memories and sensations flooding her mind and body, returning her to a different library.

She wanted him even more now.

He wanted her even more now.

Their shared desire was as unspoken as their agreement to resist it. She sensed that though they came to the decision for individual reasons, they were at least as in sync about this consensus as they were physically.

They had so much to do, so much to plan and learn about each other and the world they would build for their child.

They wanted the same things, even the ones they couldn't have.

Her brown eyes locked on his green.

He was beautiful—slightly amoral or not.

She was far past being able to tell which he was, only that a part of her was convinced he was hers.

Either way, it didn't matter. He fascinated her.

Like magnets, they stepped toward one another, erasing the space between them in synchronized movements, as if greater powers had choreographed them.

He opened his mouth.

She licked her lips.

His eyes locked on the motion, and he swallowed.

"The baby," she said.

He nodded. "We need to talk about the baby."

She nodded, heat rising to her cheeks, her skin tingling and alert. "First and foremost."

The tension between them stretched tight, egged on by the heat, and the sumptuous library, and the man she had already proven she was willing to risk everything to touch.

And then he was closing the space between them on a strangled oath, his arms coming around her.

Jenna sighed into his mouth as he took hers, her body weeping with the relief of giving in and the end of the tension of resisting her attraction to him.

Her body was a cascade of needs, a rush of wanting him that demanded everything all at once—sensitive, hot and famished.

She wanted to bite him, wanted to savor him and wanted him inside her, ravishing and soft and gentle, all at the same time. The immensity of the conflict came out as a growl against his lips, which, devil that he was, only made him smile.

The experience of kissing him the first time had been an awakening, and earlier, in the kitchen, a dreamy whisper. Now, it was an incendiary, sparking a fire he'd built deep inside her, her skin flushed hot and her nerve endings blossoming into sensitivity greater than she knew what to do with.

She was transcendent, the incredible rushes of pleasure leaving her desperate for more, holding on to her form as long as it took for the entire universe to break apart.

When his hand cupped her breast over the thin, soft fabric of her dress, she moaned into his mouth. As if the sound had aggravated him beyond control, he swept her into his arms before carrying her to the sofa, where he lay her down, never breaking their kiss.

Her hands explored his chest and shoulders, adoring the softness of his sweater against them as they trailed toward the hemline. There, she slipped her fingers beneath the fabric of his clothing to feel his hot skin pulsing beneath her hands.

His breath caught at contact, and a hot rush pulsed at her center. That this man, powerful enough that he could direct an international espionage program, trembled for her—plain, Priory Jenna—shook her to the core.

Abruptly hating that clothing separated them, Jenna pulled him close, driven by an urge to fuse with him that she knew he felt just as powerfully.

And then his pocket trilled, vibrating and ringing a

jaunty tune absolutely out of place amidst the hungry sounds of their breathing.

Gasping, she looked around, momentarily disoriented as he pulled back to slip the device out of his pocket and hold it up. In that moment, he was disheveled and real and completely within her reach, his clothing off-kilter, and hair tousled where her fingers had run through it. And he looked as shaken as she was.

"It's the king. I have to take this," he said, distancing himself from her more effectively with the words than even the large steps away he took as he straightened his shirt and moved to answer.

It was as if a bucket of icy water had been spilled over her.

Jenna shivered, now cold where she had been on fire only moments before.

Incredibly, it seemed the king's reach extended even further than she had ever imagined. The monarch had somehow managed to insert himself into yet another shameful encounter with Sebastian, despite the fact that he was hours away and no longer her employer.

But, she thought, as she pulled herself back together, the sound of Sebastian's muted conversation low in the background, this time the interruption hadn't come too late, after things had already been said and done that couldn't be taken back. He had saved them from repeating that folly at least.

The last thing that she and Sebastian needed was to be intimate again.

They *needed* to sit down and have some serious conversations. They *needed* to hammer out their plan for parenting together.

The combustible attraction between them had only increased, but it would only burn them both. That was more clear than ever.

And none of that talking was going to happen in his

sumptuous library. The two of them needed a less sensual space, a place where they wouldn't be tempted to explore anything other than the future of their child.

So, rather than wait for him to finish his business on the phone, Jenna gestured to excuse herself, ignored his motion to stay and made her way back to the kitchen to wait for him.

In a kitchen, with space between them, they would surely be able to talk.

CHAPTER NINE

HE HAD TO return to the capital.

Frustrated by the timing, even while acknowledging the summons had saved him from making a grave mistake, Sebastian hung up the phone and followed Jenna out of the library, knowing he would find her in the kitchen.

She was the hash-it-out-in-the-kitchen type.

It was simple and straightforward, unlike whatever information the king had for him, which could only be delivered in person.

Generally, this was the kind of information Sebastian lived for—secrets so big they could barely be uttered for fear of the consequences—but right now he had more important things on his mind.

Though perhaps the break and space would be blessings in disguise. Keeping his distance from her was proving more difficult than he'd anticipated, which only meant the threat she posed to him was greater. Clearly it would be a more challenging balancing act to walk and maintain the tightrope of his control while she remained within arm's reach.

Finding her in the kitchen, as he'd expected, he quickly briefed her. "I have to go to the capital. I'll be back tonight."

Shaking her head, she opened her mouth, likely to demand more of an explanation, but he held up a hand. "I'll tell you more later." It was a request.

That he stood to wait for her answer, that she had the power to say yes or no and have him obey when he allowed no one else that privilege irked him, but it was pointless to fight. She had it and he was completely at her mercy.

Finally, she relented with a short nod. "Fine. We need to talk, though."

"We do. Tonight," he promised, surprised to hear himself offering promises and more commitment than was necessary. Master of shadows and manipulation that he was, promises were something he didn't make lightly. He knew too well that promises were a form of honesty that could too easily be weaponized.

And as unusual as the promise was, what followed was even more so.

Turning to leave her there, he reached out to take her hand, absently, thinking nothing of the impulse, until his fingers grazed hers and caught.

Before he understood his intention, he had snagged her arm, an echo of the afternoon of the gala, and spun her around to him. Drawing her closer, the movements as natural and fluid as they were foreign, he pressed a kiss first against her forehead, and then one to her lips, and then released her.

Only was it as he swept his phone from the countertop that he realized he'd kissed her goodbye, and only as he left Redcliff did he realize how good it had felt to have a reason to come home.

It was dark by the time he returned hours later than he'd anticipated.

Queen Mina was pregnant.

Babies, it seemed, were in the air and catching.

The information set off a strange mixture of reactions

within him. Royal offspring and heirs were expected and Sebastian had protocols already established for the consequent expansion of his intelligence protection program required by their existence.

He had expected the news to be purely professional. He had known the monarch socially his entire life and had come to respect him immensely as a colleague and ruler, but he would not have said they were friends.

Never would he have imagined that, rather than a mild sense of pleasure that a man he liked had reason to celebrate, Sebastian's mind would instead jump to projections of future playmates for his child.

How would Jenna react?

How would she feel to know that the monarch was pregnant, as well? And Helene, too. Had she heard that her former partner was not only newly married, but had come back from her adventures pregnant, as well?

Yet again, Sebastian didn't know.

Driving into the garage and turning off the car, Sebastian noted as he got out and entered the house through the private door that he had spent more time at Redcliff in the past twenty-four hours than he had in the previous five years.

With Jenna in residence, the long drive between here and the capital seemed shorter.

To his pleasure, he found her back in the library, her legs curled up under her in one of the large chairs. A fire crackled cozily beside her.

"I lit the fire," she said, by way of greeting. Her voice was cool and tired, letting him know that she'd had a long time to circle around the topics at the top of her mind, including everything they still needed to discuss regarding their child.

Keeping his tone mild, he said, "I'm glad. You should make yourself at home."

She eyed him closely. "What did the king have to say?" she asked. She was probing, testing how much he could, or *would*, tell her.

The urge was there to share without reserve, so he hedged. "Let's take a walk," he said. She would come back to the question, he knew, but the invitation bought him time. Only Jenna seemed to have the ability to put him in the position of being short on said time.

She held his stare for a moment, those deep dark lances of hers piercing him without hesitation, and then nodded.

"There's a chill in the air outside," he said.

She flashed a small smile at his words, as if they'd surprised her. Walking past him, she said, "I'll grab a coat," leaving the room to, he presumed, retrieve her coat.

They met again in the kitchen, both of them somehow knowing that was where they would reunite.

He had installed her in his preferred bedroom, the one near his office, as opposed to the master suite, which he had taken, and he knew she knew the way.

In preparation for their walk, her attire was a study in contradictions.

She wore a long, tailored overcoat above her airy red dress and had matched it with a pair of floppy boots.

Together, the boots with the dress should not have worked—the style part country maiden, part grizzled dairy farmer—and yet it did, and somehow elegantly.

She brought the masculine and feminine, the sophisticated and the natural, into perfect balance effortlessly.

With her long braid, she looked entirely ready for a moonlit stroll in the countryside. Did he, he wondered, look as carefree and natural? Did he present the picture of a hearty and happy man of the landscape? Somehow, he doubted it. But he took her arm nonetheless, leading her outside through a side door that led into the woodland trails that constituted his landscaped forest garden.

Though they were here to discuss the future, one made infinitely more complicated by the intensity of the attraction that flared between them, walking through the moonlit woods with Jenna—even when that moon was little more than a thin sliver in the sky—came with a sense of peace that Sebastian had never experienced before.

The day with her had been a conflux of emotions, his control tenuous at best. At worst, well…at worst it had been the sweetness of kissing her in the kitchen and the inferno of touching her in the library.

Had he once again chosen the mistaken course with her? Should he have installed her somewhere other than Redcliff, at a more comfortable distance?

The idea offended both the father and the man within him. He refused to keep any child of his at a comfortable distance and he had at least enough control to keep his hands to himself. Was that not one of the basic tenets of manhood?

The day's ups had been a testament to the strengths of his plan and the downs, merely a side effect of delaying this conversation too long.

Once they'd laid down parameters—one of which would be physical distance—neither would get carried away.

The trail ahead of them was lovely, wide and laid with a soft, sound-absorbent natural bedding of shredded bark. In the dim lighting, her hair shone like a raven's wing, her thick eyebrows drawn together making her look like a grave woodland witch from another era.

"What did the king say?"

What a strange thing it was to walk with Jenna in the woods.

Another woman might have gone immediately to the most pressing issue at hand—their baby—but not Jenna. She was a terrier and, though she continued to bafflingly rebut the idea, a professional.

Duty to the monarchs was more than a job to her, it was a part of her being. Her rejection of the reality of that— her rejection of the attempts that had been made to reinstate her to her position as guard—was the only lie he'd witnessed her utter.

Truth had always proven to be more powerful than lies, but he understood that people more often feared it than revered it. His father had belonged to that category of people.

But not Jenna. She had proven fearless in the face of the truth time and time again. He wondered what scary truth hid beneath the lie this time, but he did not ask. Now wasn't the time and if it was large enough to scare Jenna, it was best to approach with caution.

"The queen is pregnant," he finally answered her question.

Coming to an abrupt stop at his side, Jenna sucked in a hiss of air at the news, her hand coming to her abdomen in a protective gesture.

Ever the defender was Jenna, he observed, even when the heartache was her own.

"That's wonderful," she croaked thinly.

Eyeing her, he was ruthless, if only for her sake. "It's not. It hurts you to find out this way."

She winced, but did not deny it. "I'm happy for her."

He knew she told the truth, the way he always recognized truth when he heard it, but he could see that her joy for her friend was not strong enough to take away the sting.

An unfamiliar surge of irritation with the king rose in him. It was Sebastian's job to remain unequivocally in the king's corner, but in firing Jenna so impetuously, Zayn had made a huge mistake—and because that mistake had caused irreversible hurt to Jenna, it was an unforgiveable one.

But the queen, whom he knew thought of Jenna not just as an employee, but a true friend, had already told her husband as much before insisting that he retract his dismissal of her guard.

When the king had capitulated, however, and tried to rectify his mistake, Jenna had refused his calls, just as she had refused the queen's.

It took a lot of spunk to ignore a king's telephone calls. Sebastian had been proud of her.

But spunk didn't heal hurt feelings, and he suspected that what she needed was to talk to her friends.

While he excelled at planning in the shadows, he was powerless to address her current hurt. She had to take the first step.

More information, though, could potentially encourage the movement.

Information regularly inspired him to action, even when it hurt. Perhaps *especially* when it hurt.

"She is spending her pregnancy at the Summer Palace," he said.

Jenna nodded. "That makes sense. Will Hel accompany her?"

He could see the wheels of her mind turning. It was not customary for primary security to accompany the royal family to the summer palace, but the queen would miss her friends with such an extended stay.

Sebastian shook his head. "She will not. Helene is on maternity leave, as well."

"What?" Jenna's screech in reaction to the news was less reserved than it had been to the queen's. "But she—" She cut herself off before she revealed what he assumed was private information.

Idly intrigued, as he always was at the prospect of clandestine information, he set aside his curiosity at whatever barrier had previously existed to Helene having a child— a future that was somewhat expected of the head of one of the oldest families in the country—keeping his attention instead on Jenna.

When she finally spoke again, her voice was tired and quiet. "She didn't tell me."

Recalling the phone records he'd monitored, Sebastian said, "You only spoke once."

Jenna nodded. "Right after she got back. I was so glad she had returned safely, but when she tried to convince me to come back to the capital, I just couldn't. I cut her off and made an excuse to get off the phone. I never gave her a chance."

Although he had his own suspicions as to the answer, Sebastian asked, "Why?"

Jenna looked up at him, startled by the question. "I—" she started and stopped. Looking away, she said softly, "I don't belong there."

Had she not been serious, he would have scoffed. "You are one of the most qualified royal guards we have seen in over a decade, Jenna. Your service record is impeccable and you've only improved over the years."

She shook her head. "It's not about that. I'm invisible there, no one sees me," she said.

Lifting an eyebrow, he asked, "Isn't that what a guard is supposed to be?"

Again, she shook her head in a negative. "To the majority of people, yes. But not to everyone."

"I don't follow," he said, though he was beginning to understand.

"Helene has been my best friend for nearly a decade, and yet the gala was the first time I had ever been to her home. She and the queen have been the only people to see me, to be my friends in a real and meaningful way where I thought we were more than our roles, that we were the kind of close that opens and changes for each other, but neither of them shared their pregnancies with me."

"You haven't shared yours with them, either," he pointed out, happy to play devil's advocate if it meant presenting her with a more complete view of her situation. She was intelligent and savvy, but no one could truly see themselves.

Eyebrows drawing together in a frown, she waved her hand at him. "It's not the same."

"I think it might be closer than you think," he countered.

"No. It's not. They belong in that world. They understand the rules and where they fit. I thought I did too, but I was wrong."

"Aren't you the one who refused their calls?"

"Because they would only try to get me to come back," she said.

"Because you belong there," he pressed.

"I don't, Sebastian," she insisted. "Helene belongs there. She was born there and couldn't be invisible if she tried."

"And the queen?"

Jenna waved the point away. "She's the queen. She belongs wherever she wants."

"She wants you at her side."

"To be her friend on a payroll. What kind of friendship is that? What kind of real life? I wanted to join the rest of the world when I left my home for the capital, to find a place for myself amidst the bustle and noise. Well, the place I found was a background fixture and I don't want to continue consigning myself to that kind of echo of an existence. I thought I could have both and it turns out everyone else was right and I was wrong. I can live in the foreground of my life and be seen as a woman with value and skill if I'm willing to give up a career and get married like my Priory friends, or I can go back to the capital and return to being an interchangeable body in blue, only one that is pregnant with a new blemish on my record. That doesn't sound like belonging to me."

Like anyone in a spiral of shame and self-loathing—a

mental and emotional cocktail Sebastian was intimately familiar with the signs of from the rare visits he'd had with his father throughout his childhood—she was painting a cherry-picked picture of her life to date, but he knew better than to point that out directly. "Being only the second woman appointed to the royal security force and graduating at the top of the military academy can hardly be considered an echo of an existence, Jenna."

"Of course, they can. Achievements don't constitute a life rich with love and warmth and laughter. Honors don't make a family or a home."

He raised an eyebrow, eyes darting pointedly to her abdomen. "Your condition contradicts that."

She made a noise in the back of her throat, hand once again protecting her belly, as if to shield their child from her next whispered words. "Pregnancy doesn't make a family, Sebastian."

He resisted the urge to laugh. She was correct. Pregnancy did not make a family. Attachment and dedication to one's children made a family, and—based on her self-censoring for the sake of baby ears that had not yet formed—he'd say she was more than halfway there already. To her, he said, "As I understand it, it does."

She shook her head. "Love makes a family."

Sebastian scoffed, mildly surprised to hear a woman as intelligent and down-to-earth as Jenna utter such a clichéd line. "Love makes people selfish and weak. A mother and father committed to their child's future make a family."

Distaste feathered her face. "That sounds like a business arrangement."

"We'd be lucky if more people took parenting so seriously," he countered, not exactly sure how they had gotten here from discussing her illusions.

"Well, why don't we get right to it then? Okay. I'm to

assume you've got a number of proposals regarding the future of our offspring, then."

Irritation flared Sebastian's nostrils as he reminded himself that she would have no way of knowing that she mocked one of the great lessons of his life. As cherished and adored as Jenna must have been, she had no sense of what it was like to have parents with no plans, proposals, or even thoughts for their child.

"I do, most of which I'm sure we'll get to. We were, however, talking about your inane notions of not belonging."

She gasped in outrage. "Inane? Pardon me for noticing and caring when the people around me consider me a set piece."

"A set piece? I recognize the general cluelessness of most of the capital's citizenry, but that's a bit theatrical, Jenna."

Jenna scoffed. "Outside of the king and queen and Hel, I think you were the first person in the capital to ever see me."

Her words stoked his ego, but that would not soothe the hurt inside her, a hurt that was clearly older than the ones that lay between them. "I have to disagree, Jenna. Your work is admirable and noted. You were personally selected by the king to safeguard the queen. Your name is regularly cited as an example for the young girls of the nation. Put simply, you are remarkable, and it does not go unnoticed."

"I am not. I'm too Priory for the capital, and too capital for the Priory. To return to the palace is to accept a life without love and family and ordinary companionship. A life in which my most important relationships live and die at the whim of my employment. I want to build my own real home, rather than simply visit the one I grew up in on leave. I want to know the families of my closest friends and have their children call me Auntie, not Sergeant Moustafa. When I packed up my quarters alone after I was dismissed,

I realized how truly little I had to show for the past decade of my life. My entire life fit into three boxes and there was no one there to say goodbye to me when I left. I don't want a life like that, where my presence or absence makes no difference. Even if leaving means giving up everything that I've dedicated myself to for the past two decades. All this time I thought I was following my dreams when it turns out I was merely living for the crown. I want a life for myself, as well. A life for our baby."

"Ah yes. A life for our baby." He spoke softly, not wanting to prod the tender feelings radiating from her. He could have argued, of course, pointed out to her that her absence had made more than a difference, that she had kings and queens and dukes and duchesses begging for her return, that she even had the head of intelligence engaged in the effort, but he didn't.

Like in any operation, finesse was required in dissolving illusions.

If she was determined to remain blind to the impact she had on the lives around her, he wasn't going to force the issue. Inevitably, she would come to the realization on her own.

For now, he was content to let the subject fade as they got to the grittier matters at hand.

"I want you and the baby to stay here at Redcliff. Beginning immediately," he said, anticipating and not being disappointed by the surprise that flashed across her face. It was good to be the one throwing *her* for loops again.

"Live with you?" she repeated.

He nodded. "Beginning immediately. You can enjoy a long and luxuriously pampered pregnancy, followed by a harrowing labor you will never completely forget, and then both you and our child can reside here at Redcliff, where we will raise them together."

"You've got it all figured out," she said quietly.

Eyeing her closely, he gave a slow nod. "Only if you agree."

"And if I don't?" she asked.

"I anticipated your agreement."

The bald statement elicited a dry laugh from her. "How do you propose *we* raise our child when there is no *we*?"

Hardness came to his voice. "I will be a part of my child's life, Jenna."

Rather than being intimidated, her voice grew in strength to match his in intensity. "I'm glad to hear it," she said, "I would expect no less. Nevertheless, we are not in any way, shape or form a parental unit, or a unit of any kind for that matter. Therefore, we have to decide how we are going to manage this together." She punctuated her words with one hand while the other rested over their growing child.

"Acknowledging that you've only recently become aware of it, we have had a long and productive track record of working very well together. I don't imagine parenting will be any less demanding than ensuring the security of the royal family. I am confident we have the required skills," he said.

"Did it occur to you that I might not want to stay here that long? Wrecked thought it may be, I have my own life."

"No one is suggesting you don't have a life, Jenna," he said, dismissing her flare of temper as he would a child's fit. "In fact, I believe it was I who suggested the opposite. What we are talking about is a matter of practicality. Here you have all of the resources of Redcliff at your disposal to ensure our child has the safest and healthiest environment to grow up within. As we are both aware of the fact that you are not currently employed and are residing with your parents, I would think it was the obvious best solution, with the smallest impact to your life, to prepare for the birth of our child and raise them in residence here, cared for with the whole world at your fingertips."

Anger lit her eyes with a peppery spark at the same time as it brought color to her cheeks, visible even in the low night light.

"And what was your plan for the two of us, in all of your wisdom?"

He shrugged, hedging. "I assumed we would have our hands full with parenting."

"And what happens when you get tired of playing house? Or when you identify your next conquest?"

"This is not a game to me, Jenna," he said, deadly serious. "You are carrying my child and heir."

"So, you plan to give up philandering when you become a father?"

"It had been my plan," he said testily.

Her breath caught at his words, but she stubbornly clung to the point she was trying to make.

"What about me? What happens when I am ready to move on? I told you I wanted a full life, with love and family," she pushed.

Something dark and dangerous moved inside him at the idea of Jenna moving on from him. He did not own her, he knew it logically, but that made her no less his. They were having a child together. That meant something more than romantic pleasure. Fair or not, he would not accept the image of her with another man. Yes, it meant a lifetime of fighting the desire that existed between, that threatened to carry them away with a force equal to the canyon carving the Soleil River he loved, but whatever logic worked in her mind, he was certain that its conclusion matched the picture in his mind: the two of them raising their child together. There was no room in that picture for another man. In fact, the mere idea lit his blood with cold fire.

"I would advise against that," he said.

"You can't just keep us locked away forever," she said softly.

Agitated he sped up, strides lengthening as he replied, "And I don't intend to."

Catching up to him, she said, "What did you intend with all of your grand plans? You have many of them I assume."

He did. He had begun putting details into place as soon as he had learned she was pregnant.

He had not questioned that the child was his. He had a sixth sense for truth, and this situation was no different.

He had not attempted to sway or control her behavior. He respected her...knew she had the integrity to mother his child. Nor had it even crossed his mind to take their child from her. He had simply begun making arrangements for their future.

She should be pleased. Instead, she pushed and resisted him. He liked it so much better when she went along.

Though, perhaps he should be grateful she was pushing back. The consequences, his mild irritation, were nowhere near so transformative as the alternative.

Because this was Jenna, he tried again. "None of this needs to be difficult, Jenna."

"I want to get married someday, Sebastian." The statement was soft and delivered without heat, her voice tender almost, as if she wanted to gentle the fact that she was once again throwing his carefully laid plans all to hell. "I want to have a satisfying career and I want to be a wife and I want our child to grow up in a happy, normal family."

His skin felt hot and itchy at her words, his breath constricted, but he resisted the urge to fidget or rub. She asked for things he could not give her for reasons he would never be able to make her understand. Jenna had grown up with regular people, people who could pursue love without it destroying them. He had not. He knew the damage that the obsessive pursuit of love could inflict on a child. It was not her fault that the same tendency lurked in his own blood, that in his DNA lay the same programming. It wasn't even her fault that she had been the catalyst that triggered and activated the potential of his latent disease. No, she wasn't to blame for tempting him, but it remained his duty to protect them both from disaster. "Absolutely not. Marriage is not an option on the table between us." He would not repeat his father's mistakes, even with a woman like Jenna. The price was too high.

Nodding, she placed a gentling hand on his forearm. "I wasn't asking you, Sebastian. I know we didn't plan this, but before it happened, I had always planned to marry and have a family. I still want that."

"You've gotten what you wanted then. You have your very own family now."

"What you're offering is not the same thing, Sebastian."

"The only difference is a piece of paper, Jenna."

She shook her head. "If you think that, I feel bad for you."

With a strange growing sense of dread rising, reaching up to slowly grip and squeeze him around the throat, his voice was more clipped than he intended when he said, "A legal document does not make a stable family, Jenna, and you're a fool if you think so."

"You're right, and that's not why I want it. I want what the paper represents. I want that confidence for my child. I want them to grow up secure in the knowledge that the people who love them will be there for them, a steady, unshakeable unit, bound together by love, commitment and a proudly public promise. I want them to know that no matter what they choose or decide in their lives, they will at least always have a loving family to come home to that is proud of them, even if they make a mistake. I want them to see passion and fire and purpose and to know that they don't have to choose between those things and their dreams and that anything that asks them to, be it person or situation, it isn't right for them." A look of surprise came to her face, as if she had only just heard her words by saying them out loud. "I want what my parents gave me," she added softly, "even if all it does is blow up in their faces."

Love and family. She wanted love and marriage and a happy family. Of course, she did.

He could not offer her that. But what he had to give her was just as good, if she would see it that way. "No other man will care for you as thoroughly as I would, Jenna. You have to sense that's true."

"That might be true, but it's not the same thing. Whatever this strange obsessive thing between us is, it isn't the same thing that carries couples through the highs and lows of a lifetime together, through the difficulties and triumphs of parenthood, or the inevitable desert-like stretches of distance and resentment. I want the thing that does that, Sebastian. I want a fully realized life, Sebastian, not a career and a business partner I raise kids with. I want what my parents have."

"You don't want what they have. If you did, you would have never gone away to chase your dreams in the big city. I read your academy admissions essay, Jenna. I'll buy that you want wholesome and secure, and I can give you at least a version of both, but we both know that's not all you want. You want fast and world-changing, too."

Again, her hand fluttered to her belly, but she remained serious. "I wanted those things, Sebastian, and look where it got me. Pregnant, alone and no closer to fitting into the world than I ever was—further from it now, in fact. I have to think about what's best for our child. I have to think about what happens when someone better comes along for you. What happens to me when you find a woman you *do* want to marry?" She spoke with her hands, gesturing between the two of them as they walked.

She wounded him though she didn't know it, couldn't know that the intensity of his need for her was so immense that he had not even seen another woman since laying eyes on her. She said she was invisible when it was she who had made every other woman on the planet disappear.

"I can assure you, that won't happen. If I will not marry you, what makes you think I would marry anyone else?" he asked.

"It's too late for silly fears and games, Sebastian. You're going to be a father," she said.

And it was too late for him to stop this train, however much she might deserve the answers she wanted.

He would give her the truth.

"I will not marry you, Jenna."

"Wh—?" she stuttered for a moment as if his bald statement had gone through her chest, before pulling whatever question she had been about to ask back before it escaped. Then she caught her breath, balled up her fist and released it. "I know. That's exactly why we're having this conversation. We need to talk about the future. For our child."

He gave her credit. The words had come out even if her voice had a faint tremor.

"Marriage no longer makes a difference as to whether or not our child will inherit Redcliff, in case that addresses your concerns."

Jenna gasped. "Do not insult me. Wealth is the furthest thing from my mind and you know it." When she wagged her finger at him while she spoke, it gave him a window into her childhood—and one into what a future with her might be like.

But marriage was not required for that future.

"Marriage is not on the table. A stable future with the father of your child, however, is."

"And if that's not enough?" she demanded, stubborn and strong and gorgeous, a knight without armor, defending honor and goodness.

But if honor and goodness thought they could take away

what had rapidly become the most important part of his life, he would destroy them both.

"Think about the baby, Jenna."

The words worked like a charm. The righteousness went out of her, leaving exhausted resignation to sweep over her.

Seeing clearly now, she turned to him, stopping them both in their tracks. Her gaze was like a high beam in the night making him certain she saw exactly what he was doing but had lost the will to do anything about it.

"Does it always have to be your way, Sebastian?" she asked.

He held back the wince that wanted to be let free. Whatever she had seen of him, it had revealed too much.

He said, "It's better this way."

Her lips pressed into a firm line while her eyes darted around his face as if she looked for the key to unlocking him. Finally, she asked quietly, "Better for who?" before stepping back from him and continuing along the path.

Her dress, where it showed from beneath the long jacket she wore, was as dark as a blood blot test.

Catching up to her in a matter of strides, he could see the wheels of her mind turning.

"Better for you," he answered. "Our baby. Me," he added.

Her face said he'd surprised her with the admission but she had lost none of her leeriness with him. "Why?" she asked.

"I won't have to worry about you as much."

"If the king can manage, you can, too."

"The king had no choice in getting married."

"This is a *choice* thing?" she asked, incredulously.

"Yes, Jenna. I *choose* not to get married."

"Why?" she demanded, volume rising.

"Because of you, Jenna. It is clearly enough of a challenge to resist our attraction when we are merely colleagues, but I am willing to face the risk for the sake of our child. This is not simply a fear of commitment, Jenna. It is a choice between being a functioning human being and a slavering mess waiting to jump at your beck and call. I choose to provide a better example for our child than that. I'm not not choosing you, Jenna. I'm choosing to be a man, rather than a puppet and a fool."

She was unmoved by the eloquence of his dilemma.

Placing her hands on her hips, she said, "Well, I am *choosing* not to consign myself to a life as your live-in nanny and nursemaid."

With an exasperated oath, he swore, "I will not lead my family down the same path of folly as my parents. What lives between us, the thing that neither of us can seem to deny or resist, is dangerous. It's a cancer preying on our child's future. We both excel in our chosen fields and have experience navigating complicated and delicate situations with tact. We will come together on the matter of our child's future."

At his side, she nodded, uncowed by his low outburst. "I agree. We will. But not like this. We'll do it like normal people in our situation. I will accept your offer to stay here through my pregnancy and the birth of our child. Once I have a new job, the baby and I will move into our own residence, and the two of us will share custody."

Nothing about the dismal vision she presented aligned with his plans, but why would it? This was Jenna he was dealing with.

Irritation growing into something larger as she pulled away from the future he wanted, he rasped out, "It's too late for that."

They had gone too far.

Again, she stopped, turning to him, her face compassionate. "It's not. We have to be adults about this." She smiled softly, the expression, he assumed, supposed to be comforting. "But it isn't too late to get to know each other."

"It's too late to go back, Jenna," he said. "I've already been inside you. I know that's not enough commitment for you, but it changed everything. As to *knowing* each other…? If you don't know me by now then it's best you not find out exactly what kind of creature you've already invited in."

Her lips parted, breath halted. The tip of her tongue darted out to moisten them and her cheeks flushed, not with fear, but heat. She felt what he felt, whether she acknowledged it or not.

"I already know," she said, hushed as she stared at him, her eyes bursting with the want of him.

He couldn't risk answering her unspoken invitation, so instead he snarled, "You only think you do." And then he turned around to stride back to Redcliff, leaving her to stroll on or follow after him if she liked. He had exhausted his interest in persuading her.

CHAPTER TEN

JENNA WAS AWOKEN in the morning not by unfiltered daylight streaming in through the massive windows of the room Sebastian had given her, as she had expected, but instead by the powerful urge to use the restroom.

Stumbling in that direction she observed that this was because sometime while she had been sleeping, light-blocking screens had descended to cover the windows.

Whether it had been Sebastian's doing or merely something automatic, she didn't know. After he'd stormed off in a fit like that, she wasn't feeling particularly inclined to give him the benefit of the doubt.

Even after stepping into the bathroom that still shook her. Groggy, irritated and filled with memories of her openness beating against Sebastian's closed-off mindset she might be, but she really loved this bathroom.

Washing her hands, the reflection of the tub in the mirror was a siren call, luring her to come and stay awhile, to submerge herself in water and let its wholesome warmth fill her system, working its way into the kinks and knots of her muscles, creating space for relaxation in the way nothing else could.

She had always loved baths, was a true believer in the power of a soak to provide both soothing and profound relief to most of one's physical and emotional woes. But, as if God was truly testing her, even that simple pleasure was denied to her.

Her doctor had advised against long soaks in hot water—it was apparently not good for the developing being in her womb. She was welcome to take lukewarm baths, they'd said, just nothing that might cook the baby.

Motherhood, it seemed, demanded sacrifices long before you had the reward of an actual child.

Of course, it did. And like everything else in her life, she had foolishly rushed headlong into it.

The bath was just another reminder that she'd been impulsive and thoughtless to the point that her body and life were forever and irrevocably changed.

Her stomach rolled and a wave of slick nausea overtook her. Steadying herself on the counter she drew in a deep breath. Standing alone like this, ruminating and mulling and brooding, wasn't good for her. She needed some food in her stomach, and she needed—she searched herself, scanning for any clue inside—action.

Everything had happened so fast and disastrously that she hadn't had time to be present to her body's newfound awareness and tenderness—she had become sensitive to even her own thoughts, it seemed.

But if pregnancy was making her more sensitive, it was at least also making it easier to see her needs.

She had always been a woman to find solace in physical activity. She couldn't get Sebastian to see what he was so obviously and stubbornly blind to, and she couldn't take a hot bath, but she could work out. She remembered the way to his home gym.

Returning to the bedroom, she made a beeline for her bag. In her hasty sweep of her closet at home, she had lost out on bringing along workout gear. But that barrier was easily surpassed by selecting one of the many dresses she'd swept up.

This one was lilac colored and wide cut. It was made from a high-stretch material that flowed with her every move, no motion restricted. It was perfect for a woman who liked to move fast and feel pretty, just like her, because it had been made specifically for her. It was another of her mother's creations.

But her mother didn't make pants.

Because of that, even though Jenna had no problem with pants and had worn them happily for training and while on duty, in truth, she always felt slightly more comfortable in a dress.

But the most wonderful thing about the dresses Jenna's mother made for her was that they'd been made so that she could fight in them. They were always wide and open and made of fabrics that flowed with her movements, rather than getting caught up in her legs.

Her mother knew her and loved her, even if she didn't always understand her.

Jenna would need to carve out and guard a space like that for her baby in the world, with the same fierceness her mother had carved hers.

She hoped she picked up the skillset soon, because after once again letting Sebastian run roughshod over her the night before, she knew she was currently nowhere near doing so.

She wasn't ready to be a mother, to step into the role that her mother had modeled so well—and, despite Sebastian's assurances that they could be a parenting team, she wasn't ready to be a single mother on top of it all.

She didn't know any unwed mothers.

Motherhood was a sacrament to the Priory. One that distinctly *followed* marriage.

A mother was entrusted with guarding, protecting and nurturing the most precious charge on the planet: another soul.

The fact that she'd been sent home in disgrace the last

time she'd been entrusted with the charge of another soul did not bode well for her potential.

Jenna's own mother ran their household and managed the farm books—cooking, cleaning, rearing and administering with grace—while also enjoying multiple painstaking handcrafts, including quilting, knitting, dressmaking, taxidermy and leather tanning.

Everything Jenna's mother did, she did for the express purpose of nurturing her family. Her mother was the center of their family, their source of light and joy, effortless in her work.

But Jenna wasn't ready for that, not really. Yes, she was dutiful and hardworking and had diligently mastered all of the required skills, but until Sebastian, her eyes had been solely trained on bigger prizes and shinier dreams.

They still were, if she were being honest, even if she had tarnished those dreams.

Obviously, there was no way she could go back to her old life now that she was pregnant, she knew that, despite the fact that the queen and Hel and even the king had called multiple times, mortifyingly leaving the message with Jenna's mother that her position was still available to her and that the king had had no right to fire her. But even if Jenna had been sorely tempted to take the queen up on her generosity, it was out of the question now.

Her pride had begun failing on that point, but her pregnancy had come in to shore it up. There was no going back. How would her coworkers ever trust in her again?

The queen remained on the island where the Summer Palace was based, leaving Helene off duty for the time being, free to help transition all of the assets and fortunes of the d'Tierrza family to her new husband's long-lost Andros family name.

Jenna had spoken with Helene one time since leaving the capital—when she'd safely returned from her stolen adventure, and as glad as Jenna was that Helene was back safely, that she had the wonderful and utterly shocking news to share that she'd fallen in love and married, talking to her friend had been like pouring acid in her wounds, reminding her of the depth of all she'd lost and leaving her drained, sad and lonely.

But even if she couldn't return to her old life, even if the specifics of it barely even existed anymore, she could still find a relevant future for herself and child.

Unfortunately, she was also deeply cognizant of the fact that, even with all her skills, training and experience, given her condition, she didn't have many options. She was a professional security woman and her résumé reflected that, but she had a feeling that, regardless of what the law said, potential employers would quickly look over her when they found out she was expecting.

Nobody wanted a pregnant security guard, regardless of whether or not she was fully equipped to do the job.

Well…maybe not *fully* equipped. But she could cope as long as she didn't get the morning shift.

Dr. Milano had assured her, though, that she didn't have much to worry about when it came to the activity level of her chosen profession at her last appointment.

"Should I stop or pull back on my fitness and practice regimen?" she'd asked.

"No," the doctor had said with a sound somewhere between a snort and a cough. "That'd be like quitting training in anticipation of a marathon!" The doctor had laughed again at the last word, as if the idea was true comedy.

If Jenna hadn't known the doctor so well, she might have felt like she was being made fun of.

"I'd heard pregnant women needed to rest," Jenna had said.

Shaking their head, Dr. Milano had said, "Not in general. My advice is to maintain your current level of activity.

Your body will tell you when to be delicate with yourself. Otherwise keep fit. You've got one of the biggest workouts of your life ahead of you."

The doctor had laughed again and though Jenna knew the comment was meant in fun, she'd found it mildly irritating, nonetheless.

It was a lot of anticipatory pressure.

As was the endless barrage of decisions she needed to make.

Standing beside the doorway, just before she stepped out into the minefield that was her situation with Sebastian, she let the weight of just how worn-out she was settle over her shoulders, if only for a moment.

It was a bone-deep tiredness that had settled over her the second she'd identified the king's voice in the library and stayed with her ever since—through packing, through the drive home, that first night back in her old bedroom, through the doctor's visit when she'd learned she was pregnant alone—and there was no sign of rest in sight.

Not if she was going to become a mother.

There would be a birth—the biggest workout of her life, apparently—and then an entire new human to care for, a new livelihood to find and maintain, and all of it on her shoulders alone, because despite his words about commitment, the plain fact was that Sebastian had stormed away when things had not gone his way. She had to assume he might do so again in the future.

Far away from the d'Tierrza library, outside the capital and the wealth and the speed, no powerful attraction or flowery internal voice could convince her that she had any kind of future with Sebastian.

He was a duke—stupidly handsome—and one of the wealthiest and most dangerous men in the nation.

Men like him didn't end up with Priory girls, and besides, he'd already made it abundantly clear that marriage was not on the table between them.

Priory girls married nice men who enjoyed children and got softer with age.

Jenna couldn't even picture Sebastian in the same room as a child.

She could not recall ever seeing him occupy the same space as one. Not once, in all her time in the capital.

And as far as softening went, well, age would only make him tougher and leaner. With age, he would dry and tighten, his senses growing keener, his skin thinner, his patience lessening.

He was certainly not the kind of grandfather to play hobbyhorse and sneak treats.

Though, that wasn't entirely true.

She could picture him sneaking candy to his grandchildren—with deadly efficiency and outrageous intrigue, in fact.

He would love it, and so would they.

But where did she fit into that picture?

She didn't know the answer, just like she didn't know what to do for herself or about Sebastian or anything else, for that matter, and dammit, she wanted to take a bath.

But a vigorous workout would be a close second, she told herself, not believing it for a second.

When she didn't encounter him in the kitchen through the time it took her to prepare a light, stomach-soothing breakfast of biscuits, lemon ginger tea and cucumber spears, Jenna assumed she would not be encountering Sebastian today.

Still sulking, she thought with only mild spite as she put her dishes away. They had prodded too close to things he wanted kept private and she had not fallen in line like a good soldier last night, but he could go ahead and sulk for all she cared. She would not be manipulated by what was so obviously a tantrum.

Therefore, she was surprised when she found him in the workout room.

He froze upon her entry, his body deceptively still as he held himself midrep on the seated press machine, the muscles of his upper arms flexed and hard, his thighs planted and still engaged though the focus was on his upper body. As always, the man had gorgeous form.

"Sorry. I'll come back later," she said, mouth oddly dry for having just finished her tea. And how was it that he managed to look so good, even as she was less than impressed with him?

At her words, he sat forward, shaking his head. "No. Don't let me chase you out."

"It's fine, really," she said. She was quite familiar with being chased out.

"No. It's not. I want you to be comfortable here. With me."

A part of her wanted to laugh at the idea. *Frustrated, attracted, confounded*…there were a lot of words that described how she felt about Sebastian, but *comfortable* was not one of them.

Unfair, the romantic voice inside her chimed in with, and she was startled by it. It had been conspicuously absent since she'd learned about her pregnancy. *You're always comfortable with Sebastian*, it insisted, and again to her surprise, in reviewing her encounters with him, she couldn't deny it. She was always comfortable with Sebastian, even in the most shocking situations. She might also be impassioned and baffled as well, but she was always comfortable.

She'd proven that the line between comfort and settling was a very thin one for her, though. She had to remember it for both her sake and their child's.

"No, really. It's fine. I'll come back later." His presence, even after the way he'd left her on the path the night before, was too distracting to work out anyway.

"I'm sorry, Jenna. I shouldn't have left you like that last night. I—" He stopped himself from completing whatever thought he had been close to sharing. "It doesn't matter. I'm sorry. It was unacceptable and it was my responsibility. You don't have to run away from me." His gaze was clear and direct, respectful and open for her to assess the truth of what he said.

She didn't want the words to begin to work and untangle the knot of irritation and frustration she felt toward him, but like magic, they did.

"It's okay. I'm sure it won't be the last time emotions get high. Thank you for apologizing," she said.

He made a noise in the back of his throat. "Before I met you, Jenna, I might have disagreed. Now, I'm sure you're right. Our child can only benefit for having such a wise mother."

Jenna smiled, though the statement didn't bolster her. The verdict was still far out as to what kind of mother she would be. Letting out a little laugh, she said, "Not my wisdom. My mother's. More than once I've seen her comfort the new mothers of our community, saying, 'When children are involved, you'd better have tissues.' I'd say children are smack-dab right in the center of what we've got going on."

He nodded, green eyes measuring her. "Among other things." Rising to his feet, he walked to where she still stood near the entrance of the room. "I can't be your husband, Jenna. But I am committing to raising our child with you."

It was, at least, a start. With resignation, she smiled. "I appreciate that. I know a lot of men in your situation would not take that position. We'll figure the rest out as it comes. But really, get back to your workout. There's nothing so urgent you need to stop on my account."

Staring at her for a beat, he said, "You were coming here to use the space."

She nodded. "I was, but I'm good at waiting my turn." She turned, knowing he would continue to insist she remain there if she didn't take the steps to actually leave.

"Before you go, Jenna," he called from behind her.

Turning, she asked, "What?"

"Is it safe?" he asked.

"What?"

"Working out. For the baby?"

If she had not detected a thread of vulnerability in the question, she might have poked fun at him. "More than. The doctor made it loud and clear."

He nodded, and she smiled, touched that he'd cared. The child she carried was his of course, he should care, but it was nice to be included within his net of concern.

She turned once more, again on her way out when he called, "Jenna."

Again, she stopped and looked back at him, "What?"

His eyes had a mischievous look in them that was less sexual than his intense gazes but no less wicked. "Were you planning on working out in a dress?"

Eyes narrowing slightly, she said, "I was."

"Seems rather restrictive," he observed.

Lifting an eyebrow, she crossed her arms in front of her chest, aware that she no longer spoke for herself, but femme folk everywhere in the ageless battle of the sexes. "You'd be surprised."

"By how your impractical fashion choices could facilitate your abduction? No. That's, in fact, exactly what I'm pointing out." He delivered his speech looking down his nose with his head tilted to an arrogant degree.

Jenna scoffed. "Anyone who tried would be in for a rude surprise."

"You deny your attire puts you at a disadvantage then?" he pressed.

She met him head-on, a thrill rising in her blood. "I do."

"I challenge you to a sparring match then."

Her mouth dropped open and a look of impish delight lit his eyes—a look she was well versed in, having witnessed it often in the faces of each of her brothers growing up. He thought he could beat her, and he thought he could prove a point, and because of it, she was honor-bound to prove him wrong.

Her skin flushed at the thought, reminding her that, for all the momentary similarities, he was not one of her brothers. He was a man she had trouble keeping an appropriate distance from under the best, and honestly, most restrictive circumstances.

Wrestling was out of the question.

Even if the thought of it, the idea of moving her body the way it loved to move rather than doing a circuit of repetitions on machines, made both her blood and heart sing.

She shook her head and forced a light laugh, "Not this time."

"Jenna Noelle Moustafa," he said, in a perfect imitation of every playground bully that had ever existed, raising her hackles in the process. "You're scared."

Holding firm, she said, "I am not. I'm mature. And I never told you my middle name."

He shrugged, falling back slightly into a light defensive stance. "I know everything."

"Not quite everything," she said, and then she attacked, faking him out with a feint to the left before sliding right to slip inside her protective barrier. "For example, you don't know what my favorite color is."

And then she danced away, out of his reach and around the nearest machine.

Her pursued her unhurriedly, jade eyes never losing

her though she continued to maneuver and weave through the equipment, making her way to the area of open mat in front of the room's requisite floor-to-ceiling windows. Here, at least, she could make out the faint trace of mesh barrier in the glass.

She wouldn't have to worry about throwing him through.

He met her on the mat and they circled one another, eyes locked, their bodies once again transported to a world of their own. The question was: What was he willing to commit?

He knew her on paper, her stats and biography. He did not know her favorite color. The question was now: Would he want to? He said he did, but so far, she had seen him push his own agenda.

Did he care to know something that trivial about her, for the sake of knowing her, the future mother of his child, or did he only care that she was qualified for the position?

Shaking his head, voice bemused as if the fact he faced off with her and the fact that she confounded him were both novelties, he said, "I don't."

"It's pink," she said, the word light and airy, as gossamer-thin as the feelings that hovered in the shadows of her heart while the bulk of her attention tuned to the opening she knew would come. "Well, rose, really," she amended.

She couldn't read the emotion that flashed across his eyes when he said, "I would never have guessed," but he wasn't mocking her. She could see he meant it, but she had no idea if the fact was good or bad to him and not sure if she truly cared.

He'd given her the opening she'd been waiting for. Ducking to go low, small quick steps carried her in on his left.

Rather than try anything dramatic, she merely placed her two fingers against his rib cage before retreating backward, darting and twisting out of his reach as he tried to grab the flowing fabric of her dress.

At a safe distance, as if they were not eyeing each other during mock combat, she said casually, "You've already told me your favorite color, so I get to ask you something different." Bouncing back and forth from one foot to the other, she finally asked, "What's your middle name?" She kept the pressure of her question light, even as it was personal and pointed. Again, she was testing him. How much of himself was he willing to give her?

He answered without hesitation. "Reynard."

"Oh!" she brought a hand to her mouth, letting down her guard with a little gasp. "That's adorable!" She was surprised. The name was sweet and sophisticated, more whimsical and aspirational than she would have imagined coming from the image she had of his parents.

"I wouldn't know," he said, tersely, before jabbing into the opening she'd left, his hand reaching out to her.

Moving with less control than she'd have liked, she was still quick enough to evade him, laughing as she said, "It suits you. Your turn."

"My turn for what?" he asked.

"To ask a question," she answered.

She realized as she moved, her body engaged and enlivened, that she was fully into their game, her mind and heart having left the ominous weight of the previous night behind them.

Sebastian remained quiet for a beat longer, breathing and shifting his weight as he thought of his question, and Jenna wondered if maybe it felt unnatural for him to try to think of a question to get to know someone on a personal level. He was used to analyzing everyone around him, but how many people did he really know?

The thought brought a strange pinching sensation to her chest, one that felt surprisingly like empathy. Was it possible that for all he knew and manipulated about the world around him, he didn't understand the deeper emotional connections that propelled it?

He dispelled her urge to dwell on the tragedy of his backstory, however, with his next question. "How many times have you thought about my body since the library?"

She felt color come to her cheeks again. The flirtation was unexpected after he'd revealed that he thought that what existed between them was dangerous, but rather than dance away, she engaged with him.

"It's not your body I've been thinking about," she said, voice unintentionally thickening with the truth of it as she spoke. He stopped circling and she flashed him a brilliant smile, a reckless sense of freedom pulsing in her veins.

If he'd thought to get the upper hand with suggestive language, he'd been thoroughly put in his place by her bold response—exactly as she'd planned.

He had tried to use words to glamour her into letting her guard down, but instead, she had turned the tables and thrown him for a loop. She danced into his space again, moving with precision, her person momentarily in the flow zone, stepped a leg behind his, gripped his pant leg and rolled both of their bodies onto the ground.

To her, the entire series of movements had been as gentle as swaying in a hammock. For him, a sudden loss of balance followed by a crash.

Because she had been prepared for the change in their positions when he hadn't, she could turn the momentum of their weight and their fall against him to flip him over once more until she sat atop him.

Then she cocked her arm back, curled her hand into an iron fist and hammered it straight to the space one centimeter from his nose.

"I win." She grinned down into his surprised face before

rising to her feet, flashing him a salute, and leaving him in the gym just to prove that he didn't always get to be the one to have the last word.

Later that evening, they made dinner—a mild chicken alfredo liberal with cheeses she'd only ever eyeballed before at the market counter—and ate together casually, sitting side by side at the kitchen island watching the sunlight disappear from the river canyon, leaving a trail of watercolor hues in pink, orange, purple and teal.

They had just finished exchanging stories of their worst professional mistakes and disasters when, reaching for their glasses of water at the same time, the backs of their hands brushed.

Clearing her throat lightly, Jenna said laughingly, "While I will never agree with your absurd idea that falling in love is some kind of calamity, I absolutely concur that it's important we keep our relationship nonphysical. Regardless of whatever else happens going forward, we don't want our relationship to leave our child confused and uncomfortable."

Sebastian nodded at the same time as he seemed to take too large a bite, which required some effort to swallow and a sip of wine to chase down.

"And have you spent any more time considering my offer?"

Watching him closely, she asked, "Which part?" Knowing him, as she was slowly beginning to, the more time she spent with him, she knew there had to be a reason why he was so adamant they live together to raise their child.

"Living here at Redcliff."

It felt cruel to tell him the truth, but she wouldn't lie to him. "No. I just don't think that's a realistic idea, Sebastian. Parenthood shouldn't consign one to monastic existence."

He winced, the expression subtle and fleet, flashing

across his face in the blink of an eye, but she caught it. When he spoke, his tone was measured and even. "I didn't get the impression that sex was that important to you."

He thought he could nudge her into his way of thinking by using her inexperience and faith against her, but she was savvy enough to not let him.

"You alone know the limits and excess of my interest in sex, Sebastian. That's not in the least what I meant and you know that, too."

He looked away from her, sipping his wine and staring out into the darkening canyon. Then he let out a breath and turned to her. "Again, it seems I owe you an apology. That was uncalled for. I am rather turned off by the idea of living apart from my child, even within the confines of a normal custody arrangement. However, I recognize I am not the only one with skin in this game, as they say."

For a moment, she only stared at him, conscious that the absurd statement was both a genuine apology and an attempt at being humble. Then, doing her best to keep her words neutral, she said, "Well, there's that at least."

He looked at her closely before a smile cracked his serious face. "You're the only one I apologize to, Jenna. Not even the king."

If he'd intended to metaphysically reach into her chest and squeeze her heart, he'd achieved his aim, the words knocking into her, revealing far more than she thought he realized.

Mistaking her quiet for continued pique, he offered, "Come to the library, we'll have dessert."

Did he mean to draw up the ghosts of their past?

She had barely recovered from his casual confession and here he was again throwing off her equilibrium. Heat infused her cheeks.

Awareness lit his eyes, desire adding an edge to the green fire that always glowed there, but when he opened his mouth, he only offered an explanation. "Tea and bon-bons in front of the fire. Nothing else."

There was honest intention in his words, the look in his eyes held firmly in control, no machination behind his invitation. He was committed, she sensed, to charting the course they'd set.

But though she should be relieved, as they rose to put their dishes away and she joined him in making their way to the library, the heaviness in her heart could only be labeled disappointment.

CHAPTER ELEVEN

HE WAS LOSING control of things with Jenna. Sebastian could admit that in the privacy of his own mind as he opened the library door for her.

First, there had been the kiss in the kitchen—a certain slant of light and a reluctant confession were all it seemed were required to break him of his resolve when it came Jenna.

Then, again, in the library, surrounded with the scent of books, which had now become inexorably linked in his mind with the transcendence of having her, her hair gleaming as it had that original afternoon, and staring into her eyes had been all it took.

He had been luckier in the gym, losing just the bout when she'd landed that knockout punch of a smile, and not his integrity.

So why would he risk leading her into the library yet again? Especially when the ease growing between them continued to erode his guard…

But he knew it was because while he knew he couldn't give her what she wanted, and they didn't dare explore the passion that lived between them, he could at least give her tea and chocolates.

Hampered and tied as he might be, he still had enough control to do that.

But he was not fool enough to believe they could share the love seat.

Guiding her to one of the large armchairs, he indicated that she should sit while he went to the hidden kitchenette to prepare their tea. When it was finished, an array of sweets and treats laid out for her on a small platter, he rejoined her in the sitting area, strategically sitting across from her in the matching armchair.

They could not be lovers. But it was imperative that they become at least something resembling friends. Studying her as she bit into the first delight she'd selected, he reflected that that was a journey he was completely unfamiliar with.

"This is divine, Sebastian. I've never tasted something so delicious. It's like I can pick apart each individual flavor. Vanilla, almond and that oozy, creamy chocolate."

With her eyes closed, her voice full of her sensuous enjoyment, her presence trailed over his nerves like silk. The smooth pleasure of it—the oozy creaminess of *its* tone—only further grated at the shards of his control.

With a pained smile, he said, "I'm glad you like them."

Her glow in the soft lighting was threefold: the luminance of her spirit, the sheen of her glossy hair, and her enjoyment of the sweets.

He watched, transfixed, the same as any wild creature caught and frozen in the headlights.

When she opened her eyes, they were laughing, their dark brown wells lightened to become amber pools bubbling with fun and ease. For this moment, she was not dogged by the *should* and *ought* that drove her and her radiance was enough to illuminate the sky.

Sebastian swallowed. "Would you like to pick out a book?" he asked, aware of how close he was to some kind of precipice, knowing he needed to step back, yet remaining reluctant to do so.

As if his question had only now reminded her that she was in a library, she scanned the room, her eyes landing on the section of new books he'd curated for her. Her delighted smile impossibly grew upon alighting on the titles.

"I've been meaning to pick up this one for ages now," she said, reaching out to run a finger down the crisp spine of one of the paperbacks.

Sebastian shivered as if the touch traveled across his own skin.

Abruptly, he rose to select a title for himself, walking to the section farthest away from her. It didn't matter where he went, the titles in this room were only those he loved, could reread again at any time, whatever his state of mind. And that was fortunate, because he needed space between himself and Jenna more than a specific story.

Steadying himself with a breath he pulled a book from the shelf in front of him at random. Of course, it would be Jung. *Modern Man in Search of a Soul*. Reading the title, he almost laughed. It fit that his torture would be narrated as such. The cosmos was possessed of dark humor in spades.

Ultimately, a laugh did escape, and with it, some of the tension. He would take being the butt of the universe's joke if it came with putting the situation in a little perspective.

For his child, he could risk navigating the treacherous territory of his desire for Jenna, particularly as it was the only way to come out on the other side as partners—but the effort didn't need to be given the same valiancy as a war campaign.

Returning to the reading area, he found Jenna already immersed in her book, and this too provided an opportunity: it was easier to remain appropriately distanced around her when her energy and focus were directed elsewhere.

For a moment he watched her read, noting the rate at which she devoured pages as compared to her sporadic reaches for treats or sips of tea.

Jenna read like she did everything else, with her full self.

He settled across from her after pouring himself a cup of coffee. They read that way for a time—long enough that the next time he reached for his cup the coffee inside had gone cold.

Returning it to the coaster, he looked up to find her watching him with a soft smile.

"It was too late for more coffee, anyway," she said quietly.

He didn't know how long she had been watching and the fact made him feel oddly vulnerable. It was too easy to let his guard down around Jenna.

But still he smiled at her. "It's never too late for coffee."

"You'll be up all night."

He shook his head, "By this point, I'd have to mainline caffeine for it to affect me."

"It sounds like you have a problem," she said teasingly.

Taking her in, bathing in her gentle humor, he said, "Among others. You might say I have an addictive personality." And she was the greatest temptation. But it was his problem to manage the temptation. Or face the consequences. "It runs in the family."

After a pause, she said, "Tell me about your family." The demand was tentative and probing, as if she didn't expect him to oblige but was too curious to risk not asking. Of course, she would be curious. His family history was her child's history, as well.

He could do no less than tell her.

But where to start? How to reveal the sordid truth of his parents' past to her so that she would know the dangers his rules and demands protected her from while assuring her that he would never falter in the same way and bring that chaos into her or their child's life?

Where should he start?

Jenna was as far from his parents as it was possible to

be—innocent, open, free from manipulative tendencies—singular, as he'd told her repeatedly. But what if there were limits to even her compassion? A part of him trembled at the possibility of telling her the story of his family and seeing condemnation in her face for the role he'd played.

At the age of ten, three years into his boarding school career with only one visit from his father—his mother hadn't liked the feeling of the large gothic school building in Austria where they had sent him—he had stopped longing for the kind of relationship with his parents that he'd witnessed among his peers.

He accepted that whatever it was that he was lacking—whatever cold wrongness that existed in his heart, as his father had accused, that had led him to betray his mother and suffer his consequential exile without even the slightest urge to shed a tear—was the same thing which had finally stopped him from longing for that. A light came to his schoolmates' parents' eyes, even the coldest, when they landed on their progeny.

He hadn't been able to recall his mother ever looking at him like that.

His father had been no better.

It had taken three years of waking up far away from home without so much as a whisper for him to realize they just didn't care about him, were completely indifferent.

How would Jenna react?

With no real plan, he opened his mouth and said the first words that came to his mind. "My mother was unfaithful to my father."

Jenna froze, the orbs of her large eyes widening and darkening until they matched his black coffee in color if not temperature. Unlike his coffee, her eyes were filled with beckoning warmth. They called to him, jolting through him, energizing him in a way the beverage never could, gently drawing more from him.

With words, she kept it simple. "I'm sorry," she said softly.

He shrugged her words away. She had nothing to do with the old story. "You didn't do anything."

She ignored the brush-off, asking, "Did it tear your family apart?"

He looked away, a sound escaping that tried to be a laugh but didn't quite make it. "No."

"What happened?"

"At first, my father ignored it. When he no longer could, they lived brief, separate lives."

Understanding oozed out of her, free for the taking when he wasn't sure he wanted it.

"And what about you?"

"At first, I was a tool they used to manipulate each other. Eventually, they sent me to boarding school with rare visits home—where I was always alone—until my mother died when I was thirteen. After that it was year-round school until I turned eighteen. Then, my father died, too. University and early adulthood were a bit wild." He would take those hazy and blurred memories over the crystal-clear snapshots from the years before.

Her bleeding heart ached for him. It was as clear as if the organ had been on her sleeve.

Simultaneously soothing and strangling, her compassion reminded him of a wool sweater, itchy and uncomfortable in its warmth, even when he was shivering from the cold.

"That sounds lonely," she said.

Offering a smile that didn't reach his eyes, he said, "Compared to what you experienced, I imagine it does. But as far as the denizens of the capital go, it's par for the course. That's hardly the worst of it."

"What could be worse?" she asked.

She employed the most sophisticated technique to gather information—she genuinely wanted to know—and like any good mark, he opened up to her. "Before I realized he already knew, had known all along, I tried to tell my father. I was afraid he wouldn't believe me, so I laid out a case. I took pictures, saved messages my mother had exchanged with her lovers. I collected it all and presented it to my father."

"Sebastian, that's terrible," she said.

He let out a dry sound. "Oh, my mother made that very clear afterward."

She frowned, her eyebrows coming together over the bridge of her nose in the way that never seemed to fail in disarming him. "I didn't mean it was terrible that you did it, Sebastian. It's terrible that you felt you had to. And for your father to tell her that the information came from you?" That she was disgusted on his behalf soothed a deep sense of injustice he hadn't realized he'd been carrying.

His father had mishandled the information.

Sebastian nodded. "He told her all of it. He told her that I had cried as I showed him my evidence. He was trying to make her feel bad, but she didn't. Instead, she called me a crybaby sneak and said that it was unnatural that I would do such a thing to my own mother. And then she walked out."

"How old were you?"

"Seven."

"And your father just let her say all of that to you?" Obvious horror spread across Jenna's face.

"Why shouldn't he? He hadn't even stood up for himself with her. Why would he stand up for me? All in the name of love and marriage. She was the only thing he ever wanted. After she'd gone, he looked at me and told me it was my fault for chasing her away with my spying and that we would have to do everything we could to get her to forgive us."

The frown of her eyebrows was so fierce he felt compelled to cross the space to her, to give in to the driving urge to place a soft kiss there. He could lie to himself and tell himself it was because she looked so sad. He would do it to comfort *her*. "It was a long time ago. It's all right," he assured her. "And it's probably about time we said good-night."

In talking to her, he had opened a floodgate, and one that he didn't entirely understand. All he knew was that he was open and exposed and did not know what would happen if they didn't cut this off now.

Eyes intent, she once again searched his face before lifting in her seat to capture his face between her palms and brush a light kiss against his lips before lowering back down and taking his hand. "It's not all right, but thank you for sharing," she said, sounding like maybe the information had been enough to satisfy her for now.

But of course, it hadn't.

"Why didn't they separate? Why did they stay together when it was so clear they did not love each other? It obviously wasn't for your sake."

The wound was old, but he still winced at her bald statement, even as he shook his head. "My father did love my mother, was head over heels for her, even after he knew she'd been chronically unfaithful." He spoke evenly, as if he was sharing the morning news rather than revealing the most painful of his family secrets.

"What?" This she clearly could not understand.

"My mother was beautiful and charming. Half the men in the capital loved her at one time or another. My father just never stopped."

"That's not love, Sebastian. That's something else. Obsession. Lust. Addiction. Something else."

That she could hear his story and still cling to such naive notions was a testament to her will to believe the best. He appreciated that about her. But even to preserve that sweetness, he would not sugarcoat the most painful lessons of his life.

"Whatever you call it, it made him weak. It sucked the integrity and honor and goodness from him until he was a shriveling husk, willing to sacrifice and abandon his son. My children will have better." Even for Jenna, he would not repeat the mistakes of his parents. He would break the cycle of visiting the sins of fathers upon their sons.

"What they had was a sickness, Sebastian, and I am so sorry it swallowed you up with them, but it wasn't love. And it isn't the same thing as what we have between us."

It was a wonder she had been able to maintain the level of optimism she had while rising through the national security ranks.

"Do you know that for sure, Jenna? I certainly don't. Before you, my personal code might have been shadowed, but I had never crossed it. Now? I've lost count. And before me, you were living the life of your dreams."

The noise she made in the back of her throat was surprisingly cynical. "Hardly. I was a ghost in the life of my dreams, Sebastian. Just like with your parents, it's not enough. It's not the same thing."

He had to admire the tenacity of her will to cheer him.

"Everyone knew but him. It was mortifying to hear them talk about him. About my mother. That he was a fool and she was a slut was at one time the most popular topic in the capital. In fact, I learned that word overhearing gossip about her."

He'd heard it over and over again, with even greater frequency than the times he had overheard the whispers and snickers about his idiot father—the only one who didn't know about his mother's infidelity. But, of course, like everyone else, he *had* known.

"Oh, Sebastian."

It was incredible the amount of compassion, understanding, and balmy, soothing sympathy she could pack into the single word of his name.

After his childish intervention attempt had backfired, Sebastian's father had consoled himself with booze and gambling until death.

"I survived," he said, shrugging her softness away. "In fact, I thrived. I tore down the old house, and I made an incredibly successful profession out of having all the information and never playing the fool. In a way, you could say I am grateful. The lessons they taught me will ensure our children never have to experience the same thing."

Even if that meant a lifetime of wrestling with the dragon that was his desire for Jenna. Even if it meant asking the same sacrifice of her. He had to. He hoped she understood now, in a way that she hadn't before, why it had to be this way.

CHAPTER TWELVE

PRACTICAL JENNA, THE girl who had always loved to run and jump with her siblings far more than plan imaginary weddings with her cousins, stared up at Sebastian where he stood over her chair, her mind filled with marriage and parents and everything else they'd discussed.

Inside, she wrestled to put his revelations together with his reasons for why things had to be the way they were between them, and also her own wants and needs.

Was it time to accept that certain dreams had already become impossible? That, as Sebastian had said, because they had been together and were now tied for life, she needed to set aside the full picture of her dreams?

While she had never doubted that consequences could be irrevocable, perhaps she had also never truly respected her circumstances as such.

He would not give her the life she'd envisioned for herself, but given what he'd revealed, she suspected that had more to do with old childhood wounds than her worth in his eyes or a playboy's fear of commitment.

Perhaps it was enough, then, that he had promised to care for her and her child.

She would go back to work eventually, of course, but it was no small thing that he had offered to support her and their child. Security, even without love and passion, was more than many women in her situation could hope for.

Their arrangement would not be in keeping with the Priory tradition, but he was right that she had become comfortable breaking with tradition long before she'd met Sebastian.

And though their parents would not be a unit, it was clear that her child would not lack for love from either of them, even if Sebastian had not used the word.

That he felt it was clear in his actions.

He had swooped in and addressed all of the greatest concerns that had been dogging her, outside of nausea and hormones, out of that love. It seemed he would swoop in and take care of her whole life if she let him. If she was willing to agree to his terms.

But was she?

Only if he would meet her halfway. Reaching out, she caught his hand and it was a warm pulsing beacon in her own.

Her mind returned to the imperative desire that had driven her during their encounter in the d'Tierrza library, more urgent now, more immediate, than it had even been during that first clandestine meeting: she wanted him, and he needed her—to bring him sweetness and light, to temper the darkness of his memories with the offer of a more hopeful future. She was the only one who could do it.

In a world in which she was the preternatural outsider, she had finally found a place made only for her—as long as she was willing to compromise.

Here in the secluded library with him, far from the judgment of even the sun, she realized she was.

Right or wrong, what had been true, from the moment they'd first spoken all the way through until now, was that there really wasn't much she wasn't willing to compromise in order to touch the complicated man before her.

But everyone had their issues, and hers, stark and clear at the end of another long day, which had followed over two months of long, hard days, was that the only place she had ever felt truly at home was in the arms of the man in front of her.

And she was done fighting it.

They'd crossed too many lines, incurred too many irreversible consequences. The only thing left to do was lean in and accept the fall.

If she was going to fall, though, she was taking him with her.

"Take me to your room, Sebastian," she said.

He fought it. In his eyes played out a fierce battle against the nameless force that drew them to each other, as desperate as if his very life depending on it.

The air thickened around them, turning as full and pregnant as she was, until on a frustrated oath, his long fingers came down to curve around her arms and pull her to her feet.

And then he was drawing her through the blur of hallways.

They stopped in front of a door she had not yet entered.

He turned the knob and her heart leaped to her throat.

Inside, the room was palatial.

Far bigger than any single room in the rest of the house, the main suite at Redcliff lived up to every bit of Sebastian's hedonistic reputation.

The walls were dark slate gray, the paint thick and smooth. White trim and accents ensured the deep hue didn't turn the space into a dark cave.

Thick, soft lambskin rugs covered much of the honey-colored hardwood floors, an invitation to play a glossy, luxurious and very adult game of The Floor is Lava.

The centerpiece of the room was a massive bed, its free-standing four-post frame both elegant and minimal. Tall and square, it was made from butter-smooth iron, its lines crisp, clean and almost Puritan for all that it shouted the erotic intended purpose of the room.

The bedding was all ivory, with a thickly stuffed down comforter and a battalion of plush pillows. At the base of the bed, a slash of inky black—a glossy throw blanket lying there like an indolent velvet panther.

Abstract art graced the walls, innocent and sinuous inkblots and lush swirling lines suggesting bodies entwined, snapshots of pleasure and breathless gasps.

There was no doubt the room was built for sex, and at the same time, it could have graced the cover of a magazine.

It was a room like Sebastian.

A charming black-and-white-tiled kitchenette adjoined the room, as if activities here might lead to a need to refuel so desperate that the walk to the kitchen could not be managed.

Other doors led to mysterious places, but her interest in the room faded as her survey led her back to Sebastian, the source of it all.

His green eyes glowed, drinking in her reaction to yet another thing he'd made.

"It's gorgeous," she breathed.

His eyes lit, unmoving from her. "It certainly is."

The soft, warm lighting of the room made her simple lilac dress look elegant.

She didn't care.

She shrugged it off impatiently before undoing her braid, her eyes on Sebastian the whole time. When she wore nothing but panties, she nodded, and the movement sent a ripple through the cool hair falling against her back.

The muscles of his jaw tensed, his eyes burning a swath across her body, and she felt like the most beautiful creature in the world.

He crossed to her, still fully clothed in yet another one of his "rich man's impersonation of the ordinary" costumes— this time jeans and a simple soft sweater.

She brought her hands to his shoulders. He put his own

hands on her waist, setting off shivers of electric shock where their skin touched.

Without meaning to, he had once again revealed his need and asked for her, and once again she was giving herself up. As before, there was a sense of the inevitable.

Unlike before, however, this time she knew the firestorm she walked into—had already faced its irrevocable consequences.

He was no softer now than he had been. He made no promises, had flatly refused to give the assurances she demanded even as he denied himself.

But he had opened.

There was no room nor time, nor energy left for games of cat and mouse.

They had to join, become partners on one team. Their child demanded it of them.

The words didn't matter. The intent did.

And the intent in his eyes was as clear as it was powerful.

It didn't matter that he was fully clothed—he was naked to her.

He was subject to the needs and fears that drove him, the need for her, vulnerable and hating it, biting at the bit as surely as a wild colt. The fear of what feeding that need might make of him. He had no freer will in the matter than she did.

"Take off your clothes." She didn't know where the commanding voice she spoke in emerged from, low and utterly assured of obedience as it was.

He undressed for her, his form like a Grecian statue in its perfection.

But disrobing was as far as he was willing to go at her direction.

His urge to dominate clawed for release as his gaze raked across her, sending pulses down her spine. His inner beast paced closer and closer to the surface—to what she knew would be her ultimate delight.

They stared at each other for a long moment, energies circling, breathing synchronized.

And then she blinked, and he was upon her, sweeping her into his arms and carrying her to the bed, eyes locked the whole way.

He laid her in the bed gently, as if she were delicate and not a trained guard raised with four boisterous older brothers.

His body was even more beautiful than she remembered, his colors more alive, his scent more necessary, weaving into her system, comforting and assuring and settling, the chemical elixir her body craved most in its current condition.

After kissing her lips and her jaw, and leaving a trail of kisses down her neck, he worshipped her breasts, his touch intuitively responsive to her incredibly sensitive and tender flesh. His caresses and kisses, licks, and featherlight nips left her breathless, her back arching, legs rising to wrap around his waist and draw him closer, urging gravity along with the force of her desire.

She wanted to be joined with him as powerfully as she wanted to draw the ecstatic agony out—until she could no longer take it and simply exploded in his arms again.

At the rate he was building her, pushing her higher, nearer that exquisite precipice, she knew it wouldn't be long, certainly not as long as she wanted.

She wanted the stretched-out, languorous experience that their passionate rush in the library had lacked.

She wanted to melt and reform and melt again, over and over with him, all night long.

And there was so much she wanted to do to him still, so many places she'd yet to touch and taste and feel. Things she'd heard of in passing, things her peers had quickly stopped discussing whenever she'd come around.

Images of them—graphic, wet, fleshy—flashed through her mind, and alongside the mastery of his hands and mouth, she couldn't resist.

She burst into thousands of pieces, her atoms spraying everywhere, in all directions at once, as she called his name at the top of her lungs.

Beneath her noise, she could feel his growl vibrating across her skin, possessive and feral.

Rising back to whisper in her ear, he tsked, "Jenna, Jenna, Jenna. I never said you could come."

Still not sure if she was any more than the series of throbbing pulses whose hold on her system had only slightly abated, she somehow found the ability to shiver.

She shocked herself further by saying, "I guess you'll just have to do it again," the words flowing from a part of her she was only now becoming acquainted with.

Hands departing her breasts, he rose over her. "I like it when you talk back to me."

Staring up at him, sex and sin incarnate, she could not believe this, even imperfect, was her life.

All of that force, and it was focused on her.

His eyes had the light of the predator in them, lazily trailing up and down her body, wicked delights promised in their depths as they considered the plains and valleys of her figure.

"You still have your panties on," he observed.

Surprised, she glanced down. Sure enough. Off-white and virginal, the forms of daisies woven into the lace.

"Take them off," he said.

It was a command.

She obeyed, breathlessly lifting her hips to slide the garment away.

Once again, he observed her, saying nothing. Her skin

heated beneath his examination. Little about her figure had changed as a result of her pregnancy yet.

Just her breasts were fuller, more sensitive at this stage.

"Open your legs."

Another order.

At this one, her skin flamed, but again, she obeyed.

Spread before him, he continued to stare, eyes darkening. His tongue darted out from between his lips to moisten them, and she swallowed.

His face was shadowed—the expression on his face as he took her in that of a starving man staring at a feast.

"I am going to eat you all up, Jenna."

It was a statement, a promise even, and she shuddered in anticipation.

He didn't disappoint. Her hips bucked when his lips pressed against her intimate folds, the moan escaping high and musical. He smiled his devil smile against her—she felt it—and then she was lost to the expert manipulation of his tongue and lips until they were both drowning.

Recalling his erotic censure, she danced on the edge, holding herself back from crashing.

He rewarded her with greater temptation, hand replacing tongue, long fingers gently stroking as he repositioned his body over hers.

She could no more control the moans and whimpers that escaped her than she could resist the need in his eyes. But because he had not told her to, she somehow held herself on the line of oblivion.

When the hot, thick tip of him pressed at her entrance, trailed and teased along its crease before slightly pressing against her opening only to tease her by pulling back again, she whined.

It took her a moment to recognize the plaintive begging sounds as her own.

Above her, Sebastian was strained, his face a blend of

pain and pleasure that she couldn't look away from, both of them frozen for the moment by the strength of their passion.

And then he gave them both what they wanted, what they needed more than their next breath of air. He plunged into her, calling her name as he did, and she broke into a thousand pieces, pieces that she knew only he would ever be able to put back together again.

When she coalesced beside him, it came with what could almost be called peace.

The wave they'd been desperate to escape had come for them, and though they had truly settled nothing—only clouded things, in fact—and she did not know what awaited them, there was relief in finally being out to sea.

The darkness of the room did not press on Sebastian, nor was it filled with ominous recriminations, as he would have expected after having so thoroughly and utterly lost control.

Instead, it was an embrace, as intimate as the one in which he held Jenna, whose deep, even breathing told him she was sleeping.

Was this what his parents had felt, each time they'd fallen back into each other after yet another dramatic separation?

As much as the hard voice inside him wanted to insist that the answer was yes, that he needed to self-flagellate in order to atone, he could not believe it was.

He couldn't associate his parents, chaotic and broken as they were, with the feeling of wholeness that surrounded him.

Again, Jenna had proven him wrong.

Even knowing he was only temporarily sated—that it was just a matter of time before he would want her again, and intensely—he knew he was no more likely to emulate his father than he had been before he'd succumbed.

If anything, he felt more committed to the future that

he'd mapped out for the three of them. Having Jenna like this, sharing his home—he was absolutely certain this was what was best for their child, to belong to a healthy and complete whole.

Her compassion had led them through his fears. His reason would lead them through hers.

More confident than he had been in a long time that he would be able to persuade her toward accepting his vision for their future, he drifted off to a deep and dreamless sleep, a smile on his lips.

CHAPTER THIRTEEN

BY THE LIGHT of day, Jenna's conscious noted, what had been clear and certain the night before was more muddled and murkier.

Whereas in the library, his heart and soul bared to her, Sebastian's great fears and the wounded boy inside him were so obvious that she could not help but provide comfort and soothe. Upon waking up alone in his bed, however, she didn't know if she had perhaps done more harm than good.

It had certainly felt that way when she'd drowsily reached for him, only to find him gone. Was he even now reconstructing the distance between them—undoing the progress they'd made toward finding ease in each other's company and the capacity to raise a child together without being a couple?

Judging from the way she'd come to full alertness the instant she realized her fingers caressed empty sheets, she feared she knew the answer.

Urgency to find out for sure, to hunt him down and demand he account for his feelings, the urge now more important than ever, pushed her, but she refused to let it lead.

Instead, she was measured and slow in her movements as she slid out of bed and located her dress on the floor. Shrugging it on, she left the room sedately, careful not to let the door fall closed behind her.

If she walked into a new minefield, she was not going to go in rushed or frazzled.

But it was not a minefield she walked into.

Instead, it was breakfast. A buffet of light options greeted her. Watermelon and berries, toast, egg whites and pineapple—everything fresh and bright—released delicate scents, strong enough to entice, but not so strong as to make her stomach roil.

And Sebastian.

Though she couldn't put her finger on it, something had changed in him since last night. It wasn't his clothes, though those were as fresh and perfectly suited to him as ever. He wore a simple white T-shirt and slimline khaki pants. His feet were bare.

The intimacy of that, the scene not unlike ones she had witnessed between her own parents, broke the frayed threads of her resolve even as they attempted to rebraid themselves.

He smiled upon seeing her, the skin of his face easy in the expression, no longer tight and fighting to rein in and hide the attraction he felt for her.

He looked…happy.

"Good morning, Jenna. I made breakfast." The little boy that had been hiding inside him, the wounded soul she'd glimpsed last night, was on full display and eager to please her.

And it had been absolutely worth it, she realized.

And she would stay with him—even after the baby was born.

Was it even a sacrifice if she had what she wanted for all intents and purposes, if not in name?

A fluttering sensation in her abdomen answered, her stomach flipping and settling, anchored if not as steady as she would have liked.

Their child would have a family, if not a traditional one.

Sebastian would shine as a father, and if the only thing she had to sacrifice for all of it to be true was the title and role of wife, she would have gotten off easy.

Finding enough to root in the resolution, enough good to muddle through, she put on a bright smile and said, her voice oddly stretched, "Thanks. It looks wonderful and I'm starving."

CHAPTER FOURTEEN

SEBASTIAN WATCHED JENNA, her dark hair spilling across the pillows, the long olive contours and planes of her body supple and relaxed in sleep.

She breathed slow and deep and her body was angled toward his, her head tucked into the crook of his arm.

Watching her first thing in the morning, he was filled with unprecedented peace. It had become one of his most treasured portions of the day.

"You're staring. I can feel it." She hadn't opened her eyes yet, but there was a smile threaded through the grumble in her voice.

He continued, shameless. "I will never get tired of waking up with you in my bed. No matter how many times I've memorized it."

Things had shifted between them in the time since all of his intentions had fallen apart, and with them, new possibilities opened. He had risked a sliver of vulnerability with her, and the reward had been paradise.

Since then, he had shifted his main office to Redcliff and spent every spare moment with Jenna. Every day, they cooked and ate together, they chatted and read, they exercised and strolled—and every night they fell asleep exhausted and utterly spent.

She had entered her second trimester, and against expectation, her morning sickness had worsened and, in that time, he had become as expert at managing scents and flavors and spice as she had.

And, early and out of the blue, their baby had quickened, dancing around with such frequent enthusiasm within its mother's still toned and tight abdomen that even Sebastian had had the opportunity to catch a flutter.

He could think of no other time period in his life in which he had been happier. And, though they had not discussed the future again, since that night in the library when Jenna had so clearly seen and understood what drove him, he looked forward to the future. Just as he'd wanted, it would be filled with Jenna, his work and his child.

She cracked open a single glorious brown eye, only to immediately squint in the dappled light that the paned skylights let in. Soon, her other eye followed suit.

With alertness came the focus and warmth that the cold, lonely thing inside him couldn't get enough of—all of it flooding in, as if her eyes were two buckets, slowly submerged in an ocean of her heart.

It was a process he could sample every morning and still look forward to at the end of each night.

"Doesn't that steel trap mind of yours have more important things to memorize? Secret codes, launch sequences, priceless national intelligence..."

"Good reasons to keep it fresh on you, wouldn't you say?"

She smiled, blushing, somehow sweet and innocent still despite the fact that by now he'd had his hands all over her in every possible way—and only wanted to put them there over and over again until the end of time.

The wanting would never stop, he realized.

"Did you sleep well?" she asked, echoing the first morning he'd stayed in bed with her. As he had nearly every day since.

Sebastian shook his head. "No. I haven't had a full night's sleep since you've joined me. I'm exhausted."

Jenna chuckled though he only spoke the truth. "You're uncontrollable."

He didn't bother to deny it. Instead he pulled her hand to his lips to softly nibble the tips of her fingers. "And we have so much time until the afternoon…"

Jenna scoffed but made no move to pull her hand away. "Spoken like a decadent city duke."

"I'll accept decadent, but Redcliff is deeper into the country than your own home."

She scoffed. "You were always at the capital."

He shrugged. "There are more women in the capital."

"Right," she said flatly, eyebrows becoming a straight, unamused line across her face. "Well, I'm going back to my room now." She swung her legs over the edge of the bed, at ease and saucy, even absolutely naked.

It stole his breath away.

Until she brought a hand to her stomach and moaned.

Sitting up, recognizing the signs of her nausea, he let himself be guided by the powerfully possessive urge to care for her that had developed within him over the past month or so—since he'd stopped trying to deny it.

Sliding from the bed himself, he found one of his softest T-shirts for her and untangled her panties from the sheets. She muttered a dark thank-you, and he was tempted to smile. But only tempted.

By now he'd learned that his amusement would not be tolerated at the moment.

"Time for breakfast," he said, holding a hand out once they were both dressed.

She took his hand and went with him willingly.

The habit—taking his hand and going with him—was one of his favorite things about her.

Holding back his smile, heedful of the inner knowledge

that the morning bear version of Jenna had no interest in his amusement, he walked them back to the kitchen at the heart of the house.

Jenna didn't want words. She wanted relief. And, as ever, he'd hunted the information down until he could provide it.

After tweaking and more research, he'd perfected his morning offering to her, food as remedy, and, like everything he did, he'd been extremely effective. It had become their morning ritual that he prepare it for her first thing once they got to the kitchen, before he even had coffee.

It was a small thing, the least, in fact, that he could do to show appreciation for the physical burden she took on for both of them. It was a way he could show that even though he couldn't give her everything she asked for, he could give her what she needed. He could provide care.

She had shown him something that night in the library. It was not he who had been faulty or unworthy. It was something in his parents.

By so clearly seeing his childhood intentions, with no hint of castigation, she had vindicated and validated his instincts. He *could* see the right course of action, not merely the most expedient. Keeping her safe then, giving her the life that those same instincts had driven him to plan for them, was the least he could do.

He had not been wrong in that, and he was not wrong in this. She wanted their child to have what she had had. He did, too. And so they would, even if not exactly the same construction. They would have a place to grow.

With so much nurturing, it was no wonder Jenna had become the woman she was. In small ways, he'd tried to show her over the past month that he could not only match but surpass her upbringing in terms of attentiveness and care, if not tradition and structure.

She would be a wonderful mother and he would make sure she had every support she needed.

The thought warmed him as they walked—as it always did.

In the kitchen, he set the wilting Jenna at one of the stools tucked under the large kitchen island's thick marble countertop and flicked the switch on the countertop kettle.

She lay her forehead on the marble—no doubt appreciating its smooth coolness in the face of her furnace-like metabolism—and he prepared her tea.

When the tea had finished steeping, he added a half teaspoon of honey to the hot liquid and laid six ginger cookies on a plate. No more, no less. This was the first course. They had a routine.

When three of the cookies were gone and her color steadier, Jenna aimed a much stronger smile at him. "I'm human again."

Leaning in close, he kissed the space below her ear, where her jaw and neck met. "I'm glad to hear it," he said, savoring the shiver of her response.

The catch in her breath.

She drew in a long, slow inhale, her nostrils fanning slightly with its strength. She was smelling him, he realized, and her body sighed closer to his. The attraction between them was only enhanced, magnified by the side effects and superpowers of her pregnancy.

By the time she trembled out her exhale, he was hard as rock and ready to take her at the island.

Her mind was on more mundane subjects.

Voice steadying as she spoke, she said, "Every day, I'm surprised again at how well it works. The internet is full of old wives' tales that only make things worse."

He continued kissing her neck, murmuring, "I do my research and don't leave things to luck."

She chuckled softly, breath turning shallow. "No, I don't suppose you would. I mean, except for contraception," she teased.

Smiling against her skin, he made his words temptation against her neck. "How am I to know you didn't sabotage and entrap me, Jenna, my sweet? It's very bold of you to highlight my behavioral contradictions. There are leaders of nations who would hesitate to do so."

Again, she shivered against his lips. "Spoken like an espionage mastermind." He could hear the smile in her voice, knew it was there on her face without looking, but also knew the fact took her aback—that she realized that was what he truly was, saw it without illusion, but still chose to lean into him. Each time was a tiny stitch repairing the idea that there was something evil about his thorough nature.

His lips traced her skin, imbuing his words with his wicked intentions. "And yet, you're still here. What does that say about you, Jenna?"

"Only terrible things, I'm sure. In fact, I can't for the life of me think of a reason why I'm even here with a playboy like you." Her voice was saucy and airy, even as it dared him to name a reason.

He closed in on her, enveloping her smaller frame from behind, arms coming to wrap around her middle, taking the weight of her breasts on one forearm while the other hand remained free to play. "What can I do to jog your memory?"

"Hmm…" she murmured, and he could feel the vibration where their skin connected. "I have to think like a mastermind myself if I'm going to take one on. That means information. Give me information." The words were as heavy and thick as her breasts.

He smiled into her skin, inhaled her scent, and mind, and soul. "It's so sexy when you talk dirty."

Always down for a game, a blush rose on her cheeks and wickedness flashed across her eyes. "Tell me—" She stopped, exhaling as his fingers found her nipples. Then, drawing another heavy breath, she continued, "Something that would break you."

He stilled.

The air around them thickened and pulsed in time with his erection, the intensity of its sudden rage and drive for dominance on par with the vulnerability she'd so casually asked of him.

She wanted a secret, a weapon she could use if the moment arose—the dark currency he dealt in on a daily basis, that he knew the power of.

She asked for a bit of the shadow he wore like armor, and she knew it, her brown eyes unflinching and bold in the request.

For compromising, this was the price she asked of him—a stake to drive in his heart. To make himself vulnerable.

So be it.

His hands traveled back down and over her breasts and lower, his fingers dancing along the bare skin of her belly until he reached the top edge of her panties. He slid them down as he pressed closer to give her what she wanted.

"No husband on earth has ever wanted his wife the way I want you. Will never stop wanting you... What's between us, Jenna, goes so far deeper than something as paltry as marriage," he said, positioning himself to enter her from behind at the kitchen island with the watery light of the morning streaming through. Then, lower, softer, he confessed, "I've never cared about anyone or anything as much as I do about you."

"Sebastian." She turned his name into a gasped interjection, sharp and his for the taking right as he placed himself at her entrance.

Outside the sky cracked open, rain pounding down from the clouds against the roof and windows.

But he held back at the gate, their breath suspended, her wet heat searing and teasing him. He had given her the stake. Did he risk now laying himself bare?

He resisted for as long as he could, held the line until there was nothing left of him to grip. And then he worshipped her as they both required.

Thrusting inside her, his erection harder than it had ever been in his life, he gave her his greatest fear: the knowledge that she held the power to hurt him, as deeply as his parents.

She met him with every deep stroke, received him with shuddering moans and gripped him for more in exchange for the power to ruin him.

"Sebastian," she cried again, and he heard the question in the word as much as he felt it in the increasing strength of her body's rhythmic pulses around him.

He had given her what she wanted, and she teetered on the edge. She wanted to fall.

Entirely in her thrall, he could do no less than give her what she wanted.

The orgasm that ripped through was her strongest yet, gripping him in a vice storm unlike any he'd entered in his long, bacchanalian life. So strong she stripped him of his control, tearing him into pieces as she went on, milking him until he was wrung out and dry.

They collapsed against the island together, their heavy breathing suddenly loud in the soft morning light of the kitchen.

She moved first, her palm slowly creeping across the shining marble surface to intertwine her fingers with his and squeeze. And with the gentle pressure, the tight, angry knot in his chest, the little boy who couldn't forgive his father for being a fool, loosened.

Returning her squeeze, he drew in a deep breath as he lifted his weight from her back. She straightened with him, snuggling back against his chest instead. He wished he could have said the move didn't warm him, but lies were a weak man's defense, and while he might have a weakness in Jenna, he was not a weak man.

He wrapped his arms around her and held her close for another moment and breathed her in deep, wanting her only more for the new weapon she held over him.

Straightening, he adjusted her shirt before placing his hands on her hips, holding them with gentle pressure as he eased out of the lock of her body. Her breath hissed out as he did, resisting the movement.

Lodged thick and tight within her as he was, it felt as if higher powers than their bodies protested the breaking of the primal connection.

Moving slowly so that he didn't chafe her as he withdrew was its own oversensitized communion, and he was present for its entirety until all he could feel was cool air all around him.

Watching it as he was, he noticed traces of blood and stilled.

"Jenna," he said, a strange rushing sound in his ears.

"Hmm...?" she replied, turning to look at him.

He lifted his fingers, where faint traces of blood lingered. As an experienced adult male, he was familiar with women's bodies and wasn't squeamish about a bit of blood. As a prospective father, however, he had no sense of the level of danger. Without the requisite knowledge, he was at a loss for what to do, starring at what could be normal or could be disaster, absolutely powerless.

For her part, the color fled Jenna's face, pale panic chasing the pigment away from even her freckles. He had seen that kind of reaction once before in his life, before his mother had passed out after she had witnessed him fall from a tree and sustain a compound fracture as a child.

Sebastian braced Jenna immediately, though he doubted that was what was happening to her.

She was a royal guard. She couldn't faint at the sight of a little blood. He refused to believe it.

Instead, she turned frantic, separated from him to twist

and face him. Steadying herself with his arm, her grip clawlike in its ferocity, she gingerly probed herself with her other hand. When her fingers came back laced with blood, too, she said, her voice pitched low with fear, "We have to go to the hospital."

CHAPTER FIFTEEN

SEBASTIAN ASKED NO questions as he drove. Or maybe he did, and she just hadn't heard them.

Either way, when they parked, and he opened her door, she realized the journey from Redcliff to her doctor's office had passed by in a vague blur, the colors seeping and bleeding together, aided in their distortion by the fall of rain.

She was glad it was raining.

Her mother had had a miscarriage. She remembered it.

The very late pregnancy had been an exciting surprise to the whole family.

At six, Jenna had been so excited to pass on the baton of being the baby of the family.

She had already filled two boxes of arts and crafts for the new baby when it had happened.

Her mother had been so sad.

Jenna's doctor had assured her that while miscarriage was relatively common in the first twelve weeks of pregnancy, with the increased morning sickness she'd been experiencing and safely making it past her first trimester without any trouble, she likely didn't have anything to worry about it.

A nurse ushered her into the back, asking Daddy to wait in the lobby while they took Mama's vitals. If they had come by for a routine check-up, Jenna might have had time for the expression on Sebastian's face as he memorized everything around them.

Emotions flashed across his countenance, but she didn't pay attention.

"Here, love, you know the drill." The nurse's voice was soothing, calm and easy as she handed her the sample container as if emergencies like this happened all the time.

In Jenna's line of work, she knew they did.

Just not to her.

She was the one who saved other people from emergencies. She was not the one who had them.

Except now she was the one sitting in a hospital gown on a table in a silent exam room.

Her heart stuttered.

And then Sebastian was there, his presence like a shadow in the room, and something in her felt marginally steadier.

Coming to stand beside her, he took her hand.

The doctor came into the room, stopping her where she was. "Well, Jenna," she said, looking at the chart in her hands, "that entry was nearly as dramatic as when you came into the world bottom-first, but I—"

Dr. Milano, the grandparent-like figure that Jenna had never seen uncomfortable in her entire life, stopped talking upon noticing Sebastian glowering darkly at Jenna's side.

At first, the doctor stared at him in mild wonder. Then she squared her shoulders and gave a glare of her own. "Glad to see this pregnancy isn't some kind of miracle. You never know with a woman like Jenna."

Jenna's mouth dropped open. For good and ill, the staff at the country hospital that Jenna had grown up going to didn't always maintain their professional distance. Only Dr. Milano's breach of etiquette reminded her that this was Sebastian's first time accompanying her to the office, though. He had missed the early appointments while she remained at her parents, and she had not yet transitioned to the more frequent visit schedule of later pregnancy.

For his part, Sebastian's hand tightened around Jenna's, but he sounded easy when he said, "Agreed."

The response wasn't what the doctor had expected and resulted in some wary eyeballing before she finally turned back to Jenna. "We'll do an ultrasound, but it is just us being extra cautious. In my opinion, everything looks well within the realm of normal pregnancy bleeding. You're still feeling terrible every morning?" the doctor concluded cheerfully with the question.

She nodded. "Like clockwork."

"Excellent," the doctor said. "That's the best sign that everything's still on track. Ready?"

Nodding, Jenna lay back on the table, positioning herself as she had the very first visit. This time, thankfully, she had progressed past the wand. She had become leagues more comfortable with Sebastian in the near month they'd lived together but hadn't quite progressed to wanting him in the room during invasive medical procedures.

Sebastian positioned himself on the opposite side of the bed from the ultrasound machine and doctor, his entire posture thrumming with an intensity that had nothing to do with desire but was no less fierce for it.

The doctor prepared the jelly, warning, "This is going to be cold," before spreading it on Jenna's lower abdomen.

Jenna's heart beat furiously in her chest, a strange pressure mounting. The doctor had said they thought everything was fine, so why did Jenna's sense of warning refuse to wane?

She was at the hospital with the father of her baby for the first time—it made the fact that they would be parents real in a way that all of their talks and time spent together had not.

And then the room filled with the thundering hoofbeat sound that heralded the beginning of a new era in her life.

Beside her, Sebastian froze, his entire focus halted and held by a sound, stopping him as powerfully as it did her—she felt it all as if experiencing the shock along with him through the special bond they shared.

"There's the little one. Sounds strong and healthy," the doctor said, ear cocked, listening to the sound, moving the wand around, and watching the screen until exclaiming, "Ah. And there we are."

The grainy black and gray and white of the screen showed an obvious head and body. Limbs and bones appeared and disappeared on the screen as the doctor moved the wand around over Jenna's abdomen, happily chattering away while the baby's heartbeat thundered in the background. "Baby looks good, now let's find the placenta, shall we... Ah, yes. Here we go. Attachment is strong, and the cord is nice and thick and not tangled in there."

The doctor's words were comforting, affirming.

Jenna barely registered them.

Her baby was beautiful. It was a blob with bones and a head, yes, but it was a perfectly formed head. Genius bones. And though she knew it was absurd, she could have sworn she saw Sebastian in the shape of its little skull.

Her child was astonishing, instantly the most amazing being she had ever seen in her life.

And seeing that perfection for the first time, hearing the drum of the heartbeat that would be the rhythm of its entire life, Jenna knew that what had been enough in the face of all of Sebastian's trauma, and over the past month—playing house and making love—was by no means enough now.

In fact, *enough* wasn't even the right bar to set.

Magnificent. Spectacular. Abundant.

She and her baby deserved not what they could get, but the very best life could offer. Looking at them, it was suddenly, irrevocably and abundantly clear that they were part of something large and longer, the vast length of human history, and that each and every linked soul in it was a kind of miracle, utterly and absolutely deserving of every specific dream and wish their heart desired—herself included.

She could never accept *enough* for her baby. Her mother could never accept *enough* for her, and so on, unbroken, backward and forward. She could not settle.

And leaving things like this, the future ambiguous in its lack of specific key features she had always wanted it to include, would be settling. For her, for their baby and even for Sebastian—though he still didn't get that he too lost out by denying them what she wanted.

But accepting anything less than exactly what she wanted would be settling. Like sins revealed in the face of God, filled with a new awareness of her baby, she could no longer do it.

In the halogen lights of the doctor's office, in the face of the being whose presence was the manic galloping sound in the room, she realized it was never a matter of *enough* but *how much*—how much life and joy and love she could shove into the precious short time she would have to be her child's world.

Like cosmic curtains had been opened, clarity flooded Jenna. Her baby deserved a whole family. *She* deserved a whole family. And her baby also deserved a rich childhood full of laughter and warmth and pride in family and confidence in place and belonging—a strong starting place from which to jump off from when the time inevitably came for them to leap off and create their own belonging and place in the world.

Just like she had had.

Sebastian had been right when he'd insisted that she belonged in the capital, and in the queen's guard. He'd been trying to tell her, he'd even shown her, but it was only now she was seeing—she belonged wherever she put in the time and effort to be. She belonged in the place she had been building for herself all along. Destiny wouldn't carve a place for her, it merely provided the tools and circumstances with which she could build one for herself. And, as she'd always known but seemed to have recently forgotten, it was up to her to establish its shape and boundaries. It was up to her to identify her moral standard and stick to it. She had to do what was right according to the voice inside. She could not settle. Not even out of love.

With the tsunami of fear for her child broken, the bright light of understanding had dawned, and in it, she was left to see exactly the wreckage she was dealing with, and it was love. Absolute, devastating love. The thing Sebastian had so feared had gone right ahead and snuck up on Jenna, caught her in its net and convinced her to forget her integrity as surely as it had his father.

But she had learned.

She would have to pick up and repair all of the parts of herself that had been willing to accept anything less than the fully realized life experience she wanted for herself and her child—including all of the rubble of the rest of her fears, desires, loneliness and illusion.

She loved Sebastian.

But as much as she wanted him, and loved him, she couldn't have him, not with what he offered.

If it wouldn't mean losing sight of the mesmerizing creature on the screen, she would have squeezed her eyes shut in resistance to the dawning realization.

As it was, it was their child on the screen that gave her the strength and insight to finally make her stand.

The joy of sharing this moment with Sebastian in the flesh, after the threat of danger had passed, was matched only by her dread of knowing she had to walk away from him.

He could not have them if he could not give them the life

they needed. His wounds and misconceptions could not be allowed to shape the direction of their lives, no more than her own could.

She would call her friends back and apologize. She would return to her job because it was her passion and calling and she was good at it and loved it.

And she would be a phenomenal mother, just like her own.

"Well, everything looks good to me. I'd say you can head home. No strenuous exercise for a week or so, but as long as you don't have any more bleeding you can probably just get back to life as normal."

Sebastian's voice croaked out, as if rusty, thick and heavy, "Thank you, doctor."

The doctor nodded after another assessing glance. "Glad to meet you."

"Likewise," he said in a voice she'd never heard him use before. She couldn't call it the real him, but it was warm and friendly with genuine happiness.

He was being cordial to the doctor caring for his unborn child.

The doctor stepped out with the admonition to take as long as they needed, and then they were alone in the room.

Without words, Sebastian wrapped his arms around her, enveloping her in warmth that seeped into her pores and tempted her to accept less than she should.

But she had a responsibility to her baby. Sebastian would provide for them while she was on leave and after, ensuring their child would have everything it could ever want or need.

But Jenna didn't need to live with him for that to be true.

And more than that, she no longer could.

It didn't matter that she wanted him exponentially more with each taste she got of him. It didn't matter that he wanted her with equal intensity. It didn't even matter that they seemed to have been *carved out of the same stone*, as Priory tradition waxed poetic.

What mattered was the environment and example she provided for their child.

Mothering was about more than meeting basic needs.

It was about creating a home bursting—overflowing, really—with love. It was about showing through actions how to be a decent person in the world. It was about being present and there for the little things so that you could be trusted with the big. Mothering was about getting in arguments and holding the space to get over them, without the fear that things might fall apart. About showing that people grow and change but that authentic love remains.

It was about what her parents had built for her and what she wanted to build for the developing human she carried.

Mothering wasn't about all-encompassing obsessions and secrets and shame—it didn't have room for things like that.

Mothering was about love.

She loved Sebastian, and wanted his love in return, but whether destiny had ordained it for her or not, she could not accept him with anything less. That would only be bad for everyone involved.

She wanted him to love her enough to respect the vision she had for her future.

"The baby is safe, Jenna."

Sebastian's voice cut through her thoughts, drawing her attention to the long stretch of time that she had gone without speaking.

He thought she was still worried about the baby.

Turning to him, she opened her mouth to correct him. "No. I—" But he didn't let her finish.

Instead, he kissed her, and in it she felt his fear and wonder, as well as an overwhelming wash of possession, of her, yes, but of their baby, as well—all of it as if they were her own emotions.

If there had been any doubt as to his cherishing of her, she had none now. And if there had been cause to question his intentions toward his child, his reaction had obliterated it.

She should have expected it.

Sebastian did not dote on or love anything. He lifted it up on a pedestal and then proceeded to decimate any threat thereto.

It was not the same thing, Jenna knew, but it was Sebastian.

Of course, his child would be treated the same.

The tidal wave of all of the emotional highs and lows of their past month together—mornings and nights, making love as if they were honeymooners, cooking and eating together, relaxing and reading together, the nausea and conversations about the baby and moments just being quiet together—infused their kiss.

It was going to kill her to let go of the only place that had ever naturally felt like it belonged to her.

It felt like kissing him goodbye.

All she could do was ride the wave as it carried her through to its inevitable end. She could not stop the tide.

He pulled back, eyes closed as if he lingered, savoring the taste of her on his lips.

The tears that had threatened throughout the episode sprung up and made their move now, filling and spilling in heavy, fat drops.

He opened his eyes. Alarm flashed through their mesmerizing emerald depths.

"What's wrong, Jenna?"

"I can't do this, Sebastian." Her voice broke.

His eyes narrowed. "Can't do what?" he asked.

"This. This crazy thing between us. This is no kind of

family for a child. We have to stop. I won't live at Redcliff. I told you it's too late for games. I'm not willing to play house. If you don't want a family, I'm going to find a man who does."

He stilled, becoming almost unreal with his lack of motion.

"Unacceptable," he rasped, his voice implacable. Then, he added, the words hushed, "You know how I feel about you."

The vulnerability was a dagger in her heart, but she could not relent. "I haven't blamed you, Sebastian. Not once have I blamed you for the wreck that my life has become since you've come into it. I take responsibility. I went with you willingly, over and over again. That's my fault. But I'm stopping it here, and you're going to let me. You're going to walk out that door and wait for me to call you and you're not going to monitor my calls, and you're not going to have me followed. And you're going to do it because if you don't, it will become your fault, and I *will* blame you, and, for whatever reason, *that, of all things*, matters to you." She had wrung out every word her heart had been holding up its sleeve, including nuggets she hadn't even understood before saying them out loud.

The thing she saw—the bond she felt that defied her sense of herself as a modern woman of the world—he felt it, too.

He felt it and didn't know what to do with it, didn't recognize it for what it was, because he had never felt it before.

Her heart broke for him.

But her child didn't deserve to inherit his wounds.

She didn't deserve less because of them.

And it wasn't her job to save him from himself. If he wanted what she represented, he could do the work.

His dragon eyes glowed, showing her words had hit their mark.

Looking at him, she noticed for the first time that he was completely disheveled—for him.

His hair was tousled, the midlength sandy blond waves lying akimbo as if he had recently run a hand through them. He wore jeans and a crewneck T-shirt, and his face was shadowed with a day and a half's worth of growth. He was the most human looking Jenna had ever seen him.

But she wouldn't break.

"I will never stop wanting you. Why can't that be enough?" His voice was ragged and harsh.

She shook her head. "It's not the same thing."

"Isn't it? I can't say I've seen otherwise."

"I know, Sebastian. And I feel sorry for you. We are the masterminds behind our own lives. You taught me that. But you're so afraid of repeating your parents' mistakes and cruelty that you've consigned yourself to living half a life. You have to be the one to change if you want something more." She didn't imagine people often felt sorry for him, but if he was too much of a fool to see what blossomed so obviously around him, she couldn't help him. She couldn't save him from himself, any more than he could save her.

His expression said as much.

His words were tight, but he managed to squeeze out the words with dry derision. "Don't worry on my account."

Her eyes narrowed at him.

"I wanted you the moment I laid eyes on you, Jenna. I didn't care what walk of life you came from, about your abilities, none of it. That's more than the king can say about the queen. Everyone calls what they have love. Why can't you do the same with this?"

"He loves her, Sebastian," she said, aching for this man who could see through everyone he encountered but could not see what was so obvious to all those around him.

"It's another word for the same thing."

She could not allow him to evade, could not let him slide

around her defenses, not without meeting her demands. There was too much at stake. "Love and marriage are about more than physical passion and obsession."

"And so is this," he said, gesturing between the two of them. "I told you that you were singular, Jenna. That wasn't a lie. What is between us is, as well. You think that what exists between us is normal, like it happens like this all the time because it's the only thing you know, but it's not."

"Our child deserves a real family, Sebastian," she said. "I deserve to be loved."

"Loved?" he said darkly. "Sweet Jenna. I drink from you until there is nothing left. I possess you, body and soul, until you can't remember if you ever had a dream before I came into your life. I thought once would be enough. I was wrong, and now I need a constant supply—and you do, too. Love pales in comparison to how I feel about you. You think our child needs a happy family, fine, but don't for a minute lie to yourself about what you want, Jenna. You won't be happy with something as watered down as love when you could have me."

The truth of his words lanced through her, impaling her, lodging in her chest, pinning her to a lonely future.

Her hand came to her abdomen by habit, reminding her. *Not lonely.* She wouldn't be lonely for a long time.

She would have their child, and her friends, she thought, realizing that something had shifted inside her. She could pick up the phone and call her friends and family at any time. She always could. The knowledge gave her the strength she needed to hold her ground. She loved him, but she wouldn't be a martyr.

"You're wrong. I know you are the only one for me. A part of me has known it from the beginning. You're not the only one who knows things. But life sometimes requires sacrifice, even a once-in-a-lifetime one. Our child is worth that sacrifice."

She was breaking apart inside, but it was okay. For the first time since they'd parted at the d'Tierrza gala, she could feel her inner compass again—could sense the magnetic pull of *truth* in her cracked-open and bleeding chest. "It's all or nothing, Sebastian. I deserve that."

He stepped back from her as if the movement hurt him, his eyes sliding toward the blank screen of the ultrasound monitor that had only recently given them their first image of their child. Then, as if he were a thousand years old, his bones brittle and fragile and rigid, he walked out of the room.

He hadn't spoken, but he had given her his answer.

She watched him go, staring after him, numb for an eternal instant.

When he had been gone long enough that the sounds of the clock ticking and her breathing had become overloud to her ears, she put her face in her hands and cried like she was a baby.

CHAPTER SIXTEEN

SEBASTIAN SAT BEHIND the wheel at a lonely fork in the road.

A right would lead him to the capital, where he could lose himself in work, raking his mind through the muck in order to forget what kind of man he was.

A left would take him to Redcliff, the house that he had spent the past month transforming into a home with Jenna.

His mother had hated Redcliff—she had thought it too far away from the city, too high in the mountains, and too rainy and foggy. She had called it moldy.

Jenna was nothing like his mother, but for one similarity—her uncanny ability to bring a Redcliff man to his knees.

Sebastian had sworn he wouldn't be like his father, that his weakness would not live on beyond him.

He had come so close to keeping his word.

And then he had encountered Jenna.

Jenna's face, aching as he left the hospital room, was seared into the backs of his eyelids, taunting him every time he closed his eyes.

He knew he was a cold man, but here he was, at a new level, abandoning the mother of his child after she'd put her heart on the line.

The immensity of impending fatherhood swept over him once again, washing over him with a sense of vertigo more concrete than ever before, now that he had seen and heard his child.

A right was his life in the capital, unchanged, pretending to be the city's most notorious playboy, all the while immersed in the work of maintaining the international security of the country.

A left, a family life.

Fatherhood, watching his child grow, evening walks and morning after morning with Jenna.

But that was wrong.

A left wouldn't bring him any closer to a future with Jenna. If it could be so simple, he'd have already made the turn. Only giving her everything she wanted from him would bring him closer to a future with Jenna. Only letting go of his inner demons was good enough for her.

He had fought and striven to be a man far removed from his parents his entire life, and in rigidly controlling his life, in ruthlessly filtering what emotions he allowed in and out, he had merely repeated their mistakes.

He had made himself into the impossible-to-love creature that he'd always feared he was, and now that creature was hell-bent on bringing the same fracture to his own burgeoning family. And it was all because he couldn't deal with his own feelings and fears—his obligations—like an adult.

The choice was clear when he thought of it that way. There was no choice.

Tearing himself open and letting her shed light into the deepest corner of his shadow was the only option. Facing his fears to give her what she wanted, over and over again—endlessly—was the only way.

Jenna was the mother of his child, identified by a plan and process he'd had no role in, but that had somehow led him to the right woman. She had loved even with the barriers he had put up to stop it from happening.

His body and what scarred bits remained of his soul had

recognized her, and his need for her, long before the strategic mind that he was so proud of had.

In much the same way, his heart now dragged the same resistant mind toward acknowledgment of what his instincts had known immediately: he was in love with her.

It didn't matter if they were married or not, she already had the power to make a fool of him, as his mother had his father.

He was clearly a fool, driving away like an ass instead of standing beside her.

Beside the mother of his child…and the woman he loved.

The admission slammed into him like a wrecking ball, demolishing the last protective wall that stood between him and the truth.

He loved Jenna.

Utterly and absolutely. He had from the moment he'd laid eyes on her, and so he had also been right.

Because he was a man who had no qualms and much means when it came to protecting and pleasing that which he loved, she was the most dangerous woman in the world.

And the only defense the world had against her was the fact that she was alive with an inextinguishable inner goodness and light. That she didn't ask for the whole thing on a silver platter—only that he love and adore her and the child that grew within her.

He didn't turn toward the capital or toward Redcliff. He turned the car around and drove back to the hospital.

CHAPTER SEVENTEEN

IT WOULD HAVE been impossible to hide the fact that she'd been crying when she finally left the hospital room, so Jenna didn't bother trying. Thankfully, after her dramatic entrance and results, the nurses appeared comfortable assuming she was going to be fine.

Had it been worth it? Issuing an ultimatum to Sebastian like that—putting everything she wanted out there on the line. She thought so, even if inside she felt like a thousand tiny pieces of dull shattered glass scattered across asphalt.

Humpty Dumpty had a great fall. All the king's horses and all the king's... she thought idly, suddenly very clear on the fact that she needed some air, fresh air, not the recycled stuff circulating inside the hospital.

Outside the maternity ward now, strolling through the regular hospital, the word *king* bounced around in her head giddily.

She had ignored phone calls from the king. Multiple.

She stopped in her tracks, in the middle of the hallway between the chapel and an elevator bank. She needed to call Mina.

Changing course, she found the nearest courtesy phone and dialed quickly. And because she didn't just belong, she didn't just matter—rather, she shone wherever she went and made an irrefutable place for herself wherever she wanted—she was the kind of woman who had the queen's personal direct number memorized.

Mina picked up before the completion of the first ring.

"Hold on, I've got to get Hel on the line," she said, not giving Jenna a chance to protest.

Jenna smiled, the sound of her friend's voice and her rush to do things right as soothing to her soul as her mother's homemade chicken soup.

The call was short, her friends somehow sensing the delicate, easily tired nature of her new enlightenment, but it was more than enough. They would work out the details in the months to come, but she was returning to the queen's guard—and receiving all the associated maternity leave and pay.

She would need it now that she had drawn her line with Sebastian.

Stepping into the gray toned drizzle of the day was the final reset she needed.

She had come out a side entrance, one that faced the rising rolls of hill that disappeared into fog that obscured the road to Redcliff.

Misty and green, quilted with distant farmsteads, much like her own family's, the view was one of her favorites in all of Cyrano—the view of home. Tourist brochures extolled the beaches and wine country, and locals adored the big city, but Jenna thought the sloping green landscape of the near interior leading all the way up to the upper reaches of the cliffs, was the most beautiful stretch of land of all.

Staring at it, her hair and dress and coat growing damp in the increasing rain, it wasn't enough that she could feel his memory in her body, she also saw Sebastian everywhere.

She saw him in the colors, in the harsh planes and valleys, in the red in the clay-rich soil. In the earliest days of Cyrano, Redcliff lands had extended all the way to the coast, including her family home. It was only after unification that Redcliff had become landlocked.

Perhaps that was why she had never worried about being out of place when she was with him—because they came from the same place, even if not the same walk of life.

Unlike with her closest friends, or within her career, or even back in the place she grew up, she had never felt out of place with Sebastian. The cosmic thing between them made everything ordinary and human that separated them—incredible wealth, titles, centuries-old traditions—seem small by comparison.

But even cosmic connection was not enough reason to settle.

They would either travel this road together as full partners or they wouldn't. It wasn't a path they could travel halfway and then turn around. That would be too hard on everyone's hearts.

Harder than the feeling in her heart now. At least now, she was the only one who had to deal with the pain of letting Sebastian go. If she had delayed, her child would have experienced this pain, too.

Turning her face up toward the rain, she let out a long sigh before setting out on her way home—not Sebastian's, which had somehow slipped into the mental definition, but the home she'd grown up in.

No one had answered the phone when she'd called her parents from the hospital room, but she lived only a few miles away. Even pregnant she could walk. Growing up in these hills, she'd walked in the rain many times before. It was too depressing to wait for a cab.

A little water was fine. It could hide her tears if she needed to have any more outbursts.

She was walking along the long hospital drive when the car pulled up beside her, slowing to drive at her walking speed.

It was Sebastian.

Jenna squinted through the rain and the tinted windows.

Her reflection staring back at her in the shiny glass assured her that her hair and dress were plastered to her, while her heart beat fast.

The streamlined contours of his car promised speed and intensity, the color that tempted you to look past it only to dare you to look away once you peeked. It blended in, even while it stood out. It kept secrets and watched with a thousand eyes. It was a spy, just like its creator.

It was a truly fantastic car, just like the man inside.

But she wasn't going to backtrack because he had a nice car.

She was thoroughly soaked to the bone and extremely sensitive to the fact that today pregnancy seemed to have stolen her soldier's toughness. Or perhaps that toughness had never been more than a thin facade. Maybe she was always a marshmallow.

She was a defender, there was no doubt of that, but maybe that was as far as it extended. Maybe she had never been hard, or smooth, or impenetrable, or whatever else it was people in the capital admired. And maybe it didn't matter. Maybe she could be a guard and still be soft, because that wasn't where her value and skill came from.

It had to be. Because that was who she was.

And she was both good enough and deserving.

The car doors hinged upward, and a dark figure stepped out.

"Jenna?" Sebastian asked.

"Sebastian." She lifted a hand to block the light from her eyes and watch the figure by the vehicle.

He stood there in the rainy, overcast afternoon, his clothes disheveled, face ravaged, but for the light that shone in his eyes. The same burning intensity that had changed her life that long-ago day on the balcony.

He opened his arms and she ran to him, sobbing once again as he picked her up, wrapped her in a hug so tight, she couldn't breathe and didn't care.

"I'm so sorry, Jenna. There's no excuse for leaving you like that, for what I said. I was a fool, and I'm sorry. I love you, Jenna. There is no other woman I would choose in the whole world to be the mother of my children, and no other woman I want, and therefore no other woman that I could possibly trust enough to spend the rest of my life with. Come back home with me. Be the mother of my child, yes, but more than that, be my wife."

He wasn't down on one knee. She didn't imagine he ever would be—at least not in public.

He was not the kind of man who knew how to bend. And he might be a little ruthless.

But he was hers, her home in the world, irrevocably and absolutely.

She spoke into his neck, clinging to him not for dear life, but for dear love. "Yes."

And then he was kissing her, long and hot and possessively, with so much passion she was surprised steam didn't rise from their soaked bodies.

He kissed away her fears that she was too plain, too poor and too Priory to ever find love.

He kissed away her fears that she would never truly belong in the capital, carving and viciously protecting an irrefutable and powerful place for herself by his side in the glittering world of wealth—a place in which she could be herself, raise her child and return to her job, a lifetime in the company of her two dearest friends becoming just the icing on the cake.

He kissed away her fears that he couldn't give them a real family, full of the kind of love that grew healthy, happy children, utterly obliterating every shadow of a doubt that haunted or lingered.

Sebastian loved her but didn't *only* love her.

It went far deeper than that.

They kissed, standing in the pouring rain until she wasn't sure where she ended and he began, and then he led her to the car that she wasn't sure wasn't a spaceship and drove them back home, to Redcliff.

There, they would make a home for their family—honest, wholehearted, and utterly unique. And for the times when work meant they would need to stay in the capital for a longer stretch of time, they could create a new private paradise, designed by Sebastian and brought to life by the energy that flared to life when two pieces that fit together found their perfect, destined whole.

EPILOGUE

Two years later

"I'M GLAD WE'RE in agreement, gentlemen." Sebastian raised the toast, and the two men he spoke to touched their glasses to one another's.

Sebastian, Zayn and Drake were arranged in a half circle—Sebastian standing, Drake and Zayn seated—set apart at the outdoor bar from the soft grassy play area where three women formed a small ring around a trio of tiny seated humans, the babbles and ham-fisted gestures of which seemed to indicate the beginnings of a beautiful friendship.

Each of the tiny humans hovered around ten months old. The two girls, the Royal Princess Elke Aldenia d'Argonia and the young Amira Andros, heiress to the largest duchy in Cyrano, were both sturdier in their seat than the lone boy, but Reynard made up for the fact that he kept collapsing with the volume and power of his voice at each tumble.

Sebastian's son was a talker. More of a roarer, actually.

So much so that, while it remained as strong as ever, an enduring flame, the peace Sebastian found at his many homes was no longer a quiet peace.

It was, however, still rooted in Jenna. Always Jenna.

It blew him away to reflect on the era of transformation that she had ushered into his life. There had been more fraught and tenuous firsts than a man as jaded as himself had a right to.

He cherished every one, bringing to family life the same focused intensity he brought to everything on the short list of things he loved, a list that included: Jenna, his child, espionage and architecture. It wasn't lost on him that her coming into his life had nearly doubled the list. She'd gone and grown his heart to nearly twice its original size.

And it was twice as much to love her with.

He loved her with the immensity of his full will behind him.

He'd gained much to lose, but if he was more vulnerable now than he had ever been, it was because he loved more, and was therefore justified in being that much more cunning and ruthless in removing any threat thereto.

And this was a part of the reason the three men held their small conference at the sunny poolside bar.

Each man held a drink: the king, the pirate and the spy.

It was a good setup for a punch line.

It was an even better setup for an ironclad national protection team.

By land, by sea, by shadow—they would watch and guide Cyrano into its bright, modern future—as directed by their wives, of course. Their children needed a playground, after all.

The three men had just finished their toast, officially setting Sebastian's latest plan in motion.

The king was Zayn d'Argonia. His role needed no explanation. His job was to rule. He was the king.

The pirate was Duke Drake Andros, now the wealthiest landholder in the nation. He was also a retired admiral and privateer who had reclaimed his birthright and in the process found the love of his life in Helene d'Tierrza.

He would watch the seas—a critical role for an island nation.

And then there was Sebastian, the reformed playboy duke, now a world-renowned architect. Publicly, he had become the incredibly exclusive architect who designed only three houses a year. Privately, his hands were filled with adoring his small family and leading Cyrano's intelligence forces.

Three men, tied to one another through the country they ran and the women that ran them.

They were colleagues and, after the past year and a half or so, friends—a rare thing for men as powerful as they were.

And it was all because of the eagle-eyed women who stood at a distance from them, watching over their babies.

His Jenna, Queen Mina and the Duchess Andros—or, more truly, the queen and her loyal guards and most trusted companions, as storybook worthy as the Three Musketeers.

But for Sebastian, there was only Jenna.

After taking his fiancée home that day in the rain, they had flowed right into a honeymoon-like bubble, exploring the rest of Redcliff and each other simultaneously.

He lured her the same way every time, and she always indulged him.

"Let me show you the greenhouse," he would say.

And she would go.

"Let me show you the pools."

And she would go.

And so on and so on, until she was glowing and he was inspired to build more houses.

He began drawing up plans for their home in the capital immediately after they returned home that day.

Not too long later, and after many sumptuous dinners, Jenna was into her wonderfully energized and nausea-free third trimester and the specs for their townhome were complete. They had enjoyed their private library many, many times. Now they were ready to return to the city.

And, possibly because of all the home-cooked food, to his, her, and her entire family's delight, the bump they'd been waiting for and despairing of ever seeing finally made an appearance.

The king and queen celebrated their wedding in December, the date moved up to accommodate the queen's pregnancy, and it was such a stunning winter ceremony it set off a new cold-weather wedding trend.

The queen shocked the world and none who knew her by choosing her two guards as her bridesmaids. And then, one by one, the babies had arrived. Mina's, then Helene's, and then Jenna's.

Helene had delivered early and Jenna late, after all the plans had been made and executed.

All the babies were happy and healthy and wealthy.

His son was the cutest—in Sebastian's well-informed opinion.

Following in the footsteps of his father instead of his mother, Little Reynard had not arrived in the early morning but waited until the night was at its darkest point to make his debut.

Before his son's birth, Sebastian had known Jenna was strong—a woman with a warrior spirit.

After, he feared her for the goddess that she was.

He might have the power to pull strings and make nations move, but she pulled life from the unknown and brought it screaming, whole and healthy into the world.

And of course, just two weeks before Reynard's arrival, he and Jenna had been married, the occasion taking place on a sunny spring day at Redcliff.

At Sebastian's insistence, the ceremony had been outrageously expensive. To Jenna's delight, it was suffused with earthy warmth and love.

Jenna's mother had made her dress. Helene and Queen Mina and her sisters-in-law were bridesmaids.

With colorful silk ribbons and flowers, an abundance of handmade lace, and iced lemon and ginger chiffon cake—imported from faraway producers and hothouses or handmade—surrounded by the people she loved most in the world, the wedding had been everything Jenna had ever wanted. She'd made a point of both telling and showing him afterward.

He had appreciated the sentiment, but Sebastian needed no thanks. Jenna coming down the aisle in her layers of lace and satin, the empire waist and deep-V cut of her dress setting off the warm glow of her olive skin and glorious fullness of her breasts, her long hair loose and flowing beneath the veil that rested atop her head like a medieval lady's—also handcrafted by her mother—all for him was all he would ever need.

She had been so beautiful that, after the queen got permission to share a photo on her social media channels, a bridal magazine asked to purchase photos from their day for a special edition.

Jenna's embarrassed shock at the request would always make Sebastian smile. She had no idea that becoming a trendsetter came along with becoming the Duchess of Redcliff.

She would get used to it as time went on, but he doubted she would ever feel invisible again.

He didn't worry that the attention would change her. She would always remain his honest and true Jenna, no matter how many people took notice, just as he would always be wicked and she would always love him anyway.

The fact of it never failed to give him pause.

She saw him, complicated and shadowed, and loved him anyway, shared her light, let him drink his fill over and over, never minding the endless ravenous hunger he had for it. Jenna had made him do a double take, and so he had taken her. And he would, again and again, until the two of them were no more, and all the world was left to their children.

A world he intended to preserve and protect from every threat—political, economic and environmental—so that those children might enjoy it half as well as Jenna had taught him to. That would be enough.

And because of the miracle that she was, he wasn't alone in the endeavor.

He had her, and he had the men at his side.

"Now, stop that, Amira," Helene shouted suddenly. "You leave Auntie Jenna's braid alone!"

Swirling the ice around in his drink, listening to the satisfying clink of the frigid cubes against the priceless crystal, and the happy chaos around him, Sebastian took a sip.

The cool liquid burned down his throat, its fire nowhere near a match for the one that burned in his eyes as he observed the woman with a long dark braid and the green-eyed little boy who sat at her feet, his dark mop a match for her own—Jenna and Reynard—his whole world.

They had faced their dragons, hunted down and worked out the scars from the past that hindered them, and because of it, Sebastian realized, even more important than their impressive lineages and legacies, their children would not inherit their wounds. And what was that, if not happily-ever-after?

* * * * *

COMING SOON!

We really hope you enjoyed reading this book.
If you're looking for more romance, be sure to
head to the shops when new books are
available on

Thursday 25th November

To see which titles are coming soon, please visit
millsandboon.co.uk/nextmonth

MILLS & BOON

THE HEART OF ROMANCE

A ROMANCE FOR EVERY READER

MODERN

Prepare to be swept off your feet by sophisticated, sexy and seductive heroes, in some of the world's most glamourous and romantic locations, where power and passion collide.

HISTORICAL

Escape with historical heroes from time gone by. Whether your passion is for wicked Regency Rakes, muscled Vikings or rugged Highlanders, await the romance of the past.

MEDICAL

Set your pulse racing with dedicated, delectable doctors in the high-pressure world of medicine, where emotions run high and passion, comfort and love are the best medicine.

True Love

Celebrate true love with tender stories of heartfelt romance, from the rush of falling in love to the joy a new baby can bring, and a focus on the emotional heart of a relationship.

Desire

Indulge in secrets and scandal, intense drama and plenty of sizzling hot action with powerful and passionate heroes who have it all: wealth, status, good looks…everything but the right woman.

HEROES

Experience all the excitement of a gripping thriller, with an intense romance at its heart. Resourceful, true-to-life women and strong, fearless men face danger and desire - a killer combination!

To see which titles are coming soon, please visit

millsandboon.co.uk/nextmonth

MILLS & BOON

Coming next month

A CONTRACT FOR HIS RUNAWAY BRIDE
Melanie Milburne

'Could you give me an update on when Mr Smith will be available?'

The receptionist's answering smile was polite but formal. 'I apologise for the delay. He'll be with you shortly.'

'Look, my appointment was -'

'I understand, Ms Campbell. But he's a very busy man. He's made a special gap in his diary for you. He's not usually so accommodating. You must've made a big impression on him.'

'I haven't even met him. All I know is, I was instructed to be here close to thirty minutes ago for a meeting with a Mr Smith to discuss finance. I've been given no other details.'

The receptionist glanced at the intercom console where a small green light was flashing. She looked up again at Elodie with the same polite smile. 'Thank you for being so patient. Mr...erm... Smith will see you now. Please go through. It's the third door on the right. The corner office.'

The corner office boded well- that meant he was the head honcho. The big bucks began and stopped with him. Elodie came to the door and took a deep calming breath but it did nothing to settle the frenzy of flick-knives in her stomach. She gave the door a quick rap with her knuckles. Please, please, please let me be successful this time.

'Come.'

Her hand paused on the doorknob, her mind whirling in ice cold panic. Something about the deep timbre of that voice sent a shiver scuttling over her scalp like a small claw-footed creature. How could this Mr Smith sound so like her ex-fiancé? Scarily alike. She turned the doorknob and pushed the door open, her gaze immediately fixing on the tall dark-haired man behind the large desk.

'You?' Elodie gasped, heat flooding into her cheeks and other places in her body she didn't want to think about right now.

Lincoln Lancaster rose from his chair with leonine grace, his expression set in its customary cynical lines- the arch of one ink-black brow over his intelligent bluey-green gaze, the tilt of his sensual mouth that was not quite a smile. His black hair was brushed back from his high forehead in loose waves that looked like they had last been combed by his fingers. He was dressed in a three-piece suit that hugged his athletic frame, emphasising the broadness of his shoulders, the taut trimness of his chest, flat abdomen and lean hips. He was the epitome of a successful man in his prime. Potent, powerful, persuasive. He got what he wanted, when he wanted, how he wanted.

'You're looking good, Elodie.' His voice rolled over her as smoothly and lazily as his gaze, the deep sexy rumble so familiar it triggered a host of memories she had fought for seven years to erase. Memories in her flesh that were triggered by being in his presence. Erotic memories that made her hyper aware of his every breath, his every glance, his every movement.

Continue reading
A CONTRACT FOR HIS RUNAWAY BRIDE
Melanie Milburne

Available next month
www.millsandboon.co.uk

LET'S TALK
Romance

For exclusive extracts, competitions
and special offers, find us online:

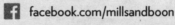 facebook.com/millsandboon

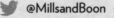 @MillsandBoon

@MillsandBoonUK

Get in touch on 01413 063232

For all the latest titles coming soon, visit
millsandboon.co.uk/nextmonth

MILLS & BOON

Desire

Indulge in secrets and scandal, intense drama and plenty of sizzling hot action with powerful and passionate heroes who have it all: wealth, status, good looks…everything but the right woman.

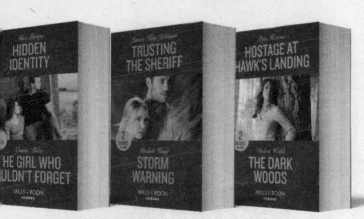

MILLS & BOON
MEDICAL
Pulse-Racing Passion

Set your pulse racing with dedicated, delectable doctors in the high-pressure world of medicine, where emotions run high and passion, comfort and love are the best medicine.